This book is dedicated to

Bobbe

who is an inspiration with
her ability to always
look at life with
the glass half full.

Also by Pamela Frances Basch

EACH TIME WE SAY GOODBYE

ACKNOWLEDGEMENTS

Again, my thanks go out to the dedicated team of people who have given me so many ideas on how to make my stories better. I could not have done it without you and I am deeply grateful. Your thoughtful feedback, editing and innovative ideas on marketing my stories has been invaluable.

My sister, Vivian Foster, at www.bookscribe.co.uk
My daughter, Amy Sager, at bebetterstudios.com for designing the
beautiful cover
My friend June Donnelly
My daughter Vanessa Talbott
My husband Gary Basch
And, last but not least, my very special anonymous friend.

Also, it is impossible to express how much I appreciate those of you who have taken the time to give me such great reviews and feedback for EACH TIME WE SAY GOODBYE. It's hard to be objective about one's own writing and receiving these reviews and encouraging emails has not only spurred me on, but also given me the confidence to continue. Your enthusiasm for wanting to read this book, the second in the series, has been amazing and I will always be deeply indebted to all of you. Thank you.

Thank you also to all the staff at CreateSpace. It's comforting to know I can always rely on getting prompt and professional assistance just by sending an email or making a phone call.

CHAPTER ONE

NOVEMBER 2005

Thea Chamberlin was having a bad morning. No matter how hard she tried, she couldn't dispel her despondency. Even her artwork and the luxury of having uninterrupted time to finish her drawings did nothing to spark her interest. Her creativity was dead, and she sat staring at the walls seeing nothing.

She missed the children—their chitter-chatter and the running of their footsteps. They filled her with hope even though she worried about them all the time, especially Jessica. Thea was constantly amazed at their remarkable resilience, considering all she had put them through. But how could she have possibly known the consequences of her actions? She was only an innocent girl, twenty years old and in love, and her fairytale wedding was just the beginning of the downhill spiral. She hugged herself and rocked back and forth on the hard wooden chair, overwhelmed by wretchedness, unable to pull her mind away from the harrowing memories. Neither her marriage to Michael, nor her relationship with Kenny had given her the happy ending she was seeking. Of course, her expectations had been much too high, especially of Kenny, but she had persevered, tried so hard to make the relationships work, and they had all suffered just because she was afraid to be alone.

To her dying day, she would always blame herself for putting Jessica in harm's way. Totally unaware of Kenny's jealous and psychopathic friend, Bart Robinson, she'd had no idea he spent all his waking hours trying to think of ways to hurt Thea and her family in revenge for his warped perception of the anguish she had caused in Kenny's life. When things had come to a head between her and Kenny and she had finally asked him to leave, Bart pounced. Something had snapped in his sick mind, and he had hidden in the bushes waiting for Jessica to get off the school bus. Had Thea stayed home, instead of attending Kenny's court case, none of this would have happened. She had told Jessica to get off at the Country Store instead of her usual stop, but she had forgotten and lost the note for the bus driver. Thea could only imagine Bart's rough treatment of her daughter when he dragged her into his car, and Jessica must have been in such pain when her leg became entangled in the seat belt. She believed Jessica had passed out at this point because her daughter remembered nothing of the rest of her ordeal, thank goodness. But why was she allowing her mind to travel down this dark road, especially when she was already miserable? Going over and over the events of that fateful day only served to deepen the guilt, and stack up the pile of regrets. Enough was enough.

What she needed was someone to talk to, someone to cajole her out of her mire of self-pity—this sinking sensation was a familiar enemy. The leaden sense of dread sat on her chest like an elephant, and she was terrified. She reached over and ran her finger down the smoothness of the coffee mug; the chill of the earthenware matched the chill in her bones, and she felt as though all the warmth from her body had leached into the room. It took her a moment to realize the phone was ringing, and in a way she was glad for the interruption, although talking was going to be difficult.

"Yes," she said.

"Thea, is that you?"

"It's me," she said. "Hello, Ellie."

"Didn't sound like you. I just wanted to make sure all was well with you and the kids."

Thea made a super human effort to lighten her voice. "We're making progress. The kids are so much more settled now that there's just the four of us, and we're all so relieved Kenny has gone. We're trying to forget about all the bad experiences and move on, but I can't say life's been easy," and she sighed into the phone.

"You know what they say about sighing—it's a woman's silent scream!"

She wanted to tell Ellie she was okay, but today she wasn't. "The responsibility of trying to bring up three kids on my own scares me sometimes."

"Did you ever think of making a fresh start somewhere else?"

Wasn't that tantamount to running away?—something she had to stop herself from doing constantly. "I've thought about it, and while I know a change of scenery would probably be good for me, I'm not so sure leaving here would be a wise decision for the kids. Moving would be such an upheaval for them..."

Ellie jumped in and prattled on. "Thea, you know you would always be welcome here in Massachusetts. The apartment over the store is empty. I've just used the space for storage. I know it's small, but you and the kids could probably manage there for a while, and I think the empty rooms are waiting for you. At least until you get on your feet."

"So much time has gone by, though, and you know the saying—*you can't go back*. There's a lot of truth in the old cliché."

Thea was surprised Ellie didn't give up, but she appeared undaunted by Thea's negativity. "I know, but I just wanted to at least give you the option."

"Don't think I'm not tempted, because I am, and I will definitely give your offer some thought."

Ellie changed the subject. "How's Jess doing?"

"She seems to be okay. The cast is now off her leg, and you should have seen her face when she saw how dry, pale and hairy her skin was where the cast had been—it really freaked her out! Physically she's healthy, but mentally, I'm not so sure. It's as if she is always looking over her shoulder except when we are all in the house together. I'm still taking the three of them to school and then I pick up Jessica after her morning kindergarten session. Peter and Izzie ride the bus home."

"Are you still working at the Country Store?" Ellie asked.

"I am. I've also started drawing again and I'm in the process of putting a stack of greeting cards together..."

Ellie interrupted and said, "If you ever want to send any my way, I'd love to sell them at Aladdin's Cave. Do you remember how much our customers loved them?"

"I do," Thea said wistfully, thinking back to those happier days. "We had such good times together, didn't we? Then Michael had to come on the scene and I ruined everything by falling in love with him."

"Thea, if Michael hadn't come into your life, it would have been someone else. I agree the timing was awful, but you were ripe for the plucking," Ellie said.

"I know, but I was so happy with you, and we had so many plans. I'm sorry I didn't keep in touch. I was full of such good intentions. Makes me realize how thoughtless I was."

"Don't be such a silly goose. You needed to spread your wings. I was just as much at fault, but it took me a while to get over the hurt of losing you."

"Now you're giving me a guilt complex, and it doesn't take much."

Ellie soldiered on. "Sorry, I didn't mean to upset you, and look, I have to go. Customers, they are awaiting. I just wish we were closer so we could sit and hash this all out."

"I know, and I do appreciate your calling me."

"Promise me you'll think over my offer. I'm willing to give you a full partnership. Goodbye for now, and remember I love you," and she was gone.

Thea sat staring at the silent receiver in her hand, willing the comfort of Ellie's voice to come back. She paced up and down the kitchen. The phone call had been unsettling; their conversation had seemed stilted, and somehow unreal. There was so much she hadn't told Ellie. Why couldn't she talk to her anymore? Was it just because they'd lost the thread of communication over the years? She found life terrifying—she was scared of so many things. School was tough for the kids. She felt as though they were all tainted because of Kenny's accident, and even though neighbors and townsfolk had truly rallied around during and after Jess's abduction, they all seemed to be steering clear of her now. And the children were suffering too. It was as though some of Kenny's misfortune had rubbed off on all of them. Damn it. Sometimes life just wasn't fair, and now the kids were paying for her mistakes.

She sat down and picked up one of her pencils, absent-mindedly rolling the slender piece of wood between her fingers. At least the conversation with Ellie had pushed her out of her misery—given her something to think about—and maybe making a fresh start wouldn't be such a bad idea. Thea's mind took her back to the days when she had worked with Ellie at Aladdin's Cave—a colorful and thriving art emporium—in a town with which she was oh so familiar, nestled at the foot of the Berkshire Hills. They were such happy times, and the fact that Ellie had now presented her with the opportunity for a full partnership in a business she truly loved, was sorely tempting. But why now? Was there something in Ellie's voice or was she imagining the change in tone? Twelve years had passed since they had worked together, so she was a little puzzled. Taking Ellie up on her offer would certainly solve some of her money worries and make her less dependent on Michael, even though he continued to be exceedingly generous with his child support. She sighed and thought how reassuring a steady source of income would be. Her current job at the Country Store working for Bill and Margaret Gilson was becoming mundane and tedious, and she needed more contact with people other than the local townsfolk.

Perhaps it would be a good idea to move away and put her checkered past behind her. This way, she and the children wouldn't have to worry about Kenny always lurking in the shadows because, try as she might, she couldn't quite believe he wasn't going to cause further problems. But how could she tell Bill and Margaret, and Nan, their daughter, she and the children would be moving away? Breaking the news to Nan wouldn't be so difficult because she was in Boston most of the time, but it was an entirely different story with Bill and Margaret who had constantly given her a shoulder to lean on. She just couldn't shake her guilt for all the trouble she had showered upon them. If it weren't for her and the complications resulting from the bust up with Kenny, Lady, their beautiful black Lab, would still be alive. Her list of misfortunes was never-ending, and she shivered. She got up from the table, pushed her drawings aside and resumed her pacing, deep in thought. What's to say she wouldn't bring Ellie bad luck too? After all, she'd already let her down once.

Thea couldn't think anymore, and she needed to get out and run before she drowned in her own pool of self-pity. She glanced at the clock, and she had about an hour before she would have to pick up Jess—time enough to iron out the kinks. She loved to run, and she reveled in the way the strenuous exercise always lifted her spirits. She had an easy, natural stride, and she soon felt as if she were running on air. With the rhythm of the music playing through her earphones, she was able to dispel her despondent mood, and even though she was a little disheveled and sweaty when she went to pick up Jess, she was much more cheerful.

Jess seemed to have grown taller in the last couple of months and seeing her five-year-old daughter without her plaster cast pleased Thea. Her face wasn't quite as round, but her shiny black curls were just as unruly as she ran to meet her mom. Much to everybody's dismay, she had lost her voice after the abduction, and it was only the thought her father might come back into their lives that forced her vocal cords into action. She had needed to be heard because she vehemently opposed the idea of spending any time with Michael. Needless to say, Thea was thrilled to have her little chatterbox back, but dismayed to learn how strongly Jessica feared and disliked him.

Thea still had the occasional conversation with Dr. Andreski, the intern who had tended to Jess after the accident. He had provided excellent and loving care, and even though he couldn't treat Jess as an outpatient, he still wanted to keep tabs on her. He also counseled Thea and she listened carefully to his words of wisdom. He said she should encourage Jess to ask questions; advised she would probably fear for her safety—this was certainly true—and if she started any role-playing with her toys, the activity would not necessarily make the fear go away. He sometimes told Thea things she didn't always want to hear, such as how children were severely impacted by trauma and had a much harder time understanding and recovering from the event. This was not only vividly real for Jess, but for ten-year-old Peter, too, as he had been the first person to come upon the horrific scene where he had found his sister twisted and unconscious and his mother with a bullet wound in her side. He had also been devastated to see Lady, the Gilson's brave and wonderful dog, lying motionless. She was the one who had taken the bullet which would surely have killed Thea and she who had knocked Jess's abductor backwards onto the rocky ground, causing a head injury from which he never recovered.

Thea dragged her thoughts away from all the bad memories and bent down to take her daughter in her arms, but Jess pushed her away. "Ugh, you're all sweaty," she said.

"Sorry, I just came back from a run."

"Well, duh," Jess said. "I can see that."

Thea felt her hackles rising in response to Jessica's rudeness, and trying hard to keep her temper in check, she said, "That is no way to speak to me, or anyone else for that matter."

"Sorry, Mom," and she turned to give Thea one of her beautiful smiles, looking contritely at her mom with her big blue eyes. Jess, out of all her children, was always the straight talker, but somehow her comments were harsher than they used to be, and Thea was hard-pressed sometimes to remember her daughter was only five. Hearing unwanted truths was the price she paid for demanding honesty from her children.

"How was school?" she asked as she helped Jess carry her bag and lunch box to the car.

Jess shrugged and said, "It was okay."

"Is there something you're not telling me?"

"No..." and she paused.

"Come on, Jess, talk to me. You know I will try and help."

They had reached the car, and Jess clambered into the back, got into her seat and strapped herself in. "I don't think the other kids like me anymore," she said quietly and her eyes filled with tears.

"Why? What's happened, pumpkin?"

"We had to get into teams to work on a project, and nobody wanted me on their team, so Miss Simms had to choose one for me. Then the kids wouldn't talk to me, and they used to be my friends. I just don't know why. What have I done?" and she burst into tears.

"Oh, sweetheart, I'm so sorry," and she gently wiped Jessica's face. "Let's go home and then we can figure out what to do. Okay?"

"Uh-huh," Jess sadly agreed.

Thea's mood was as black as the clouds darkening the sky. The current upset would mean setting up a meeting with Jessica's teacher. When things went wrong with the children, she felt such a pain in her heart. So now it was Jess as well as Peter who was running into difficulties. Izzie seemed to have remained unscathed, but she always had been a rather solitary child, so being ostracized wouldn't be such an issue for her.

They reached the house and Jess just sat in her car seat looking glum. The day was like a train in a tunnel. Earlier Thea had felt a pinprick of light, only to be doused by her daughter's worries and the relentless falling of the rain only made things even more miserable. "Come on, Jess, let's go inside before we get soaked."

Once in the house, Thea took her daughter in her arms and let her cry her heart out. Smokey, Izzie's cat, rubbed herself against Jessica's legs, and eventually the little girl gave one last giant hiccup and even managed a tiny smile. "How's my brave little soldier, now?" Thea asked.

"Mommy, I'm so sad cuz I used to have lots of friends. 'Member how they all signed my cast and did funny drawings? Now, it's as if they can't see me."

"I'll come into school with you tomorrow and ask if I can be in class with you."

"No, no. That won't help," Jessica said, shaking her head frantically. "That'll just make things worse."

"All right then, what do you think would be the best thing to do?" Thea asked.

"I don't know. I just don't want to go to school anymore."

15

Thea was at a loss. "Let's get you out of your school clothes into something more comfortable, and then we need to get to the store. Maybe going to visit Uncle Bill will take your mind off things."

"Oh Mommy, I don't really want to see Aunt Margaret and Uncle Bill. I'm just too sad. Could we stay home, please?"

Her daughter's reluctance to leave the house had become a regular occurrence. Jessica used to love her afternoons at the store, but lately she had not wanted to go, preferring to stay home with her mom. She used to be such a happy-go-lucky child, and Thea remembered the days when her daughter couldn't wait to get to the Country Store and spend time wandering around looking at all the merchandise, totally immersed in her own fantasy world. She would curl up with a book, or sit on one of the round stools at the counter, swinging her legs back and forth as she chatted happily to Bill and Margaret, without a care in the world, giving Thea the opportunity to work away in the little back room checking the inventory and recording each item on the computer. Now Jess was much more fearful and with good reason. Although she had little recollection of the actual abduction, she was now deathly afraid of any man she didn't know. She was also becoming increasingly reluctant to accompany Thea to the store, which was creating a huge problem because Thea needed to work. She was going to have to change her hours, give up her free mornings, so she could be with Jess when she came home from school after her morning kindergarten session. She hoped Bill and Margaret would understand because they loved Jessica and only wanted the best for her. Could she ask them to weather yet another of her bumps in the road?

"Tell you what, Jess, let me call the store, otherwise Uncle Bill and Aunt Margaret will be wondering where we are. I'll just go there in the morning instead. Then you and I will spend some time together and see if we can find our own little ray of sunshine on this rainy day. How does that sound? Why don't you go off and look for a game we could play, or a book we could read together?"

Jess said, "Thank you, Mommy," and went off to the room she shared with her eight-year-old sister, Izzie.

Thea waited until her daughter was out of earshot and then picked up the phone and dialed. Margaret answered, and Thea explained about Jess's rough morning at school and how she wanted to stay home. She asked if she could come in the next morning instead, and she heard Margaret sigh. She was as worn out with Thea's troubles as Thea was herself, but she agreed. She said she hoped Jess would soon be feeling better, and to give her a hug from her, and told Thea she would see her in the morning. "Thank you," Thea said, and hung up. In the old days, Thea wouldn't have given into Jessica's likes and dislikes, but now things were different. Her mind kept going to Ellie's offer, and the more she thought about the prospect, the more appealing the idea became. Certainly, life would be better in a place where no one had knowledge of her recent past, where there could be no prejudices against her children because of her association with a rotten man. Melford Point was a small town. All the locals were acquainted with her business, and she felt stifled.

The afternoon passed pleasantly enough, and she and Jess enjoyed each other's company. She was saddened, though, because she believed her daughter would really have been better off playing with a friend her own age, but she seemed perfectly content spending time with Thea, emerging the winner of a lively game of Chutes and Ladders.

Peter and Izzie weren't surprised to find Jess and their mom at home. In the days before the abduction, they would sometimes still be at the store as it was only a couple of blocks away, but now Thea always made sure she and Jess were at the house. She didn't want Peter and Izzie to be alone, to be latchkey kids.

There was a great deal of chatter around the dinner table as usual, and she wondered whether she should mention her phone call with Ellie and the job offer, but something held her back. Peter's eleventh birthday was coming up at the beginning of December, and she wanted to know what he would like to do. The mention of her brother's birthday was a welcome distraction for Jessica. She got all excited about making his cake, and turning to him, asked what flavor he would like. She loved to bake and even though she couldn't do it all by herself, she did as much as possible. Her mom was really good about the mess! He said, "Chocolate, of course!" He just wanted to have a couple of friends for a sleepover—Ian being one of them—the boy who had helped him when they were looking for Jessica when she had gone missing. He considered himself too old for the parties Thea always gave with all the crazy games; although he still liked "pass the parcel," so he agreed to make a concession, but only just this once. The girls were thrilled and asked if they could join in, and he said, "Sure." The game comprised wrapping a gift in many pieces of paper and then Thea would have the kids all sit in a circle. Music would be played, and each time the music stopped, the child holding the gift would unwrap

17

a layer and so on until the person who removed the final piece got to keep the prize. There would still be parties for Izzie (her ninth in May) and Jess (her sixth in August), and Thea was thankful both their birthdays weren't until next year, by which time she hoped her enthusiasm for party giving would have returned.

CHAPTER TWO

Margaret turned to Bill after she finished talking to Thea, and he could tell by the slump of her shoulders, she didn't have good news.

"They're not coming, are they?" he said, running his hands down his shop apron in a gesture of disappointment.

"She said she'd come in the morning and make up the time, but that's not really the issue, is it?"

"No, it isn't. Do you believe as I do that the family seems to be slipping away from us?"

"The whole situation is weighing me down. I wish Nan was home because she's always able to get through to Thea."

"I know, lass. I know it's hard, but I do think we just have to let them be. Keeping the store running is taking all my energy, and worrying about the Chamberlins just makes my day even harder. I must get back to these deli orders. Let's talk about it later." Irritatingly, of course, he was right. Now was not the best time to have this discussion.

Margaret decided to make herself a cup of tea, and she took comfort from the familiar by sitting at the table where she did all her baking, listening to the soft swish, swish of the meat slicer. She was tired, and not only her legs ached, but her heart ached too. She and Bill had always looked out for Thea, and despite the added worry and complications, they couldn't imagine life without her. Notwithstanding the up and down nature of her character, they loved her, and Margaret had taken her under her wing right from the start, recognizing her need to fit in. She, herself, was an 'outsider,' and the folks in Melford Point were disappointed Bill hadn't married a local girl, but they eventually accepted her. Thea's marriage to Michael had given her a partial foot in the door, and once Bill had accepted her too, their lives had quickly become entwined, especially when Nan and Thea became firm friends. Margaret and Bill had joyfully supported Thea through the births of her children, and they had welcomed each tiny infant with open arms, but seeing Thea through her divorce from Michael put a strain on all of them, and her relationship with Kenny was the last straw. She had buttoned her lip with a great deal of difficulty as she had no right to criticize: after all, Thea wasn't a true daughter, only an 'adopted' one. She'd felt sorry for her and tried to fill the motherly void since Thea's parents lived in Massachusetts and didn't like to travel to Maine. Being nurturing by nature, she just didn't understand their lack of support, and there was many a time when she wanted to pick up the phone and scream at them.

Without even realizing what they were doing—and it certainly wasn't anything they'd planned—she and Bill became surrogate grandparents to Peter, Izzie and Jessica. They often commiserated with one another, saying how bringing up their daughter Nan had been a breeze in comparison. She and Bill would have liked more children, but their wish was never fulfilled, and despite the disappointment of not being so blessed, they were content with their lives. They were simple, hard-working folk who looked at the world with their glass half full, and the Country Store was the hub of the little town. She and Bill managed the store, as had his parents before him, and Margaret sensed he was secretly concerned there was no heir to take over from them when they were too tired to run the business anymore. He had high hopes Peter might be the one, but Margaret was realistic and doubted whether a boy with such a brilliant mind would have any interest in staying in a small town in Maine. After all, his father was a successful lawyer, and even though Peter saw nothing of Michael, sometimes the apple doesn't fall far from the tree, so following in his father's illustrious footsteps wasn't out of the realm of possibility.

Margaret stood up and took her empty mug over to the dishwasher. She rarely sat during the day, and the lunchtime crowd was coming in for their sandwiches, so she put a smile on her face and happily took their orders. She loved working alongside Bill, and he winked at her, and the simple gesture gave her all the encouragement she needed to get back on track. She and Bill were holding their own, and the store was manageable at this time of the year, but decisions about staffing had to be made before the next holiday season. The Country Store itself had changed little over the years, but there were now more tourists and more summer residents as a result of the increasing number of cottages, which seemed to have sprung up like mushrooms all over the place. Even though the work was physically demanding, so far she and Bill had managed to cope, but they weren't getting any younger, and the future worried her. They took pride in ownership, giving good value for money and Margaret's baking was the best for miles around. She loved the bantering back and forth with the townsfolk and all the accompanying gossip, although she never passed on what she heard. She created rhyming games in her head in order to remember everyone's names and took great care in treating each of her customers equally.

Thea had brought unwelcome drama into their lives and threatened Margaret's safe, uncomplicated world. She vividly remembered the first day they had met. She had looked up at the jangling of the doorbell to see Michael towering over Thea as she walked in front of him and into the store. She had hesitated, pausing briefly to take delight in the colorful merchandise and inhaling the smell of baking until he firmly put a hand on the small of her back and pushed her gently forward. He was at his most charming and eloquently introduced Thea as his new bride, to which she had responded with a soft, "Hello." The pungency of his cologne had mingled with the subtleness of the rosewater she had worn, and the scents had lingered in Margaret's nostrils long after they had gone. Thea, all bundled up in a long navy-blue coat, had looked at Margaret and Bill with a shy smile. "I'm pleased to meet you," she had said, pulling off her gloves and holding out her tiny hand. She and Michael had sat down at the counter and ordered lunch and Margaret observed them while she prepared their sandwiches. Thea had seemed such a child with her soft, reddish-sandy colored hair framing her face, compared with Michael's dark handsomeness, and even though they were so obviously in love, they weren't easy with one other—there had been no comfortable bantering back and forth between the two of them. Even Margaret had found it difficult to keep the conversation going, and in all honesty, wished they would leave and was much relieved when they finally did so.

She had always considered Michael somewhat of a mystery, and she no more understood him than she did the rest of his family, with the exception of Mimi, Michael's grandmother. The Chamberlins lived in some kind of elitist world inside their huge house up on the bluff as if they were royalty. Margaret had gotten mad when the family had wanted nothing to do with Thea and the children once the divorce was final and she would have liked nothing better than to have given them all, apart from Mimi, a piece of her mind. She and Bill had loved Mimi, who was a frequent customer, and despite the sparkling diamond earrings and the extravagant rings she always wore, she had no airs or graces. She was just absolutely charming, and she and Bill would exchange stories when he wasn't too busy. It was all so sad the way things had turned out because the marriage had at least been ticking along with Mimi as the anchor, but as soon as she died the ship was cast adrift and all those who had loved her quickly fell overboard, especially Michael. She left a huge void in their lives, and Thea tried to fill the emptiness with Kenny after Michael had left. Margaret and Bill made a valiant attempt to pick up the pieces for the sake of the children, but Margaret was tired of being in the middle. She and Bill still kept a watchful eye, and she was saddened by the current situation with Jessica, disturbed by the fact she chose to stay home rather than come visit. The little girl loved them, especially Bill, and she sensed he was hurt, but Margaret believed Jess would come around eventually. There was no way she could resist a special Uncle Bill hug for too much longer, and she fervently hoped this was the case for her husband's sake. But enough reminiscing—she needed to get back to work.

CHAPTER THREE

Thea was finding it hard to fall asleep. She had too many things preying on her mind and she wasn't looking forward to the morning when she would be faced with cajoling Jessica into going to school. She would have to speak to Miss Simms and hoped she would be able to snag a little of her time before class started. She was puzzled by the children's behavior. How could such little ones be so cruel to each other? Hopefully, Miss Simms would be able to shed some light. Eventually, she drifted off into a restless sleep, only to be woken by Jess who was standing by her bed, looking exceedingly forlorn. "I can't sleep, Mommy. Can I come into bed with you?"

Having her children in bed with her wasn't something Thea encouraged, but she just couldn't turn Jess away, so she pulled the covers back, patted the mattress, and said, "Hop in. Let's ride to the Land of Nod together." Times like these always made her think of how close she had been to losing her, and she snuggled up to her daughter. Even though she didn't really want to admit it, she found Jessica's presence truly comforting. Thea hummed a gentle lullaby and soon they were both fast asleep.

They were both awakened by the alarm. Jess just groaned, turned over and went back to sleep. Thea went downstairs to make a pot of coffee and to wake Peter and Izzie. She had to drag Jess out of bed, and she was surprised she didn't make a scene. Soon they were all eating breakfast, munching contentedly on cereal, or scrambled eggs and toast. Peter looked up at his mother, chewed madly, swallowed and said, "Mom, can I ask you a question?"

"Sure," she said, wondering what was coming.

"Do you think it would be all right if Izzie and I rode the bus in the mornings as well as the afternoons?" Jessica looked up from her bowl of cereal in alarm and Thea thought Peter's timing couldn't have been worse.

Thea hastened to reassure her youngest daughter. "Not to worry, Jess. You don't have to ride the bus. I will take you to school for as long as you want." Jessica sighed and went back to eating.

"So, you don't mind, then, Mom?" Izzie asked.

"Not if you're both sure that's what you want to do. Is there a reason why you don't want me to take you anymore?"

"We just don't want the other kids to think of us as big babies. We don't need to give them any more reasons to tease us—things are bad enough already," Peter said.

Thea looked worriedly at her two older children: Peter, so dark, resembling his father, and Izzie with her reddish hair just a little darker than her own. "Is there anything specific you need to tell me about? Would you like me to talk to your teachers?"

"I don't think it would help. Someone always gets picked on for some reason or another. I have a couple of good and loyal friends, and they get me through the days," Peter said.

"Izzie, how is it for you?" Thea asked.

"I'm not really having any problems. All the kids pretty much leave me alone."

Thea didn't really want to hear what her children were saying because she felt as though she were the cause of all their problems. She understood—from her own experience—school was a battleground, but she had hoped her children would go through the system mostly unscathed. They had been doing fine until all the scandal associated with Kenny's hit-and-run accident had become common knowledge. Peter had already instigated one fight, albeit in defense of his sister, and she could see he was brewing for another. He had a hard time controlling his wicked temper, and his anger scared him as much as it scared her. After all, he had plenty to be angry about.

"You'll have to come with me this morning, but I'll go into the office and make sure the bus stops to pick you both up tomorrow. Does that work?"

They both nodded.

Thea was surprised Jess wasn't making a fuss. She was awfully quiet, but got into the car with the other two, and didn't say a word, which was most unusual for her because she was always the chatty one. Izzie sensed something was wrong, but she didn't want to set her sister off, so she didn't say anything, either. They reached the school and Peter and Izzie tumbled out with their huge backpacks and hurried off, soon getting lost in among all the other kids pouring into the building.

Thea turned to Jess and said, "Stay put. I'm going to park the car so I can come in with you." Jess just looked at her.

"Okay, missy—school bag, check; lunch box, check," and she was rewarded with a glimmer of a smile. Once inside the hallway, they headed towards the kindergarten classroom and Jess was definitely dragging her heels. The kindergarteners didn't have lockers, but just hung their bags and coats on pegs and tucked their lunch boxes into cubbies below, with their names taped above. The room was brightly decorated and hummed with activity. Thea caught Miss Simms's eye in the hope the teacher was sensitive enough to realize Thea needed to talk. Thea was observing the other children's reaction to Jess as she hung up her coat and stashed her lunchbox, after which she went and sat at her desk. As far as she could tell, everything seemed to be pretty normal. Miss Simms turned to the class. "Please sit quietly and look at your reading books. I will just be outside the door for a minute, and you know I have eyes in the back of my head, so no misbehaving!"

"Yes, Miss Simms," chorused the children.

Once in the hallway, she turned to Thea. "I'm sorry, but I don't have much time. You can't expect five-year-olds to sit still for very long. Could you come back at recess at ten o'clock and I will get someone to cover for me?"

"It's just that I'm so worried about Jess."

"I know, but I promise I will keep an eye on her. I'll meet you in the office. See you at ten?"

Thea had no choice but to agree even though meeting at ten o'clock would mean she was missing yet another morning of work, but making time to talk to Jessica's teacher was much more important. "Please tell her I will be back during recess." Miss Simms nodded, shook Thea's hand, and went back into the classroom.

Thea wandered down the corridor to the office, her shoes making soft squeaky noises on the highly polished floor, to inform the admin about the bus pickup for tomorrow. She wondered whether she should make appointments with Peter and Izzie's teachers, but decided to let sleeping dogs lie. Ruth, the school administrator, looked up as she walked through the door, "Good morning, Mrs. Chamberlin. How can I help?" She always felt like saying, "I'm not *Mrs. Chamberlin*—I'm *Ms.*," but since she had decided to keep Michael's name for the children's sake, there didn't seem much point in splitting hairs over a mere triviality. She explained about the bus, and Ruth confirmed there would be no problem. "Just Peter and Izzie, then?" she asked.

"Yes," Thea replied. "I shall continue to drop off and pick up Jess for as long as she needs me to."

"Very good," Ruth said, making a note on the list of bus routes, and nodding her head with its perfectly coiffed and lacquered hair without so much as a strand out of place. Thea had never seen her look any different, although there did seem to be a little more than the usual subtle hint of blue in the silvery gray today. Despite her advancing years, she was an efficient, steadfast and loyal employee totally devoted to the school. Thea had no doubt she would pass the message along and thanked her before walking out of the office.

Thea stepped out of the warmth of the building and shivered. The sky was overcast with low-hanging clouds, and she wondered whether there would be snow. Normally, she loved the winter months, but she wasn't sure she had the energy to tackle all the shoveling this year. The children would be thrilled, though, to have snow days, to be able to skate on the local pond and be part of the after-school ski program. She tried to focus on the positive and decided to go to the Country Store rather than making another phone call. She was worried because she was pushing Bill and Margaret to the limits of their patience. She pulled into one of the parking spaces set slightly on the diagonal all along the northern side of Main Street. The Country Store was buzzing with activity, and the brightly lit windows revealed the tantalizing merchandise within. She knew the regulars would be inside having their morning coffee, and she took comfort in knowing there would be friendly faces. She glanced at her watch, saw it was nine o'clock and decided she was probably a coward for picking one of the busiest times of the day; she was well aware there would be little opportunity for a private conversation with either Bill or Margaret. She knew she was putting off the inevitable, but she did at least want to give them the courtesy of putting in a personal appearance.

The bell jangled as she pushed the door open. Nobody took any notice of her except Bill, who looked over to see who had come into the store, and his chubby face lit up when he saw her, and she smiled in return. She loved Bill with all his funny sayings, and so did Jessica, and she felt sad when her daughter didn't want to come visit. Margaret was taking a batch of scones from the oven and had her rather broad back turned towards Thea. "Those smell delicious," Thea said, noticing Margaret seemed to have lost a little of her sparkle. She, too, was round like Bill, and she had an exceptionally pretty face with features that would never age, even though her skin might wrinkle. There didn't seem to be any sprinklings of silver in her soft, brown hair; Bill, on the other hand, was completely gray. His wiry hair sprung out around his ears and around the back of his head, but his pate was bald and shiny. He always made Jess laugh by saying he could never go outside without a hat because some giant bird might come and take him away to its nest as some kind of gleaming treasure!

"Hello, my dear," Margaret said, placing the tray down on the scrubbed pine table, removing her oven mitts and giving Thea a hug. "It's good to see you."

"I can't stay long."

"Oh, and why's that?" Margaret said, stepping back and looking at her intently.

Thea heard the coldness and disappointment in Margaret's voice, and said, "I have to go back to the school and meet with Jessica's teacher. She suggested I go at ten o'clock because there's a situation I need to deal with right away. The other kids are being unkind to Jess, and I need to find out why and what we can do to put things right. I know my letting the work pile up here isn't fair to you, but when things go wrong with the kids, I'm the only one who can sort it out. Unfortunately, I can't be in two places at once, and I'm just so terribly sorry to be letting you down like this."

Margaret was at a loss for words. Her heart went out to Thea because she was a kindly soul, but she was tired of being taken for granted. "Thea, I don't know what to say. We're trying to run a business here. We do need to sit down and talk but now's not the time," and she turned to take the cooling scones off the baking tray. She didn't offer Thea one.

Thea realized she shouldn't have come. It wasn't fair to burden Margaret with her problems when she was trying to serve her customers, so she tentatively made a suggestion. "Would you mind coming over tonight after the children have gone to bed so we can talk this through? I would come here, but I don't have anyone to stay with the kids."

"Sure, I can do that. See you later," and Margaret returned to her work. Bill gave Thea a little wave, and she went back out into the cold.

Thea was desperate for someone impartial to talk to. Margaret and Bill were great, but they were too emotionally involved. She could pick up the phone and call Nan she supposed, but she hated phone calls. She used to be so active in the community, but she had withdrawn from the volunteering because of the kids, and she didn't trust anyone to look after them but herself. She had never intentionally asked Bill and Margaret to babysit, although, of course, they had because they loved spending time with the children. The Gilsons had trained Izzie and Peter to help out at the store, an activity they had both enjoyed, and even though Bill couldn't pay them because they were underage, he used to slip them pocket money. Thea wondered now whether they had been more of a hindrance than a help, but she didn't think so. They were bright kids and Peter was big for his age, so he was able to help carry boxes and stock shelves. Izzie worked with Margaret drizzling icing on scones, and helping to mix up the huge batches of different kinds of cookies. There were machines to do most of the really hard work, but those still had to be manned, and the dough still had to be put on the baking trays. Her daughter had become extremely proficient, and Margaret had sung her praises many times. Then, for some reason, it all stopped, and Bill and Margaret had hired a couple of older kids to take care of what Izzie and Peter had once undertaken. Of course, this was quite understandable as her children's help was sporadic at best once the school year started and they were busy with homework, compounded by soccer for Peter and dance for Izzie. Thea wondered whether Bill and Margaret were pulling back to ease the hurt just in case they did all decide to leave, even though she had not given them any reason to think they would move away. She put the car in gear, reversed out into the road and made her way back to the school, weary from trying to figure out the complexities of life.

Miss Simms was as good as her word and was waiting for Thea just inside the office door. She said, "Come with me and we'll find somewhere quiet to talk. I have about twenty minutes."

Thea nodded and followed the slim, conservatively dressed young woman, with her dark hair pulled away from her face into a neat bun, back along the hallway and into a small room off the teachers' lounge. The room was set up informally with four fairly comfortable chairs and a coffee table on which someone had placed a rather tired arrangement of artificial flowers. Thea sat at the teacher's invitation and said, "Miss Simms..." at which she interrupted and said, "Please call me Monica."

Thea looked into the teacher's light brown eyes and continued. "Can you please tell me what happened yesterday? Jess was very upset because she told me none of the children picked her when groups were being formed for a special project."

Monica was brief but kind. "I'm truly sorry. I didn't realize she had taken it so much to heart. She has been much quieter lately, and when she does say anything she comes across as being a little bit rude. She didn't get picked by the other children simply because she just isn't fun to be around anymore. I know that's no excuse, but five-year-olds aren't sophisticated enough to play silly games and leave someone out on purpose. Unfortunately, they chose other children to be in their groups, and Jess got left out. I tried to fix the situation as best I could, but sadly, the damage was done."

Thea sighed, looked down at the worn oriental carpet beneath her feet and swallowed the lump in her throat before looking up into Miss Simms's plain but kindly face. "I hate to admit it, but I think the time has come to get professional help for Jessica. In the meantime, I will talk to her about her rudeness, and if you could find some way to boost her confidence, I would be grateful. Is there maybe another child who needs help? Someone who Jess could spend time with, take her or him under her wing, to make her feel important again."

"I'll see what I can do." Monica paused, trying to think what would be best. She was well aware the family had gone through a rough time, but she didn't have the right to say anything. Thea looked at her expectantly, and she continued. "Jessica seemed to be okay until her plaster cast came off; after that she seemed to lose her identity along with the cast. Most likely, it was some kind of security blanket for her." Her heart went out to Thea.

"Monica, I think you're right. I have to find some way to bring back the old fun-loving Jessica. I truly appreciate your time and your honesty, and I know she's in good hands. I believe she's comfortable with you and I know she likes you otherwise I don't think I could have persuaded her to come to school today. I know I'm asking a lot, but if you could find a way to improve her morale somehow without the other children thinking you're playing favorites, I would be so thankful."

"Mrs. Chamberlin, I will do what I can. I don't like to see the children in my care unhappy, and I will certainly keep an eye on her. If you would like her to see the school psychiatrist, please let me know, and I will make an appointment for you."

Thea stood up. She and Monica shook hands. "Thank you for taking the time to meet with me at such short notice. You've given me hope, and it's reassuring to know you will be taking steps to help my daughter. Could I ask just one more favor? I know you're busy, but if anything like this happens again, could you call me? It would be so comforting to have the benefit of your first-hand observation, so any future situation can be dealt with right away before it gets out of hand."

"Of course. Now I really must get back to class. I will most definitely keep an eye on Jessica and call you if a problem arises. I'd also be happy to meet with you again. Just call the office and they will set up a time for us."

"Thank you," and Thea turned, gave Monica a brief smile, and left.

Monica watched her walk away. Mrs. Chamberlin seemed so alone somehow. She walked back to her classroom, pondering on the way as to how she could help Jessica. She wasn't the only troubled child in her class, but what saddened the teacher most was how Jess had changed. She had only been in kindergarten for such a short period of time before the accident, and she had been a joy—one of those kids who make teaching worthwhile. She had put on a brave front when she had first come back to school, and the other children had gathered around her, eager to read what had already been printed and drawn on her cast, wanting to add their own marks. She reveled in the attention and smiled with delight when Monica had produced some brightly colored stickers. With Jessica's leg prominently resting on one of the chairs, each child had lined up for a sticker, after which, one by one, they happily applied them to her cast. Jessica had been over the moon.

Monica suddenly thought show-and-tell would be a good idea. She could ask them to bring in something really important to them, and she wondered whether maybe Jessica would bring in her cast. As soon as she was back in the classroom, she made sure she gave a special smile to Jessica and those other children who really needed her help. In a way, she was grateful to Mrs. Chamberlin for making her more aware of all the children and their different personalities. She was a sensitive young woman, and Thea was right when she said Jessica was in good hands.

Thea sat in her car, and she couldn't stop shaking. Having a satisfactory conference with a teacher gave her a sense of pride, but this session with

Miss Simms had been difficult, leaving her perplexed and doubting her parenting skills. Although she now felt she had an ally in Monica Simms, there was the question as to whether she should seek psychiatric help for Jessica. Her mind was running a mile a minute as she attempted to figure out what would be best for her daughter. The problem was she didn't actually believe in the psychiatric approach because it seemed as though people went into therapy, talking about their problems for years, and never getting any better. She thought massage was a much better option, but she needed to run the idea by a professional. This wasn't a decision she could make by herself, but she believed—based on her own experience—massages alleviated pain, anxiety and depression. Obviously, Jessica would have to be comfortable with the concept, and Thea would make sure she was with her for every session. The therapist would also have to be female because of Jess's fear of men she didn't know, and she needed someone with whom Jess could build up a relationship of trust, someone who would listen to her and give her an overall sense of wellbeing, thereby restoring her self-esteem. She remembered the infant massage class she had attended with Peter shortly after he was born. He had been a fractious baby, and Michael was no help. "Can't you do something," he would say as if it were all her fault. She went to the class as much for her own sanity as for Peter's and took comfort from the other mothers, even though she was too shy to make friends. In any case, she would have had to go to their houses because Michael would never have tolerated what he would have termed "an invasion" in their own home. It had never occurred to her to stand up to him, and their line of communication had completely broken down. She had still loved him, but she had no longer respected him: he had bullied her once too often. She had also fiercely protected Peter from Michael's frustration, and the time spent massaging her son and singing him lullabies had been mutually beneficial. They had formed an unbreakable bond and the same could be said for Izzie and Jessica. Deprived of touch as a child, she had been determined not to make the same mistake with her own children.

Thea pulled herself back into the present and wondered whom she should go to for advice about the massage therapy. Maybe she should start with Jenny, the art therapist, with whom Jess had had sessions shortly after she had come home from the hospital. On the other hand, perhaps Dr. Andreski would be the best person to call, or the pediatrician who had carried out Jess's outpatient care. At least she had options, and thinking the idea through had made her realize she wasn't totally alone. She glanced at her watch. She had about forty-five minutes to kill and wondered what to do with the time and decided to do a quick run to the closest coffee shop as she had a sudden longing for a vanilla latte. She was cold, and the thought of a hot drink was irresistible. She parked outside the quaint little place called the "Coffee Pot" and once inside, the warmth and the pungent aroma of roasted coffee beans enveloped her. She inhaled deeply, ordered her drink, and sat by the window so she could watch the world go by. She didn't think she'd see anyone she knew at this end of town, so she relaxed. She was always worried she might run into Kenny, but he would be much more likely to frequent Will's Diner. She enjoyed the attractiveness of her surroundings and the warmth of the gas logs burning in the hearth as they helped to lift her mood and dispel the gloom of the day.

Thea waited at the bottom of the school steps for Jess. A cold and nasty wind had whipped up, so she pulled the hood of her coat over her bright hair and rammed her hands into her pockets for warmth. Her daughter's face lit up when she saw her mom, and she ran down the steps as best she could with all she had to carry. Thea lightened the load, gave her a hug, and they headed for the car. Soon they were both safely strapped in, glad to be out of the cold, and Thea asked Jess how her day had gone. Jess was all chitter chatter, said there was going to be show-and-tell tomorrow and she had to take in something important to her. She also said Miss Simms had had a quiet talk with her and said she was sorry about yesterday. "That made me feel so good, Mom, cuz she saw I'd gotten left out. She has also asked me to look out for Johnny, who's new. He only came a week ago. So she said I'm not the only one who gets left out sometimes."

"Sweetheart, that's wonderful," and Thea blinked madly so her daughter wouldn't see her tears. She recognized the need to broach the subject of Jess's rudeness, but decided to leave the unwelcome task until later. The positive note in her daughter's voice heartened Thea, and she said a silent thank you to Miss Simms for her caring and sensitivity. She was so glad she had gone in to see her today. Thank goodness five-year-olds, unlike adults, didn't have the ability to dwell on things, and she was ever so pleased to have Jessica in a much better frame of mind. Now the next piece of crisis intervention would be her meeting with Margaret later. She prayed she'd be able to handle that amicably, but she still had the afternoon to get through, and who knew what might happen!

Fortunately, her worries were unfounded, and the next few hours were uneventful. As soon as Peter and Izzie came home, she told them they were all set to ride the bus from now on, and they thanked her profusely. She managed to take Jessica aside and suggested she needed to think a little bit more about other people's feelings and how she said things. As soon as Thea mentioned Miss Simms and how she'd noticed Jess was sometimes a little bit rude in school, Jessica looked worried. "I'll try to say nice words, Mommy. I really will. I don't want to let Miss Simms down."

"Okay, pumpkin, that's good enough for me because I know you will try your absolute best."

"I will, Mommy, I will. Now I have to go and find something for show-and-tell."

Thea was content to be home with the children, within the safety of her own four walls. The wind had definitely become more menacing, and she felt bad Margaret would have to go out in the miserable weather later. She knew it couldn't be helped as they needed to talk, but she wasn't looking forward to hearing what Margaret might have to say. She was so tired, and again, she realized how starved she was for adult company—a friend her own age. If they stayed here in Melford Point, she was going to have to find someone to stay with the children so she could get back out into the community and have a few hours to herself. But whom? She just didn't have a clue, but she would go mad if she didn't do something to change her current circumstances. She believed, emphatically, she did not want another man in her life, but she longed for a confidante, someone to share the load. She ran water in the teakettle and put a tea bag in her favorite mug—a special gift from Nan—with the words "Wild Woman" painted in bright bold letters on one side of the shiny surface, and they had puzzled her when she had first read them. She had never been *wild*, not by any stretch of her imagination, but Nan must have sensed something! A latent personality trait waiting to explode—she fervently hoped not. She had enough trouble dealing with her current moods, although a little fun for her and her alone would be truly welcome.

Tea in hand, Thea went off to the living room, flipped on the gas logs and curled up in the corner of the sofa. She loved the coziness of the room with the bright pillows and throws she'd carefully chosen, and she snuggled beneath one of the softly woven afghans. She was reading *The Magician's Assistant* by Ann Patchett, and picking up the thread of the story from where she had left off was easy, and she was soon immersed in the lives of the characters. She and the children were regular visitors to the library, and because they had a hard time keeping track of all their books and seeing as Izzie was pretty organized, she had agreed to take charge and remind them of the due dates in an attempt to make sure they didn't pay too many fines. Occasionally, on a Saturday, they would pick out a video, and they resumed the beloved ritual once Kenny had left. It was so much fun to make popcorn from scratch and snuggle together to watch the movie, although it was becoming increasingly difficult to find a storyline on which they could all agree. More often than not, they ended up with more than one and Peter and Thea would watch his choice after the girls had gone to bed. Being allowed to stay up later than his sisters gave them some one-on-one time together, giving her the opportunity to keep the lines of communication open—something she considered a necessity. She tried to have time alone with each of her children, but this was becoming increasingly difficult because of the absence of a babysitter in their lives.

Supper was done, dishes were washed, baths and showers taken, and bedtime stories read to Jess and Izzie. They were both fast asleep, and Peter was in his room reading. He was currently devouring all the Harry Potter books, and so far, he had seen all the movies. She told him Aunt Margaret was coming over, warned him not to read too late, kissed him on the cheek— even though he got all huffy—and said, "Good night. Sweet dreams."

"Goodnight, Mom," he replied and snuggled under the covers, already immersed in his book.

Thea decided to make a pot of decaffeinated coffee just in case Margaret would like some and the familiarity of the task helped to keep her restlessness at bay. In a way, she wished Bill was coming too, but she understood his wish to avoid what he called "woman talk" like the plague and he would have felt awkward, so it was probably best he was staying home. She sat at the kitchen table and looked through her most recent drawings, but this wasn't her creative time of the day, so she put them away.

Bill insisted on driving Margaret to Thea's. "You're tired, lass. You haven't sat down all day. I'll go start the car and make the inside nice and warm," and off he went. She wearily put on her coat, wrapped a scarf around her neck, and waited for Bill to bring the car to the side door. He was such a kind man, and she loved him dearly. She thought of all Thea's misfortunes and wondered why fate had chosen to deal her such a rotten hand of cards, but had seen fit to grace Margaret with the highest in the pack. Of course, Bill was a man in a million, but it didn't seem fair Thea had ended up with two rotten eggs. Still deep in thought, she saw the lights of the car and stepped out into the alleyway. The wind grabbed her scarf and tried to rip the strip of soft fuzzy wool from her neck. Boy was it cold! Bill was holding the car door open for her, and he said, "Quick, quick, woman. Hurry up and get in. I'm freezing my buns off out here!" She smiled and folded herself into the warmth, and he shut the door, climbed in the driver's side, and they were off. "This was such a good idea. Thank you," she said. He reached over and squeezed her hand, and the warmth of his fingers caressed her own.

Thea was standing at the kitchen window trying to prepare herself for her meeting with Margaret, and although she was nervous, she was relieved when the Gilson's car eventually pulled up outside the house. She waved to them and waited until Margaret was on the porch before opening the door in an attempt to keep the wind from sucking all the warmth out of the hallway. "What a night. I'm not sure I'm ready for winter. Let me take your coat. I made a pot of decaf. Would you like some?"

"How thoughtful of you, and I'd love a cup. It's so nice and warm in here," Margaret said, still struggling crossly to unwind her scarf, which seemed to have gotten entangled around her neck. "Oh, this wretched thing!"

"Here, let me help," and Thea gently unwound the scarf, hanging it on the hallstand with Margaret's coat.

Margaret followed Thea into the kitchen. Thea kept a tidy but warm and inviting home, and she stood looking at all the children's drawings on the walls. They were so bright and cheerful in their simple acrylic frames. The walls were a soft yellow and the tiles on the floor black and white. The room was large enough for a scrubbed pine table and mismatched chairs with colorful seat cushions. A bright pot of gerbera daisies, vibrant in their oranges, reds and yellows, sat in the center of the table, and Margaret reached over to touch one of the flowers. "I love your kitchen," she said.

Thea smiled, and said, "Come, let's go sit in the living room. I can turn on the gas logs, and we can relax."

"Don't make me too comfortable, dear, or I shall fall asleep."

Thea was fully aware the evening wasn't the best time of the day for Margaret and admired her even more for braving the cold to come and see her. "Thank you for being here," she said.

"I wanted to come. It's just that I'm on my feet all day and I usually end up falling asleep in front of the TV, but talking will keep me awake! I really wanted to find out how you're doing and, of course, I have a vested interest in hearing what you have to say."

Margaret took the comfy chair by the fire and Thea tucked herself into the corner of the sofa, drew in her breath, and said, "I've let you down, haven't I?"

"Oh, Thea, no. That's not true. But I do have to be honest with you, scary as it is. Bill and I have a business to run, and we're not getting any younger. I don't want to lose you, and I don't want you to take what I am about to say the wrong way, but we have to have someone who is reliable. I know life's difficult for you..."

Thea interrupted, her hands gripping the front of the couch. "I don't have anyone I can leave the children with and Jessica's going through a tough time. It's impossible to second-guess her. I just don't know quite how she's going to be on any given day and she needs me. Much as I hate to say this, I really think you should find someone else to do inventory for you."

Margaret nodded as if she had known all along what Thea's decision would be. "I was afraid of that," she said. "You need an outlet, though. You can't isolate yourself with the children. It's not healthy. I wish we could help you more, but with Nan away all the time..."

Thea didn't allow Margaret to finish her sentence. "You, Bill and Nan have come to the rescue so many times. The three of you have been my real family, and I will forever be in your debt for all you've seen me through. Without you, the kids would be in much worse shape than they are. I'm embarrassed to think about how much you've helped us over the years, especially when Jess and I were in the hospital. She wouldn't have recovered as quickly if you hadn't taken the time to stay with her, especially at night because I was too weak to be with her myself. You've done enough. Now I need to stand on my own two feet."

Margaret looked at Thea. "Easier said than done. It's not wise to be too independent. I'd like to tell you a story told to me by my friend, April, many years ago—a story I've carried with me ever since... Just up the road from April's home was a field in which there were two horses. From a distance, each appeared to be like every other horse, but if you stopped your car, or were walking by, you would notice something quite astonishing because the larger of the two horses was completely blind. The horse's owner, out of the kindness of his heart, had chosen not to have him put down, but had instead made a good home for him by giving him a companion, and if nearby and listening, you would hear the sound of a bell. If you looked around for the source of the sound, you would notice a bell attached to the halter of the smaller horse. The tinkling of the bell would let her blind friend know where she was so he could follow her. If you had time to stand and watch these two horses, you would see how the smaller one was always checking on her friend. He would listen for her bell and then walk slowly to where she was, trusting she would not lead him astray. When she returned to the shelter of the barn each evening, she would stop occasionally and glance back, making sure her friend wasn't too far behind to hear the bell. Like the owners of these two horses, God does not throw us away just because we're not perfect or because we have problems or challenges. He watches over us and even brings others into our lives to help us when we are in need. Sometimes we are the blind horse being guided by the little ringing bell of those whom God places in our lives. Other times we are the guide horse, helping others to see. Good friends are like this... You don't always see them, but you know they are always there. Please listen for their bells and they'll listen for yours. So you see, Bill, Nan and I are your friends as you are ours. I want to help you and the children get back on your feet." Margaret paused when she saw Thea's tears, and said, "I'm sorry. I didn't mean to make you cry."

Margaret got up and went and sat next to Thea and put her hand on her knee, and Thea covered Margaret's hand with her own, noticing how swollen Margaret's knuckles were and how her gold wedding band seemed to have settled into the flesh of her finger. Thea was at a loss for words and sat silently while she attempted to pull herself together. Finally, her voice thick with tears, she said, "I would like to believe in God, but I don't."

"I wish you and the children would come to church one Sunday. I think you would be comforted by the spiritual community, and there are all sorts of outreach programs, including a youth group that might be good for Peter. I know you think of yourself as an 'outsider,' but I'm one too, and the town has accepted me. Mainly, because of Bill, I know..."

"Margaret, I promise I'll think about it. As far as being an 'outsider' is concerned, I was accepted as Michael's wife, but after the fiasco with Kenny, people are steering clear of me now. How can I expect others to have any respect for me when I have so little respect for myself? I'm afraid I have a long uphill road to climb in order to get back into Melford Point's good books. Even the children have been tainted because of my mistakes. Unfortunately, I've made a bit of a mess of things."

"You know, Jim still asks after you whenever he comes into the store."

Again, Thea didn't know how to respond, so she sat back into the couch and removed her hand from Margaret's.

Margaret continued, "So you see, it wasn't just Bill and I who rallied around. There were other folks too."

Thea nodded. "I know and don't think I'm not appreciative of all the help we've received. I will always be grateful for the wonderful way in which all the Melford Point people supported us, and I want to thank you for being honest with me, not beating around the bush."

"Well, if you think you're okay, I'm going to call Bill and have him come pick me up. I know we could talk all night, but I think we've said enough for now."

She wasn't okay, but she nodded anyway, and in an attempt to bring some normality into her life, said, "Would you and Bill come and have dinner with me and the kids on Sunday? I would like that very much."

"We'd love to, and I know I can speak for Bill—it will be like old times. I'm pretty sure he misses the kids even though he doesn't say much."

Margaret stood up and so did Thea. She gave Thea one of her famous hugs, but Thea could sense neither of their hearts was quite in it. Things had changed between them, and she didn't know how to bridge the gap. Thea helped Margaret into her coat and gently wound her scarf around her neck. "Thank you for coming," she said. "I wish my mother had been half as loving and as wise as you."

Margaret touched Thea's cheek, noticing the dark shadows beneath her beautiful eyes, said, "Goodnight, see you Sunday," and stepped out onto the porch where Bill was waiting. Thea blew a kiss and quickly shut the door. She stood watching from the kitchen window as Bill got Margaret all settled and then drove away. She really needed to go to bed, but she was antsy, so she rinsed out the mugs, threw away the stale coffee and set everything up for the morning. She reflected on their conversation, and she wasn't sure they had achieved anything except to avoid hostility, and the fact she was now out of a job was downright scary.

Margaret was right, of course, about isolating herself, but she just couldn't see her way out of her present dilemma. Interesting that Margaret had mentioned Jim Hudson. Jim used to be Kenny's boss, and she wondered whether he still employed him. She had known Jim for a long time and had met him and Kenny when she used to go to Hudson's Hardware and Lumber back in the days when she and Michael were first married. Those were such happy times. She and Michael had been so much in love, and she was nesting. She would pick up those little cards with all the various paint colors and bring them home to choose the ones she liked best. Sometimes when she needed advice, she would talk to Mimi. She had a flair for decorating, and they had taken many a shopping trip, picking out a pillow here, a throw there, and scatter and area rugs for the newly stripped and refinished wooden floors. Michael loved her so much then and would be delighted at the smudges of paint on her nose, but she didn't want her thoughts to take her there—reminiscing was just too painful.

Jim had loved her from a distance for many years, but she lived in blissful ignorance of his feelings. She was equally unaware of Kenny and had no idea he was besotted with her. She never gave it a second thought when he always seemed to appear as if from nowhere to ring up her purchases, and had she known, she would never have allowed him to deliver orders to the house. She still didn't get it, even when he would hang around afterwards exchanging pleasantries and making a nuisance of himself. She tolerated him just out of kindness, but eventually, she would tell him to shoo, saying, "I've got work to do." He always refused the tip she tried to press into his hand. As far as Jim was concerned, she was equally blind and blissfully ignorant of his love for her until she saw the way he looked at her during one of his visits while she was recuperating in the hospital. How easy life would have been if she could have returned Jim Hudson's love with an equal passion of her own, but she was numb then, and was numb still. She had also made a promise to herself not to bring any more men into the children's lives—they had suffered enough because of her poor choices. But she was getting exceedingly tired of her current sackcloth and ashes routine. She was procrastinating, and she knew it.

CHAPTER FOUR

Little did Jim know Thea was thinking about him at the precise moment he was thinking about her. He was in his workroom lovingly whittling away at the little animals he made as a hobby, and he wondered as the piece of wood beneath his fingers began to take shape, whether Jessica still had the seal he had placed in her hand when she was in the hospital recovering from her injuries. If he'd had a crystal ball, he would have been able to see she kept the seal on a special shelf in her bedroom where she could look at the whimsical creature all the time. He remembered adding whiskers made out of waxen thread and he smiled. He realized there was a market for the tiny carvings, but he found it much more satisfying to give them away as gifts to children in need, and even occasionally to the elderly folks at the local care home. He used to donate them anonymously, but not anymore. Seeing the delight on the children's faces melted Jim's shyness and they loved him. He wove colorful and amusing stories about each of his carvings and their eyes would light up, especially when he gave each child one to keep. The same went for the elderly, some of whom lived in the past. Occasionally, one of the animals would remind them of something, trigger a memory, and they would look at him with tears in their eyes, and say, "Thank you so much." Reaching out to these people helped to fill the yawning gap in Jim's personal life, and on days when he was feeling particularly lonely, made him realize his own good fortune.

Jim wanted to contact Thea, and he thought the best way would be to write her a letter, but the idea seemed so old-fashioned in these days of electronic communication. He wasn't much for computers, but eventually he caved and ordered a system for the hardware store—a necessary evil to keep up with the times. He had hired a professional, and a rather introverted young man had trained him in the intricacies of the software programs so he could, in turn, train his employees. Once he'd gotten over his initial fear, he actually enjoyed the input of data. He found himself fascinated by all the information available at his fingertips and was thinking about getting a laptop for home.

Jim lived on the outskirts of town in the big, old rambling house, which had been in his family for three generations. He was acquainted with many folk in the trade, plus he was very handy himself, so with expert help at his beck and call, maintaining the house was easy; besides which, it was a labor of love. But he was tired of all the empty rooms, and he longed to fill his home with Thea and her children. He wanted to marry her and be a father to Peter, Izzie and Jess. He loved them all.

The day was drawing in, so Jim neatly tidied up his workbench, took one last look at his current project, pleased with the way it was shaping up. He didn't add any more logs to the stove because, even if the fire went out, there would be some residual warmth from the cedar-clad walls should he decide to go back into the workshop the next day. There were no pipes to freeze, the building was solidly constructed and fully insulated, and it was his haven. He trudged along the path through the yard to the house, pulling the collar of his jacket up around his neck in an attempt to protect himself from the wind. As soon as he opened the side door it was nearly blown off its hinges, and he struggled to pull the door shut as he stepped backwards into the kitchen. He, too, had been procrastinating, mainly because not much time had elapsed since Kenny had moved out of Thea's house, and Jim sensed she probably needed some breathing space, but he just couldn't wait any longer. He filled the teakettle and went off to get some writing paper, and he could hear the dang thing whistling while he rummaged around in his desk. The only paper he could find was a lined pad, and he decided to make do with that: after all it's the message that counts, not the paper it's written on.

Eventually, he found himself sitting at the kitchen table with a mug of strong sweet tea, trying to think about what to say, and after much deliberation, he just told himself to get something down on paper. He could always start again if he wasn't satisfied with what he had written.

Dear Thea,

I'm sure you are surprised to hear from me, although Margaret has probably told you I'm always asking after you and the kids. I know this letter will probably be unwelcome because I'm sure you are still finding your feet after all that happened, but it's easier for me to write down how I feel rather than phoning you.

I don't want to interfere, but just thought I would fill you in on what is going on with Kenny, just in case you're afraid he is going to show up on your doorstep. I couldn't turn him away, so he is still working for me. He is one miserable and down-trodden man, but surprisingly, quite sober. I think he would really have liked to go to prison rather than just being fined and doing community service. He is also constantly reminded of what he did because of having to send a monthly check to the Bainbridge family. I think he sees Melissa's face each time he seals the envelope. He must be living in holy hell knowing he caused the death of somebody's child. He's too mired in his own misery to be a threat to you and the children anymore, and I believe, as long as he stays off the booze, you have nothing to fear. We all keep fairly close tabs on him, and this includes his mother and brother. Anyway, enough about Kenny, but I thought you'd like to know.

I'm still carving my little animals and have even gotten brave enough to deliver them in person to the needy children in the area and also to the elderly folks at the local care home, some of whom I know anyway. It is very gratifying. Does Jess still have the seal I carved for her?

Thea, I would like to be your friend—nothing more. I would love to have you and the kids in my life to give you support. I know it's none of my business, but I did find out from Margaret and Bill that even though Michael wanted to come back into the children's lives, it didn't work out. I would like to spend some time with Peter. I could teach him how to carve, kick a soccer ball around and just do some "man stuff." He's going to be eleven soon, isn't he? That's a tough age for a boy.

I think of you on your own, and wonder how it is for you. I wonder whether you have a shoulder to cry on, someone to talk to. As you know, living in a small town isn't easy. It's like being on the front page of a newspaper all the time. Let me help you build bridges. I won't pressure you in any way, and that's a promise, and I don't break my promises.

I'm sorry about the notepaper, but it's all I could find! I hope you can read my scrawl and please write back if you feel like it, or you could call me at home.

Jim

He suddenly noticed he hadn't touched his tea and the once steaming drink was now stone cold. He was as happy as he was ever going to be with what he'd written, so he pushed the chair backwards away from the table, stood up, and went off in search of an envelope and a stamp before he changed his mind. He would mail the letter in the morning. He congratulated himself on, finally, putting an end to his procrastination and reaching out to Thea, something he had wanted to do for such a long time—now fate would determine what would happen. Deep down, he knew this was a last-ditch effort on his part because if she wanted nothing to do with him, he would have to find some way to move on, but at least he would know where he stood.

CHAPTER FIVE

Thea woke to the sound of the alarm, and she lay in the darkness, reluctant to leave the warmth of her bed. The bedroom was still dark, and she noticed the wind was no longer howling, and the tree outside the window with its stark winter branches was no longer scratching the pane. Pushing the curtains aside, she was relieved to see there wasn't any snow because she certainly didn't relish the thought of shoveling. Once downstairs, she wandered around the kitchen in her slippered feet, with her robe wrapped tightly around her, making coffee and setting the table for breakfast. She suddenly remembered Jess and show-and-tell and wondered whether her daughter had decided what to take because she was renowned for constantly changing her mind. Thea turned on the radio and listened to the news. She often wondered why because there always seemed to be such doom and gloom, but the voice of the newscaster did, at least, give her a sense of contact with the outside world. This particular station only gave news on the hour, followed by a lively variety of music, and sometimes she needed a little background noise. Smokey was rubbing against her legs and making soft mewling sounds, so she opened a can of food for the cat and this task reminded her about the need to clean out the litter tray—a sometimes forgotten responsibility. Izzie was pretty conscientious, and they were quite good about reminding each other for Smokey's sake, but they both considered the chore a necessary evil.

She poured herself a cup of coffee and then went off to take a shower. She was relieved in a way she didn't have to worry about going to the Country Store anymore, but she was going to miss the companionship. She had failed to mention Ellie's offer to Margaret, and she wondered why. She decided it was probably because there was no point in upsetting her unnecessarily; after all, everything was still very much up in the air. She didn't like secrets, but sometimes it was best to bide one's time, although the benefit of Margaret's wisdom would have helped to alleviate her anxiety over making yet another ill-fated decision.

She made scrambled eggs and toast for breakfast and the children talked to each other between mouthfuls. They seemed to be in good spirits, and Peter and Izzie bantered back and forth about what they had to do at school, pulling faces at some of their least favorite classes. Soon they were bundled up and out the door. Since Jessica's abduction, the bus stopped outside each child's house, and this was so much better than when the children had had to walk to the corner. Due to the change, Thea could now see them get onto the bus, and this was as necessary as the air she breathed. She took comfort in knowing at least there was one positive thing that had come out of their dreadful experience; the kids might get harassed on the bus, but at least they were safely on it. She watched out of the window until the bus was gone and then turned to Jess and asked whether she had decided what to bring for show-and-tell. "Oh yes," Jess said, her face bright with anticipation. "I am going to take the little seal Mr. Hudson gave me when I was in the hospital. He's very, very special."

Thea was surprised, but gave Jess a squeeze and said, "What a wonderful thing to choose."

Jessica was excited and looking forward to telling her classmates all about the little seal and how he had come into her possession. She thought he was magical, and she couldn't wait to share her story. She had made a little nest for him out of a tiny cardboard box, and she cradled the treasured item in her lap on the way to school. The box was inside a small brown paper bag because she didn't want anyone to see the seal until it was her turn. She wondered what Johnny would bring, and she went off to find him as soon as her mom had seen her safely inside the school.

There was a great deal of excited chatter among the children that morning. Jessica found Johnny and asked him what he'd brought and he said he'd forgotten. He seemed so forlorn and bedraggled, and he didn't look as though he had anyone to brush his hair and make his skin all bright and squeaky-clean. He was thin, and the elbows and the cuffs of his dark green sweater were worn and frayed, and the sleeves were a little bit too short. His sneakers were grubby and downtrodden and looked to Jess like hand-me-downs. She wore hand-me-downs too, but not shoes because her mom said each person's feet were different, and that was certainly true of her and Izzie. Her sister had slender pointy feet, and Jess's were square and wide. Jess looked into Johnny's face, took his hand and said, "You can share mine. We'll go up together. Okay?" He looked at her and mumbled shyly, "You don't have to do that."

"I want to. If you do."

He nodded and his sad little face broke into a happy grin. "We'd better go sit down, or we'll get in trouble," he said and Jess rewarded him with one of her brightest smiles.

Miss Simms had decided to begin the day with show-and-tell because she understood the children would be much too excited to concentrate on anything else. She told them she was going to call them up one by one in alphabetical order. "I know it's not fair for those of you with names further down the alphabet, but next time I'll go backwards so the A, B, C's, and so on, will go last." The kids thought Miss Simms had come up with a great idea.

There were about six children before Jess, and they had brought in a variety of objects including a dog-chewed Frisbee, a book about dinosaurs, a brightly colored hand-knitted scarf, a wooden music box with a dancing ballerina, a really neat kaleidoscope, and a potted plant grown from a grapefruit seed. Then it was Jessica's turn, and she stood up when Miss Simms called her name. She took a deep breath and plucked up all her courage and asked whether Johnny could come up with her because they were going to share what she had brought. Miss Simms readily agreed and said, "This is a little irregular, but Johnny is new so it would be helpful for him to have someone to show him the ropes. Come on up, you two."

Jess waited for Johnny to catch up with her, and hand in hand, they walked to the front of the class. She asked him to hold the bag while she carefully took out the little box and removed the lid. He smiled when he saw what was inside. Jess took out the seal and held the little carving gently in her hand. "I think it would be nice if Johnny could take the seal around for everyone to see while I'm telling my story. It's also really, really smooth and great to feel." Miss Simms agreed, and the children sat waiting expectantly, all eyes on Johnny.

Jessica ran her hands nervously down her skirt, took a deep breath and began, trying to speak slowly so her words wouldn't all run together. "The seal was carved by Mr. Hudson, who is a very kind man. He owns the hardware store in town and he came to visit me in the hospital when I hurt my leg. I was also asleep and couldn't seem to wake up so he put the seal into my hand. I believe he put magic into it cuz it helped me get better. He has a workshop where he makes lots of animals, and I'd like to go there someday so I could say a real thank you. That's all," she said and gave a little bow. Johnny brought the seal back, and Jess returned the carving to the little box. "Thank you," she whispered to him as they returned to their seats. "You're welcome," he whispered in reply.

Miss Simms was heartened by the change in Jessica, and truly impressed by her vocabulary and the way she had come across. She was always able to pick out those children whose parents had read to them from an early age—it made such a difference. Suggesting Jessica take Johnny under her wing was a good idea, and she hoped in the developing relationship, each could give the other a helping hand. The rest of show-and-tell flew by and was a huge success. She loved teaching five-year-olds—they were such sponges—but they were only able to sit still for short periods of time. They soon became excited and restless, and she was always glad when the time came for recess so they could go and run off their excess energy. The day was cold, but bright and sunny, a stark contrast to yesterday's gray skies with the threat of snow. She watched Jess and Johnny chatting away happily to each other, and she noticed some of the other children were beginning to gravitate back to the little girl, seeking her company. She would have to give Mrs. Chamberlin a call, and she couldn't wait to tell her—judging by what she had observed today—that Jess had actually weathered this particular bump in the road rather nicely.

Once she had seen Jessica safely inside the school, Thea decided to go to the Battered Women's Shelter, a place where she used to volunteer, but first of all, she needed to find a phone and call the Country Store, so she went into the school and asked Ruth if she could use the one in the office. She still wasn't sure why she didn't have a cell phone, but if she were to be truly honest with herself, she was just plain scared of the things! Ruth was more than happy to let her use the phone, and Bill answered. "Hi, lass," he said, when he realized it was Thea.

"I have a free morning," she said, "and I wondered whether you would like me to stop by and do some work for you. I forgot to ask Margaret last night about how you're going to manage while you look for someone to take my place."

"No one will ever be able to fill your shoes, lass," and the warmth of Bill's voice was almost a palpable thing. She would like to collect that warmth and keep it in a box to comfort her on those days when she was particularly low.

"Thank you. What about this morning, then?"

"Please stop by if you would to visit with us, and I don't want to upset you, but the work is being taken care of."

"Oh," she breathed, and felt the wind go out of her sails just a little bit. *That part of my life really is over*, and she was surprised to find it was actually a relief. "Not to worry, Bill. I was going over to the Battered Women's Shelter if you didn't need me, but just wanted to check in with you first. See you and Margaret on Sunday, right?"

"Yes," Bill said, thankful the conversation was over. "We're looking forward to it."

"Bye, then," and she hung up, thanked Ruth and walked out of the building back to her car.

Thea turned out of the school parking lot and headed towards Route 1. She went past the harbor and through the center of town, and twenty minutes later came to a driveway on the left-hand side of the road leading to a large Victorian house. Anyone driving by would have no idea the house gave shelter to abused and battered women and their children. The location was kept confidential in order to keep their abusers from finding them. This particular shelter was small and only able to accommodate four families at a time. However, no one was ever denied assistance and beds were always made available until the next day when a place would be found at another shelter further away. The fate of these women was a cause exceedingly close to Thea's own heart. The two relationships in which she had become entangled were abusive to a certain extent, but to a lesser degree than those of the women she encountered at the shelter. Michael had eroded her self-confidence and Kenny had made her jumpy, but she had never feared for her life. Michael had left of his own accord, and Kenny had not put up much of a fight when she had asked him to leave. She felt incredibly lucky. She also recognized her good fortune in not having any money worries. Michael had owned the house outright where she and the children lived, so there was no mortgage, and at the time of their divorce, he had agreed to put the house in her name and pay her generous child support. He felt guilty and wanted to look good in the eyes of the community, and this was definitely to her advantage. Even though out of necessity, she had to swallow her pride for the children's sake, she was eternally grateful for the help he gave them, and she took none of his financial assistance for granted, but being dependent on Michael made her vulnerable. Fortunately, he was an intelligent man, and even though he took no part in the rearing of his children, he wanted what was best for them. What he couldn't do for them emotionally, he did financially. Kenny was just Kenny: kind and gentle when sober, but a monster when drunk. Thea didn't even want to think about the dreadful aspects of their relationship. What a fool she had been.

She pulled up in front of the house and got out of the car. She was a little nervous. She couldn't remember exactly when she had last visited the shelter, but she had to make a start somewhere to make a life for herself. She was a little uncertain as to what kind of reception she would get, but nothing ventured, nothing gained. The doors of the house were always locked, and the windows on the ground floor were always closed. No one ever opened a door without checking to see who was there first. Both the front and the back doors were solid wood with a peephole inserted in each. Barbara Jennings was the manager, and it was she who was on duty. "Well, Thea Chamberlin, how wonderful to see you. Where have you been?"

"I wish I could say a holiday in the South of France, but no such luck. Let's say life hasn't exactly been a walk in the park."

"Come on in."

Thea stepped into the hallway, and the smell enveloped her: the scent of bacon left over from breakfast, shampoo from one of the showers, disinfectant, and just the presence of humans. The odor wasn't unpleasant, but the place definitely had an aroma all of its own.

"Let's go into the kitchen, and I'll make a fresh pot of coffee," Barbara said, and Thea followed along behind.

"I can't stay long," Thea said, "as I have to pick up Jessica from school, but I really wanted to see you. It must seem as though I dropped off the face of the earth and I feel bad for not being able to help out."

"Of course we heard through the beating of the drums what had happened. Are you fully recovered?" Barbara asked, turning and handing Thea a mug of steaming coffee.

"Physically, I'm fine. The wound has healed nicely, but I still have nightmares. However, I didn't come here to talk about me." She thought back to how the shelter had started and how Barbara had given her the history when she first filled out an application. They had opened their doors ten years earlier, and Barbara was the one who had staffed the first overnight, full of trepidation, wondering if a woman would call or if she would remain alone in the old Victorian house with its strange noises. A woman did call: a woman in distress who found her way to the shelter where she was welcomed by Barbara, and the two of them stayed up all night talking, both of them testing the waters. The woman was taking a giant step in reaching out for help and Barbara was taking a huge leap of faith in thinking she could actually provide her with some.

There were ten women in all who formed the original core group: some of them battered, bruised and emotionally scarred, and some not. None of them had any specific skills, but together they forged a vision, first to establish a hotline for women to call for help, and then a safe place to which they could escape. The shelter was opened on a shoestring on an interest-free loan, which enabled the group to buy the old three-story Victorian house. Size and location were ideal, but the house needed a great deal of renovation. They did much of the work themselves.

The shelter was still small, but over the years Barbara and the other members of the group—not all the original core—had worked tirelessly to try to change laws and policies. They constantly met with resistance, indifference and a lack of compassion. The age-old question was always asked, "Why does she stay?" Barbara thought it was the wrong question. She firmly believed the question should be changed to, "Why is he violent towards women?" She hoped by taking the focus away from the woman and placing the onus on the man, the ingrained beliefs and attitudes of the culture would eventually change.

Lack of funding was always a constant battle, and Thea understood the program couldn't survive without committed volunteers. In the past when she was active, she often helped out with childcare. She enjoyed volunteering because she loved to hang out with the kids and give busy moms a break. She would come to the shelter for a couple of hours, bringing Jess with her while Peter and Izzie were in school. It wasn't much, but she sensed what little time she could give was appreciated. There were always openings for volunteers to answer crisis and business lines; assist staff and residents; perform light clerical work; assist youth advocates and/or supervise children; organize donations, and assist with the general upkeep of the shelter. The highest burnout was the on-call advocate, who would be the first person to reach out to victims after the arrest of an abuser. There was also always the need for someone to man the reception desk, answer phones and connect clients with the resources they needed.

Thea took a sip from her coffee and looked at Barbara. "How have you been?" she asked as she relaxed and took comfort from her surroundings.

She had spent many hours in the big friendly kitchen with its oversized stove and two large refrigerators; a huge table dominated the room around which all the women would sit and there were always highchairs available for the little ones. Gleaming pans hung from the ceiling on a huge rack, herbs grew in brightly colored pots on the windowsills and the walls were painted a sunshiny yellow.

"We keep fighting the good fight. It's the little things that get you down. One of the refrigerators died the other day and, unfortunately, we were unable to save some of the food and I hate waste," she said. "Then we had to scramble to find a replacement, and even though we get a good discount because of being a charitable organization, forking out money for a new fridge was still money we could ill afford."

Thea nodded. "It's awfully quiet in here. Where is everyone?"

"Group cognitive therapy class at the Community Center. It's great because there's daycare, and the class gives the moms a break."

"Is this something new?" Thea asked.

"It is, and I'm thrilled. We've got a really good group of volunteers this year and it seems as though we are finally on the map." Barbara smiled. "A couple of them are young and enthusiastic with plenty of energy, so together with the Legal Shelter Advocate we have been able to hire, things are humming along."

"Is Michael still helping with the Legal Advocacy Program?"

"Not on a regular basis, but we do know we can call him if we are in a bind, which I find reassuring because there isn't really anyone else with his level of expertise. What about you, do you have any contact with him?" Barbara asked.

"Not really. He wanted to come back into the children's lives, but he's left it too late. In fact, it was the thought he might become part of our lives again that jump-started Jessica's voice. She didn't speak after the accident, and we were all so worried about her. I'm so thankful for the return of her speech, but extremely saddened she was so adamant about not spending time with her father. It's rough on Peter. He really needs a dad."

"I can understand that."

Thea glanced at the cat-shaped clock on the kitchen wall, the tail swinging back and forth beating out a steady tick, tick. "Oh gosh," she said. "Look at the time. I really must get going, but before I do, would it be helpful if I came over in the mornings when I'm free? Unfortunately, I can't offer you regular hours because of Jess. She needs me to be available for her at the drop of a hat, and it really is one day at a time with her right now, but I would like to be able to help out."

Thea looked at Barbara who smiled, temporarily relieving the tiredness of her face. Her eyes were kind, a deep brown with a ring of dark lashes. Although, there were streaks of silver in her shoulder-length chestnut brown hair, it was still silky and wavy. Thea remembered the times when Barbara would tie her hair back, impatiently pulling the heavy strands away from her face because they got in her way. Thea always thought this change in her appearance had made her seem older somehow and just a little bit intimidating, and she wondered whether anyone else had felt as she did. "Thea, I'm not sure that would work, but let me give your offer some thought, and I'll let you know. I'll talk to the other volunteers and see how best we could use your time. I thought you were working at the Country Store though, so how would any hours you could give the shelter fit in with your job there?"

"I'm not working there anymore. I let them down too many times because of having to be with Jess, so they found someone else. I'm really digging a hole for myself here, aren't I? Why should I think I could be of any use to you, either?"

"Hey. Don't sell yourself short. You were wonderful with the kids, and I'm sure we could use you. Unfortunately, the decision isn't one I can make by myself; there are other people to consider. But, I'm pleased you stopped by."

Thea smiled, picked up her pocketbook and gave Barbara a hug. "It was so good to see you," and she turned and walked out of the kitchen and through the hallway. Barbara followed her to the door and said, "I'll be in touch."

Thea gave a little wave and got into her car and watched as a van pulled in and drew up outside the house. The doors opened and suddenly there were women and children all over the place. She waved to them and then waited until they were all safely inside before driving away. She imagined them all in the house together making lunch for themselves and the children, comforted by having other women around to talk to—women who were all in the same boat—no longer helpless and alone. Finally, they had people to go to bat for them. Their options would be reviewed, even though each woman would be supported in making her own decisions. They would also receive advocacy assistance from staff when meeting with legal, medical, social services or other local agencies. Thea remembered it was all terribly complex and she had really only stayed on the fringe. There were times when Thea had just listened, and because she had a quiet stillness about her, the women felt as though she could be trusted. As part of her training, she was sworn to secrecy and could not discuss cases with anyone outside the realms of the shelter. It was amazing what the staff did for these women, even though sometimes the women went back to their abusive situations and would make many attempts to break away before finally being strong enough to be on their own. A lot of times, they would go back to their abusers because the financial hardship was too horrific. All they had left were shattered dreams, to which Thea could relate only too well.

Talking of dreams, she still hadn't decided what to do about Ellie's offer. She really was sitting on the fence, and she had mentioned the proposition to no one. Deep down, if she truly admitted it to herself, she was petrified of making yet another mistake. She needed to sit down and make a list of pros and cons, and the thought of moving away and making a fresh start literally threw her into a panic. She was desperate to talk about the whole situation with someone, but she just didn't know whom to turn to.

Thea arrived at the school a little early, so she parked the car and went inside and sat on the bench outside Jessica's classroom. She was eager to know how her morning had gone, and she was looking forward to her daughter's company. Oh my goodness, this was sad, wanting to spending time with a five-year-old! Soon the bell rang, and she heard the scraping of chairs and the excited chatter of voices. Miss Simms opened the door and was delighted to see Thea sitting there. "Mrs. Chamberlin, how nice to see you." She walked over to Thea who stood up. "You will be pleased to hear Jessica did a wonderful job of show-and-tell, and I'm sure she'll tell you all about it. Sorry, I don't have time to talk now," and she smiled at Thea, turned away and walked over to the kids who were lining up so they could be chaperoned out of the building where they would either catch buses or be collected by a parent. Thea didn't want to mess up the carefully supervised routine, so she waved at Jess and then walked with her and the rest of the children to the big double front doors. Once outside, she grabbed Jess's hand, smiled at Miss Simms and mouthed a whispered, "Thank you," and then they were on their way.

Listening to Jessica's chatter warmed Thea's heart. Her daughter talked about "her friend Johnny" and how he had helped her and how she had shared her seal with him because he didn't have anything of his own to show. Thea let her ramble on, giving her a big hug just before she climbed into her seat. "I think this is a cause for celebration, and we should go out to lunch. How about The Pantry?" Jess was all over that because she loved their cinnamon raisin bagels, toasted with butter if you please, and Thea knew she could get one of their healthy salads. It meant driving out of town, but what the heck. She was elated by her daughter's happy mood and just didn't want to go home right now.

The Pantry was small and cozy, and their favorite table—the one with a small bench on each side, right by one of the windows—was vacant. Each table had a tiny vase of bright and seasonal flowers and right now the vases were filled with mums. The walls and the ceiling were covered in old-fashioned tiles made out of tin in a shade of cream. There was a Christmas tree permanently in one corner decorated according to the seasons and Jessica loved it. The owner collected anything to do with Red Riding Hood, and the dolls, wolves, red capes and baskets were a feast for the eyes. Jess never got tired of looking at everything, even though some of the items were rather high up and difficult for her to see, much to her frustration. Thea put Jess's school bag on one of the benches to show the table was taken, after which they went to the counter to order. Jess, very plainly but politely, asked for her bagel and Thea chose the chicken oriental salad with a honey mustard dressing. They turned to go sit down, and Thea nearly bumped into the woman who had come up behind her. "Hello, Thea," the woman said.

"Janine, it's nice to see you. Jessica, this is Mrs. Mitchell."

Jessica looked at her and said, "Hi."

"Pumpkin, why don't you go and sit down and I'll be right with you?"

"Okay, Mommy."

"How's book club?" Thea asked.

"Still going strong, although we probably won't meet as often now winter's on its way. Would you like to start coming again?" Janine asked rather half-heartedly.

Thea could hear the reluctance in her voice and chose to ignore it. "I'd love to if you could all come to my house. I don't have anyone to leave the kids with right now."

Janine said she'd check with the group and Thea felt as though she was an object to be put on a shelf, like a food mixer, only to be pulled out when it would be useful, but she couldn't blame Janine, or Barbara for their lack of enthusiasm.

Their lunch orders were ready, so she said goodbye to Janine and told her she hoped she would see her soon, although she realized she didn't really care whether Janine called her or not. Her salad was crisp and tasty, and she savored each delicious mouthful, watching Jessica as she happily munched her bagel, getting butter all over her face. "So, you had a really good morning, then?"

"I-did-and-could-I-have-Johnny-over-to-play-after-school-one-day?"

"Whoa, slow down. You're running all your words together. Tell me all about Johnny."

"Did you know he's Ian's brother?" she said between mouthfuls. "And he looks a little worn out. At least his clothes do. I think he should come to our house and make cookies with us. Being with us would make him all better as he seems kinda sad and lost."

"Ian's a nice boy, so I'm sure Johnny is as well. And of course he can come over. I'll send a note with you tomorrow, and you can give it to him so he can ask his mom."

Jessica smiled, "You know he didn't start school when we did cuz he was sick and I missed school cuz I was sick, too, so I think that's why we're best pals."

Peter and Ian were friends and had formed a strong bond, especially after Ian stuck by Peter's side in their search for Jessica. They were each troubled in their own way, and Thea was glad of their friendship, firmly believing the boys drew strength from one another. Peter had never gone over to Ian's house, but Thea had made sure Ian was always welcome in theirs. She didn't know the story behind his family life, but he was polite and respectful; he and Peter always had a good time, and this was what truly mattered. She had thanked Ian for what he had done on that dreadful night; he had merely shrugged and said he'd been glad to help. And now, if Jessica wanted to add Johnny to the mix, she was more than happy to accommodate her youngest daughter. Maybe she could extend a hand of friendship to Ian and Johnny's mother. Perhaps she was in trouble and needed help.

When they got home, there were three phone messages waiting. One from Nan, saying she would be home on the weekend. Thea was thrilled and hoped she'd be able to come with Bill and Margaret for Sunday dinner. The second was from Ellie, saying she was just checking in and had Thea given any more thought to her offer. The third was from her mother, and this was odd because she rarely called. She felt a little shiver of apprehension. She went off to help Jessica change out of her school clothes and to make sure all the butter was washed off her face and hands. "Well, pumpkin," she said. "Do you need anything?" Jess shook her head, eager to be immersed in her own little world. "Okay then, I'm off to make a couple of phone calls."

She called her parents' house first because she was concerned, and her mother answered the phone. "Hello, Thea, is that you?" she said.

"Yes, Mom. What's up?"

"Your father had a bit of a fall yesterday. He's all right, but I thought I should let you know."

"How did it happen, Mom?"

"It's my fault. I left the vacuum cleaner out, and he tripped over the cord. It was stupid of me."

"Accidents happen," Thea said. "Please don't blame yourself. How badly is he hurt?"

"Fortunately, he just sprained his ankle. I called a friend, and we took him to the Walk-In Center—so much easier than the Emergency Room. They have an X-ray machine there, and there was nothing broken, so they sent us home with instructions to alternate hot compresses with cold. Frozen peas work nicely! They showed me how to bandage his ankle properly, so I'm playing nurse now."

"Can I talk to him?" Thea asked.

"Not right now, dear, he's resting, but I'll have him call you later. Is that all right?"

"Of course, and thank you for telling me. I wish I were closer so I could help out."

"I know," her mother said. "You're a good girl. Bye for now." And she was gone.

Thea sat down. What was she going to do when her parents were no longer able to look after themselves? They weren't loving and warm, but besides her children, they were the only family she had. Her dad sometimes asked about the kids—her mother rarely did—but there was no point in dwelling on their shortcomings now. At least the current situation was resolved, but the fact her mother had never learned to drive complicated matters. She had been surprised to hear her mother had called a friend as she and her father were rather solitary, but it was comforting nonetheless to know they weren't totally alone.

Next she phoned Nan. The conversation was brief because she was at work. They both said how much they were looking forward to seeing each other, and Nan said she would be there sometime in the afternoon on Saturday.

Thea didn't really want to call Ellie, so she decided to put off the inevitable by making herself a cup of tea. She heard Jess chattering away to her dolls and animals. She had never felt obligated to amuse her children because she had wanted them to develop imaginations and learn to be self-sufficient. Of course, there were times when she had to fill in as a play-mate when no one was around, and she was always willing to show each of her children how to do things. They shared her love of board games and puzzles and they had all spent many hours playing all sorts of games. During the long winter months, there was usually a colorful jigsaw puzzle set up on the card table in the corner of the living room. TV was limited to Saturday morning cartoons and the occasional movie when they all had cabin fever on a day when they were snowed in. All of them were avid readers, including Jessica, who was just beginning to figure out the words.

She pulled herself away from her thoughts, took her tea into the living room and picked up the phone. Ellie answered right away, and without even so much as a hello, said, "I had a thought. I wondered whether you and the kids would like to come for Thanksgiving."

"Goodness, you have taken me by surprise, but I honestly don't think my car would make the journey! It's a long drive," Thea said, hoping she didn't sound too negative.

Ellie was undeterred. "I know. Maybe it's just wishful thinking on my part. I would so love to see you."

"And I you. I don't know what to say. I wish we could all just close our eyes, click our heels just like Dorothy, and arrive at our chosen destination. I'm not going to discard your invitation without giving it some thought, and perhaps I could rent a car. I just know mine won't make it. It's okay for running around locally, but I don't trust the elderly beast. I will also have to discuss the idea with the kids. We've all become rather insular and don't travel far from home, but I'm sure a change of scenery would do us all good."

"I haven't given you much time to think about it, have I? When do the kids get out of school for Thanksgiving break?"

"They have early dismissal on Wednesday, and I'm sure if they missed school Wednesday morning it wouldn't be any big deal, but I'd have to find out. On second thoughts, Thursday might be the better day if we leave really early. They're off until the next Tuesday, but I think I would have to drive home Sunday, or maybe early Monday morning. We can play it by ear, depending on how tired the kids are. Let me think about it. I must say I'm sorely tempted because I could look in on my parents at the same time. I heard from my mother today, and she told me dad had a fall. Just a sprained ankle, she said, but I wonder if there's something she's not telling me."

"I could stop by and see them if you'd like me to," Ellie suggested.

"Oh, Ellie, would you? It would put my mind at rest. They'll probably be mad at you. Just tell them I was worried so they can blame it on me! And don't say anything about a possible visit because I don't want them to be disappointed."

"It's no problem at all. As you know, they live less than thirty minutes from the store and it's even closer from my house. So you'll think about coming, then, and let me know?"

"Sure," Thea said.

"Have you thought any more about the partnership offer?" Ellie asked.

"I have, and I honestly don't know what to do, but perhaps coming to visit would make the decision for me. I wouldn't hesitate if I didn't have the children to worry about, and if I do say yes, we wouldn't be able to come until the end of the school year."

"I know, and I understand. Talk to you soon."

"Bye, Ellie, and thank you." Thea hung up the phone just as Jessica appeared in the doorway.

"Who were you talking to, Mommy?" she asked.

"Come sit next to me, and I'll tell you," and she patted the sofa. "First, I talked to your grandma..."

"The grandma who lives far away?" Jessica interrupted.

"You are absolutely right. Apparently Grandpa fell over the cord of the vacuum cleaner and sprained his ankle. Grandma took him for an X-ray, and there are no broken bones, so he doesn't have to have a cast."

"I'm pleased about that cuz it wasn't fun except the signing part when all my friends got to write their names or draw a picture. Will he have to have crutches, cuz they're no fun, either?"

"I don't know." Thea smiled at her daughter and continued. "Then I talked to Nan, and she told me she was coming home on the weekend and would be arriving on Saturday." Jessica received this piece of news with a great deal of enthusiasm. She clapped her hands and bounced up and down on the sofa.

"Then..."

"You mean there's more..."

"Yes, there is. Do you remember me talking about Ellie?"

"Is she your friend with the shop in the place I can't say?"

"Yup, she's the one—in Massachusetts. I'll say the word slowly so you can remember. Ready? Mass-a-chu-setts. So, repeat after me. Mass-a-chu-setts."

"Mass-a-chu-setts," Jessica said proudly.

"By George, she's got it! That's my girl!"

"What did you talk to Ellie about?" Jessica wanted to know.

"She surprised me by inviting us all to go and have Thanksgiving with her."

Jessica's jaw dropped. She wrapped her arms around herself and put on her thinking face. "This is seeeerious," she said. "We always have turkey day with Uncle Bill, Aunt Margaret and Nan. They would be so sad without us."

"I think they would understand if we really wanted to go."

"Do you want to go, Mommy?" Jessica asked.

"Only if you, Izzie and Peter want to go, too."

Jessica sat and thought for a moment, and then she said, "I think we should talk about it again later."

Thea gave her a big hug. "I love you," she said, and Jess hugged her in return.

"I love you too, Mommy."

"Let's go write a note to Johnny's mom before we forget. Do you know his last name?"

"Hm. I don't think so."

"No worries. I'm sure Peter knows. We'll ask him when he gets home. Okay?"

Jessica ran off to find paper and a pen and Thea thought about what she had to do that afternoon. She was also rather taken aback by Ellie's invitation. Why now? It just didn't make any sense. Did Ellie have some kind of ulterior motive? She just didn't know. She dragged her mind back to the present, deciding life was definitely taking on some interesting new twists and turns.

It was Thursday, which meant ballet class for Izzie. Thea needed to plan the meal for Sunday, get groceries at some point, and she should also clean house. Peter's room was a disaster, but the girls were pretty neat, and this was a blessing. At least Izzie was tidy, and she encouraged

Jess to put her stuff away although she was constantly battling with her sister. She thought about converting Michael's old office into a bedroom for Izzie, thus creating a winter project they could work on together. She felt bad denying her eldest daughter the right to a room of her own, but they both understood Jessica's need of her sister's comforting presence; besides which, Thea wasn't even sure Izzie was ready to make the break. Time would heal, and even though Jess still crawled into bed with Thea when she couldn't sleep, it was happening less and less, so maybe the time would soon come when she would be able to be on her own. As a mother, she was fully aware the middle child was sometimes lost in the shuffle, so having a special project with Izzie would be a good thing. Of course, the project could only happen if they were staying, but she was running ahead of herself. The house fit them like a glove, and was the only home the children had ever known. There was a Ping-Pong table in the basement, as well as an area with a huge floor to ceiling mirror and a barre where Izzie could practice her dance. It was a good hangout for friends and somewhere to vent some of their energy when the weather was too cold and snowy to go outside. There was a treadmill and a stationary bike, together with weights and an exercise mat—equipment Thea used when she had the time. She glanced at the clock; Peter and Izzie would soon be home from school.

Jessica appeared with paper and a pen, and they sat down together and wrote a note to Johnny's mom. "Let's start with *Dear Mrs....* and then we can fill in the blank when Peter gets home. Jessica nodded.

Thea wrote... *My daughter, Jessica, is in Johnny's kindergarten class, and they have become friends. She wondered whether it would be possible for him to come home with her after school one day to play. I would be happy to bring him to your house at the end of the afternoon. If you would like to meet me and see my home before agreeing to this, I will quite understand. You can reach me on my home phone, and the number is 207-555-9981.*
Sincerely,
Thea Chamberlin

"Is the note okay?" Thea asked after she'd read it out loud. Jessica nodded. "Could you find an envelope, do you think?" and Jess happily ran off to accomplish her mission.

In the meantime, Thea turned on her laptop and decided to look up the cost of rental cars. She went to the Expedia site and plugged in Yarmouth, Maine (there was nothing in Melford Point) and the number of days for which she would need the car. She was horrified at the prices. Enterprise seemed to be the most reasonable, but even their rate was eighty-nine dollars a day for a standard SUV and one hundred and twenty dollars a day for a mini-van. She was aware the car would come with a full tank of gas, but she still had to factor in the cost of getting to Massachusetts and back, plus returning the car with a full tank. Could she afford to do this? She had money in the bank because she was frugal with the child support Michael provided, and by living modestly and saving over the years, she had been able to build a moderate nest egg for herself and the children. Much as she would like to be less dependent on him, she was sensible enough to realize if they were to have any kind of life, she needed his support. Not a day went by she didn't say a silent "thank you."

The front door burst open, and there were Peter and Izzie standing in the midst of their discarded backpacks, coats, scarves and hats, although after she gave them *the look*, they started to make an effort to tidy up. "Hello, you two," she said. "How was school?"

Peter shrugged, "Oh, you know, same as always,"

"Izzie, anything new for you?"

Izzie's pretty freckled face lit up in response to her mother's question. "We had a great art class and Mrs. Mackenzie loved my painting. In fact, she asked me to show how I had done it to some of the other kids. I was shy at first, but everybody was so nice and seemed to want my help."

"How wonderful. I'm so proud of you," and she gave her daughter a hug. "Now, Peter, there must be something in your day that stands out."

"Not really," he said, refusing to look at her, and Thea wondered what he wasn't telling her.

Jessica appeared from around the corner and asked Peter if he knew what Ian's last name was cuz she wanted to invite his brother, Johnny, over to play. He said it was *Wilkinson*, so Jess turned to Thea and said, "We can finish the letter now, can't we, Mommy?" waving the piece of paper back and forth. "We surely can," Thea replied. Soon the letter was safely in the envelope if a little creased, and she wrote *Mrs. Wilkinson* on the outside. Jessica licked the edges and pulled a face at the taste of the glue. "Ugh," she said, and went off to put the letter in her school bag.

Jessica seemed to have forgotten about their potential trip, so Thea decided not to say anything until they were sitting around the dinner table. They all had a snack, after which Izzie put her ballet stuff together. They then all piled in the car, Peter grumbling all the way, especially when he heard they were going to get groceries while Izzie was in class. He thought he was old enough to stay on his own. After all, he was nearly eleven, but Thea said, "No way!"

Thea dropped Izzie off at the studio, and drove quickly to the Hannaford in Yarmouth. Once inside the store, Jess chatted away happily asking how she could help. Thea wasn't fooled. Her daughter was playing the "suck it up to mommy" game because Peter was being less than cooperative. She was choosing, with her air of self-righteousness, to totally ignore her brother who was trailing along behind them, dragging one foot after the other and glaring at his sister. He used to be so helpful, and although Thea had little patience with his moodiness, she did understand how he felt, so she made no attempt to cajole him out of his fit of pique. She sensed he was at loose ends with the soccer season coming to an end, but there'd be basketball and skiing soon enough. She decided to pick up a frozen chicken for Sunday, together with potatoes, stuffing, broccoli to steam, and carrots to bake with honey. She asked the kids what she thought they should have for dessert, and Peter actually responded by saying, "How about one of those meringue thingies."

"You mean a pavlova?"

"Yes, that's it, with raspberries and whipped cream and chocolate drizzled over the top."

"Sounds like a plan. Why don't you go off and get a dozen eggs—the organic, cage-free brown ones, please."

She also picked up tilapia for their supper. The fish was mild in flavor, and the children loved it dredged in breadcrumbs and baked until it was all crispy on the outside, and together with oven-fried sweet potatoes, it was one of their favorite meals. They only had dessert on weekends, but there was always fruit.

Thankfully, Thea didn't see any familiar faces while they were standing in line at the checkout because she wasn't inclined to be the least bit conversational. Jess had surprised her by reminding her to pick up kitty litter and food for Smokey. Peter helped with the bags and his mood seemed to have lifted somewhat. Physical exercise was key to his sense of wellbeing and helped to keep his anger at bay, but it still took a great deal of arm-twisting to get him on the treadmill on the days when the weather was bad. And even though he begrudgingly agreed he always felt better afterwards, he would have much preferred to be outside kicking a soccer ball around—it was an uphill battle and one he frequently lost.

Izzie was just finishing up when they arrived at the studio. She looked flushed and happy and went off to change. The teacher, Simone Beauchamps, came up to Thea and asked if she could have a word. "Of course," she responded and turned to Peter and Jess and asked them to sit and wait for Izzie. She followed Simone over to the corner of the room, admiring her slender figure. There was something about dancers—they had so much poise and her daughter was among them.

"Mrs. Chamberlin, as you know, each year we put on a production of *The Nutcracker*. Rather than giving Isabel a minor role such as the ones she's played in the past, we would like her to play Clara. I have not asked her yet because I wanted to get your permission first."

Thea was delighted. "I'm absolutely thrilled. I will discuss it with her. I want to make sure she'll still be able to manage her schoolwork. I'm assuming it is going to be somewhat time-consuming, much more so than when she played the minor roles."

"There will be more rehearsals for her than last year, but I don't think it's anything she can't handle. Isabel is a gifted little girl and is perfect for the role and just the right age for our local production. There will be three performances in total on the twenty-first, twenty-second and twenty-third of December, with a matinee on the last day. It will be in the auditorium at Pinecrest, the private girls' school in Yarmouth, a venue with which I am sure you are familiar. Will you be able to get her there?"

"Yes, of course. Will our being away at Thanksgiving interfere with rehearsals?" Thea asked.

"No, because rehearsals won't start until the children go back to school on the twenty-seventh of November. The schedule will involve a couple of Saturdays, together with evenings in the week since we don't have too much time. However, Isabel is proficient in the role so it should be fairly easy for her. Please let me know what she says as soon as you can."

"We'll talk about it tonight, and I'll call you tomorrow. Thank you for choosing her."

"Isabel was an easy choice, *trés facile*. She is very talented, *extraordinaire*, and a delight to work with. I enjoy her immensely," and Simone smiled. "You should be extremely proud."

Thea said, "Oh, I am." She looked at Simone, with her almond eyes and high cheekbones, her dark sleek hair pulled into a knot on the top of her head. She was quite beautiful, her posture flawless, and when Thea caught a glimpse of herself in the mirror, she automatically pulled her shoulders back and sucked in her stomach.

The three children looked up expectantly as Thea crossed the room. She gathered them together, cut off their questions mid-stream, and said they'd talk at dinner. She told them there was going to be a lot to say, so she said she was sure they would need the *talking stick*!

Dinner was a lively meal, and once the kids were full, they all started talking at once, and Thea held up her hand. "Who needs the *talking stick*?" she asked.

"You do," they all said, and handed her the piece of driftwood they had collected from the beach just for this purpose, because they wanted to hear what she had to say.

Thea leaned back in her chair, held tightly onto the piece of wood, and looked particularly important. "I have excellent news for Izzie," and she smiled at her daughter. "Ms. Beauchamps would like you to play Clara in *The Nutcracker*. Izzie, how do you feel about her offering you the part?" and she passed her the *talking stick*.

"Oh, Mom," she said. "It's a dream come true. I've had visions in my head for so long of playing Clara, I could do it in my sleep."

"So, I'm guessing that's a yes!"

"It is, it is!!"

"Will you be able to fit the rehearsals in with all your school work? I don't want you getting over-tired."

"Oh yes, I'll make sure I do all my homework and rest as much as possible. I don't want to get sick."

"I'll call Ms. Beauchamps tomorrow and give her the good news. I'm so proud of you."

Peter congratulated Izzie. He was pleased for her. Jess then asked for the *talking stick* and proceeded to tell them all about her show-and-tell experience and how, even though she'd been kinda scared, it had been fun. She also mentioned she had told her classmates she would like to thank Mr. Hudson personally one day. Thea was surprised, but told her maybe she could help her write a note to Mr. Hudson, and Jess thought her mom's idea a good one.

Peter was beginning to feel left out. Then his mom dropped the bombshell about Ellie inviting them to Massachusetts for Thanksgiving, and this piece of news rendered him and Izzie speechless and left Jessica with a smug expression on her face because she had already known. Peter blanked out. He just couldn't handle it. Things had just been getting sort of normal, and now his mother wanted to take them away from the Thanksgivings they had always known. He knew he was being unreasonable, but he just sat at the table with his arms folded and said nothing.

Thea looked at them all and realized her news had gone over like a lead balloon with her son and decided she would have to talk to Peter on his own. "I know this has come out of the blue, and it's only an idea. I'm certainly not going to drag us to Massachusetts if you don't want to go, but I thought doing something different for a change might be fun. Getting out of town and having a change of scenery is tempting." She got up and started cleaning off the table. "Let's get the dishes done," she said, and they quietly set about doing their assigned chores, their heads full of their own thoughts.

Izzie went off to finish her homework, and Jess to continue whatever game she had started before supper. Peter turned to leave the kitchen, and Thea asked, "Do you have time to talk to me, or do you have homework?" He shrugged and didn't move. "Please come back and sit down." He reluctantly went back to the table, sat in one of the chairs and started tilting it back and forth, much to Thea's annoyance. She sensed his need to get a rise out of her, but she refused to take the bait. "So you think going to Massachusetts is a bad idea?" Again he shrugged and refused to meet her gaze.

"Peter, please look at me and tell me what's wrong."

He glared at her across the table, folded his arms in a gesture of defiance and said, "I don't want to go."

"Why?" she asked, summoning up all the patience she could muster.

"I like our Thanksgivings with Uncle Bill and Aunt Margaret. It just wouldn't be the same. We don't even know Ellie, and why now, Mom?"

"Because Ellie has offered me a partnership in her business. I would also like to be able to go and see my mom and dad. Apparently, Dad had a fall and even though Ellie said she would look in on them, I'm still worried Mom is making light of what happened."

Peter was finding his mom's revelations difficult to digest, so he leaned forward and ran his hands through his hair. "Now it's beginning to make sense," he said. "Do Jess and Izzie know about Ellie's offer?"

"No, I wanted to discuss it with you first. I respect your opinion, and you've always looked out for me. I think you're a little lost because you don't have to protect me anymore now that Kenny's gone. Am I right?" she asked, looking into his handsome face. He had leaned back but was no longer rocking the chair.

"Everything's just weird," he said. "I really am at loose ends now soccer's finished. I felt as though I was really part of a team, but now I don't have to get together with the other kids, they don't seem to want to spend any time with me, except for Ian, and surprisingly, Marty, even though we had that awful fight. I just can't figure it out because I haven't done anything."

Thea chose her words carefully. "Don't you think it might be a good idea for us to have a fresh start...?"

Peter interrupted her. "How would that help? Wouldn't we just be running away? You always said we should deal with our problems, not run away from them."

"You're right, but the whole sorry mess has taken on a life of its own, and although we have so many happy memories, we have some horrific ones, too. I know you're scared, but so am I. I'm scared to leave, and I'm scared to stay, but I promise you I won't take the three of you away from here unless you all believe moving would be a good idea. In any case, we wouldn't be able to go until the end of the school year. Would you do something for me?" she asked.

"Sure," he said, and Thea noticed his tone of voice was a little more positive. She had boosted his self-esteem in valuing his opinion, and she could sense their reconnection.

"Would you take some time to think about what I've said and then make a list of pros and cons?"

Peter nodded, and she said, "Once your list is done, we'll be able to see whether you think this would be a good move for us as a family. Do you have any questions for me?"

"Where would we live?"

"There's an apartment above the store, and even though it's small, we could make do while we look for a house. That's one of the reasons why I wanted us to all go for a visit, so you could get to know Ellie, see where we would live and where you would go to school."

"What would happen to our house?"

"I'm not sure, but I would probably have to sell it back to your dad unless he doesn't want it anymore. Even though the house is in my name, I'm not sure I can put it up for sale without getting his permission, but we're jumping ahead of ourselves."

"I love our house, Mom, but it would be nice to make a fresh start somewhere without the ghosts. I'm always wondering whether Kenny will come back."

"Me, too," she said. "It makes me jumpy. I know this house is the only home you've ever known, but to be honest, home for me is where the four of us are, and it would be nice to feel completely safe, wouldn't it?" She got up and walked around to where Peter was sitting. "Can I have a hug?" He got up, and she put her arms around him. It was getting awkward because he was almost as tall as she, but it felt good to hold her son. She always said a good hug cured all ills, and she felt Peter relax. She stood back and smiled at this man-child of hers and said, "Thank you." He grinned back at her, and she could tell he was doing better. She had enjoyed their conversation, but having to concentrate and come up with the right words was hard work, and she was mentally exhausted.

It was bath time for Jess as there wasn't time in the morning for all three children to shower. Peter and Izzie were quick and efficient, but you couldn't hurry Jess, so bathing at night was the best solution. Soon the house was quiet. Thea went off into the living room and curled up in the corner of the sofa and started making her own list of pros and cons, wondering how many items on the list would be similar to Peter's. She was glad they had talked. She needed to talk to Izzie too, but her daughter was so excited about her role in *The Nutcracker* it would be difficult to get her full attention. Anyway, she would wait and see what Peter came up with and then they would all sit down and revisit the question of whether they should go away for Thanksgiving or not. The decision would have to be made soon so she could make all the necessary arrangements. She told herself to feel the fear and do it anyway, although she was feeling far from brave, and terribly alone.

The morning dawned bright, clear and unseasonably cold, and she watched Peter and Izzie climb into the bus. The bus made many stops, so she had about thirty minutes before she had to take Jessica, and when she went out to start the car to warm it up the wretched thing was as dead as a dodo bird! She said, "Shit, shit, shit," and pounded the steering wheel. How in heck's name was she going to get Jess to school on time? She took a deep breath and went back into the house. This was a hiccup she didn't need just when Jess was finally looking forward to going to school, and she cursed herself for not heeding the warning the car needed a new battery.

She picked up the phone and called the school, telling them what had happened and saying she would get Jess there as soon as possible. She then called the garage where she had the car serviced and asked if someone could come and give her a jumpstart. The truck was out on another job, but Eric, the proprietor, said they would be there within the half hour. Apparently, her car wasn't the only one reluctant to start in the frigid temperature, and she blamed herself for forgetting to put the car in the garage before she went to bed—so much for her peaceful morning.

Jessica could sense something wasn't right because it was time for them to leave, and they weren't going anywhere. "What's wrong, Mommy?" she asked. Thea bent down, put her hands gently on Jess's upper arms, and told her the car wouldn't start. "Oh, no!" Jessica exclaimed. "I'm going to be late for school." She pulled herself out of Thea's grasp and sat down miserably.

"It's okay. I called the school and the man from the garage will be here soon. He'll use his special cables and get the car going, then I'll take it to the garage and get a new battery so it won't let us down again."

But Jessica wasn't to be consoled. She sat on the hall floor with her legs sticking straight out in front of her and kept saying, "I don't want to be late. I don't want to be late. I don't want to be late," until Thea felt like banging her own head against the wall; she gritted her teeth and left her daughter sitting in the hallway with the face of doom. She wandered into the kitchen and decided to call Simone Beauchamps to tell her Izzie would love to play Clara. It was early, so the answering machine kicked in, and she left a message because she certainly didn't want Izzie to miss the opportunity.

After what seemed much longer than thirty minutes, she heard a truck trundle into the driveway. She threw on her coat, rammed a hat on her head and went out to meet it. "Thank you so much for coming so quickly. I need to get my daughter to school."

"Not to worry, ma'am. We'll have your car running in a jiff. Can you pop the hood?"

Thea's fingers were stiff with the cold, and she glanced up to see Jess's face peering out of the living room window. She pulled the lever and heard the hood snap. The man from the garage opened it up all the way, attached jumper cables to both his vehicle and hers and then asked her to try to start her car. It was reluctant to turn over, but eventually the engine roared into life, and she breathed a huge sigh of relief. "Thank you," she said and pressed a ten-dollar note into the man's hand. "I'll settle up with the garage once I've dropped my daughter off, but this is for you. I'm sorry, I don't know your name."

"It's Harold." He smiled, revealing nicotine stained teeth, and said, "Glad to be of service," got into his truck and backed out of the driveway.

Thea went back into the house to get her gloves, praying the car wouldn't stall out. "Come on, Jess," she said. "We're only going to be a little bit late. It's bitterly cold, so you need your hat and gloves today." She pulled the soft pink woolly hat down around her daughter's ears, and made sure her hands were snug inside her mittens. Then they were off. "Drive fast, Mommy," Jessica said, and Thea drove like the wind, hoping she wouldn't get caught for speeding, which would definitely be the last straw.

She left the car running and took Jessica into school. She knocked on the classroom door and apologized to Miss Simms for being late and disrupting the class. Monica just smiled and got up to help Jessica put away her stuff. "Jessica, don't worry. You weren't the only one who was late this morning."

"See you later," Thea said to Jess and mouthed, "Thank you," to Miss Simms. The car was still running, thank goodness, so she didn't waste any time getting to the garage where she asked Eric if she could wait while they replaced the battery. He ran a greasy finger down the list of appointments, and Thea's heart sank when she saw how many there were. "If you can't do it right away, do you have a loaner?" she asked. "I only have the one car, and I need to be able to pick up my daughter from kindergarten at eleven-thirty." He lifted his baseball cap and vigorously scratched his scalp. "I won't be able to do it until this afternoon, and that's pushing it. You could go to the Midas in Yarmouth."

"You don't have a loaner, then?" she asked, looking at him miserably. "I'm not sure I'd have time to go into Yarmouth and be back by eleven-thirty, and I'm afraid to turn the car off. Isn't there anything you can do?" She was beginning to think the situation was hopeless when Eric's face suddenly lit up. "I think my nephew is in your daughter's class," but then his face fell again. "It won't help though," he said, shaking his head, "since he rides the bus." It was quickly dawning on Thea that Eric wasn't terribly bright, and she was rapidly running out of time if she had to get the car fixed elsewhere.

"Is there someone on your list who might be persuaded to give up their slot if you called and explained the situation? How long does it actually take to change a battery?"

Eric ignored her first question, scratched his head again and said, "About an hour." Thea took a deep breath. She was getting increasingly frustrated, but it wasn't Eric's fault she was so helpless. She was trying so hard to be independent, and she didn't want to call Bill or Margaret. In any case, dragging one or other of them away from the store would hardly be fair.

"Look," Eric said. "I'll call Midas in Yarmouth and see if they have the battery you need. That's the best I can do. What year and make is your car?"

Thea told him it was a 1995 Volvo, and she crossed her fingers. He turned away from her and plucked the grubby phone off the wall, and he obviously knew the person at the other end because the conversation was quickly over. He said she was in luck since they did have those batteries in stock and she breathed a sigh of relief. He told her Midas was by the mall, and the person he had spoken to understood she was short of time, so they were going to fit her in as soon as she got there as a favor to him. He said to ask for Mike and to mention Eric's name. He apologized again for not being able to help her. She said, "Thank you, anyway," and made a dash for her car. It was only nine-thirty, but she still felt panicky. Fortunately the traffic was light, and she made the journey in about twenty minutes. She pulled up outside, left the car running, and headed for the office. There was no one there! There was a door leading into the work area; all the bays seemed to have cars raised up on lifts, and the sight of them in mid-air didn't fill her with confidence. She went from bay to bay asking each mechanic whether he was Mike and eventually she found him. "Mrs. Chamberlin?" he asked and smiled, showing perfect teeth. She caught herself staring at him because beneath all the grease was an exceptionally nice looking young man. "Yes," she said, nodding vigorously, hoping he hadn't noticed.

"If you drive your car around to the back of the building there's a space we can pull it into and get it fixed."

"Okay and thank you. I really, really appreciate you finding the time to do this for me," and she made a dash for her car. Mike's gaze followed her longingly—he thought she was quite lovely.

Thea waited in the office and made herself a cup of coffee. The garage had one of those single-serve machines and the coffee was fresh, delicious and piping hot. She was still all right for time as long as Mike could install the battery by eleven o'clock. She amused herself by reading the rather dog-eared magazines, none of which were particularly interesting, but she was so relieved to have found someone to help her and felt proud of her independence. See, she *could* look after herself. Time was ticking by, so at ten forty-five she went off to see how much longer Mike was going to be. She also realized, while she was thinking about what the replacement of the battery was going to cost, she hadn't paid Eric. She would stop by once she had picked up Jess.

Mike looked up as she walked towards him, and even though she was all bundled up, he could see how slender she was. He was sure she had beautiful legs inside those tight jeans and the expression written all over his dirty face was one of admiration. "Almost done," he said, looking at her intently.

"Thank goodness. As you know, I'm a bit pushed for time so can you tell me how much it is going to be, and I will write you a check while you're finishing up?" He watched while she removed her gloves, noticing she wasn't wearing a wedding band, and he thought how nice it would be to spend time getting to know her. "The battery is eighty-five dollars, and labor is forty-five, so the total will be one hundred and thirty."

"I'll just go back into the office and write out the check for you," and she could sense his eyes on her as she walked away. It felt good to be admired, but she certainly wasn't going to act on his obvious attraction. Her newfound independence was much too precious.

Thea handed Mike her check after he had driven her car around to the front, and told him how much she appreciated him helping her out when she was in such a bind. He said, "My pleasure," and did a little bow. He was thinking how sorry he was to see her leave, and she was thinking he probably flirts with all his young female clients. She left without so much as a backward glance, got into the car, slipped a CD into the slot and sang with Katie Melua all the way to the school.

Thea was in plenty of time for Jess, and once they were both in the car, she told her daughter she had to make one stop on the way home. Jess just nodded and was soon engrossed in a book she had picked out of the school library that morning. Thea saw the book was Dr. Seuss's *Green Eggs and Ham,* and she was looking forward to sounding the words out with Jess once they got home.

Once they reached the garage, she had to coax Jess to get out of the car. "But, Mommy, it's so cold," she whined.

"I know, but you can't stay in the car by yourself, and it will be warm inside. Did you give Johnny the note for his mom?"

"I did, and he seemed really happy. I hope his mom says yes."

"I don't see any reason why not. After all, Ian's come to our house a few times, and we haven't eaten him yet!"

Jessica giggled and said, "Oh, Mom. You're so silly."

Thea held Jessica's hand, and they walked into Eric's office, but he wasn't there. She could see Jessica wrinkling her nose at the smell of gasoline and the strange odor all service stations seemed to have. She pushed open the door leading into the work area and noticed it was much smaller than the one at Midas. The mechanics were only able to work on three cars at a time, and she found Eric at the far end. Jessica was in awe because she had never seen the underside of a car before. She stood well back because she wasn't sure how it stayed up so high, and she didn't want the car to fall on her. Eric was tightening lug nuts on one of the wheels of a shiny red Volkswagen and turned to face Thea when she said, "Hello."

"I've come to pay you what I owe you for jump starting my car this morning, and I'm sorry I left in such a hurry without settling up."

"Everything worked out at Midas, then?" he asked. "And this must be your daughter."

"Yes, this is Jessica. Jess, say hi to Mr. ... I'm sorry, I don't know your last name."

"It's Aldrich, but you can call me Eric. Let's go into the office, and I'll write up a receipt for you."

Thea was getting used to him removing his cap and scratching his head, but she could see Jessica was summing him up, and Thea hoped she wouldn't say anything!

Jessica wasn't used to seeing someone with such grubby hands and she thought his head must be pretty dirty too! He seemed like a nice man though, and she was glad he had helped her mom.

Once the check was written, and Thea had a rather grease stained receipt in her hand for thirty-five dollars, she thanked him once again, and Jessica said, "Bye," and they were on their way.

It was gratifying to have the car roar into life, and as soon as they were home, she tucked it safely away in the garage just to be on the safe side. She grabbed the mail before she took off her coat and boots and then went into the kitchen to make herself some lunch. There were no messages, so she hoped she and Jess would have a nice quiet afternoon with no more surprises before Izzie and Peter came home, but she should have known better because life is never predictable.

Thea glanced at the pile of mail. There were a couple of bills, the local Melford Point news, a couple of catalogues, and a letter. She picked up the envelope, glanced at the return address, and wondered why Jim Hudson would be writing to her. The only way to find out was to slit open the envelope, but she wasn't sure she wanted to. Life was pretty simple right now, and she just didn't want anyone to upset the apple cart. She pulled out the letter and the paper smelled faintly of the wood Jim used to carve his animals, and she thought about coincidences and how Jess had mentioned last night she would like to thank Mr. Hudson in person.

It was a nice letter, and she could certainly do with a friend, but could you really have a friendship with a man? She found his offer to reach out to Peter heartwarming, especially as Peter was starved for male companionship. He was at that critical age where he needed a stabilizing influence, but what did she really know about Jim? Why was he still single after all these years? Could she trust him with her son? She would write back to him even though it seemed rather silly sending a note when they lived so close to each other, but she had found his thoughtful words comforting and felt they should be acknowledged. She would phrase her own letter in such a way so as not to give him any encouragement, but right now she needed to see what Jess was up to, so she put any thoughts of letter writing out of her mind.

Thea found her daughter sitting on the bed pretend-reading to a couple of her bears. Needless to say, she hadn't changed out of her school clothes. "Would you like me to read your new book with you?" she asked, and Jessica said, "Maybe later." So Thea kissed her, told her she was going to make zucchini bread if she would like to help, and went back to the kitchen. Jessica couldn't resist a baking challenge, and soon they were grating zucchini and madly stirring batter. They used applesauce instead of butter, and even though Jess wasn't terribly keen on the green bits, she just ate it with her eyes shut so she couldn't see them because the bread really did taste delicious.

Peter and Izzie were glad to be home. The weather was so bitterly cold, and even in the short distance from the bus to the house, the wind attempted to whip their hats off their heads and their scarves from their necks with its icy fingers. They were quite literally blown into the hallway, winded from their mad dash up the driveway, much relieved to be inside. Izzie, trying to catch her breath, managed to say in no more than a whisper, "Oh, bliss, Mom's been baking."

Thea appeared in the kitchen doorway and smiled at them both. "Phew, what a day. After you left this morning the car wouldn't start and I was mad at myself for not putting it in the garage. Luckily, I was able to get a guy from the local service station to come and jumpstart it, but we were a little late for school and, of course, Jess wasn't pleased. Then I had to go to the Midas in Yarmouth because the local garage was too busy to fit me in. Fortunately, it all worked out in the end, but I was a bit worried, I can tell you. How was your day?"

"We didn't go out for recess, so we had to run around the gym," Peter said. He turned to Izzie. "Did they make you run around the gym, too?"

"Yup," she said. "But I loved it because I really like to run, and it was much better than being outside. What did you and Jess bake, Mom?"

"Zucchini bread," she said. "And Jess was the best helper in the world."

Jess looked up from her drawing and said, "I was. I stirred and stirred until I thought my arm would drop off!"

Izzie smiled at her sister and said, "It's good to be home and to have such wonderful things to eat. We're so lucky." Thea smiled at them all and realized how grateful she was for these children of hers because, despite all she had put them through, they were good kids with big hearts.

Soon they were all tucking into slices of bread with cheese and apple wedges washed down with glasses of milk. "Have you given any more thought to Thanksgiving?" she asked, hoping maybe Peter had discussed it with his sister.

Izzie said, "We thought it would be okay if you would really like to go, especially if you need to check in on Grandma and Grandpa. Do you think they will like us better now we're older?"

"Maybe they will," Thea said. How could they not like these children of hers? But it was wishful thinking on her part, and she knew it. "Thank you for being so thoughtful," she said.

After supper, Thea waited until Jessica was fast asleep and eventually Izzie went off to join her sister. Once she was safely tucked in, Thea gave her a big kiss and thanked her for the nice things she had said. "You made Jess feel good, and it's so important for us to boost her morale. She's also beginning to get her confidence back at school, and she loves her teacher. How are things going for you?" she asked.

"I'm okay. I just keep my head down and do what I'm asked. I have a couple of good friends to eat lunch with so I'm all right, really I am."

"You'd come to me, wouldn't you, if you needed any advice? I don't like to think of you trying to figure everything out by yourself. You're a little bit like me, I'm afraid: not very good at asking for help, but not afraid to give it. Don't let anyone take advantage of you."

"I'll try, Mom, and of course I would come to you," Izzie said and grabbed her mom's hand.

"What are your thoughts about playing Clara? Are you sure you're going to be able to handle all the rehearsals as well as your schoolwork?"

"I'm very excited. It's something I really, really want to do. I'll make it work, I promise, and I'll catch up on my sleep whenever I can."

Thea looked into the face of this daughter of hers, so like her own. Both Peter and Jessica were dark, whereas Izzie was fair. Their eyes were blue, but Izzie's were the gray-green she and her daughter had inherited from Thea's father, with the same thick lashes.

"What about Massachusetts? Are you really okay with making the great trek? I know you would like Ellie. She loves kids and is a lot of fun. You will think you have died and gone to heaven when you see Aladdin's Cave. The store is absolutely crammed with every imaginable art supply."

"I think it would be an adventure now I've got used to the idea, and we'd all be together, and that's what matters."

"You are the best." She leaned over and gave Izzie a hug. "I love you so much. Sweet dreams."

Izzie smiled sleepily and said, "Goodnight, Mom. I love you, too."

Thea then went off in search of Peter and found him at the kitchen table frowning over a bunch of math problems. There was a time when she would have ruffled his hair, but he wasn't a little boy anymore. She just squeezed his shoulder and she felt him tense, and his negative reaction saddened her. She didn't want to lose the connection with him. "Am I bothering you?" she asked.

"No, Mom, I just have to concentrate on my homework. I'm just trying to remember how we were told to solve these equations. I might have to call Ian if I can't figure them out."

Peter was the brightest of the three. He needed to be constantly challenged and was in an advanced math class. She was secretly pleased the problems were proving difficult, forcing him to use his brain to its full capacity because he was easily bored. Unfortunately, he was well beyond her own level of math, so she was of no use at all.

"Sorry I can't help," she said and turned to the sink to fill the teakettle. Once she had brewed a steaming mug of tea, she went off to the living room. "Come find me when you're done."

"Okay, Mom."

Thea slipped a CD of soft piano music into the stereo system, tucked herself into the corner of the sofa, and immersed herself in her book. Peter eventually appeared. "All done?" she asked. He nodded and sat down right by her feet.

"Did you do the pros and cons list by any chance?"

"I did. Let me go get it." He quickly returned, list in hand, and she asked him to read it to her.

"Okay, here goes.

Pros:

1. Getting away from the bad memories.
2. Going to a new place where no one would judge us.
3. Being safe because Kenny wouldn't be just around the corner.
4. Making new friends with people who don't know our past.
5. Living in a new house with no ghosts.
6. Maybe getting to know Grandma and Grandpa.

Cons:

1. Leaving Uncle Bill and Aunt Margaret and Nan, although she doesn't actually count since she isn't here much.
2. Leaving Ian. He really is such a good friend.
3. Not being able to work in the store during school vacations.
4. Going to a new school would be very scary. Not just for me, but for Izzie and Jess, too.
5. Not being near the beach.
6. And what would we do if we didn't like Massachusetts and wanted to come back?

That's all I could think of."

"You did a great job. It's interesting, isn't it?—your pros and cons seem to be even in number. I haven't finished my own list yet, but I think it would be similar. You put a lot of thought into this, and I truly appreciate the time you took." Peter smiled and squeezed his mom's foot. "How do you feel about going to Massachusetts for Thanksgiving? I talked to Izzie, and she seems to have gotten used to the idea," Thea said.

"Now I've had a chance to think about it, I think it would be fun to go somewhere different. Are you going to tell Izzie and Jess about the partnership and the possibility of us moving there for good?"

"I don't know. What do you think?"

"I think they should know. But I'm not sure whether we should tell them before we go or after we come back. Because if we hate Massachusetts, we won't go, right?"

"Absolutely," Thea reassured him. "We are all in this together as a family." She wondered whether she should tell him about the note from Jim, but she hesitated because she thought it might just muddy the waters.

"What are you thinking about?" Peter asked.

"I received a letter from Jim Hudson today. You remember him, right?"

"Yes, of course I do. He was so helpful when Jess was lost. He came to the hospital and gave her the little wooden seal. I like him a lot."

"He said he would like to spend some time with you. He says he could teach you how to carve, kick a soccer ball around—you'd probably be better than he is—and just do some 'man stuff.' What are your thoughts? I think he's lonely. He lives in that big old Victorian house all by himself so you'd be doing him a huge favor."

"I'm not sure, Mom. I'll have to think about it. I don't want to get to know him and then start enjoying being with him if we're going to be moving away."

"I know. That's why I almost didn't tell you and I feel exactly the same way, but I do, at least, have to give him the courtesy of a reply. I also didn't want you to miss the opportunity to have a good and positive man in your life. I think we should both sleep on it, and touch base tomorrow. Do you agree?"

Peter looked thoughtful, his brows furrowed in concentration. "We could give him an answer when we get back from Massachusetts because, then, we'll have a better idea of what we're going to do."

"You're so smart. I'll give him a call tonight just to be polite and explain the situation. Is there anything else you want to talk about? Oh, one more thing. When are basketball try-outs?"

"Monday and Tuesday, then the games will start after Thanksgiving."

Thea had no doubts he would make the team. "Boy, between your games and Izzie's rehearsals, we're going to be busy, aren't we? It's a good thing skiing doesn't start until January."

"Would there be skiing in Massachusetts?" Peter asked.

"Yup. There are some ski hills in the Berkshires."

"That's good."

"Off to bed with you. I'm glad we had this talk." She got up to give him a hug, which—much to her surprise—he returned. "Night, Mom," he said.

"Love you," she whispered.

"Love you too," he said softly in reply, and she sensed he was beginning to accept the idea of the possible changes in their lives.

Thea heard the clock in the hall strike nine, and she had a sudden longing for the comfort of her nightgown and soft, fleecy robe. She was tired after her busy day and the action-packed week had seemed never-ending. She thought about the story Margaret had told her about the blind horse, and she wondered whether Jim was a bell of friendship. He hadn't mentioned Nan in his letter, which worried her because Nan had carried a torch for Jim for years. They had gone out together for a little while, but the magic just wasn't there for Jim. They had both wanted it so badly, but in the end, Nan just went back to Boston to lick her wounds and throw herself into her work. Thea was of the unspoken opinion the relationship would never have really worked between the two of them. Jim was so solid and dependable, and Nan was so restless; she just couldn't see her settling down in Melford Point. Despite being born here, Nan was a city girl at heart. Thea was excited at the thought she was going to see her tomorrow because she had missed her dreadfully. Of course, she could always call or email her, but Thea liked face-to-face relationships. She never was one to spend hours on the telephone, and email was good for quick questions, but not for pouring one's heart out.

With her teeth freshly brushed, and her face scrubbed of what little makeup she wore, she went downstairs. She was all toasty in her nightgown, robe and sheepskin slippers, and wherever she went there was always a faint scent of roses because of the soap she used and the subtle perfume she wore. She picked up the phone and called Jim and it was a good thing, for his sake, he was at the other end of a telephone line because he would have found her irresistible.

"Hello," she heard him say.

"Jim, it's Thea. I got your note, and I wanted to say thank you."

"I hope you didn't mind me writing. I thought it better than phoning out of the blue."

"I was surprised." Suddenly there was an awkward silence since neither of them knew what to say. Finally, she said, "I'm not good at talking on the phone."

"Me either. How are you and the kids?"

"Recovering. Jessica took the seal you gave her to school for show-and-tell. She told me she would like to thank you in person, but there's a problem."

"Is she all right?" he asked.

"She's fine, getting better each day, and some of her spunk and confidence is coming back, but that's not it. I've been offered a partnership in the store in Massachusetts where I used to work before I married Michael. Ellie, my long-time friend and mentor, has invited us for Thanksgiving, so the kids and I can check everything out and see if we want to move permanently. I told Peter about your letter and how you offered to spend time with him. He said he would like that but didn't want to build a friendship with you if we were going to be moving away. I told him I was going to call you and explain the situation, and if things go terribly and we do decide to stay here, I will contact you when I get back. I'm sorry..."

Thea heard Jim sigh. "I understand, but of course I'm disappointed." She could hear the sadness in his voice, and she was beginning to wonder whether she should have just let sleeping dogs lie, rather than picking up the phone. She decided against telling him Nan was coming home tomorrow since she really didn't want to get into anything personal. "How are you getting to Massachusetts?" he asked.

"I'm planning on renting a car. We'll leave at the crack of dawn on Thursday as, hopefully, there will be less traffic and return on Monday because there's no school. It will be good for us all to have a change of scenery."

"I'd be happy to drive you," he said.

"I do appreciate the offer, but this is something I need to do. I need to stand on my own two feet. I've been leaning on other people for far too long."

"Maybe I could take you to pick up the rental car," he said, realizing he was clutching at straws. He was beginning to sense her slipping away, and he just couldn't bear the thought of losing the comfort of her voice. He didn't want to let her go.

"Again, I appreciate your offer, but I plan to drive over in my car and leave it at the rental place."

"If you're sure there's nothing I can do..." Suddenly there wasn't anything more to say. Thea could hear the disappointment in his voice, and it dragged her down. "I'll call you when we get back, okay?"

"I'll look forward to it. Stay safe," and he was gone.

Thea sat slumped at the kitchen table and covered her face with her hands. Her chest ached and she felt so empty and alone. The house seemed too quiet. Smokey came and rubbed herself around her ankles, and she bent down to stroke her silken fur. "It's not my fault Jim's so unhappy, is it?" she asked the cat, leaning down to pick her up. Suddenly she was weeping, overwhelmed with sadness because she had made Jim miserable, and she wanted to comfort him but knew she couldn't. The cat wriggled in her arms and struggled to get down, and thoughts of Lady came to mind and how she would give anything to have the big black Lab here right now. Dogs understood. Cats just didn't.

Maybe she should send Jim a note. Their conversation had become stilted and awkward in an attempt to keep away from the personal, and she hadn't wanted to give him false hope. Writing always lightened her mood, so with that thought in mind, she dried her tears, made sure the doors were securely locked, and went off to bed. She had just got herself all settled nicely with a pad of paper and one of her favorite pens when the phone rang.

"Hello," she said tentatively, hoping it wasn't Jim calling back. It wasn't. It was Ellie.

"Hey, are you all right? You sound a bit shaky," Ellie said.

"I just had a rather difficult conversation with a friend. I'll tell you about it when I see you."

"Does this mean you're coming?" Ellie asked.

"Yes, we are, subject only to the non-availability of a rental car, and I will call Enterprise first thing in the morning."

"This is fabulous news. I'm so pleased. When do you think you'll get here?"

"I'm planning on us leaving at the crack of dawn Thursday morning because there will be less traffic and the kids won't have to miss any school. Then we will return Monday as early as possible. Does that work for you?"

"Sounds great. I have plenty of room. I'm looking forward to seeing you so much and meeting those rug rats of yours!"

Thea smiled. She could sense the lifting of the cloud of doom. Jim was not her problem. He was a grown man, and she couldn't help it if he had carried a torch for her for all these years. She had never given him any encouragement. "Thea, are you still there?" Ellie asked.

"Yes. Sorry. I was just realizing how talking to you has brightened up my day. Did you manage to stop in and see Mom and Dad by any chance?"

"I did. You will be pleased to know they seem to be coping just fine. Your dad is hobbling around, but they have a wonderful neighbor who has been a godsend, so you can rest easy. I'm sure they'll be happy to see you though."

Thea didn't share her optimism, but she didn't voice her doubts. "Thank you," she said. "You've taken a load off my mind. What would you like me to bring?"

"Absolutely nothing," Ellie replied. "All I ask is you get yourselves here. I can't tell you how excited I am."

"Don't make us too comfortable. We may never leave."

"You know that would be just fine with me, don't you?"

"Yes, I do know, and it's comforting. I will call you in the morning as soon as the car is all set, and thank you so much for reaching out to me."

"Goodnight, my friend," Ellie said. "Sleep well, and I'll talk to you tomorrow."

"Goodnight. Love you," and Thea hung up the phone. Suddenly, writing to Jim didn't seem such a good idea, so she turned off the light, snuggled under the covers, and fell fast asleep.

Thea was awakened from a deep sleep by a thunderous banging on the front door. She shot out of bed and ran down the stairs in a flash. Peter was standing in his bedroom doorway. "Go and be with the girls," she said, "and stay away from the windows."

The thumping on the door became louder and more insistent, and she sensed it was Kenny even before she heard his voice. "Thea, let me in, you bitch!" His words were slurred with drink.

"Kenny, you know I can't do that. Go away or I'm going to call the police."

She heard him move away from the door, and she dashed into the kitchen and pushed a chair under the doorknob. The door was secure, but it wasn't a solid door as the top half had square panes of glass. She picked up the phone and called Jim. She had no idea of the time, and the phone just kept ringing and ringing. Suddenly she saw Kenny's shadow at the door, and he raised his arm and broke one of the panes with the rock he held in his hand. He reached in and made an attempt to undo the lock. Thea heaved the kitchen table in front of the chair and jammed it hard up against it, forming what she hoped would be an effective barrier. She was breathing hard when Jim finally answered.

"Jim," she whispered in desperation. "It's Thea. Kenny's here at the house and he's trying to break in. Should I call the police?"

"You really should, but can you hold him off until I get there?"

"I'll try, but please hurry."

Kenny had his arm through the hole, and she shrieked in alarm. She could see he'd cut his hand, and it served him right.

"Open the fucking door or I'll break all the glass!"

Thea looked around for something she could hit his hand with. In his inebriated and groggy state, he was having trouble finding the knob to twist so he could release the lock, and this worked to her advantage, buying her a little time. The door was double locked, but Thea needed to get the key out because if he managed to undo both locks, she doubted her barrier would hold. She needed to distract him until Jim got there.

Kenny lifted his arm to strike the window again, but the rock fell from his blood-covered hand. As he bent to pick it up, she managed to lean over and pull the key out of the lock. Then she stepped back just as he hit the pane of glass above the one he had already broken, but somehow it held fast.

"Kenny, what good is breaking into my house going to do? You're just making matters worse for yourself."

"How could things be any worse than they already are?" he yelled. "You ruined my life."

Petrified and shivering, she forced herself to keep talking. "And how did I do that? Did I pour the alcohol down your throat? No, Kenny, you did that all by yourself." His arm was back through the door, and he was still fumbling for the lock, but he'd used his right arm to break the glass, and the lock was to the right so finally it dawned on his befuddled mind he needed to switch arms. Thea picked up the heavy skillet from the top of the stove and whacked his hand as soon as he put it through the door. He let out a bellow of rage and pain and pulled his arm back through the hole. Now he was really angry and so was she. "Get away from my house, right now."

"You've broken my hand, you bitch," and he started kicking the door. Thea could hear Jessica's screams and she got even angrier. It was a good thing there was a door between her and Kenny otherwise she would have brained him. His presence was messing with her children and where the hell was Jim? She was just about to call the police when she saw the headlights of his truck and she heard him running around the side of the house.

"Come on, Kenny, do you want to end up in jail? Look, you're bleeding, man. Let's get you home."

"I'm not goin' nowhere until she lets me in. The bitch broke my hand," Kenny moaned.

"Serves you damn well right," Jim said, trying to keep his anger under control. "Come on, you need to go to the Emergency Room." It was the last thing Jim wanted to do, and if he hadn't been concerned for Thea's and the children's safety, he would have just as soon left Kenny to his own devices. "Just be thankful Thea called me instead of the police."

Kenny just howled with rage and lunged towards Jim. Jim had had enough, and he smacked Kenny firmly on the jaw and knocked him out cold. Thea was standing in the kitchen shivering. She couldn't really see what was going on, but she heard the sharp crack of Jim's knuckles meeting Kenny's jaw and then the thud as Kenny fell to the ground. Jim peered through the hole in the door. "Are you all right?" he asked.

"Yes," she replied. "A bit shaky, and I need to get to the kids. They must be terrified. I'll patch up the hole to keep the cold out. Will you take Kenny away, please?"

"I called Kenny's brother before I left, and he should be here soon. The two of us will get Kenny out of here. I'll come back in the morning and fix the door. Okay?"

Thea could hear Kenny stirring. "Please get rid of him," she whimpered. "I can't take any more."

"Go to the kids," Jim said, "and I'll see you tomorrow."

She ran from the kitchen and went to find the children, but they weren't downstairs. Peter, wise beyond his years, had taken them up to Thea's bedroom where they would be further from the ruckus going on in the kitchen. Thea took the stairs two at a time and looked at the three of them all snuggled in her bed. Peter sat between his sisters, and they were all clinging on to each other—the girls' eyes were wide with fright, and she could sense Peter's anger. She held out her arms to them, and Jessica kept saying over and over, "I'm scared. I'm scared. It's the bad man. It's the bad man."

"The bad man has gone sweetheart. You're safe," and she took Jess in her arms and hugged her tight.

"Mommy, I was so frightened."

"I know, baby, so was I." She leaned over and gave Izzie a hug too. "My brave girl," she said.

"Why didn't you call the police, Mom?" Peter asked.

She got up to look out the window. Kenny's brother's car had just pulled into the driveway, and she could see from the illumination of the headlights Kenny was leaning drunkenly on Jim. Phil went to help, and between them, the two men got Kenny into the back of Phil's car. She breathed a huge sigh of relief as she watched them leave, and she still couldn't figure out how Kenny had gotten to the house.

Peter glared at his mother in anger and exasperation, and said, "Mom, I asked you a question."

"Sorry, Peter." She looked at his scowling face. "Thank you for looking after the girls and bringing them up here. That was a smart thing to do. In answer to your question, I didn't want the police involved because then all the town would know."

"But, Mom, he deserves to go to jail."

"I know," and she sat down on the edge of the bed. She tried to pull herself together for the kids' sake, but now the ordeal had passed, she was in the throes of a bad reaction and couldn't seem to stop shaking. Peter, worried about her going into shock, jumped out of bed and came to sit beside her. "Here's your robe, Mom," he said, holding it out to her. "Put it on and you'll feel better."

"I have to go back into the kitchen, but I don't want to. There's a hole in the door, and I need to put some cardboard over it to stop the cold air coming in. Please stay with the girls and I'll be right back."

"Can't I help?"

"I would love you too, but it's a bit of a mess, and I'd rather you didn't see it. What you can do, though, is find me a good sturdy piece of cardboard and some duct tape, and I'll stay with the girls until you come back." She looked at Jess and Izzie and said, "Why don't you two snuggle under the covers and try and get some sleep." She kissed them both and told them it would be all right, it really would.

Peter returned in a flash. She suggested he get into bed with the girls and try and get some sleep, but he didn't want to. "I'll just stretch out on the chaise until you get back."

Thea pulled a pillow and a couple of blankets from the linen closet. "Here," she said. "You might just as well make yourself comfortable. I'll be as quick as I can." She put on every available light because she didn't want to be in the dark. She pulled the kitchen table away from the door and slid it back to where it belonged, but she left the chair there. She recognized her own insecurities, and ridiculous as it may seem, having the chair securely under the door handle made her feel safer. She didn't want to look at the hole in the door with Kenny's blood all over it, and she certainly didn't want the kids to see the mess in the morning. She cut the cardboard to the size she needed, which was hard to do because her hands were shaking so much. She then used copious amounts of tape to secure it over the hole. She then put on a pair of rubber gloves and set about cleaning the blood off the inside of the door, stuffing the stained paper towel right down into the bottom of the trash can. She scrubbed the skillet rigorously, hiding it in the far right-hand corner of one of the lower cupboards, absolutely convinced she would never use it again. She did what she could to make the room seem as normal as possible, and with the exception of the door, felt as though she had succeeded. The bright and colorful kitchen where they had shared so many good and happy times would never feel the same to her ever again. She needed a hot drink, so she made herself stay long enough to accomplish the task. What was the saying about getting back on the horse? Well, she had certainly done that.

Back upstairs the girls had finally fallen asleep, and Peter was looking a little sleepy himself. "Hi, champ," she said, sitting down on the chaise by his feet and cradling her hands around the hot, sweet mug of tea. "I'm so glad we're going to Ellie's. It gives us all something to look forward to."

"Uh-huh," Peter agreed.

"Do you want to stay on the chaise or come into bed with the girls and me?"

"I think I'll stay here, but I may change my mind," he grinned mischievously.

"Oh, you," she said. "What would I do without you?"

"Have less fights!"

"Too darn right, and I could rent out your room to someone who is tidy and doesn't keep food and smelly socks under the bed!"

And they both giggled, relieved they had survived one more ordeal in the saga of their family life. She kissed Peter on the forehead, swigged the last of her tea, went off and brushed her teeth and climbed into bed with her daughters. She lay there for a while remembering how, after the abduction, she had become obsessed with trying to make her children safe by keeping them with her so nothing bad could happen. Being focused on having them close so she could keep an eye on them every minute of every day, just wasn't practical, but she was scared. She always did her utmost to be a good mother, but even with the best of intentions, she still seemed to attract trouble, still seemed to put her family into undesirable situations. Finally, she drifted off to sleep, comforted by the soft breathing of her children, and the purring of Smokey, as the cat circled and finally settled herself at Thea's feet.

CHAPTER SIX

Exhausted by their Friday night ordeal, the Chamberlins slept in. The day dawned gloomy and overcast, with no bright sunshine to wake them up. Eventually, Smokey got the ball rolling by crawling up the bed and pushing her furry face into Izzie's. At first, the little girl was bewildered to find herself in her mother's bed, and then she remembered the horror of the night before. She glanced over at the clock, and it was already eight thirty, much later than she and Jessica would normally get up. She slid out of bed, tucked Smokey under one arm, and crept out of the room. The wooden floor felt cold under her feet, and she went off to find her robe and slippers. Izzie was a bit nervous about going into the kitchen, but at least it was daylight and she felt much braver than she had the night before. She flipped on the light and looked around her, but the room seemed much the same except for the cardboard over the upper half of the door and the chair pushed up under the handle. She fed Smokey and then poured a bowl of cereal for herself, adding some milk and getting a glass of orange juice. She didn't want to think about last night, so she concentrated on her role in *The Nutcracker* and all she needed to learn. She wasn't really sure what she felt about the trip to Massachusetts. She supposed it would be fun with them all going together, but their first Thanksgiving holiday without Uncle Bill and Aunt Margaret would be strange. She missed them and she smiled to herself when she suddenly remembered they were coming over for dinner tomorrow. It would be good for her mom to have lots of people around to help her forget about last night. She shuddered at the thought of Kenny and recalled how horrible things were when he had been living with them.

Peter continued sleeping, with one arm flung out of the covers, and he was making soft, little breathing noises through his lips. Thea's arm had become numb where Jess was lying on it, so she gently pulled it out from beneath her daughter and noticed Izzie and Smokey had gone. She could hear the TV faintly, and found it reassuring to know that at least one of her children was in their normal Saturday morning routine. She thought, with a start, about Izzie going into the kitchen on her own, but she had done a good job of cleaning up, and in any case, there was no way she could protect her daughter now. All the fear of the night before must have worn Jess out because she was still sleeping soundly. Thea got out of bed and shook her arm to get rid of the pins and needles, put on her robe and slippers and went downstairs. She put her head around the living room door to ask Izzie if she was all right. "I'm fine, Mom," was the reply.

"Honest truth?" Thea asked.

"Honest truth," Izzie said.

Thea, like Izzie, wasn't really sure whether she wanted to go into the kitchen, but the thought of a hot cup of coffee was too tempting to resist. She found it reassuring to have something mundane to do, and as soon as the coffee started brewing, she went upstairs to check on Jess. She wanted to be there for her in case she was still frightened and she was so mad at Kenny for being the instigator of the recurrence of her daughter's terror. She knew it was unrealistic to believe, even with Jess's apparent return to normal, her fears were gone. She sat on the bed and looked at this beautiful daughter of hers and Jess suddenly sat bolt upright, her eyes wide with fright. "Bad man, Mommy? Is he gone?"

"Yes, he's gone. Mr. Hudson took him away, and do you know what?"

"What?" Jessica asked.

"Mr. Hudson's coming over sometime today to fix the kitchen door, and while he's here, you could thank him for the seal."

Jessica's face lit up, "That's great," she said.

"Come," and Thea held out her hand. "Let's go see what we can drum up for breakfast." Jessica shuffled over and slid out of the side of the bed, and Thea caught her and gave her a big hug. "How's my brave girl?" she asked.

"Not sure."

"I'm here to listen if you need to talk." Jessica slipped her hand into Thea's and they went downstairs together leaving Peter still in the Land of Nod.

Thea poured coffee and toasted frozen waffles for her and Jess, after which Jess toddled off to watch cartoons with Izzie. Jess seemed to be okay. Her daughter had frowned at the broken door and said it looked ugly, and Thea reassured her the ugliness would be fixed soon.

Peter eventually stumbled down the stairs; his hair all disheveled and falling over his face. He, too, glared at the kitchen door. "What!" she said. "You don't like my taping job?"

He just pulled a face. "Not bad for a woman," he said, grinning at her.

She grinned back at him and said, "Enough of your cheek, young man!"

"Hah!" he said. "Any chance of some delicious scrambled eggs with buttery toast?"

"I'll check in with the cook," she said, "but I do believe it's her day off."

He played along with her, "In that case, we'll just have to do it ourselves."

Soon there was the sound of butter sizzling in the pan—not the same one she had used on Kenny—eggs being beaten and toast popping. She went off to see if either of the girls wanted any, but they said they were full, so she and Peter made the most of each other's company. "Goodness, is that the time?" she said. "I need to call Enterprise. Be a love and clear the table, would you please, and then if you could tackle your room..." Peter interrupted her with a groan, and she just gave him one of her disapproving faces!

Enterprise answered on the fourth ring. She explained she would like to rent a minivan if there was one available and she would need it from some time after three o'clock on Wednesday afternoon until late Monday. They told her she was in luck because they had just received a cancellation and her immediate thought was this was meant to be. After asking if she could park her car there, to which they agreed, she gave them her credit card information and sealed the deal. She was nervous but excited at the same time and pleased to have something to look forward to. She longed to see Ellie, and she knew the children would love her stories. It would also be somewhat of a guilt reliever to be able to stop in and see her mom and dad.

Soon she and the kids were busy with Saturday morning chores. She hauled the vacuum cleaner out of the closet and went off to Peter's room. He had his music blaring, but he turned the volume down when he saw his mom, and he did seem to be making an effort to sort out the chaos. "Rental car is all set, and here's the vacuum cleaner. Try not to suck up anything other than dust!" she said, at which he pulled a face, and she left him to it. Jess and Izzie were sorting laundry, and in amongst all the chaos, she heard the phone ring. She ran like a mad thing into the kitchen and grabbed the receiver off the wall. "Hello," she said, slightly out of breath.

"Thea, it's Jim. I was wondering whether it would be convenient to come over and assess the damage to the door. I can then measure up, go off and get what I need and then come back later. Is that okay with you?"

"Perfect. How long do you think you'll be?"

"About half an hour."

"That'll work," she said, thinking to herself it would give her time to get dressed. "See you in a little while and thank you."

"No problem. Bye, Thea."

She went off to find the children to tell them Mr. Hudson would be coming in about thirty minutes, said she was going off to get dressed, and suggested they might want to get out of their jammies, too. She threw on a pair of comfortable jeans and a sweatshirt, tied her hair back, washed her face and cleaned her teeth. Sometimes she wore a touch of makeup, but not today. She certainly didn't want to give Jim any encouragement. Little did she know it wouldn't have made any difference what she was wearing or how she looked, Jim would have loved her anyway.

Thea set the children to their tasks, and it always surprised her Izzie liked to clean. She was such a methodical child and went off happily to dust the living room. Jessica was sitting on the floor in the midst of a pile of laundry with her arms folded across her chest looking totally disgruntled. "Do you want to get dressed?" Thea asked.

"I can't find anything to wear," she said, thoroughly down in the dumps. Thea held out her hand and said, "Come. I know just the thing," and she rummaged through Jessica's closet and came out with the much-loved purple sweat suit. "Let's hurry because I think Mr. Hudson is almost here."

"How do you know, Mommy?" Jess asked with a puzzled expression.

"Because I have magic ears."

"You don't!"

"Oh, but yes I do," and she gave Jess a big hug and her daughter's eyes grew as large as saucers when they heard the doorbell ring. She took Jess's hand and they ran into the hallway, and they both said, "Who is it?" and Jim played along. "It's Mr. Fix It. May I come in?"

Thea asked Jess in a very loud voice whether Mr. Hudson had passed the test, and Jess yelled, "Yes," in response.

"Shall we let him in, then?" and Jess nodded. Thea opened the door, and Jim stepped into the warmth of the hallway. "I thought I was going to freeze to death out there, so I'm really pleased I passed the test."

Jess became shy all of a sudden and tucked herself behind Thea. She looked up at Mr. Hudson, and she liked what she saw: his soft light brown hair and his warm brown eyes which seemed to twinkle with little smiley lines crinkling out on either side. Izzie poked her head out of the living room and said, "Hi." Peter was occupied with his vacuuming and had taped a *Busy, Men at Work* sign on his bedroom door! Jim smiled down at Thea, all five feet of her, and she apologized for the chaos, but he loved it. It wrapped itself around him and temporarily assuaged his loneliness. "What chaos!" he said, and she laughed. "I'll just go through to the kitchen and check out the door."

Thea and Jessica went back to sorting laundry and once Jess had found a task Thea believed she would enjoy, tidying her bookshelf, she went off to find Jim. He turned to look at her.

"I'm just going to get you a new door," he said. He had removed the chair propped beneath the handle and had stepped outside to assess the damage. "It's a mess as you can well imagine, and I have a door I can fit into the space without having to do much rejiggering. Does that work for you?"

"How much will a new door cost?"

"It's on me. I feel as though this whole mess is my fault," and he sat down heavily on one of the kitchen chairs.

"Don't be ridiculous," she said. "It's just as much my fault for getting involved with Kenny in the first place."

"Then we're both to blame."

"Damn right," she said and smiled at him. "I'm almost afraid to ask, but where's Kenny now?"

"We had a heck of a time with him last night. He was bellowing like a stuck bull over his broken hand, but with Phil's help we were able to sober him up and get him to the Emergency Room. His hand was X-rayed and the broken bones re-set. They had to splint his hand rather than applying a plaster cast because of the cuts from the glass, some of which had to be stitched. I can tell you, lady, you did a real number!"

"I would have killed him if he'd broken through the door and threatened my children," she said.

"I know you would. Any mother would have done the same."

"He should be in jail, you know. I should have called the police, but it would have been all around the town like wildfire and would have made it worse for the kids, just as the stigma of being involved with Kenny has started to fade. Where is he now?"

"He's at his brother's house, and he's certainly not going to be able to work for a while."

"Good," she said. Jim didn't like the way the conversation was heading, so he said, "Let me go off and get the door." He made himself leave before the desire to take her in his arms became too overwhelming. "I'll be back before you know it."

"Thank you," she said. "I'll make a fresh pot of coffee while you're gone."

They all stayed out of the kitchen while Jim installed the new door until Thea suggested to Peter he should go and see whether Mr. Hudson needed any help. Jim said, "Sure," and asked him to hold the new door in place while he took the old one to the back of his truck so the boy wouldn't have to see Kenny's blood. He then had Peter stand on a stool and help him screw in the hinges. He also gave the boy all sorts of carpentry tips on how to hang a door properly, using shims where necessary. They worked well together, and Jim was happy to have Peter's company. The boy was strong, big for his age, and well coordinated. He thought how pleasurable it would be to be able to teach him all he knew: to give him skills that would be useful to him down the road.

"Well done," Jim said, and they slapped their hands together in a high five.

Thea asked Jim if he would like to stay for lunch and soon they were all sitting around the kitchen table eating grilled cheese and tomato sandwiches. Thea's dark mood of earlier seemed to have dissipated, and Jim suspected as long as there was no mention of Kenny, it wouldn't return. She was comfortable with her children, and they were polite and respectful to Jim. Jessica eventually lost her shyness and produced the little seal he had made for her and placed it on the table. She looked up at him, pleased he was sitting down because he didn't tower over her, and looked into his kindly face and said, "Thank you so much for my seal. It helped me get better, you know."

Jim struggled to keep his emotions in check and looked into her beautiful blue eyes. "I'm glad its magic worked for you."

"Oh, it did, it did," she said and clapped her hands. "And did you know we're going to Mass-a-chu-setts for Thanksgiving?"

Jim's heart sank. "Your mom did mention it to me," he said.

"We're renting a big car because it's a long drive," Izzie chimed in.

"Is that right?"

Thea observed the interaction between her children and Jim. She hadn't seen them so animated for a long time. Every now and again he would glance at her and smile. She wasn't used to respect and kindness. The only other man she and the children had ever been comfortable with was Uncle Bill, certainly not Michael, and most definitely not Kenny. She wasn't sure she wanted to encourage the burgeoning familiarity. She didn't really know Jim, and could she trust him? Why had he remained single? She couldn't believe it was because of her, but if she could have read Jim's mind, she would have known it was.

Jim suddenly sensed he was outstaying his welcome, so he reluctantly pushed his chair away from the table, saying, "I really have to get back to the store." The kids were disappointed, and they all clamored for him to stay, but Thea didn't say anything, so he knew it was time to go. He looked at her and said, "Thank you for lunch."

"It's a small token after all your kindnesses and thank you so much for fixing the door."

He grabbed his jacket off the back of the chair and pushed his arms into the sleeves. He made funny jerking motions with the zipper, and his antics made the children laugh. He gave a little bow, "Until next time..." he said, opening the new door and stepping out into the cold. Thea heard the crunch of his boots on the gravel driveway and then the throaty rumble of his truck as he drove away. The kitchen suddenly seemed horribly empty. A shiver of desolation went through her, and she ran her hands along the back of the chair where Jim had been sitting.

"Mom, would it be okay if I called Ian to see if he could come over?" Peter said, suddenly needing a friend.

Thea was distracted and didn't respond. "Mom, did you hear me?"

"What, Peter? What did you say?"

"I asked if Ian could come over."

"Sure," she said, thinking the house will have to stay a mess.

Jessica piped up and asked if Johnny could come too. When Thea nodded, she and Peter went off to use the phone in the living room.

"Do you need a friend, too?" she asked Izzie.

"Not today, Mom."

"Are you okay?"

"I'm fine. I need to practice," and she went off to the basement. Her daughter was very serious about her ballet, and the installation of a professional dance area was her just reward for her unwavering pursuit of perfection. As far as Thea was concerned, the expense had been worth it, and she didn't begrudge a single cent she had spent on the barre, floor to ceiling mirror and specially coated wooden floor, especially when she was rewarded by the satisfaction and enjoyment it gave Izzie. After all, what was child support for, if not to give the children pleasure?

Peter came back into the kitchen and asked her to pick up the phone as Ian's mom wanted to speak to her. "Thea Chamberlin here," she said.

"Hi," the gentle, shy voice said on the other end. "This is MaryAnn Wilkinson. I just wanted to make sure it was okay with you to have both Ian and Johnny come over. I know how kids cook up things sometimes."

"It's absolutely fine. Ian and Peter can go outside and kick a soccer ball around to get rid of some of their energy, and I know Jess has wanted to have Johnny come visit for some time now. They have become firm friends, and I'm pleased. Why don't you come in and have a cup of tea when you drop them off so we can get to know each other?"

"That's really kind of you," came the soft reply. "See you in a little while."

Thea turned to Peter who had been standing patiently. "Why don't you go tell Jess they're on their way."

She looked out of the kitchen window as soon she heard the crunch of tires on the driveway and saw a rather dilapidated car, which appeared to be in even worse shape than her own ancient Volvo. She went to the front door to greet the Wilkinsons. "Please come inside out of the cold," she said, smiling kindly. She said "Hello," to Ian, whom she knew well, and "Pleased to meet you," to Johnny, who stood awkwardly until he saw Jess, and then his thin little face lit up. Jess reached out for Johnny's tiny hand, enfolding it within her own much broader one. "Come," she said, gently tugging him off to her room, and she met with absolutely no resistance. Thea's heart went out to this little boy who looked as though he had troubles of his own. Ian was comfortable in Peter's house and soon the two of them were out in the back yard running off their excess energy.

Thea turned to MaryAnn and said, "Sorry to leave you standing on the doormat, but it's always best to get the children settled first, don't you think?" MaryAnn didn't say anything, and Thea sensed she was going to have to tread carefully in order to break through this young woman's shyness without scaring her away. "Why don't we go through to the kitchen?" she said, and MaryAnn quietly followed.

Thea suggested MaryAnn sit, and busied herself turning on the electric teakettle, asking her what kind of tea she would like, and bringing out the last of the zucchini bread. She looked frail and colorless; her silvery blond hair was lusterless and in need of a good cut; there were deep shadows under her pale blue eyes, and she looked sad. There was poverty written all over her and Thea wondered what her story might be, but thought it prudent not to ask. She placed the steaming mug of tea in front of MaryAnn, together with a pitcher of milk and the sugar bowl. "Please help yourself to zucchini bread," she said.

"You know, I feel bad because I never thanked you personally for the courage Ian showed when we were searching for Jessica. It's hard for me to talk about what happened, but your son is a fine young man and you should be proud of him."

MaryAnn looked at her, and Thea saw the first glimmer of a smile which transformed her rather long face, and she became quite animated as she talked about her son. "I'm just glad he happened to be there for you. He's a good boy. Thank you for letting him come to your home. It's a bit grim at our house sometimes," but she didn't elaborate and Thea didn't pry.

"Ian and Johnny are welcome here any time." She wondered whether she should ask about Johnny's absence from school, but decided to stifle her curiosity.

As if reading her mind, MaryAnn said, "Johnny hasn't been very well. He catches cold really easily, and it always goes to his chest. It's hard on Ian. He loves his brother, and I know he worries about him."

"It is hard on the other children when one of their siblings is a little out of sorts. Peter has an overdeveloped sense of responsibility, and he is overly protective of his sisters. It saddens me to think he has had to grow up too fast and be the man of the house."

MaryAnn said, "That's it exactly," and she seemed to relax a little, but Thea sensed she wasn't going to be any more forthcoming.

"When would you like me to pick them up?" MaryAnn asked.

"You're welcome to come back and have some supper with us. It's just going to be homemade pizza. Is there a Mr. Wilkinson?" Thea asked tentatively, "Because he'd be welcome to join us too."

MaryAnn shook her head sadly and said, "No. I'm a single mom." She looked around the bright kitchen and thought how nice it would be to have the opportunity to spend more time with Thea. "I'd love to have pizza with you and the kids if it's not too much trouble."

"Absolutely no trouble. It will be fun for us all to be together."

MaryAnn stood up, and she and Thea walked into the hallway. Thea handed MaryAnn her coat and she shrugged into it, wrapping the shabby garment tightly around her. "Why don't you come back at five?" Thea said. MaryAnn gave a little wave as she walked to her car, tugged the door open, and drove away.

It was three o'clock already, and Thea hadn't really achieved anything. She wondered whether Nan had arrived yet and suddenly realized how much she was looking forward to seeing her. She thought she might just as well make the pizza dough so she could leave it to rest. She gathered all the ingredients she needed: bread flour because it gave a much crisper crust; yeast; sugar; kosher salt; water at just the right temperature, and olive oil. She turned on the radio, and hummed away as she mixed the dry ingredients, adding the oil and the water a little at a time, kneading the dough until it became a solid ball. She loved to cook, and she, like her eldest daughter, was methodical by nature and enjoyed setting up the ingredients, using them one by one. Izzie appeared to get herself a snack and a big glass of water, looking exceedingly hot after her workout. "How did it go?" Thea asked.

"Great," she said, stretching her arms up to the ceiling and bending over to touch her toes.

Peter and Ian burst into the kitchen from the back yard. Jess and Johnny heard all the commotion and soon the kitchen became alive with thirsty and ravenous children. Thea continued with her dough making; the older children helped the little ones with their snacks, and soon they were all munching on carrot sticks, celery, peanut butter and raisins—"ants on a log" as Jessica would say—and string cheese. She told Ian and Johnny their mom would be coming to have pizza with them and was rewarded by their happy smiles. She placed the ball of dough in a large oiled bowl and covered it with plastic wrap to rise for an hour. She then shooed them all out of the kitchen so she could clean up. Jess wanted to know if they could make chocolate chip cookies, but Thea suggested they save their baking activity for another day.

"Aw, Mom..." Jess moaned.

"You and Johnny can help me put the pizzas together a little bit later. How about that?" The suggestion seemed to placate them, and the two of them disappeared. The little boy looked so malnourished especially against Jessica who exuded good health with her rosy cheeks and shiny hair. Despite all she and the children had endured, it was at times like these she considered herself truly blessed.

Thea cleaned up the kitchen, chopped up fruit for dessert and vegetables for the pizzas, by which time her little helpers had returned. She made sure they washed their hands thoroughly, and they then each took turns to roll out the dough into three separate pieces. They added sauce on all three; broccoli, mushrooms, sausage and cheese on two, and one with just chopped tomatoes and cheese. When the kitchen had been originally designed, some unknown person had come up with the brilliant idea of installing a double wall oven, and she absolutely loved it. Having the extra oven meant she could cook all three pizzas at once, and they were sizzling away when she went out to meet MaryAnn. Soon they were all sitting around the kitchen table, and she asked MaryAnn whether she would like a glass of wine or a beer without thinking whether this would be a problem for her. MaryAnn declined and just requested a glass of water, so she had one too. Ian glanced at his mother at the mention of alcohol and Thea wondered what he had to contend with at home, but it was soon forgotten. The children bantered back and forth, and her three were very gracious to their guests, making sure they had all they needed. They all declared the pizzas were delicious, and Thea was glad because they were so much more nutritious than the store-bought kind. She glanced at Johnny, delighted to see his little face smeared with sauce. He had eaten two pieces and truly seemed to enjoy his meal. All the children's faces lit up at the mention of ice cream, although she said they must also eat some fruit, so they all had two bowls, one with fruit and one with ice cream unless they wanted to mix it together.

Thea brewed some coffee and then took MaryAnn off into the living room so they could drink it in peace. "The children will clean up," she said.

MaryAnn stood to one side watching Thea turn on the gas logs and then sat in the chair by the fire at Thea's suggestion. She suddenly found herself completely overwhelmed by the comfort of Thea's home and her kindness. "I don't know how to thank you," she said. "It's been a long time since anyone has extended a hand of friendship." She paused to take in her surroundings, "This room is so pretty. You really have a flair for decorating."

"Thank you, and I don't want to intrude, but is there anything I can help you with?" Thea asked gently.

"It's not a happy story," MaryAnn said, looking down at her pale and work-worn hands. "I'm not sure where to start," she said with a sigh.

"Did you know a sigh is a woman's silent scream?" Thea said, echoing Ellie's words and trying to lighten the atmosphere.

MaryAnn raised her head.

"I'm a good listener," Thea continued, "and I promise you anything you tell me will go no further than these four walls."

MaryAnn looked at Thea and said, "We had a really good life up until..." when the doorbell rang, and the opportunity was lost. In a way, MaryAnn was relieved. She was in danger of falling apart, and while she sensed Thea's kindness and felt she could trust her, would her pride let her unburden her soul? She wasn't sure. "Why don't you go and see who's at the door."

"MaryAnn, I'm so sorry," and she truly was. She was pretty sure it was Nan, and much as she was looking forward to seeing her, she just wished she'd at least had a little more time to listen to this woman's story. She could sense MaryAnn had gone back into her shell, and it would take much coaxing to get back to the same level of comfort.

"Please don't be sorry..."

"But I am. I really would like to spend some time with you."

There was all sorts of commotion out in the hallway and soon Peter appeared with Nan in tow. "Look who I've found," he said, grinning like the proverbial Cheshire cat.

Peter had eventually gone to the door and asked who was there. As soon as he heard Nan's voice, he opened the door wide and welcomed her with the biggest hug he could muster. "My, how you've grown," she said. She peered over the top of his head and beamed at Thea. "It's so good to see you, and I just wish I wasn't so far away. But, unfortunately, it can't be helped." She stepped around Peter, and she and Thea hugged each other tightly.

"Come, Nan. There's someone I'd like you to meet." Nan's curiosity was piqued, but she certainly didn't expect to see a rather sad and careworn woman in Thea's living room.

Thea, in turn, couldn't help noticing how Nan exuded health and vitality with her slight plumpness, rosy cheeks and shiny black hair, a sharp contrast to MaryAnn's frailty.

"MaryAnn, I'd like you to meet my good friend Nan Gilson. Her parents, Margaret and Bill, run the Country Store. Nan, this is MaryAnn Wilkinson. Her son, Ian, was the boy who helped Peter look for Jess."

Nan smiled and held out her hand. "I'm pleased to meet you," she said.

MaryAnn stood and took Nan's hand in a surprisingly warm handshake. She turned to Thea and said she should really round up the boys and be on her way. Thea tried to encourage her to stay, but MaryAnn sensed Thea and Nan had a lot of catching up to do, especially when she heard Nan was only there for a short visit. Thea assured her they would get together real soon, and "That's a promise," she said, giving MaryAnn a gentle hug.

"Let's go find those children of yours. They'll probably be glad not to have to do any more washing up!" She turned to Nan and said, "I'll be right back."

Both Ian and Johnny groaned when their mother told them it was time to leave, but they knew better than to argue. Soon all three of them were bundled into their rather shabby coats. Jess gave Johnny a big hug, Ian gave Peter a high five and Thea reached up to kiss MaryAnn on the cheek and told her she would call her tomorrow so they could fix a time when they could get together again. "I'd like that," MaryAnn said, and then they were gone out into the cold of the night.

When Thea went back into the living room, she found Izzie sitting with Nan on the sofa, telling her all about her role in *The Nutcracker* and how she was getting along at school. She didn't say anything about Massachusetts because she thought her mom probably wanted to tell Nan about that. But her alone time with Nan was short-lived because Jess came in and sat on Nan's lap and Peter squeezed in on the other side of her. Soon they were all chattering away telling Nan how much they had missed her. She hugged them all tight and told them she had missed them too.

"Then, why did you go away?" Jessica wanted to know.

"Because, missy, I can't be in two places at once and if I could have spirited you away with me I would have, but I think there's someone here who would miss you too much." She reached over, put her arm around Jessica's waist and squeezed her tight; Jess responded by resting her dark curls against Nan's silky hair.

Thea sat by the fire in the chair recently vacated by MaryAnn and watched them all. How she loved them, and she, too, wished Nan didn't live so far away.

"Okay, kids. I don't think we're being very good hosts. We haven't even offered poor Nan anything to eat or drink, so let's give her a little breathing space, shall we?"

Jess slid off Nan's lap after giving her a big kiss on the cheek and said in her most grown-up voice, "And what is it you would like, my lady?"

Nan joined in the game and in a good imitation of a British accent said quite royally she would like a cup of coffee with sugar and cream. Izzie turned to Peter and said, "Will you help us lowly chamber maids grant this lady's wishes." He bowed, said, "Come with me," and they followed him out into the hallway where they burst into a fit of giggles.

"What was all that about?" Nan asked. "Your children are hilarious," and then both she and Thea were laughing until their sides ached and the tears were running down their faces.

The kids were scurrying about in the kitchen, and they eventually came back with a small tray on which there was a mug of coffee, a pretty napkin and a little bowl of ice cream. Peter carried it with great self-importance, and the girls shuffled along behind their brother finding it impossible to keep straight faces. Nan quickly grabbed the tray to avoid a mishap and they all dissolved into yet another fit of the giggles. In the end, none of them could honestly say what they were laughing at, but it truly didn't matter as the laughter felt so good and proved just how comfortable they were with each other. Thea's thoughts went to MaryAnn and her boys and wished she had stayed, at least for the sake of Ian and Johnny. Laughter was such good medicine.

CHAPTER SEVEN

MaryAnn, Ian, and Johnny were a sad little trio as they left the warmth of the Chamberlin home and climbed into the car. The engine rumbled reassuringly into life, a miracle in itself, but they were well aware it was going to be an arctic ride home as the heater only worked enough to keep the windshield defrosted. Ian and Johnny, huddled in the back, were snug beneath the pile of blankets, but she was freezing, and her coat wasn't thick enough to keep out the cold. She had thoroughly enjoyed spending time with Thea in her warm and cozy home, but even this small amount of comparative luxury only served to make matters worse for her when she realized how little she could give her own children in her present circumstances. This brief venturing into a world so much better equipped with creature comforts made the stark reality of their lives even more unbearable. She wondered as she drove carefully on the darkened road how much she would really have confided in Thea had they not been interrupted.

It was about eight thirty by the time they got home, and as she pulled into the driveway, she thought how unwelcoming the house looked. The night air was bone chilling, and she quickly bundled the boys in the blankets to ensure Johnny stayed warm until they got inside. There were no houses close by with brightly lit windows to penetrate the inky blackness, and it was downright creepy. She always kept a small flashlight in her pocketbook so they could at least see their way up the rickety porch stairs and find the keyhole in the front door—a door that wasn't as secure as she would have liked.

The hallway was chilly and dark, and she immediately switched on the light to dispel the gloom. The boys were quiet, immersed in their own thoughts. Jackets were hung, shoes removed, and they all slid their feet into their slippers. "Come," she said to Johnny and held out her hand. "It's time you were in bed." He slid his hand within her own, and she squeezed gently and smiled down at him. "We had a good time, didn't we?" He nodded and grinned and said, "Uh-huh." She could tell how tired he was, and his little lungs always seemed to be working overtime draining all his energy. They slowly climbed the old and creaky staircase, and it didn't do to lean on the banister too heavily as it wobbled alarmingly. MaryAnn had hung pictures of the boys on the wall going up the stairs in an attempt to give the place some personality, but no matter how hard she tried, her efforts did little to disguise the truly awful drab and dismal paintwork.

MaryAnn always kept the bathroom at a pleasant temperature, giving them a place to dress and undress without freezing to death. She had flannel sheets on the beds, and she filled Johnny's fleece-covered hot water bottle so he would be nice and warm. She helped him brush his teeth, noticing as if for the first time, the old and shabby bathroom with the iron-stained sink and the cracked and faded linoleum—once a pretty shade of blue.

"Are you too tired for a story?" MaryAnn asked as she dressed Johnny in the only warm pair of pajamas he had, and even those had come from the local thrift shop. In fact, most of their clothes were procured this way and what a godsend. Tag sales were another cheap source for necessities (hence the flannel sheets), and embarrassed as she was by their circumstances, she had become rather good at bargaining. She would do anything within her limited financial powers to make her children's lives as comfortable as possible. She tried to look on the bright side, but spending time with Thea had made her realize how lacking their lives were in the basic necessities, such as plentiful food and heat.

Part of the nightly ritual was the mad dash from the warmth of the bathroom to the warmth of the bed, so she turned to Johnny and said, "Ready?" He nodded, and they ran like mad and he jumped into bed, pulling the covers up to his chin. She would always get into bed with him, using her own body heat to make sure he was toasty; besides which, it was too cold to sit anywhere else to read him a story. They had a good stash of library books sitting on his bedside table and she asked him to choose and he picked one of her favorites, *Fun is a Feeling*. The drawings were delightful and the rhymes on the pages whimsical and happy—a good way to end the day. Soon her little boy was snuggled drowsily beneath the quilt and many layers of blankets. She kissed him and told him she loved him, and he said, "Love you, too."

Ian was sitting in the kitchen reading a book. The kitchen was another room she kept at a comfortable temperature, augmenting the existing heating system by the use of a fan heater. The house had been severely neglected and was old—cold and drafty in the winter and stinking hot in the summer. She turned the thermostat down as low as possible without running the risk of frozen pipes, in order to keep the heating bill manageable, and it was a roof over their heads, but by no stretch of the imagination could it ever be called a home. The landlord did at least have the ancient and inefficient oil-burning furnace serviced each spring for which she was grateful, but other than this small concession, getting anything out of him was a lost cause. He wasn't a bad man, just tight with his wallet, even though he had begrudgingly replaced the refrigerator for her when it had finally given up the ghost one hot summer night. The house was furnished, so he was obligated by the agreement she had signed to replace appliances and she had chosen a furnished house for just this reason. She had kept many of her own things, some of which were stored in the basement. She had spread the rest throughout the various rooms in a rather pathetic attempt to create a home for her and the boys, but it bore no resemblance to the house where she had lived with her husband, Sam. She wished she could have kept the house, but she was forced to sell it after his death, out of necessity to pay for the horrendous medical expenses resulting from his fight with liver cancer, a battle he had lost after only eight short months, just over three years ago.

She hadn't known what true happiness was until she married Sam. She still talked to him all the time, and she hoped if he could see her, he wasn't too disappointed in the way she was coping. She wasn't sure she believed in heaven, but she wished with all her heart if there were such a place, he was at peace. Johnny was only two when Sam died, but he was still bewildered by it all, and he went from a robust and healthy toddler to a thin and silent child with a weak chest. He had been short-changed, and she knew it, but at the time she was spread so thin with the needs of Sam, there was little energy left over for her youngest son. Ian, at the age of eight, just seemed to grow up overnight. He knew how much his dad loved him, and he wasn't frightened by Sam's illness. Amazingly philosophical, he tried to help his mom as much as he was able, and even though MaryAnn understood the life in which they found themselves was much too heavy for an eight-year-old, she didn't know what she would have done without him. Always incredibly mature, secure in his parents' love, and content within his world, he managed to cope with his dad's illness instead of being shattered by the fact his dad was slowly dying. Sam was very good with him, and they spent a great deal of time together except when the pain became too much for Sam to bear: he didn't want his son to see him crying.

Ian's patience appeared to be limitless when it came to his younger brother, and he would keep Johnny amused when MaryAnn had to stay with Sam. Spending time with a two-year-old with a short attention span was no easy task, but Johnny loved Ian and would do anything for him. However, Johnny's attitude towards MaryAnn was totally the opposite, and he tested her incessantly.

MaryAnn had few friends. She hadn't felt the need because she and Sam were so close. Theirs was a deep and abiding love and a true friendship. They had met at the University of Maine's Business School in Orono, located on the banks of the Stillwater River five miles north of Bangor. They had both picked the school for different reasons—Sam for the diversity of the student population and the opportunity to travel, as well as getting a first rate education, and the appeal for MaryAnn was to get as far away from her family as possible, coupled with the fact she was enticed by the curriculum. They had an enriching four years—Sam fulfilled his wish to travel, and MaryAnn enjoyed the internships at local businesses and her newfound freedom.

Sam was the only child of Sandy and George Wilkinson. They doted on him, but fortunately, they had enriched his life rather than smothering him. They welcomed MaryAnn, but not without reservation, to their modest home in Sharon, Connecticut. It was heavy going to begin with, but as soon as they came to the happy conclusion MaryAnn would add to rather than detract from Sam's life, they warmed to her. They never recovered from Sam's death and were of little help to MaryAnn either emotionally or financially once they had laid Sam to rest. She was deeply saddened by their reaction. She had hoped they would be able to overcome their grief to at least help her children, but Ian's stark resemblance to Sam was more than they could bear. She hardly spoke to them now, just to thank them for remembering the children's birthdays and gifts at Christmas.

MaryAnn came from a large and gregarious family in Upstate New York. They were nothing to be proud of, but there was no shortage of love, even if a few of her relatives were downright strange. Growing up in a chaotic and poverty-stricken home, she had certainly wanted something different. Out of all the motley crew, she turned out to be the bright one, and she worked hard to gain a scholarship as a ticket to freedom away from what she called the "handout society." Her dad, a mediocre worker at best, was always being laid off and claiming unemployment. Her mother cleaned houses, but never had any energy left over to clean her own, and MaryAnn couldn't wait to escape. Her brothers and sisters scorned her for always having her nose in a book and not pulling her fair share of the chores, although their criticism wasn't entirely justified—she did what she could as long as it didn't take her away from her studies. There was no privacy, and how she managed to not only graduate from high school but to do it with high honors and a scholarship to boot, amazed her family as well as herself. She was dizzy with her success. Her last summer at home was spent working two jobs so she could at least have some cash to take with her when she left for college in the fall. She was well aware she would need at least her bus fare since there was no money for a car. She had no illusions and understood she wouldn't really be missed at home, and the sister with whom she had shared a room was happy to have the extra space, but there were no hard feelings. Both her mom and dad wished her luck, and she surreptitiously slipped some money to her mom when her dad wasn't looking. "Go buy something special for yourself, Ma," she said and gave her a big kiss on the cheek. Her mother gave her a hug and said she'd put the money by for a rainy day. So, MaryAnn packed up her few belongings, boarded the bus and arrived in Orono, Maine, virtually penniless, but ecstatic.

Sam's parents were not happy to see him leave, wishing he had picked a college closer to home, but they put on a brave face. They also believed he would come to visit as much as his studies would allow, and to facilitate this, they had purchased a modest car for him as a graduation gift. The look on his face was one of wonderment and surprise as he really thought he was going to be hoofing it, but Sandy and George were smart. They realized it would be easier for him to get home to see them more often if he had wheels and that he also wouldn't be able to come up with a reasonable excuse not to. So he bid them farewell on a late September day, and arrived in Orono seven hours later, all ready to start his first semester.

MaryAnn was walking across campus one day, reading as she walked, a rather absent-minded habit of hers. She failed to look up and barreled straight into Sam. He had stopped to let her pass, amused by her preoccupation, when she veered to the right and walked into him. She gasped and dropped her book and then bumped heads with Sam when they both bent down to retrieve it. And that was the beginning of their relationship. He loved her soft silvery blonde hair and pale blue eyes and she was attracted to his shock of curly dark brown hair and his neatly trimmed beard. His brown eyes twinkled with amusement as they stood and faced each other laughing their fool heads off. "I'm sorry," she said.

"No need," he said. "Come have a cup of coffee with me." From that day forward, they became firm friends, but she explained to Sam how important it was for her to stay focused, otherwise she would lose her scholarship so she couldn't be sidetracked by a love affair. He was surprised by the audacity of her assumption he even wanted to enter into a relationship, but they both knew the mutual attraction was there. She also felt safe with Sam. She couldn't quite put her finger on the reason why, but she had grown up around enough unreliable men to believe Sam was the real deal. She had chosen to be upfront with him right at the beginning believing if he had been put off by her honesty, the friendship just wouldn't have worked, even though at the time she had run the risk of scaring him away. He was charmed by her and discovered how much he enjoyed their lively conversations. He was also a great communicator, thanks to his mom, who had chased him relentlessly around the house until he told her what was bothering him. MaryAnn told him endless stories about her quirky family, and they laughed until the tears rolled down their cheeks and their sides ached. He also discovered she was working at night as a waitress so she'd have some spending money and it became a habit for him to run her into town and pick her up at the end of her shift. It was an odd relationship in a way as they kept their distance from each other, both realizing if they started to get physical, they wouldn't be able to stop, though they didn't find it easy.

They were wise beyond their years. They didn't live in each other's pockets. They maintained their independence. Sam was reluctant to leave her and travel, but she encouraged him to go because she believed he would resent it eventually if she tried to hold him back. "We have to do things separately," she said. "It's all part of building character, and will stand us in good stead when we really zero in on what we want to do." He touched her face and told her he loved her, and she said, "I love you, too."

They discovered they had a mutual love of photography. They discussed how it might be possible to start up their own business one day; how the education they were receiving would be invaluable, and how important it was not to miss one single opportunity to learn, learn, learn. They supported each other and bounced ideas around. They helped one another with complicated assignments, pooling their knowledge, and they had excellent debates even though they didn't always see eye-to-eye. They were happy because they were both where they wanted to be, doing what they wanted to do, and their friendship was the icing on the cake. Their enthusiasm and positive energy rubbed off on everyone else, and they were exceedingly popular with their classmates.

Sam was able to ease MaryAnn's financial burden by subtly helping her out. Anything extra he had brought with him he just loaned her. His mother had stocked him up with all sorts of things he didn't really need, such as a surplus of sheets and blankets. MaryAnn wasn't stupid. She was fully cognizant of what he was doing, but she also understood it puffed up his male pride to be looking after her, to be the hunter and gatherer, so she let him give her things within limits. He would go home for the summers, but when she explained her situation to the college administration, she was given a special dispensation to stay in her dorm room, enabling her to get a summer job in the neighborhood. She wasn't too proud to beg, especially if it meant she didn't have to go home. She and Sam missed each other terribly but agreed they had all their lives in front of them to be together, so they put up with their times apart as best they could. It was an unusual relationship, and one their peers struggled to understand as few of them had any desire to be monogamous and spent their time bed-hopping with alarming regularity. However, after the initial teasing, they left Sam and MaryAnn alone and conversely were drawn to the couple by their love and respect for each other and their incredible enthusiasm for life.

When Sam first went home, his mom had asked whether he was seeing anyone special. At first he was reticent to tell Sandy about MaryAnn, but as usual, his mother wore him down, and as soon as he started talking about her, he couldn't stop. He showed her a picture he had taken, and she gazed intently at the laughing girl with the pale blue eyes and soft blonde hair. She wasn't pretty or beautiful by any stretch of the imagination, but even though she couldn't explain it just by looking at a photograph, she liked what she saw. Smiling, she turned to Sam as she handed the picture back to him saying, "I can't wait to meet her." He was pleased his mom had liked the look of MaryAnn, but he wasn't entirely sure how accepting she and his dad would be when they found out about MaryAnn's strange family! Hopefully, her endearing and funny stories would win them over, and this is exactly what happened. After sizing her up, and keeping a wary eye for any character flaws and finding none, Sandy and George welcomed her with open arms. Having grown up in such a large and dysfunctional family, she was exceedingly capable and flexible and demanded little. She had deflected so much over the years, and even though her family wasn't too sad to see her go, they weren't unkind. Life was just so chaotic and having one less mouth to feed was a blessing. The advantage for MaryAnn was she didn't feel even the tiniest bit guilty. She believed she had contributed to her family as much as she could, and it was much better she find her place in the world and be financially independent. She had no doubts she would be successful and planned to send money home when she was able. She explained all this to the Wilkinsons, impressing them with her grit and determination, and even though she wasn't the wife they had envisioned for their son, it became abundantly clear as they listened to her talk why Sam had fallen in love with her. Besides which, the two of them were such great fun to be around. MaryAnn had a great sense of humor, and her sunny outlook on life rubbed off on all of them.

She wondered now, as she sat in the kitchen with Ian, what had happened to her sense of humor. Where was the bright and confident young woman who had not only charmed Sam, but his parents, too? She knew the answer, though—Sam's death had doused the light in her soul, and she just couldn't rekindle the flame. Not only had she lost her best friend, but every single thing they had built together: the successful photographic studio and all the equipment, the house where they had lived, and their two cars. If only she could have pulled herself together, she might have been able to save the business, but she was barely functioning. Initially, she was consumed with rage at Sam's diagnosis—angry at the unfairness of it all—then came a grudging acceptance and the daily struggle of putting on a brave face for Sam, the boys, and Sam's parents. George and Sandy temporarily moved in with them towards the end. George was a tower of strength and helped her find the right buyer for the business, making sure she received a fair price for not only all the equipment, but also the good will. But once Sam was gone, George took Sandy back home where they could both grieve in private. Ian and Johnny missed their grandpa, and George did try to persuade MaryAnn to come live nearby, but she sensed it wouldn't work. Sandy was only increasing Ian's unhappiness by not being able to be with him, and she didn't think Sandy's attitude would change with time. It seemed as though she blamed MaryAnn for Sam's illness as if she had fed him poisoned vegetables or something. She could see all the *if only's* reflected through the sadness of Sandy's eyes, and she just couldn't bear it, so it was a huge relief when she and George packed up their belongings and left.

MaryAnn thought back to happier times to their small and intimate wedding, without any members of her family. She explained they had an "invite one, invite all" policy, and in any case, they had no money to pay for even a modest event, so she and Sam quite happily had a civil ceremony with a small reception at the Wilkinson's home. They invited a few of their college friends, and Sam's parents asked some of the people with whom they socialized. MaryAnn found a simple white dress at a markdown price, and the straight lines of the gown accentuated her slender figure perfectly. Sandy happily paid for the dress and the delicate veil that gave MaryAnn's rather plain face an ethereal beauty all its own. The simple wedding bands were white gold with their names engraved inside. MaryAnn didn't want an engagement ring, and she told Sam it would be annoying to wear and didn't see the point. Sam just raised his eyebrows and told her she was the most unusual but wonderful girl. She had just smiled and told him how much she loved him. He never really formally asked her to marry him; it was a foregone conclusion and neither of them was terribly romantic. Sam was just relieved he didn't have to go to great lengths to find somewhere special to propose or go down on one knee.

"A penny for your thoughts, Mom," Ian said, and she came back to earth.

"Sorry, I was miles away."

"I could tell," and he looked at her quizzically from beneath his mop of dark curly hair. "Happy thoughts, I hope?"

"Yes, they were. Did you have a good time today?"

"It was brilliant," he said. "Being with Peter rocked and Mrs. Chamberlin is so nice. I hope we can go again soon."

MaryAnn smiled at his enthusiasm and held out her hand. "Come on, young man, it's time you were in bed."

"Aw, Mom."

"I know. I hate to leave the warmth of the kitchen, too, so let's be brave and get it over with."

MaryAnn turned down the heat, and they walked quickly but quietly up the stairs as Johnny was a light sleeper, and into the bathroom where she filled hot water bottles for both of them. Ian brushed his teeth, got into his pajamas, and made a mad dash for his bed, jumping in and letting his icy toes find the comfort of the hot water bottle. He asked if he could read for a while to which she agreed, and then she said she was off to her own bed to do a little reading of her own. She didn't like being downstairs by herself. She hated the dark winter evenings and found them lonely and depressing. She sometimes thought she might, possibly, be better off taking the kids and going home to her parents, but her instinct told her it wouldn't have worked. In any case, she had wanted a better life for her children, and she couldn't believe she still found herself in a poverty-stricken state three years after Sam's death. She was going nowhere, and it was time to do something about it. Thea Chamberlin just didn't know how lucky she was not to have any money worries, but other than that, their circumstances seemed to be remarkably similar.

CHAPTER EIGHT

The chaos in the Chamberlin home had calmed down somewhat with Jess and Izzie in bed and Peter shut away in his room. Nan opened the bottle of red wine she had brought with her and Thea got out cheese and crackers.

"Thea, I have such news," she said, grinning from ear to ear. "I met someone, and I brought him home to meet Mom and Dad."

"You did. Nan, this is wonderful. Do tell..."

"His name is Stanley Weatherhill, and the most ridiculous thing happened. I had just come back from a business trip and I was standing outside Logan Airport trying to hail a cab. It was a horrible night, absolutely lashing down with rain. I had pulled up the hood of my jacket, so I had no peripheral vision. I didn't see Stanley, and we barreled into each other making a mad dash for the same cab, which didn't even stop! We both said, "Sorry," and "Let's get out of the rain," and we retreated back to the shelter of the overhang—we were drowned rats. He smiled down at me as he's extremely tall, and I looked into these amazing blue eyes. He asked me if I was hurt and all I could do was shake my head. I kept telling myself it wasn't wise to get friendly with a total stranger at an airport, and he must have read my mind because he said he was harmless. And I thought how could someone with eyes like that be harmless, but I didn't want to let him go! You know my luck with men, absolutely zero, but not this time. Anyway, to cut a long story short, he asked if I needed to be someplace right away. When I said no, he suggested we go back into the airport and have a drink, and I agreed because I thought I would be safe seeing as we would be surrounded by people. We found a cozy table at one of the bars, draped our sodden coats over the backs of the chairs, and stowed our bags underneath. I went for a soft drink because I wanted to keep my wits about me, and he did the same."

Nan paused to pour the wine, handed her friend a glass and Thea said, "Do go on. I'm bursting with curiosity."

Nan took a sip of wine and continued. "We sat there for hours. He told me all about his job at Tufts University in Medford, Mass. as a veterinary technician, and I gave him a snapshot of a day in the life of a buyer! We had such a good time. He really has a flair for telling stories, but he's also a good listener."

"I can't wait to meet him. You will bring him for dinner tomorrow night?"

"I'd love to. Now tell me what you've been up to," and she reached across the table and squeezed Thea's hand.

"I've missed you. Phone calls just aren't the same, are they?"

"No, and I'm sorry not to have been in touch more, but I've been a little preoccupied, to say the least."

"With good reason I'd say."

"How's Jess doing and, just as important, how are you? You seem different somehow."

"To answer your first question, Jess is doing surprisingly well. We had one setback as Kenny tried to break in, and scared the hell out of us. I got him good with the frying pan though!"

"You did what?" Nan asked, her eyebrows rising in amazement.

"He made the mistake of breaking a pane of glass in the back door and putting his arm through, so I grabbed my heavy skillet, which was conveniently sitting on top of the stove, and hit his hand with it! I also called Jim and he and Kenny's brother came and took him away. Jim returned the next day and replaced the back door for me, but I can tell you, we were pretty shaken up."

"Why didn't you call the police?"

"Because it would have meant a jail sentence for Kenny and I just wanted to give him one more chance, but if he ever comes near us again I am dialing 911."

"I should hope so. Maybe a stint in prison would be the best thing for him."

"I know, but going through all the steps of getting him prosecuted would have involved me and the kids. Melford Point is a small town as you well know, and I just wanted the whole thing kept quiet. I couldn't bear the idea of the kids being teased at school again."

"I hadn't thought of that. It just makes me so mad. It's a good thing I wasn't here, otherwise I would have gone and given him a piece of my mind."

"I know, but it wouldn't have helped. He was drunk, and that's when he always makes trouble. Anyway, let's change the subject."

"Yes, let's."

"Do you remember me talking about my friend Ellie?"

Nan nodded. "Yes, I do."

"She called to find out how I was doing, and then out of the blue, offered me a partnership in Aladdin's Cave, her store in Massachusetts; the place where I was working when I met Michael. She took me by surprise, I can tell you, but I told her I would think about her offer. Then she called again a week later and asked if we would like to go there for Thanksgiving. She also wanted to know whether I had thought any more about the partnership. Again, I told her it was a lot to take in, and I hadn't reached a decision." Thea paused and took a sip of wine.

"Go on," Nan said.

"To tell you the truth, I wasn't really sure, but after the incident with Kenny, I thought why not. At least we could go for Thanksgiving. The kids would have the opportunity to meet Ellie, and see where we might be living, at least temporarily, after which we would be able to make a decision. I'm sorely tempted to make a fresh start, but it's complicated, and in any case, we wouldn't be able to leave until the end of the school year. We never go anywhere so having a change of scenery will be good for us, but if we actually decide to move, it will be a huge upheaval."

"I don't know what to say. Do Mom and Dad know?"

"No. I was going to run the idea by your mom when she came over the other evening, but it just didn't seem to be the right time. Did you know I've given up the job at the store?"

"Yes. They did mention it to me."

Thea leaned forward and put her face in her hands. "I felt bad letting them down, but I had to make Jess my first priority. I know your mom and dad understood that, but they're trying to run a business, and they need reliable help. I think that chapter of my life is over, and to be quite honest, it's a relief. Please don't get me wrong. I love your mom and dad, and the kids and I would not have survived without their support, but I need more than a job in a country store."

"Thea, I totally understand where you're coming from. You're preaching to the choir here. Why do you think I live in Boston? Dad really wanted me to take over the store, and to this day, I'm racked with guilt because I was unable to stay here and support them, but it was killing me, too. It's hard to understand another's point of view when you are so content with your lot as Mom and Dad are. I can see how they sucked you in and I know Dad had his sights set on Peter, which wouldn't be right either."

"They've done so much for me, and I've caused so much trouble over the years."

"Oh, boy, we've got a good pity party going here, haven't we?"

"We sure do," Thea said, and they clinked their wine glasses together in complete agreement. "Anyway, good friend of mine, do you have any advice for me?"

"I think your plan sounds like a good one. What harm can it do to go for Thanksgiving, and as you say, a change of scenery will be good for all of you. That's all I would think about right now. I need to get back and rescue Stanley just in case Mom and Dad are eyeing him up as a future store manager!"

"Oh, my goodness, you'd better run like the wind!"

Nan started gathering up her things and put her wine glass in the sink. She turned to Thea and gave her a big hug. "Everything's going to be fine, you know. I honestly think you've come through the worst. Just go with your instincts and you'll know exactly what to do."

"Sadly, it isn't my decision alone, which makes it complicated. Ultimately, what we decide has to be what's best for all of us."

"I know, but if you moved to Mass., we'd be able to see more of each other, and I'd love to show the kids around Boston. There's so much neat stuff to do."

"It's definitely tempting. Anyway, off you go to rescue your man and I'll see you all at about five o'clock tomorrow. Tell your mom she doesn't need to bring anything. The meal is on me."

Thea stood at the front door and watched her friend walk away, the flashlight fading as Nan made a left turn onto the sidewalk. Thea closed and locked the door, checked in on Peter who was fast asleep, as were Jess and Izzie, before climbing the stairs to bed. The wine had made her drowsy, so she was quite happy to climb beneath the sheets. She lay there thinking about her day and decided she would call MaryAnn in the morning and invite her and the kids over for dinner. She was also toying with the idea of asking Jim to join the party!

CHAPTER NINE

MaryAnn dreaded Sundays. Gone were the days when the kids used to climb into bed with her and Sam. Ian would get Johnny out of his crib, and there'd be lots of whispering and giggling coming through the baby monitor! They'd appear in the doorway in their identical Dr. Denton's, Ian clutching Johnny tightly in his arms as he crept quietly towards the bed. Of course, it was much too early for a Sunday morning, but most of the time they all fell back to sleep, the two kids between her and Sam. Johnny was always slightly damp, but nobody seemed to mind. Now she lay in her solitary bed thinking about those happy times when they didn't seem to have a care in the world and she had taken the comfort of their cozy house for granted. Even though she had grown up in poverty, they had always been warm, and it was the cold and the desolation that was killing her now. She longed to be able to make a better life for her kids. She heard Johnny cough and the sound went right through her like the blade of a knife. She dreaded him getting sick.

MaryAnn had enrolled them all in Medicaid and swallowed her pride and signed up for the Food Stamp Program. She felt like a beggar, but there was no way she and the boys could exist on the small salary she made as a waitress at the local diner. She worked hard, had a phenomenal memory, and made sure she always got her customers' orders right. Some of them knew her and would smile and nod, but they were never overly friendly. After all, like Thea, she was an 'outsider.' They weren't cruel or unkind, and even though sometimes the tips were generous, mostly they were just indifferent. Fortunately, Will, the owner of the diner, had known her and Sam long before Sam's death and was sympathetic to her plight. He allowed her to bring Johnny with her while Ian was in school, and although the situation was less than ideal, it solved the problem of daycare. There was a small and shabby room that served as an office where she had set up Johnny's playpen. He was actually quite contented and would often nap for a couple of hours. Will, who loved kids, paid the little boy a lot of attention and so did the other waitresses. They all seemed to take it in turns to check in on Johnny, and he seemed pleased with all the comings and goings, even though after Sam's death he had become quieter and less demanding. He seemed to sense there was only so much his mother could handle, or maybe it was Ian's influence as he was always telling his brother to be good. Life had once been a wonderful and fulfilling adventure—now it was just a meager existence.

MaryAnn heard Johnny cough again and reluctantly got up to go and check on him. The house was freezing, and the thought of yet another day confined to the kitchen in an attempt to keep warm was almost more than she could bear. She put her hand on Johnny's forehead and breathed a sigh of relief he wasn't feverish. He opened his eyes when he felt her touch and said, "Hi, Mom."

"Hi, you," she said, sitting down on the bed. "I heard you coughing. Do you feel okay?"

"Uh-huh. I just had a little tickle."

She climbed into bed with him and snuggled him up close. "I love you, Mommy."

"I love you, too."

"Is it time to get up?"

"Today's Sunday, so there's no hurry unless you're starving."

"What's for breakfast?" he asked, loving the warmth of his mom's arms around him.

"How about pancakes? Will gave me a couple of eggs. I have flour, and there are still some blueberries in the freezer. Do you remember when we went blueberry picking?"

"I do. It was very hot, but we got lots and lots of booberries."

"We did, and I can't wait until summer so we can go again."

"Me, too. We all need some sunshine, don't we? That will make my chest all better."

"It sure will. I'm just going down to turn up the heat in the kitchen. I'll be right back."

"Hurry up," he said, and MaryAnn pulled herself away. She glanced at the clock on the bedside table, surprised to see it was already eight thirty. It had become a habit for them all to linger in bed because it took a lot of courage to make the mad sprint to the warmth of the bathroom. She dashed downstairs, turned up the heat and hurried back to her son.

"Okay mister, I think it's time to be brave. I shall make you all cold if I get back into bed with you. Ready, steady, go," and she flipped the covers back, grabbed Johnny's hand, and they were off as if they were being chased by scary monsters. The bathroom was a haven and all their clothes were in there, so they were toasty. "You first, young man, and then me." They had created the ritual out of necessity and Johnny would turn around and close his eyes while his mom got dressed. She dragged a comb through his unruly mop of hair and brushed hers up and away from her face and tied it back. The face reflected in the mirror looked tired and pale, but not so to Johnny, who said, "You look beautiful, Mommy."

"Thank you," she said, and bent down and gave him one of her special hugs. He rewarded her with one of his wonderful smiles that always transformed his rather sad little face. Everyone said he looked like her except for the rich brown hair he had inherited from Sam, although Johnny's was straight. Ian was all Sam. When she looked at pictures of Sam as a little boy, she could have sworn they were of Ian.

They peeked in on Ian as they went past his door on the way downstairs, and found him fast asleep. Yesterday must have worn him out.

"Let's go make pancakes," she whispered into Johnny's ear.

"It's a 'spiracy," he said.

"My, that's a long word for a Sunday morning, and it's *conspiracy*."

"I knew that. I 'membered the word cuz Jess used it yesterday," he said importantly.

"Do you know what the word means?" she asked.

Johnny nodded. "It means we're going to do something secret without telling anyone else. We're going to make pancakes without telling Ian!"

"You are priceless. What would I do without you?"

"Not much," he said, standing with his hands on his hips and giving her a wicked grin. He then went off and opened the fridge to find the two precious eggs MaryAnn had placed in a bowl so carefully yesterday. She prayed he wouldn't drop them because there weren't any more, but she, just like Thea, believed her children should be self-sufficient. Growing up in a large family, doing chores came as second nature to MaryAnn, and she firmly believed kids needed to play a part in the running of a household. She expected help from her boys and always had, so they never gave it a second thought. She managed to produce tasty meals out of virtually nothing, another useful and practical skill she had learned from her upbringing. The house where she grew up may not have been as clean as she would have liked and the food may have had to stretch to feed many mouths, but for the most part, the meals were wholesome. Her mother was a good cook. She had happily passed along all her skills to her daughter, and MaryAnn had started cooking for her siblings at the age of nine. In turn, she had given Ian basic lessons on how to use the stove safely and how to prepare simple meals. Johnny was still at the prep and stirring stage, but he was eagerly waiting for the day when he would be able to use the stove and flip his own pancakes.

Because the boys assisted her in the running of the house, there was never a shortage of things to do. Ian had always helped her, and when Johnny was old enough to start doing chores, the three of them had gotten together to make a list of age-appropriate tasks. She made it a game as much as she could, but it was hard without Sam. He would chivvy Ian along sometimes when he was dragging his heels over something he didn't want to do, and much as she would try to do the same thing, Ian resented her and reacted accordingly. The children's grief was almost more than she could bear. First there were tears, then Ian's anger, and once the anger had passed he became disturbingly withdrawn and subdued. There were times when Johnny unwittingly made the days worse by constantly saying, "Where's Daddy?"

"Daddy is in heaven," she would say, turning away so he wouldn't see her tears. It was too much for his two-year-old mind to comprehend and he would ask her the same question over and over until she thought she would start screaming and never stop. She would see Ian clenching and unclenching his fists, and she recognized his need to lash out at Johnny, but she would look at him with a pleading expression as if to say, "Please don't," and he would leave the room. He would storm out of the house and spend hours monotonously bouncing a basketball and shooting hoops, or kicking a soccer ball until he became calm enough to come back inside.

MaryAnn envied Ian his ability to grieve. He was able to deal with the emotions when they arose. She had to stuff hers and wait until the children were in bed so she could give vent to the terrible pain which constricted her chest and just wouldn't go away. Crying helped, but drained her of all energy. The nights were terrible and the loneliness and despair came crushing down on her like bricks from a falling building, but somehow she survived, battered and bruised as she was. She would sometimes think she had seen a glimpse of Sam, and it was all she could do to stop rushing up to some innocent stranger who would have thought her completely mad. All she needed was to see hair the color of Sam's, or a jacket of a similar style he had once worn, and it would almost bring her to her knees, tormenting her with a kind of grief that would not let her stand straight. She recognized her eyes were playing tricks, but at the beginning she just couldn't believe he had gone. Ultimately, the grief dulled only to be replaced by a mind-numbing lethargy. It was as if the MaryAnn Sam had known and nurtured had gone with him. In her place was this pale, listless shadow, and she firmly believed without her boys, she would have just faded away.

Ian eventually came down for breakfast, and she cooked up the remaining pancakes, sad to see the last of the blueberries as it was one more nutritious food no longer in the house. They had picked as many as the freezer would hold, and by using them sparingly, she had managed to eke them out. They would have to wait until the summer months before they had any more because, out of season, they were just too expensive. Lost in thought, remembering what a fun outing the three of them had had on that hot summer day, she jumped when the phone rang. She assumed the caller would be Will from the diner asking her to come into work and she dreaded the thought of having to give up her day off, but at least the kids would get a decent meal. She picked up the receiver and said, "Hello."

"MaryAnn, it's Thea. I was just wondering whether you and the boys would like to come over for supper. There will be a few of us, and I thought it would be fun if you joined the gathering. If you have other plans, I completely understand."

MaryAnn, taken by surprise, didn't know what to say. "Let me ask the boys." She covered the mouthpiece and said, "It's Mrs. Chamberlin and she wants to know whether we would like to go there for supper today."

Johnny, immediately jumping to his feet and scattering Lego pieces all over the place, said, "Yes, yes, yes."

"Ian, what about you?"

"That would be brilliant," he said.

"Thea, the answer is a resounding yes if you're really sure. I don't want to outstay our welcome. Two nights in a row and all that."

"Nonsense, MaryAnn, all the more the merrier. See you at about five," and she rang off before MaryAnn could offer to bring anything. She hated to go empty handed, but maybe she could babysit for her sometime as a thank you. Yes, she would suggest that. She couldn't believe how much she was looking forward to a social gathering. Time to come out of her shell maybe. She wasn't shy by nature, but her present circumstances caused her to withdraw, so she came across that way. Ian glanced up from his book and looked at his mom. She seemed almost happy, and he was glad.

CHAPTER TEN

The Chamberlin house was buzzing with activity and conversation. Bill and Margaret, Nan and Stanley, MaryAnn, Ian and Johnny all arrived at more or less the same time. They were all jammed together in the hallway, and Thea was trying to take their coats and sum up Stanley at the same time when the doorbell rang and there was Jim, who she had decided to invite after all. "Come in, come in," she said. "You're letting in all the cold air." Eventually they all shuffled off into the living room, and after introductions were made, Thea suggested the children go off and find something to do, saying she would call them when supper was ready. They didn't need to be told twice and scurried away. She offered soft drinks, wine and beer and she wasn't the least surprised when the ladies selected wine and the men beer. Jim came out to the kitchen with her to help and asked about MaryAnn.

"She's someone I'm getting to know because Ian and Peter and Johnny and Jess are friends. She seems nice but rather down on her luck. Her kids are great. You probably remember Ian; he was the one who helped Peter find Jess, so he has a special place in my heart, and Jess has taken Johnny under her wing. The little boy is a welcome distraction and has given her someone else to think about, so it's a win-win situation all round." She handed Jim a tray of drinks, and they headed back to the living room where there was a great deal of lively chatter.

Thea observed Nan and Stanley together and liked what she saw. He was incredibly tall and slender, and his light brown hair, which if left alone would be a mass of wiry curls, was cut close to his head. He had a rather boyish face with bright blue eyes, a small straight nose, and a mouth that tipped up at the corners. Margaret and Bill seemed comfortable with him, and she was so pleased for Nan.

Soon they were all gathered around the dining room table. Seating was a bit of a tight squeeze, but they managed. Izzie had done place cards with each of their names, and she had purposely jumbled them up. The only concession her daughter made was to allow Jessie and Johnny to sit next to each other, and she also relented when Thea asked Izzie to put MaryAnn's name next to hers. Kitchen chairs were mixed in with dining room ones, and in most instances, once you were sitting down, you couldn't get out! In no time at all, steaming dishes of food appeared and were placed all along the table. Thea had cooked the chicken and made a casserole to which she had added all but the kitchen sink to stretch the meal as much as possible. There were sweet potatoes with apple; mashed potatoes with a cheesy crust on top, and broccoli, at which the children turned up their noses, but with the magic of a little ranch dressing, were able to get down a couple of pieces! She'd also found two loaves of garlic bread in the freezer, so there was plenty of food to go around. With the pouring of wine, the conversation flowed, and Thea was happy. Entertaining good friends had gone on the back burner when Kenny was living with her, and thinking of him now, albeit briefly, reinforced how important it was to spend time with only those people who enriched her life. She smiled at them all, and they raised their glasses and said in unison, "A toast to the cook," and they all drank in her honor. She just thanked them and said how glad she was they could all be together.

Jim couldn't remember the last time he had enjoyed himself so much. He watched Thea as she bustled about, and with MaryAnn's help the two of them brought in the hot dishes. She then sat down at the end of the table looking flushed but happy, and he was pleased Kenny was out of her life. She seemed so much more self-assured, and the haunted look she had always seemed to carry around with her appeared to have gone. He also watched Jessica, and it was heartwarming to see the little girl helping Johnny and telling him he didn't have to eat anything he didn't really like, but he at least had to taste it. "That's my mom's rule," he heard her say. He had Ian on his left and Margaret on his right. The boy was certainly enjoying his food and Margaret was saying how nice it was to have someone else cook a meal. With all the baking she did in the store, he was sure this was a rare treat. He had some of his little carved animals in his pockets, and he was planning on giving them to the children before he left.

MaryAnn almost felt a twinge of happiness for the first time in a very long while. Full of food, and together with the calming effect of a couple of glasses of wine, she felt wonderfully relaxed. Margaret was sitting to her left, and she found the older woman easy to talk to. She didn't pry or probe and was happy to tell MaryAnn all about the store and how she had met Bill. She also talked about Stanley and how lovely it was to see Nan so happy, but how she felt sad because they lived so far away. MaryAnn agreed it must be difficult.

Nan was also noticing how much Thea seemed to have matured. She had always been a great hostess, even in the early days when she and Michael had first been married and before Peter was born. Back then she had been so young and terribly insecure, but now she finally seemed comfortable in her own skin and able to fend for herself. It was also good to see her so calm instead of nervous and jumpy, and Nan thought now would be the perfect time for her to come into her own without the influence of a man. She was also pleased to see such a change in Jess. Worry over the little girl after the abduction had consumed them all, but here she was playing mom to Johnny who seemed to be lapping up all the attention. Maybe Nan's own happiness and heightened awareness made her notice all these things; being in love with Stanley was her own personal miracle. She had never truly been in love in all her thirty-three years, although she had carried a torch for Jim, and it was bliss to have someone in her life to care for and to know the passion was completely mutual.

Stanley was sitting across from Jim, and they had set up an easy conversation. He had many stories to tell of his days in the veterinary world, and Jim was content to listen, as was Ian. One of the many sadnesses in Ian's life was not having a pet to care for, and he shook his head when Stanley asked if he had any animals at home. "I would love a dog," he said, "but we really can't afford one." Stanley nodded and said they were expensive to keep, but he was sure he would have one some day in the future and it would be something to look forward to. Jim told him he had a dog and if he ever wanted to come over and walk her just to let him know. "She's a beautiful collie, just like Lassie, and her name is Carrie. She's a little slow as she's getting old," he said, "but she still likes her walks." Ian smiled and told Jim he would like that. Peter, who was sitting opposite Jim, was feeling a little left out, but Jim quickly rectified this by saying he must come too.

Once they were all done with the main course, plates were gathered, and those who weren't trapped, helped carry all the dishes to the kitchen. It was then time for dessert, and there, as promised, was the pavlova in all its glory, consisting of a mound of meringue all crunchy on the outside and soft on the inside, with raspberries piled high and chocolate drizzled over the top. There was also apple crisp with a huge bowl of whipped cream and coffee or tea for the grownups. Thea sat at the head of the table and took requests and bowls were passed. The meringue was difficult to cut with its tendency to collapse and she said, "It looks as though I'm making Eaton mess," and she told them the story of the English dessert which was essentially the same thing—meringue, fruit and whipped cream, but all the ingredients were mixed together. "The dessert is traditionally served at Eton College's annual cricket game against the pupils of Harrow School and has been known by its name since the nineteenth century. A popular, though thought to be untrue myth, is that Eton mess was first created when a meringue dessert was dropped accidentally. They salvaged what they could, and it was served as a crushed meringue with strawberries and cream. Anyway, it's less fattening to do it separately, so you don't have to have the whipped cream if you don't want to!" she teased.

The party was getting rowdy, and the children were on a sugar high, so they needed to go and run off some steam. Thea was amazed they had sat for as long as they had without asking to be excused, but the grownups had made sure they had included them in their conversations, and they were all laughing hysterically when Stanley started in with his biking jokes. "A tandem rider is stopped by a police car, and the rider asks what he's done. 'Perhaps you didn't notice sir,' the officer said, 'but your wife fell off your bike half a mile back…' 'Oh, thank God for that,' says the rider. 'I thought I'd gone deaf!'" Once he had an audience, Stanley was relentless and continued, "Do you know what is the hardest part of learning to ride a bike?"

They all shouted, "No."

"The pavement."

They all groaned, and he went on, "'I've really had it with my dog,' said a guy to his neighbor. 'He'll chase anyone on a bicycle.' 'Hmmm, that is a problem,' said the neighbor. 'What are you going to do?' 'Guess the only answer is to confiscate his bike!'"

"Just one more," Stanley said, and they were all laughing too much to stop him. Nan raised her eyes to the ceiling; Stanley winked at her, and began his next story. "One day, a pedestrian stepped off the curb and into the road without looking and was promptly knocked flat by a passing cyclist. 'You were really lucky there,' said the cyclist. 'What on earth are you talking about? That really hurt!' said the pedestrian, still sitting on the pavement, rubbing his head. 'Well, usually I drive a bus!' the cyclist replied."

In the end, they pleaded with Stanley to cease and desist. Their sides were aching, and Bill's glasses were filling up with tears. It's not that the jokes were all that funny, but once you set kids off there's no stopping them and their laughter was contagious. Jessica was bouncing up and down, and said she had to pee, which set them all off again. The quickest way for her to get out was to slide off her chair and under the table, and Johnny after asking his mom if he could be excused too, quickly followed. They crawled, giggling as they went, thinking everyone's legs looked so funny from their worm's eye view!

MaryAnn couldn't remember when she'd last had so much fun. She thought of Sam and wished he could be there with her to see how happy and respectful his children were. It was so good to see Johnny laughing; he was usually such a serious little boy. She believed evenings such as this would be so much more beneficial than all the medicines in the world. She had warmed to Margaret right away and found her easy to talk to.

Margaret, in turn, sensed MaryAnn was in need of a friend although the young woman said very little, so she didn't find out anything substantial about her circumstances. *All in good time*, Margaret thought. When she learned about her waitressing job at Will's Diner, she wondered whether she would be a good candidate to take Thea's place at the store. The high school kids were doing a passable job, but their hearts weren't in it. She would talk her idea over with Bill and see what he thought. She had also cast her motherly eye over Johnny and decided he also needed some tender loving care. Margaret was also heartened by the change she saw in Thea. It seemed as though she had finally gotten rid of all the monkeys on her back, and it was about time because those monkeys had been pulling her down for far too long.

There was much confusion as they all stood up and tried to inch their way out of the dining room. Ian, Peter, and Izzie cleared the remaining dishes from the table and Thea told the kids to take a night off—she would tackle the dishes later. There were all sorts of mumblings from the grown-ups who wanted to help, but she shooed them all out. She said she truly didn't mind doing dishes, but they didn't really believe her. Jim secretly hoped he would be able to stay and help her after everyone had gone.

MaryAnn glanced at the kitchen clock and turned to Thea, "Oh my goodness, is that the time? I need to get the kids home and into bed, otherwise I'll never get them up for school tomorrow."

"I'll go round them up. They're more likely to listen to me."

Ian and Johnny appeared in the kitchen doorway with awfully long faces. "Do we have to go home?" they both wanted to know. She just raised an eyebrow and they immediately stopped talking. In any case, there was no way they were going to make a scene in front of Mrs. Chamberlin because they definitely wanted to come back again.

"Why don't you go and say your goodbyes while I get your coats," Thea suggested.

Jim shook Ian's hand and said not to forget about walking Carrie. He bent down, so he was at a level with Johnny's face and said he could come too. He then reached into his pocket and pulled out a little carved bear for Johnny and a dog for Ian. "This is what Carrie looks like," he said, and the boy marveled at the incredible detail and how much care had gone into the making of the little creature.

"It's absolutely beautiful," he said. "Thank you, Mr. Hudson."

Johnny was smiling at the chubby little bear resting in the palm of his hand. "Now I have one too. And I won't have to share Jessica's seal any more. Thank you so much."

Jim smiled at these children whom he guessed had very little, and each time he gave one of his carvings away he became aware of why he spent so many hours bringing them to life. He glanced up and caught MaryAnn looking at him. There were tears in her pale blue eyes, and he felt an instant rapport with her. Was it just a mutual recognition of their individual loneliness or something else? He wasn't really sure, but he knew in an instant he wanted to spend more time with this young woman. "Thank you for your kindness," was all she seemed to be able to say, and he was taken by surprise when he realized how much he wanted to take her in his arms.

Fortunately, the awkward moment passed as Thea arrived in the doorway with their coats, and the boys turned to her and proudly showed her what Mr. Hudson had given them. "Oh, Jim," she said. "They are truly lovely." Jim smiled and held out MaryAnn's coat for her, and she was embarrassed for him to see the shabby garment. Thea helped Johnny into his jacket, and Ian shrugged into his. MaryAnn, having recovered somewhat, turned and said how much she had enjoyed meeting everybody. Margaret said she would be in touch, and MaryAnn believed her. Once at the front door, she turned shyly and gave Thea a big hug. "I'm not sure how to thank you, but I want you to know if you ever need someone to stay with the children, I'm your woman!"

"You have made me an offer I can't refuse, so when the first opportunity arises, I will certainly call on you and we both know all the kids will be in full agreement."

Jess was giving Johnny a big hug and telling him she would see him in school tomorrow, and Peter and Ian did their usual high five and then the Wilkinsons were out the door and gone.

Thea turned to all those who had remained and said she would be right back after getting Jessica ready for bed. They made murmurings about leaving, and she said, "Please don't go. Why don't we play cards just like old times? I'd like that."

They didn't need much persuading, and while Peter went off in pursuit of a deck of playing cards, they all went back to the dining room. Izzie came and joined them and they played Up and Down the River, with Peter scoring. They had to teach Stanley the game, but he soon got the hang of it, although he lost badly. "No beginner's luck for me!" he said. Then Thea took Izzie's place, telling her daughter it was time for bed. Again, Jim slipped his hand in his pocket and produced an elephant for Izzie and a horse for Peter. They were enchanted. He also gave a dolphin to Izzie asking her to give the little carving to Jess if she was still awake, and if not, to save it for the morning. Izzie said, "Thank you, Mr. Hudson." She reached over and gave him a big kiss on the cheek, which embarrassed and pleased Jim both at the same time.

The remainder of the evening rapidly disappeared. Peter went off to bed, and the grownups suddenly noticed how tired they were, so they leaned back in their chairs and said they'd better get going, "As they had such a long way to go," and the silly comment set them all off laughing again. Once more, they all offered to help Thea with the dishes, and she said, "Absolutely not," so they gave up in total defeat. Bill gave her a hug and said she'd done them proud. She told Stanley how much she had enjoyed meeting him and gave Nan a big hug and told her she would see her before she went back to Boston. She thanked them all for coming, and then she was standing alone in the hallway shivering in the draft of cold air they had left behind.

Thea decided to check on the kids before tackling the dishes. Izzie and Jessica were fast asleep. Jess had wriggled her way out of the blankets, so she covered her up and tucked her in. Her youngest daughter had always been a restless sleeper, but Izzie, on the other hand, rarely moved unless she was sick. She left her bed in the morning as neat as when she'd first slid between the sheets. She kissed them both and then went off to see what Peter was up to. She found him sitting up in bed reading a comic book and looking exceedingly disgruntled. "What's up, doc?" she asked and sat down on the bed.

"Nothing," and he buried his face behind the lurid drawings of some evil character.

"Peter. That's not an answer. Didn't you have a good time tonight?"

"I did, but I'm tired of pretending everything's normal."

"What do you mean?" and Thea reached out and touched his leg where it lay beneath the covers.

"It's just that Mr. Hudson seemed to be paying more attention to Ian and Johnny than he did to me. I love the horse carving he gave me, but I liked the one he gave Ian better."

So, now she understood the problem; the green-eyed monster of jealousy had reared its ugly head. "I'm sure he wasn't playing favorites, but grownups can be thoughtless sometimes," she said.

"Oh, he included me *after* he'd asked *them* and he never told me he had a dog. Now he's invited Ian and Johnny to walk her and where does that leave me? Dad doesn't want me, and now Mr. Hudson doesn't want me either."

Thea didn't know what to say, but she sat silently cursing Jim. She leaned over and took both Peter's hands in hers. "I know it's hard for you, but I'm sure you'll feel better in the morning."

"No, I won't!" and he pulled his hands away. "It's all a big mess. No one at school really likes me except for Ian and Marty. I'm so fed up," and he put his head in his hands and started to cry. Thea gathered him into her arms and held him while he sobbed. For him to actually be reduced to tears was so out of character and she was mad at herself for not seeing his unhappiness.

"Peter, I don't know how to fix this. I know things are changing, and there are always going to be bumps in the road. Most of the time we drive over them without any problem and then there are the times when we are trying to do it with a flat tire. I would love to call Mr. Hudson and give him a piece of my mind for unintentionally hurting you, but I know you wouldn't want that." She sat back and gently smoothed the tears away from under his eyes.

"Maybe it will be better in Massachusetts," he said, looking at her hopefully.

"We can at least give it a try. I think it would be good for us to get away for a few days, don't you? It will be quite an adventure."

"Mom, do you think we could have a dog of our own someday? I promise I would take care of it, and I wouldn't let it be any trouble."

129

"I know you would. Let's put a dog on our wish list for some time in the future. Okay?"

"Thanks, Mom."

Thea gently removed the comic and told him to settle down and go to sleep. "Just be thankful you don't have all those dishes to wash! Right now I'd be happy to climb into bed and forget all about them."

"Why don't you?" he asked as he snuggled under the covers.

"Goodnight, Peter," and she leaned over and kissed him on the cheek.

"Night, Mom. I love you."

"I love you, too, very, very much. You are the best son any mom could have and don't you forget that." Thea saw him smile and she turned away and switched off the light.

When she got to the kitchen, she sat down heavily on one of the chairs and put her face in her hands. She suddenly felt terribly lonely and completely overwhelmed. She thought about how much she had enjoyed the evening because, for once, she had felt confident, happy and joyously independent. She had been thrilled to see Nan in her relationship with Stanley, but knew it wasn't something she wanted for herself—maybe someday, but not now. She had thought Jim would stay and help her with the dishes, but for some reason he had left. She didn't want to give him any encouragement, even though she would have enjoyed having someone to talk to, and if he'd stayed behind he could have spent some time with Peter, thus assuaging his hurt. Oh, my goodness. Why does life always have to be one step forward and two steps back all the time? She truly felt her time in Melford Point was done, and if she were by herself, she wouldn't hesitate to pack up and move away. As far as she was concerned, Thursday couldn't come soon enough so they could get on the road and temporarily forget about the current shambles of their lives. All the worry about her son had burst her brief bubble of happiness, and it just wasn't fair. Peter so badly needed a father figure in his life, and she didn't have a clue how to find one, but it certainly wasn't going to be Michael.

CHAPTER ELEVEN

Jim was halfway home before he realized he hadn't said goodbye to Thea or even thanked her for the meal—it wasn't like him to be so rude. He found himself in the middle of an ethical dilemma—unable to move on with MaryAnn without first discussing his plans with Thea—so he turned his truck around and drove back to her house before his courage failed. His change of heart worried him, and he felt as though he at least owed her an explanation, especially as he had so recently written to her expressing his wish to be friends. How could he be such a turncoat? The nagging little voice in his head was telling him he needed to be honest with her and find out how she truly felt.

Thea was sitting in the kitchen when she heard the knock on the door, and she froze. Please don't let it be Kenny. She stood up slowly and walked out into the hallway, and she could hear her heart beating in her chest.

"Who is it?" she said.

"Thea, it's Jim. Can I come in, please? It's freezing out here."

She turned both locks with shaking fingers and said, "Thank God, it's you. I thought for one horrible moment you might be Kenny."

"I'm sorry. I didn't mean to scare you."

"It doesn't take much. Why did you come back? Did you forget something?"

"No. I just wanted to talk to you, and I'm sorry it's so late."

"Please stop saying you're sorry. That's not going to get us anywhere. Would you like something to drink?"

"No, thanks."

"Why don't you take off your jacket and come in and sit down. Then you can tell me whatever it is you need to get off your chest."

He did as he was told, hung his jacket on the hallstand, and followed Thea into the living room. "I can tell you right now I'm mad at you," and she sat down on the couch and folded her arms. He perched on the edge of the chair and thought she looked like a disgruntled child.

"Why are you mad at me?"

"Because you hurt Peter's feelings."

Jim was mortified. "Please tell me what I've done."

"He said you seemed to be paying more attention to Ian and Johnny when you invited them over to meet and walk your dog. He got the impression you asked him as an afterthought."

Jim leaned back in the chair. Thea had blindsided him with her anger, and he didn't know how to respond.

"Well," she said.

"I had no intention of hurting anyone, or leaving anyone out. You know me better than that."

"Do I?"

"Thea, I'll call Peter tomorrow and tell him I'm sorry." He was beginning to wish he hadn't come, but he had no intention of leaving until he found out exactly how she felt about him. The time would never be right, so it was now or never. "I'll make it up to Peter, but I want to talk to you about something else. Can I ask you a question?"

Thea said, "Sure," but her body language still spoke volumes. He could tell she was coiled tight as a spring.

He cleared his throat and said, "How do you really feel about me?"

She didn't speak right away and he sat quietly waiting. Finally, she said, "To be honest, I've never really given it much thought. You've always just sort of been there. Your letter surprised me coming out of the blue like that. I've never had any romantic thoughts about you if that's what you're getting at. I look upon you more as an older brother, or a kindly uncle. Is that what you wanted to hear?"

"Deep down, I've always known that, but I refused to believe it. I lived in hope things would change, but the timing's always wrong for us, isn't it? I've been loyal to you in my mind, and because of the loyalty, I can't just walk away from you without telling you I would like to see MaryAnn again. It really hit home when you told me about going to Massachusetts and your possible move, and when you didn't take me up on my offer to drive you there, I should have known there was no hope for us."

"Jim, you have to understand something. I'm not the woman for you, and it's time for you to take off your rose-tinted spectacles and see me for who I truly am. I'm tainted goods, and you deserve better." Jim opened his mouth to say something, but Thea held her up her hand. "Let me finish," she said. "I had absolutely no idea you thought you were in love with me until I saw the way you looked at me when I was so sick in the hospital. I was flattered, don't get me wrong, but as far as I was concerned, it was just another complication. In the end, you would come to dislike me because the Thea you've put up on a pedestal and worshipped from afar doesn't exist. I'm not an easy person to live with—I'm not steady and constant like you. I have these periods of darkness, and they are scary to deal with. Right now, I need to be on my own to sort out what I want to do with my life. I just don't have enough energy to give to a relationship and it wouldn't be fair to the kids. I will say this, though, if I had to choose a fatherly figure for my children, he would be modeled on you. As far as your relationship with MaryAnn is concerned, go for it. You have my blessing. She's a nice young woman, and I'm just getting to know her. I'm hoping we can be friends, and I thought maybe I could be of some help to her and the kids as it looks as though she's fallen on hard times."

"You are telling me the truth, aren't you?"

"Yes, Jim, I am. I wouldn't lie to you, or anyone else for that matter. What good would lying do? In any case, in order to be a good liar one has to have a superb memory and mine's not terribly good!"

Jim finally relaxed. "You know you can always call on me, don't you?"

Thea stood up and looked down into his kindly face. "That's not going to change. Knowing me, there's bound to be some kind of situation from which I'll need rescuing. I have your cell phone number, so look out!"

Jim went to stand up, and she stepped away from him. "It's strange isn't it, to be ending something that never really began. It will be better now, you'll see, and I won't be on my own forever. There will be someone for me when I'm ready, and this time I'll do it right. MaryAnn is a lucky young woman to have you in her life. You and she will have a clean slate and, hopefully, there aren't any skeletons in her closet now you've success-fully thrown me out of yours," Thea said, grinning wickedly, taking Jim's hand and pulling him out into the hallway. "Go now, or I'll make you stay and help me with the washing up!"

Jim drove home in a relieved, but somewhat befuddled, state. The feel-ings he had for Thea were still there, but they were different. They were normal: just love and respect for a fellow human being and his heart didn't race anymore when he thought of her. He no longer imagined a life with her, and there had been no sexual excitement between them, even when she'd grabbed his hand. He didn't understand what had happened, but he felt liberated, as if he had shed a heavy burden. Suddenly he wasn't mired in hopelessness and loneliness anymore, and there was a spring in his step as he walked from his truck across the driveway and into the house. Carrie was there to greet him, making her little whining noises of welcome. She would nag at him too, in her own special language, when she thought it was time for a walk although she wasn't as keen as she used to be. He stroked the top of her head and scratched beneath her ears, and she pushed her long nose into his hands. "Come, girl," he coaxed, and she followed him outside. Business done, they went back into the house, where he refreshed her water and filled her other bowl with food, and despite being a dainty eater, she still had a good appetite. He left her to her meal and went off to the den, knowing she would soon follow.

The grandfather clock in the hallway struck nine, much too early to go to bed, but it wouldn't have mattered what hour the old clock chimed because he was wide-awake. He hadn't felt this good in years, but at the same time, he was worried he was placing too much importance on his brief encounter with MaryAnn. He knew she was widowed, but he didn't really know the circumstances. He remembered Sam when he used to come into the store, usually with Ian in tow, but he didn't recall seeing much of MaryAnn. He leaned back into the sofa and folded his arms behind his head. Carrie had come and tucked herself comfortably at his feet, and he leaned down and touched her briefly. He wondered where MaryAnn lived. He didn't even have her phone number, but that wasn't a problem because he could always go into the diner. In fact, he would take a trip there tomorrow, and with this plan in mind, he finally took himself off to bed.

MaryAnn, equally as befuddled as Jim, had taken the children home and gotten them all settled for bed. They couldn't stop talking about how much fun they'd had. Ian was still laughing over Stanley's stupid jokes and Johnny was thrilled with the fat little bear Mr. Hudson had given him. These boys of hers had so little and the frugality of their lives made these gifts so much more meaningful. The fact the carvings were so personal and not a mass-produced toy from a store was the reason they were so treasured. Johnny put his under his pillow where he could touch it with the tips of his fingers, and Ian placed his dog on the bedside table where he could see it when he woke up. He hoped Mr. Hudson would ask them over to his house soon.

MaryAnn made herself a cup of tea and sat at the kitchen table thinking about the evening. She couldn't escape her awareness of the mutual attraction between Jim Hudson and herself. She had never really thought about other men as she had remained loyal to Sam's memory and put all her energies into caring for the boys. She hadn't wanted anything to detract from her parenting. Besides which, the resulting emotional and financial devastation caused by Sam's death, had taken all her natural resources just to survive.

She thought about her relationship with Sam. It hadn't been a grand passion. It might have been if they had given into their lust when they first met, but they had suppressed their desire, and so when they finally came together, the lovemaking was mutually satisfying, but there were no fireworks. More important to both of them was their friendship and their trust in one another—the sex was just the icing on the cake. They loved their life together, building up the photography business and then there was the thrill of Ian's birth. Sam loved his newborn son, but he always made sure MaryAnn knew he had loved her first, and no matter how many children they had, she would always be the most important person in his life. She cherished him for that. She had been as fulfilled as a woman could be, and until she felt the electricity coursing through her at Jim Hudson's touch, she hadn't known such sensations existed. Now she was afraid. Except for the love she showed her children, she had subdued her ability to reach out to another human being for a long time now. She had let down her guard just a little with Thea, but she was still exceedingly fragile and withdrawn.

CHAPTER TWELVE

On Monday, Jim went off to the diner for lunch in the hopes he would see MaryAnn. He had no way of knowing what hours she worked, but he hoped if she wasn't there, Will would at least give him an idea of her schedule. He doubted Will would tell him where she lived, but Jim thought he might be able to at least persuade him into giving him her phone number. The restaurant was at the other end of town, so it took him about twenty minutes to get there. Traffic was light, and there was ample parking. As soon as he stepped out of his truck, the wind whipped around him and tried to rip the hair off his head. He pulled his collar up and walked quickly across the parking lot, opening the door to the diner and stepping into the warmth, with its accompanying smells of all those wonderful comfort foods.

Will was at the cash register and looked up when the door opened. He smiled as soon as he saw Jim and said, "Hey, man, aren't you a sight for sore eyes! What brings you to my neck of the woods? Haven't seen you in here in an age."

Jim smiled, and he and Will shook hands. "It's great to see you. You're looking good. Skinny as ever, despite all the tasty food you prepare."

"Always was a string bean. Why don't we sit down? MaryAnn, could you grab us a couple of coffees?" And there she was, and Jim's heart missed a beat. She just looked at him, and neither of them knew what to say. Jim didn't think Will had noticed anything, but to cover any awkwardness, Jim pulled the menu from its holder at the end of the table and studied it so he could order something when she came back.

MaryAnn soon returned with two steaming mugs of coffee and placed them on the table with slightly shaky hands. "What else can I get you?" she asked, and he ordered a turkey sandwich on rye toast without any fries.

"What about you, Will? Anything?"

Will just shook his head. "No thanks, MaryAnn. The lunch crowd will be here soon so it will be all hands to the pump!" and he smiled up at her.

"So how's business, Jim?"

"Can't complain. How are things here?"

"Same old, same old, but we get by. I've got good staff, and that really makes a difference. Heard you had some problems with one of your men."

"Yup. I'm still employing him, but it's not a good situation. He's off work right now with an injured hand, and to be honest, it's a huge relief."

MaryAnn arrived with Jim's sandwich, and she asked whether they wanted their coffees warmed up. Will declined and said he'd better get back to work, but Jim said, "Yes," in the hopes he would have the chance to say something to her. She nodded and turned away. Will slid out of the booth, stood up and shook Jim's hand and said, "Don't be a stranger."

"I'll try not to be," he said, and looked up to see MaryAnn standing there with a steaming pot of coffee. "Do you have time to sit for a minute?" he asked.

"Not really. I have to keep any eye out for the school bus as Johnny gets dropped off here."

"What about Ian?"

"He gets dropped off at home, and I make sure I leave here on time so he doesn't come home to an empty house. I'm sorry, I really do have to get back to work, and the bus is here. Please finish your sandwich."

Jim suddenly lost his appetite, but he didn't like to leave food on his plate, so he ate his way methodically through the meal, not enjoying it very much although the sandwich was good. The restaurant was beginning to fill up with the lunchtime crowd, and he noticed MaryAnn wasn't the only waitress. He wondered if she would come back to his table, and in the hopes she would eventually return, he waited patiently.

After a little while she reappeared, and he asked if he could have the check. She smiled at him and said, "Of course," and ripped his receipt off the pad.

"I really would like the boys to come over after school," he said quickly before she could disappear again.

"They would enjoy that. Why don't I call you when I get home? It's much too busy for me to talk to you now, but if you have the time to go and say hi to Johnny before you leave I know he'd be pleased to see you."

Jim stood up and said, "Let me go pay and then you can show me where he is."

MaryAnn nodded and walked to the next booth to take the orders of the folks sitting there. Jim left a hefty tip and walked over to the cashier. Once the transaction was completed, he just stood out of the way until MaryAnn came back to hang her order slips for the kitchen staff. "Quickly," she said. "Come with me," and they went down a dark hallway past the restrooms until they reached a door at the end. This she opened after knocking softly, so she didn't startle her son. "Hi Johnny. Look who I've found," and the little boy's face lit up with joy. "Hello Mr. Hudson," he said. "Why are you here?"

"I just came by to visit your mom, and it was a nice surprise to find you here, too." He turned to MaryAnn and suggested she go back to work. "I'll just stay with Johnny for a little while. We can get to know each other if that's all right with you."

"That's great," she said. "I'll come back as soon as I can," and she was gone.

Jim looked around Will's office and decided it was a pretty dull place, but it looked as though someone had made a half-hearted attempt to set up a kid-friendly table in the corner with a couple of chairs, and this is where Johnny had dumped his backpack. The air smelled faintly of cigarette smoke, and he didn't think it was a terribly healthy environment, but Johnny seemed happy enough. The little boy grinned at Jim and said, "Why don't you sit down, Mr. Hudson? My mom would say you're making the place look untidy!"

"She's quite right." Jim smiled, pulling out one of the chairs and sitting down. "Do you have any homework you need to do?"

"I'm in kindergarten, so we don't really have homework, but Miss Simms always wants us to practice our writing and our 'rithmetic."

"What's your favorite subject?"

"I like it when Miss Simms reads to us cuz then I feel as though I'm in the story. She's a very good reader, and I want to read like that, too. She makes all sorts of different voices for the people in the story."

"She sounds really nice."

"She is," Johnny said. "Mommy says I'm lucky, and I am, except when I get sick."

"I'm sorry you get sick, but I'm sure your mom looks after you."

"She does, but our house is cold and drafty..." and then Johnny stopped because he thought he might have said too much as he didn't want to let his mom down.

Jim didn't like the sound of that, but he sensed an unwillingness in Johnny to divulge anything more about his home, so he asked him if he had a book they could read together and the little boy turned away and rummaged in his school bag. They pushed the two chairs together and became completely engrossed in the story. The tale was a simple one and Johnny was able to sound out some of the easier words, and this is how MaryAnn found Jim and her son when she returned.

"You two look as though you've made yourselves at home, but I think we've taken up enough of Mr. Hudson's time. In any case, we'll have to leave in a little while."

Jim had been oblivious to the passing of the time, and he had truly enjoyed being with Johnny. He was bright and interesting and not nearly as shy as Jim had thought he would be. Jim had been pleased by the interaction between them, sensing the child was obviously comfortable with him. He gave MaryAnn a slip of paper with his phone number and asked her to please call so they could set up a time when she and the boys could come over. He thanked Johnny for his company, told him he would see him soon, and reluctantly turned away and left.

After he had gone, MaryAnn suggested Johnny drink the glass of milk she had brought for him and eat the banana she had begun to peel. "Did you have a good time?" she asked.

"Uh-huh. Mr. Hudson is so nice. Are we really going to go to his house?"

"You'd like that wouldn't you?" and he nodded, his mouth full of banana and his lips boasting a milky mustache!

CHAPTER THIRTEEN

Early Monday morning, Margaret called to thank Thea for the meal on Sunday, saying how much she and Bill had enjoyed themselves, and this had given Thea the opportunity to tell her she and the children were going to Massachusetts for Thanksgiving. Margaret was a little taken aback, but when Thea told her the reason why, she made every effort to be enthusiastic. They both agreed not being together for Thanksgiving would seem strange as they had always shared the holiday. She asked Thea to tell her all about their adventures when she got back and said she and the children would be missed. Thea said she would miss them, too, and quietly hung up the phone and wondered what on earth she was doing. She was glad Nan and Stanley were visiting because this meant Margaret and Bill would at least have their company. Little did she know Margaret had plans of her own.

Margaret didn't waste any time. She took Bill to one side when there was a gap in the string of customers, told him Thea and the children wouldn't be around for Thanksgiving, and wondered whether he thought it would be a good idea if she invited Jim and MaryAnn and her boys. He wanted to know why, so she told him the Chamberlins were going to Massachusetts to see Thea's old boss, Ellie, because of an offer Thea had received as a partner in Ellie's store. Bill raised his eyebrows and said, "Now, isn't that a right turn up for the book. Who'd have thought?"

Margaret was getting impatient. Bill was just standing there running his hands down the front of his apron as usual. "So, what do you think? Should we invite Jim and MaryAnn and her boys, or not?"

"Why don't you ask Nan?" he said, and turned to help a customer.

"Fat lot of help you are," she muttered under her breath and took her frustration out on the bread dough by kneading and slapping it down on the table. *This is going to be the lightest batch of bread I've ever baked,* and she smiled to herself. The dark clouds in Margaret's sky didn't stay around for long, and she turned all her attention to her task. Truth be known, she thought Bill's idea to talk to Nan a good one, not that she was going to admit it to him!

Nan was standing at the sink in her parents' kitchen in their apartment above the store filling the coffee pot with water and didn't hear Stanley coming up behind her. "Hi, you," he whispered, bending over and kissing her on the back of her neck. She leaned back into him, and he put his arms around her waist.

"Not fair," she said. "My hands are full," and she pushed back against him, but he didn't budge. "Come on, Stanley, get out of my way," she said, pretending to be cross, and he just whisked the carafe right out of her hand.

"What are you two up to?" They both turned to look at Margaret standing in the doorway and realized their game was up. They were a little flushed from their physical contact, and Nan glanced up at Stanley noticing he looked a little embarrassed.

Margaret chose to turn a blind eye. "Nan, I have something I'd like to run by you."

Nan moved out of Stanley's way so he could get the coffee going, seeing as he had stolen the carafe from her, and said, "What's up?"

"I was thinking about inviting MaryAnn, Ian, Johnny and Jim for Thanksgiving since Thea and the kids won't be here. I asked your dad, and because he couldn't make up his mind, he suggested I ask you. So, what are your thoughts?"

Knowing how her mother always needed to be looking after someone, and suspecting this to be the real motive behind the invitation because the Wilkinsons certainly looked as though they could do with some loving care, she said, "I think that's a great idea."

"That's settled, then," Margaret said, beaming at the two of them. "Enjoy your breakfast," and she winked at Stanley and left.

Once Margaret was out of earshot, Nan turned to Stanley and said, "She's mother-henning! With Thea and the kids gone, she needs someone to look after. She's got that glint in her eye, and I know she's desperate to feed the Wilkinsons, especially Johnny. That's my mom."

"We need more people like your mom. The world would be a much better place."

"Oh, don't get me wrong, I wasn't criticizing. I just thought it would be nice if it was just the four of us, but I'm being selfish. I don't get to see Mom and Dad as much as I'd like and I was looking forward to a quiet day for a change. Plus the fact it's so much work for Mom, but she won't see it that way."

Nan was so grateful to Stanley for just listening, even though she understood it was hard for him as he was such a talker. One of the things she truly loved about him was his innate ability to hear her out and gently steer her in the right direction if she was being irrational.

"So, what shall we have for breakfast?" he said.

"How about eggs and bacon? I'm famished."

"Sounds great."

"Thanks for listening to me," she said, and he leaned down and gave her a long and lingering kiss, eventually coming up for air.

"Fooling around isn't going to get breakfast made, is it?" Stanley said.

"No, it isn't, but it's a lot more fun," Nan said, wriggling out of his grasp and heading for the refrigerator.

"What do you think we should do today? It's been a while since I've had this much leisure time and I'm glad, for once, not to be on call. I'm certainly going to make the most of my brief reprieve. I hope you're going to be able to tolerate my erratic hours and being woken up in the middle of the night."

Nan stopped buttering the toast, and knife poised, unwittingly pointed it at Stanley. "You're going to have to put up with my travel schedule, so I think we're even."

"Whoa, if you're going to point knives at me I may change my mind about marrying you. Is there a violent streak in you, woman, I don't know about?"

"There sure is," and she playfully lunged at him, and he caught her and swung her around. "You really don't know me at all."

Nan served up breakfast and Stanley poured coffee, and they managed to eat without touching each other. "I think we should see what help Mom and Dad need and then maybe we could go for a hike, or is there anything else you have in mind?" and she raised her eyebrows.

"Nothing that would be appropriate in your parents' apartment!"

"It does rather cramp our style, doesn't it?"

"You know what we could do?"

"What?"

"Rent a motel room for the afternoon."

"Why Stanley Weatherhill. How could you think of such a thing? I'm blushing right down to my pretty little toes," she said in her best Southern accent.

"So, Scarlett, what do you think?" he said, winking at her and grinning broadly.

"I think it's a fantastic idea."

Margaret waited until the end of the day on Monday to call MaryAnn, grateful she'd had the presence of mind to ask her for her number when they were at Thea's yesterday. Much to her disappointment, the phone rang and rang and finally she gave up. Of course, she wasn't to know the Wilkinsons were at Jim's. She'd had a good day, made better by Nan being home. She and Stanley had pitched in and they found having someone as tall as Stanley extremely useful. They reveled in Nan's newfound happiness, relieved she no longer carried a torch for Jim Hudson. The persistence of Nan's hopeless pursuit had always bothered Margaret as Jim's unwavering love for Thea was no secret. And, in any case, even if Jim had loved her daughter and the relationship had worked out, Nan would have eventually become restless and discontented. She knew her daughter's longing for the city lights and the lure of the big shops with their glitzy window decorations, and the Country Store paled in comparison. Margaret, on the other hand, loved her life with Bill and couldn't imagine anything more fulfilling, but she worried about what they were going to do when they could no longer keep up their current pace. Always concerned about Bill's health and also her own, she was fully aware they both needed to lose some weight. They had tried many different diets over the years, but when the pounds refused to budge they became discouraged and gave up. She recalled word for word the time she'd become wedged under the sink and had to call out to her husband in desperation.

"Bill, are you there?" she had said, exploding in muffled laughter beneath the counter. "I'm stuck. Can you pull me out please?"

"Margaret, what are you doing?" and he looked down to see her extremely plump rear end protruding from the cupboard under the sink.

"I crawled in here to get something way in the back, and now I'm lodged," and she had collapsed into a fit of giggles. He had leaned over and put his hands on her ample waist and started to pull gently; finally, she had been able to get her hands into a position where she could push herself out. She had sat back on her haunches, extremely red in the face, and told him, "Now we really have to go on another diet. This is ridiculous!" But, of course, they never did.

CHAPTER FOURTEEN

MaryAnn gathered up Johnny and all his belongings and headed home. Always a little tight time-wise, the school bus arrived shortly after she and Johnny had gotten in the door. She settled Johnny in the kitchen and then headed off to change. She hated the lingering smell of food and decided to allow herself the luxury of a shower because if she and the boys were going over to Jim's, she didn't want to smell like the deep-fat fryer. She heard Ian's key in the lock, and throwing her robe on, went down to meet him. He looked up at her and smiled when he saw her coming down the stairs.

"Hi, Mom," he said.

"Hi, yourself. How was your day?"

"It was good, and I don't have too much homework."

"Must be because Thanksgiving's coming up. Guess who came to visit me today?" MaryAnn said, pulling her robe tightly around her in a somewhat futile attempt at warding off the freezing air in the hallway.

"Who?" Ian said, heading towards the kitchen.

"Mr. Hudson. Why don't you let Johnny tell you all about it? I'm just going to take a shower before I catch my death," and she headed back upstairs.

The shower left her invigorated and refreshed, and her flyaway hair miraculously behaved itself for once and fell in soft waves to her shoulders. She applied a touch of makeup, put on a red turtleneck, a gray sweatshirt, her only decent pair of jeans and—just for fun—a pair of bright red socks. She hadn't felt this optimistic for such a long time and it brought color to her cheeks, and her body felt as light as air.

The boys were deep in conversation when MaryAnn arrived back in the kitchen. Ian had spread his schoolbooks on the table, and Johnny—always wanting to be like his big brother—sat painstakingly forming the letters of the alphabet within the lines on the paper. Ian looked up from puzzling over a math problem and said, "Wow, you look really pretty, Mom."

"You sure do," Johnny said, looking at her in wonder. "Are you a fairy princess?"

Her boys' reactions pleased her, and their comments only served to enhance her sense of wellbeing even more. "Now," she said, "if I were a fairy princess and I could make wishes come true, what would you ask for?" As soon as the words were out of her mouth she perceived her mistake because she knew what they would all wish for and that would be to have Sam back; even though three years had passed, their wounds were still raw. She looked at her sons and could see the naked pain in their faces; even Johnny who had little memory of his father, still longed for him.

She swallowed and said, "Would you still like to go over to Mr. Hudson's?" She had little inclination to leave the house now, and her earlier optimism that had landed so lightly on her shoulder had now flown away, but she had to make an effort for her boys.

She saw Ian draw in a huge breath and glance at his brother, "What do you think, Johnny? Do you still want to go?"

Johnny sat with his arms wrapped around himself and looked at Ian. "I think so."

MaryAnn could see his lip quivering and she felt so helpless. She stood behind the chair on which he sat and gently rested her hands on his tiny shoulders. She wanted to take him in her arms, but close to tears herself, she wasn't sure she would be able to control herself and didn't want to frighten him further. "I think it would be a good idea to get out of here, don't you?" she said, leaning down and kissing the top of his head, breathing in not only his little-boy smell, but the faint odor of the diner and Will's stale cigarettes. He turned in the chair and stood up, putting his arms around her waist and burying his head into her sweatshirt. He looked up at her, gave her a rather shaky smile, and said, "I'm all better now."

She went down on her haunches so she could look Johnny in the eyes and give him some encouragement. "That's my boy, and I really think Mr. Hudson would like our company, so let me call him." She turned to Ian, "How about you, sport? Are you up for an outing?"

"Sure am."

"That's settled then," and she rummaged around in the bottomless pit of her large and shabby pocketbook for the slip of paper Jim had given her with his phone number, eventually finding it in amongst all the accumulated stuff. She wondered whether the state of her purse reflected the state of her mind because, if so, either or both needed a serious cleaning out. She smoothed out the now crumpled note, removed the receiver from the wall phone, and punched in the numbers. It rang a couple of times and then she heard his deep voice say, "Hello."

"Jim, it's MaryAnn. We'd love to come visit you if your offer still stands."

"Of course it does. Why don't I come and pick you up?"

"Thank you, but no, that won't be necessary." There was no way she was going to let him see where they lived as she was much too ashamed. "We can drive ourselves if you could please give me directions."

"If you're absolutely sure."

"I'm sure."

"Do you know where the hardware store is?"

"Yes, I do."

"My house is on the same street about a half mile before the store on the left-hand side, number 252. There are ducks on the mailbox. Don't ask me why, but they seemed a good idea at the time," and he chuckled. "Me and Carrie will be waiting for you."

"See you in about twenty minutes," she said.

MaryAnn hustled the boys, dressing them in the warmest clothes they had, checking they both had their gloves and hats. Soon they were out the door, hurrying into the car and heading towards town. Fortunately, there was still some daylight left, and after negotiating the traffic in Melford Point, the road was fairly clear. She told the boys to keep their eyes open for number 252 and to look for a mailbox with ducks! "There it is, there it is," Ian said, and she almost missed it, but fortunately there wasn't anyone right behind them or anyone coming from the other direction, so she slammed on the brakes and made a quick turn between the large holly bushes on either side of the tarmac driveway. The house—an imposing Victorian with a three-car garage set kitty-corner to the left of it—was secluded and quite a long way from the road. She pulled over beside Jim's truck and turned off the engine. She looked up to see his face peering at her through the car window, and she jumped. He bent down to open the door, stepping out of her way so she could get out. "You scared me half to death," she said.

"I'm sorry, I didn't mean to," he said. "I'm assuming you didn't have any trouble finding the house."

"No, the ducks were a good hint," she said, smiling up at him.

The boys were already out of the car looking a little awkward, so Jim said, "Why don't we go into the house and you can meet Carrie."

MaryAnn looked at the house as they walked. She liked the soft brick walls, partly covered by what appeared to be some kind of evergreen creeper, and she wondered what it was. There were green shutters on either side of each window and a deep burgundy red front door with a burnished brass knocker in the shape of a lion's head and a square of etched glass in the center at the top. Three wide steps led up to the door and two ornate cement urns sat on the top step, both of which were empty, and she wondered whether Jim ever filled them with flowers. The house seemed somewhat grand, and she was curious about its history.

"I don't normally use the front door," he said, "but I thought I would today as you are my special guests." He pushed the door open and before stepping inside they all wiped their feet diligently on the dark green half moon mat sitting on the top step. The entranceway was illuminated brightly by two hanging, old-fashioned, wrought iron lanterns either side of the door and the prisms in the glass cast intricate shadows on the brickwork. The Wilkinsons trooped in behind Jim, trying not to step on each other's heels, and stood in the spacious hallway, looking around in awe. There was a round oriental rug in faded blues, creams and reds on top of a wide-planked dark wood floor, but it was the sweeping staircase that caught MaryAnn's eye. It went up straight from the right hand wall to a landing, and then from there, the stairs turned back on themselves and went up to the next level. She stared up at the huge round window gracing the landing, either side of which hung two exquisite oil paintings of horses and dogs. Jim sensed her interest and said, "The one on the right is called *The Arab Tent,* painted by an artist called Sir Edward Henry Landseer sometime in the 1800's. I can't remember the exact date. This is a reproduction and my grandfather brought it over with him from England when he emigrated in 1927. The original is at The Wallace Collection in London. It's beautiful, isn't it? I never get tired of looking at it."

"Could I go take a closer look?"

"Of course," Jim said.

MaryAnn climbed the stairs with Jim and the boys followed close behind. The painting was magnificent and portrayed a large gray horse lying on an oriental rug with a light brown foal snuggled up against her; the mare's nose rested on the haunches of the foal. In the background two dogs lay sleeping on a red and blue striped blanket, and on what appeared to be the roof of the tent, two monkeys reclined in amongst the feathery branches from a palm tree.

"I'm afraid I don't know anything about horses, but it doesn't really matter, does it, because the painting is lovely," she said. "What do you think, boys?"

"I like it," Johnny said, glancing at the picture briefly and then looking up at Jim. "But where's your dog, Mr. Hudson?"

"If you turn around, you will see she's sitting at the bottom of the stairs. She usually makes a lot of noise when I come in the house, but I think she's being polite because I have visitors."

"She looks just like the carving you gave me," Ian said, going down the stairs towards Carrie who sat waiting patiently, swishing her long hairy tail across the wooden floor.

MaryAnn watched her older son sit down on the second stair from the bottom, and Johnny went to join him, leaning forward so he too could reach Carrie and stroke her. The dog lapped up the attention, but MaryAnn noticed she also had a watchful eye on Jim. She was a beautiful collie— just like *Lassie*—with her long pointed nose, now a little gray around the muzzle, and her small, but kind, eyes.

"Her hair is so soft. Do you brush her a lot?" Ian said, gently fondling one of Carrie's ears.

"I have to brush her every day otherwise her coat gets all matted. It's become a sort of ritual for us and most of the time she doesn't mind unless there's a knot and then she gets kinda grumpy."

Jim turned to MaryAnn and said, "Would you all stay and have some supper with me? It won't be anything fancy, but I'm a pretty good plain cook, even if I say so myself."

MaryAnn didn't want to appear too eager, but she couldn't imagine anything she'd rather do. "I'd like that very much, and I'm sure I won't get any arguments from Ian and Johnny, right kids?"

The three of them followed Jim with Carrie on their heels. She certainly wasn't going to let her new charges out of sight. Johnny had his hand on Carrie's neck as he walked and MaryAnn could sense the dog's protectiveness. She found the bonding of the animal with her son comforting, and she sensed he felt the same way.

Jim opened the door into the kitchen, and they were greeted by the wonderful smell of something roasting. "I put a chicken in earlier in the hopes I might be able to persuade you to stay. It should be just about done."

MaryAnn looked around the kitchen. The cabinets were old-fashioned and painted white. Some of the upper ones had glass doors, and she could see all sorts of china dishes and glassware. The countertops were a buttery yellow, and the backsplash seemed to be some kind of Mexican tile in blue, white, rust and yellow. A double porcelain sink sat under one of the windows, and a large gas stove had been placed to the left of that. The white and bulbous refrigerator, tucked into the corner, appeared to be making weird moaning noises and she wondered if it was on its last legs. The floor matched the one in the hall—wide-planked dark wood—and down the center of the room stood a large scrubbed pine table with old mismatched wooden chairs flanking either side.

MaryAnn, highly amused, watched Jim putting on an apron, and decided it didn't make him any less of a man. He tied the apron around his middle, took a couple of oven mitts and opened the door to the stove, standing back to avoid the blast of hot air burning his face. "It looks as though the chicken is well and truly done, but it will have to rest for a little while before carving. In the meantime, would you all like something to drink?"

"Just water would be fine," MaryAnn said, answering for herself and the boys. Jim handed her some glasses and a pitcher. She went to the sink to fill it, trying not to get in Jim's way even though she truly wouldn't have minded if they had bumped into one another! The boys were shown the location of the silverware, and Jim pointed to a drawer in the center of the table and told them they would find some placemats in there. He asked them to get the salad and the butter out of the fridge, and they laughed out loud when he told them the fridge's name was Mona because she moaned a lot!

They were all ravenous by the time they sat down to eat, and the chicken—cooked to perfection—turned out to be crispy on the outside and succulent and juicy on the inside. There were baked potatoes with crunchy skins and a large bowl of salad. Johnny pulled a face at the latter, but Jim saved the day with a bottle of ranch dressing. He'd also found a couple of cushions for Johnny to sit on so he wouldn't have his chin in his dinner, and MaryAnn sensed without a doubt Jim had found a friend for life in her youngest son.

Jim seemed to be comfortable with them there, and they all chatted through the meal about all sorts of things. The boys weren't afraid to ask questions, and Jim was patient in his replies. "One day, when we have more time, I will tell you the story of the house," he said. They asked him about his carvings and he said he would take them to his workshop, but they would have to save that for another day, too. She found herself liking him more and more with his kindly manner, neatly trimmed light brown hair with a touch of gray, and his warm brown eyes.

Both the boys really enjoyed their food, and left not even the slightest morsel on their plates. Jim asked them if they would like seconds and Ian said, "No thank you. I'm absolutely stuffed."

"Me, too," Johnny said, "Everything was so yummy. Thank you, Mr. Hudson."

"Jim, I'm sorry to break this up, but we really do have to be going as the boys have to be up for school tomorrow," MaryAnn said.

"Aw, Mom," they both exclaimed, scowling at her for spoiling their fun.

She ignored them, pushed her chair back and stood up. "Let's help Mr. Hudson clean off the table and then we really must leave. Okay?" Fortunately, to her relief, they remembered their manners. She helped Johnny down off his perch, and between the three of them they carried the dishes over to the sink. She further warmed to Jim for allowing her children to do as she had asked rather than overriding her instructions and saying he didn't need any help. It made her realize how sensitive and perceptive he was. Soon the dishes were neatly piled, and the leftover food put away in the refrigerator. Johnny turned to Jim and said, "Now Mona won't be hungry," and they all laughed.

Back out in the spacious entrance hall the boys said their goodbyes to Carrie as Jim helped them all into their coats. He knelt down to make sure Johnny's was buttoned all the way up, his scarf wound warmly around his neck and his hat pulled firmly down over his ears. Johnny rewarded him with a hug, nearly knocking Jim off balance, but he managed to right himself and stand up. He quickly bent down and picked up the little boy, giving him a huge hug in return.

"You're a nice man, Mr. Hudson," Johnny said, putting his mittened hands either side of Jim's face.

"And you're a nice boy, Johnny Wilkinson."

MaryAnn observed how comfortable Johnny seemed to be with Jim and she was convinced Jim's affection for Johnny was genuine. Johnny would not have responded to him in such a way if Jim had only been buttering up her son in an attempt to win her over; he was pure pleasure to be around, friendly and sincere. Ian stood smiling, watching the interaction; she could tell he wasn't feeling the least bit left out, and neither was she. If asked to explain how she felt, she would have said the four of them had already formed a strong bond because Jim had the uncanny knack of being able to treat them all equally. She hadn't felt as warm and as safe and as cherished for such a long time, and she found it hard to break away.

"What are you doing for Thanksgiving?" he said, leaning down and placing Johnny gently on the floor.

"We don't have any plans," she said, and her heart sank as she always dreaded holidays.

"I always go to my brother's, and you and the boys would be welcome to join us."

"Let me think about it. Can I let you know?"

"Of course you can," he said, shrugging into his coat. "Let me come outside with you so I can see you off."

The old vehicle rumbled into life, and she made sure the boys were safely in the back—Ian belted in, and Johnny secure in his car seat. She tucked blankets all around them, closed the door on her precious cargo and turned with her back to the car. The cold night air nipped at their noses, and both she and Jim could see their breath. She let out a little shiver. "Brrrrr," she said. She would have loved to give him a hug, but the gesture would be inappropriate because she didn't want to give her children any mixed signals, so she just held out her hand, which he clasped in both of his. "Thank you so much for inviting us over and giving us such a great meal," she said.

He relinquished her hand and thrust both of his deep into his coat pockets. "You'll let me know about Thanksgiving?"

"Of course, and thanks again," she said, moving away from him and sliding into the driver's seat. He leaned into the car and said, "Goodnight, boys. See you soon," and they waved at him and thanked him again. He closed her door and stood back while she reversed around his truck, and she caught a glimpse of him in her side-view mirror as she drove away. He looked such a solitary figure standing in the driveway, and it took tremendous willpower on her part not to stop the car and go running back to him, but she clenched the steering wheel and forced herself to keep going.

Jim watched the family drive away and went back into his empty house, locking the front door behind him. Carrie, as always, was waiting for him patiently, and he really thought he would have gone nuts if she hadn't been there. "So, what do you think, old girl?" he said, bending down and rubbing her gently behind the ears. "Did we do all right?" And if she'd had the gift of speech, she would have said, "You did better than all right."

The only thing dampening Ian's spirits was the fact he hadn't thought to ask his mom to include Peter, but then, they had all been so upset they almost didn't go. Now he didn't want to hurt his friend's feelings by telling him he'd had dinner at Mr. Hudson's. He didn't believe in secrets, and in any case, he could hardly ask Johnny not to tell Jessica. It was a problem and something he would have to speak to his mom about. She would know what to do. Despite being worried about Peter, he was happy because he'd had such a good time and the fact they might have somewhere to go for Thanksgiving truly rocked! He did hope his mom would say yes.

CHAPTER FIFTEEN

MaryAnn was surprised when the phone rang just after she and the boys arrived home on Monday because it was a rare occurrence, unlike the days when she and Sam were busily running their photography business. The call had been from Margaret, asking if they would like to spend Thanksgiving with her and Bill, Nan and Stanley. She hadn't known what to say because she didn't want to disappoint Margaret by telling her they already had another invitation. She stalled and asked if she could get back to her in a little while because she needed to get Johnny ready for bed. Finding it impossible to believe they had choices, she silently thanked Thea, because if she hadn't invited them to dinner, she would never have met any of these wonderful and friendly people and she and the boys would have had nothing to look forward to. Now they wouldn't have to spend yet another holiday alone, and she was enormously relieved.

Johnny wanted to know who'd called, so she told him it had been Mrs. Gilson and how they now had another place to go for Thanksgiving. She looked at both her sons and said, "So what do you think we should do? Who would you like to spend Thanksgiving with?"

"Mr. Hudson," they both said in unison, without any hesitation whatsoever.

"Then, that's what we'll do. Thank you for making up my mind for me."

Johnny, once safely tucked up in bed, fell asleep as soon as his head hit the pillow—one exceedingly tired, but happy little boy. Ian took himself off to his room and sat in bed reading, his feet resting on the warmth of his hot water bottle. "Don't read too long," MaryAnn said, leaning over to kiss him on the forehead, always gratified he didn't spurn her affection, and she hoped he would always be this responsive.

"I had a good time this afternoon, Mom."

"So did I."

"It was more than just getting out of the house, wasn't it?" he said, giving her a wicked grin.

"Perhaps," she said, not wanting to elaborate, surprised by her son's intuition. Was the attraction between her and Jim so obvious? She'd have to be careful.

"Mom, I don't know what to tell Peter. Mr. Hudson said he was going to ask him over too, but he seems to have forgotten."

MaryAnn wasn't entirely sure how to advise her son. "This is a tricky one, isn't it? I wouldn't tell him anything unless the subject comes up."

"But what if Johnny tells Jessica and then Peter finds out from her. Wouldn't that be worse than me not telling him?"

"I agree that it's always better to be honest. Why don't you just take the day as it comes? I'm sure Peter is busy getting ready for his trip to Massachusetts and isn't there basketball practice on Monday nights?"

Ian's face brightened considerably, "Yes, there is, so he couldn't have come anyway."

"I'll mention your concerns to Mr. Hudson when I talk to him in a little while, so the Chamberlin kids don't get left out the next time, and even if they had been here for Thanksgiving, they would have spent the holiday with the Gilsons, so I don't think we need to worry about that."

"Mom, you're the best," and she watched him as he snuggled down under the covers, relieved she'd been able to put his mind at rest.

MaryAnn went back to the kitchen and decided she needed a cup of tea. The warmth of the tea would complete her sense of fulfillment. The last time she had felt such contentment was when she was in the comfort of her life with Sam, and to be honest, she had taken much of it for granted. It wasn't until Sam got sick that she knew, with gut-wrenching awareness, she was going to lose everything. Never, ever would she sink into the trap of believing life couldn't change at the drop of a hat, for better or worse. She was running a risk embarking on a relationship with Jim, but dammit, it felt right. However, she was going to take things slowly and just let the relationship take its course, and if at any time, something didn't sit right for either her or the boys, she would back out faster than you could say 'jack rabbit.'

Jim picked up the phone after the third ring, and again MaryAnn was comforted by his deep "Hello."

"Hi, Jim, it's me," she said as if it were the most natural response in the world.

"Hello, you," he said. "Kids all safely tucked up in bed?"

"Yes, they are, but I need to talk to you about a discussion I had with Ian."

"Go ahead."

"He's very friendly with Peter Chamberlin, and he's worried about what his reaction will be when he finds out he went to your house without him."

"Please tell Ian I'll take care of it."

"As it turns out Peter has basketball practice on Monday nights so he couldn't have come anyway, but I have no doubt Johnny will tell Jessica, seeing as she's his best pal."

"I'll call Peter once we get off the phone and set it all straight. I need to tell you something first though."

"Fire away."

"I was driving home on Sunday night thinking about you and I suddenly realized I hadn't even thanked Thea for dinner, so I turned the truck around and went back. I wanted to talk to her and ask her how she really felt about me. You see, I've been in love with Thea for years…"

"Oh," MaryAnn gasped, her heart sinking like a stone.

"No, don't take me all wrong. Just listen. There was no way I could move on without clearing the air. She and I have had plenty of opportunities to build a relationship, but she's never had any interest in me. I have fantasized about her coming and living with me and my being a father to her children, but it was never going to happen. Our paths have crossed on numerous occasions, and she only ever reached out to me to get her out of a bind—nothing else. MaryAnn, you can't make someone love you. It's possible I could have persuaded her into a relationship for the sake of the kids, but it wouldn't have worked in the long run, so I've been sitting on the sidelines of her life for years. As far as she's concerned, I'm just an uncle or an older brother. Are you still there?"

"Yes, I'm here. I'm listening, but I don't really know what to say. You've kinda taken the wind out of my sails."

"There is nothing to say except there's no romance between us. I will always love her as a friend, that's never going to go away, but the fondness I have for her now is normal, not some trumped-up totally futile fantasy. I'm going out on a limb here, but I wanted to tell you I've never felt the way I did today with you and the boys. It seemed to me as if we were a family."

"I know. I felt the same way. When you were on the floor with Johnny, I looked at Ian to see if he was feeling left out and I could see he wasn't. He was just standing there with a smile on his face. He knew you weren't playing favorites, and so did I." MaryAnn made an attempt to swallow the lump in her throat, and overcome by emotion, she was unable to say anything more.

"Have you decided about Thanksgiving?"

She took a deep breath in order to compose herself and said, "I talked to the boys and we'd love to come. Funnily enough, Margaret called and invited us to be with them, but there was no contest—the boys know where they want to be."

"Ben will be thrilled and so am I. I'm not sure whose going to be there, but it's all very relaxed and informal, and I know you and the boys will have a good time. They'll have to contend with four-year-old twin girls, and they're a real handful, I can tell you."

MaryAnn decided not to tell Jim she would put up with almost anything rather than being in this house trying to pull together some semblance of a festive meal. "I can't wait," she said.

"I'll call you tomorrow."

"Goodnight, Jim." The strength of her attraction to him caught her by surprise, and she intended to tread lightly, even though she would find it difficult, as her children came first. She had to be really sure before there could be any kind of commitment because she sensed if things went wrong, it could break their hearts, especially Johnny's.

Margaret picked up the phone when MaryAnn called to thank her for her invite and to say she was sorry they wouldn't be able to come as Mr. Hudson had invited them all over to his brother's. MaryAnn's refusal disappointed Margaret, and when she gave her daughter the news, Nan immediately understood Stanley was in for a serious dose of mothering. She hoped he was up for it, although not much fazed him. They were still basking in the warm glow of their afternoon of lovemaking. They had told her parents they were going for some exercise—they just didn't elaborate on what kind! Let them think their flushed and rosy cheeks were caused by a few hours of strenuous hiking as opposed to a workout in a motel room. Fortunately, no one really asked, so they didn't have to tell any little white lies.

Thea was folding laundry Monday night when the phone rang. Izzie and Jessica were in bed fast asleep, and Peter was in the shower having come home all sweaty after his basketball practice. "Hello," she said.

"Thea, it's Jim. I've called to talk to Peter, just as I promised."

"He'll be out of the shower in a minute. I could have him call you. Did you see MaryAnn today?"

"I did. She and the boys came over for dinner. We had a good time."

"I'm glad."

"When you come back from Massachusetts I'd love you all to come over."

"I'd like that, and I know the kids would, too. I'll have Peter call you," and she hung up the phone.

Thea went off to find Peter. He was in his pajamas and rubbing his hair madly with a towel. "Who called?"

"Mr. Hudson. He stopped by last night, and if you'd been awake, I would have had him put his head round your door. He wanted to apologize for unintentionally leaving you out. He'd like you to call him."

Thea watched Peter wander off to the kitchen, and she could hear his voice but not what he was saying. She was pleased Jim had kept to his word and called. Peter came to find her, all smiles. "Mr. Hudson said he would invite us over when we get back from Massachusetts, and he said he was very sorry and a stupid grownup."

Thea breathed a huge sigh of relief—another catastrophe averted. Now, Ian and Peter would be able to continue their friendship without the green-eyed monster of jealousy rearing up its ugly head to ruin things.

CHAPTER SIXTEEN

Things were humming along nicely in the Chamberlin household. Peter seemed to be doing better as far as Thea could tell. Maybe because she hadn't said a downright no to his getting a dog had put him in good spirits and given him something to look forward to. It had been a busy three days, during which they had made copious lists trying to decide what they needed to take with them, and Peter and Izzie had knuckled down, making sure all homework assignments were completed. She and Peter had pored over the map, and he had written down the directions. Working out the scale and the mileage was a good math exercise for him, and he calculated the journey to be about two hundred and forty-two miles. She had asked Peter whether he would be her navigator, and he seemed pleased about that. Based on what they thought would be the miles-per-hour average, they determined the journey would take them less than five hours. She prayed for good weather and so far all seemed to be going their way. She had called Ellie to let her know their anticipated time of arrival and to get directions to her house. Ellie was thrilled, and said she had all sorts of plans for her and the children. She also called her mom and told her she would be coming in on Thursday and would see them over the weekend. She talked to her dad; he told her he was on the mend, was really looking forward to seeing her, and said too much time had elapsed since their last visit. His last remark really hit home.

Thea spent Wednesday packing. Nan stopped by, said she didn't want to get in Thea's way, but she had really wanted to see her since she didn't know when their paths would cross again. She waited until Izzie and Peter were home from school and then they all went off to get the minivan. "This is the beginning of our adventure. I am the captain, Peter is the navigator, you two girls will be the very important crew, and we are off to pick up the ship. The crew would usually supply the ship's biscuits, but because you were otherwise engaged today, I, as captain, took it upon myself to make sure we were fed and watered, but you must portion them out properly to make sure we don't run out!"

"But we're only going to Yarmouth, Mom!" Peter said.

"Aha, me hearties, but no matter how far the journey, we need to be prepared! We need a practice run for our voyage tomorrow. Come on you landlubbers, let's go and find our ship and make sure she's seaworthy!"

They all thought their mother had completely lost her mind, but they all saluted, said, "Aye, aye, Captain!" and climbed into the car one by one.

Thea didn't want the children to see her nervousness. She was finding the undertaking a little daunting, and she wanted to get to Yarmouth and back in the daylight because she didn't relish driving a strange vehicle in the dark. Her own car, with all its nicks and scratches and peculiar idiosyncrasies, was an old friend, but this alien beast presented a new challenge. Filling out the paperwork presented no problems, after which she found herself walking around the car looking for any signs of damage so she wouldn't be liable when she brought the vehicle back. The rep gave her a manual, showed her how to adjust the seat, how to turn the lights on and off and how to open the gas cap. The children had gathered up their belongings from their own car, including the blankets and Jessica's seat, and were standing in a cold little bunch waiting for the green light, at which point they scrambled into the van and looked around in wonder. The interior was so much more luxurious than anything they had ridden in for what seemed absolutely ages. To Thea the van seemed huge, even though it wasn't really much longer than her car—just appeared that way. The vehicle exuded comfort; she found it a pleasure to drive as it held the road well, and she found its sturdiness reassuring. She was also thankful it wasn't green, but a nice soft blue, because she had a thing about green cars—she considered them unlucky. Once home in the driveway, she silently praised herself for seizing the opportunity to take the twenty minute trip to familiarize herself with the vehicle because she now felt much more optimistic about tomorrow's journey.

Thea helped the children put out fresh clothes for the morning and then they piled all the items they wanted to take with them into the hallway. They had a portable DVD player they would have to share, and earlier that day she had picked up a couple of movies from the library to at least keep the girls occupied, although she suspected they would sleep some of the way. Once packed and organized, Izzie went off to continue with her ballet practice, and strains of the melodies from *The Nutcracker* radiated from the basement studio. Jessica, as usual, was finding it hard to make a decision on what she wanted to take, and Thea hoping to avoid a meltdown, suggested Jess have some quiet time until after supper. She knew her daughter would be much more reasonable once she had eaten because food always boosted her spirits. Peter just went off to his room, shut the door and played his own music. Thea left the children to their own resources, wandered into the kitchen, and impeded by Smokey rubbing vigorously against her legs, suddenly thought, "Heavens to Betsy! I have to find someone to look after you!" MaryAnn immediately came to mind, so she picked up the phone and called her.

Ian answered. "Hi, Ian, it's Mrs. Chamberlin. Could I speak to your mom, please?"

"Sure, hang on. I'll just go and get her. Thank you for dinner the other night. It rocked!"

Thea smiled, and said, "I'm so glad you had a good time. It was great you were all able to come." She heard Ian put the receiver down and call for his mom. "It's Mrs. Chamberlin," he said.

"Hi, Thea."

"Hello, MaryAnn. I was wondering whether I could ask you a favor and in turn give your boys a chance to earn some pocket money."

"Sure. How can I help?"

"We're leaving early in the morning for Massachusetts, and I don't have anyone to look after Smokey, our cat. Would it be too much to ask if you could come in twice a day and feed her?"

"We'd love to, but you don't have to pay us..."

"But I do," Thea interrupted. "It's not about the money. It just boosts the children's self-esteem to have a paying job to do. Bill and Margaret always used to slip Izzie and Peter pocket money when they were helping out at the store."

"Okay, I agree. I can see you've made up your mind, and we'd be happy to look after Smokey." MaryAnn smiled to herself. It felt good to be able to return a kindness.

"I'll leave the keys under the flowerpot to the left of the kitchen door—one key opens the dead-bolt and the other opens the lock in the handle. Smokey's not used to being on her own, so if you and the boys could spend a little time with her, I know she'd appreciate the company. You're welcome to use the house and watch some movies if you'd like. You'll find we have a good selection. Do you have any questions?"

"Is Smokey allowed to go outside?"

"No, she's an indoor cat, and her litter tray is down in the basement so please make sure the basement door stays open. I'll clean the tray before I leave, and it should be fine until we get back. I'll leave her food out in the kitchen with instructions. She only drinks water."

"What time are you actually leaving?" MaryAnn asked.

"At the crack of dawn, so, ideally, if you came over sometime in the afternoon, she would be all set until early the next day. We will be driving back Monday so you will only need to feed her in the morning. Are you sure I'm not asking too much of you?"

"No, it's fine. We'll just fit it into our daily routine, and the kids are off school so it will work out perfectly."

"Phew, that's a huge load off my mind. I'm not used to going away, but now I can rest easy knowing Smokey will be looked after properly. I will leave a note with a couple of numbers where you can reach me just in case you have a question, and if you have a problem, you can always call Bill and Margaret as backup. There's Nan and Stanley too, but I'm not sure how long they're staying. Now, are you sure this is okay?"

"Absolutely. Ian and Johnny will be thrilled."

"Thanks a bunch and we really will have to get together when I get back."

"I'd like that, Thea. Goodbye for now."

Thea hung up the phone and looked down at Smokey. "So," she said, bending down and rubbing her fingers along the top of the cat's head and scratching behind her ears. "It looks as though you're going to have some new friends." Smokey just pushed her head into Thea's hand and purred.

The evening passed quickly and soon the girls were safely tucked up in bed, freshly showered. Thea kissed them goodnight and told them she was planning on waking them at the crack of dawn. They groaned and disappeared under the covers. She went off to find Peter and suggested he go to sleep a little earlier than usual. She asked him whether he had the directions and he said, "Aye, aye, Captain," reverting to his role in their nautical game. "What good is a navigator who doesn't know where the ship is headed?"

"Glad to hear all is shipshape. See you in the morning. I'm off to check and make sure the biscuits are weevil-free!"

"Ugh," he said and pulled a terrible face. "We'll have to make sure we all behave ourselves because we certainly don't want to have to make anyone walk the plank!"

She smiled and kissed his cheek. "Goodnight, Mr. Navigator."

"Goodnight, Captain Mom."

The pile of belongings in the hallway was chaotic, except for Izzie's. Being a thoughtful child, she had set her small suitcase and backpack to one side—not so Peter and Jess! Thea set about organizing each item so it would be a quick pick up in the morning, after which she wrote a note for MaryAnn and put out a box of microwave popcorn for her and the boys. She double-checked the master list because she didn't want to forget anything, and she cleaned out Smokey's litter tray—the final chore. She had butterflies in her stomach about tomorrow and hoped she'd be able to sleep. A nice warm shower helped her to relax, and soon she was sitting in bed with her book in her lap. She still wasn't sure she was doing the right thing, but it was too late to change her mind now. She set the alarm for five thirty and read until she became drowsy enough to fall asleep.

The darkness was all encompassing when the alarm went off on Thursday morning, and Thea would have given anything just to roll over and go back to sleep. She slipped quickly into her clothes and went downstairs to make coffee. She went in to wake Peter, and he was less than responsive. "It's the middle of the night," he grumbled.

"Please get up, Mr. Navigator. I need your help with the crew," and she hauled the covers off him.

"You're so mean," he said. She left him groaning and moaning and reluctantly dragging on his clothes.

Izzie, who woke up as soon as she had heard all the commotion, got out of bed and started to get organized. She had tried to wake Jessica, but it was a lost cause. In the end, Thea just dressed her younger daughter where she lay and left her there while she, Izzie and Peter went into the kitchen and had a bowl of cereal. She had packed a cooler the night before, which meant Jessica could have breakfast en route. The three of them went off and cleaned their teeth and gathered last minute toiletries. She went out and started the car so the interior would be nice and warm, suddenly remembering as she walked back to the house she needed to put a set of door keys under the flowerpot for MaryAnn.

Peter and Izzie helped their mom carry all their belongings out to the vehicle. He had a flashlight in his pocket so he would be able to read the directions once they were on the road. Thea wrapped Jess in a blanket and settled her in her car seat with her teddy bear. Izzie sat next to her sister and Thea leaned in to securely fasten her daughter's seat belt. The cooler fit snuggly between them, making it nice and convenient for Izzie to get Jess some cereal and milk when she eventually woke up. They were prepared for the grumps! She took a last look around and felt a little sad they were leaving Smokey behind, but she seemed perfectly content eating her breakfast and didn't seem concerned by all the upheaval. Cats were definitely easier than dogs as dogs always gave you such a melancholy look; an expression designed to break your heart. She grabbed her pocketbook, pulled the door shut and made sure both locks were secure. She climbed into the car and pulled out of the driveway. Their adventure had begun.

CHAPTER SEVENTEEN

MASSACHUSETTS

The Chamberlins were soon well on their way, Peter doing an excellent job of navigating. They were currently on I-95 south, and when Thea asked what road they would need next, he looked down at the piece of paper and said, "I-495 south, Exit 59 towards Worcester." Checking the odometer, he told his mom they were pretty close to the exit. "Once we are on I-495, we stay on it for about sixty-two miles."

"Great job of navigating," she said. "And what's after that?"

"The Mass. Pike, and then we're going to be on that for ninety-six miles."

"Right, once we hit the Pike I think we should make a stop unless anyone needs a restroom before then."

There was no response from the girls. Jessica had finally woken up, and Izzie had helped her to a container of milk and some dry cereal. They were watching a movie on the DVD player, propped up on the cooler between them. There were two sets of earphones, so they were off in their own little fantasy world, oblivious to the trucks on the road and the traffic speeding by. Peter was content to listen to his music, look out for landmarks and keep an eye on his mom, reassured to see she seemed to be doing okay, so far.

Thea was actually enjoying the drive. Fortunately, the traffic was fairly light, with few trucks, which pleased her because overtaking the huge vehicles filled her with trepidation. She found the van extremely comfortable and, surprisingly, the children had adapted well considering they weren't used to long journeys. She felt better now she had actually left home, and there was no turning back. Her only regret was not having a cell phone, and she was ashamed of herself for being so old-fashioned—even Margaret had a mobile for goodness sake! Anyway, no good worrying about it now, but when she got home, she definitely planned on looking into getting herself a phone.

The minivan ran smoothly and seemed to eat up the miles. She checked the fuel gauge, pleased to see it looked as though they would be able to make the journey on one tank of gas. The girls had finished with the movie and were getting restless, especially Jess. "We're nearly at the exit for the Mass. Pike, and once we're through the toll booths, I promise we'll stop at the first rest area we come to. Can you hold on for just a little while longer?"

Izzie said she was fine, but Jessica groaned. "I'm tired of sitting in the car."

"I'm sure you are, but take a peek in your backpack and see if there are any surprises in there."

Jessica pouted. "I know what's in there. I packed it!"

"Come on, Jess," Izzie coaxed. "Let's have a look," and she heaved the bag up onto the seat, placing it between them on top of the cooler. Jessica's curiosity got the better of her, and she tugged at the zipper, desperate to get at the contents. Thea breathed a sigh of relief at the distraction and pressed on.

Jessica was delighted to find her mom had packed her a coloring book, some colored pencils in a special case, and a blank sketchpad. She also unearthed a pencil sharpener and a whimsical eraser in the shape of an elephant. All her woes were soon forgotten and she became totally absorbed in drawing a picture about their journey. Izzie, just as relieved as her mother to have found a way to placate Jess, wasn't sure how long the respite would last, but while her sister was occupied, she could at least read her book.

"Mom, the exit's coming up!" Peter said, pointing to the right.

"Thank goodness for that."

Thea carefully negotiated the traffic as she approached the tollbooths, managed to funnel into a fairly short line, and took the ticket handed to her by a friendly man who welcomed her to Massachusetts. She smiled at him, said "Thank you," and passed the ticket over to Peter. She paid attention to make sure she headed towards Albany/Springfield and negotiated the lane switching successfully without anyone honking at her!

"Phew," she said. "Peter, where do we get off?"

"The directions say Lee/Pittsfield."

"Is that listed on the ticket?"

Peter ran his finger down the names of all the towns and finally found their exit. "Yes, it is. And I figured out the amount for the toll."

"Okay, good job, Mr. Navigator, and as you are in charge of the booty, I know you will have the pieces of silver ready when the time comes."

"Aye, aye, Captain."

"Now girls, I want you to be on the lookout for a likely place to stop. We have choices. We can go to a rest area and eat what we brought with us, or we could stop at a service station where there will be restaurants." Of course, she knew what they would choose, but it all depended on how long Jessica's bladder would hold out. She was surprised they had managed to travel so many miles without stopping.

As luck would have it, a service area loomed just over the hill, and they were all pretty excited about the thought of some fast food—an exceedingly rare treat. Thea pulled into a parking space fairly close to the entrance, turned the car off and rolled her shoulders to relieve the tension. She undid her seat belt and turned to look at the girls. "Aha, me hearties," she growled in her seafaring voice. "We're making good time, and we're about half way there. Now I think we should go and eat another breakfast because it's not even nine o'clock yet. Come on you landlubbers, get your coats on. There be a stiff sea breeze a-blowin' out there! Don't forget to batten the hatches!"

"Whaaaat?" Jess asked.

"Mom means lock the car!" Peter said, raising his eyebrows at his sisters.

"Oh," Izzie responded, bewildered but happy to join in the game.

Soon they were trudging across the parking lot, pulling open the glass door and walking into the warmth of the building where they were greeted by all sorts of conflicting smells. After restrooms were visited and hands washed, they lined up at McDonalds. Jessica's eyes were out on stalks as she stared at all the pictures of the food way above her head; Peter thought he'd died and gone to heaven. Soon their trays were laden with hash browns, Egg McMuffins, pancakes, orange juice and milk for the kids and a much-needed coffee for Thea. Always conscious of her weight because of her dancing, Izzie never ate much, but even she seemed to be eating more than usual; of course, Peter and Jessica inhaled the food as if there were no tomorrow. Thea looked at her children, pleased to see them enjoying themselves. "How's our adventure so far?" she asked.

"It's great," they mumbled through mouthfuls.

"I'm glad you're having fun because so am I and I want to thank you for making the journey with me." She wondered about going to find a phone to call Ellie, but she couldn't leave the children by themselves, so decided to shelve the idea. They would be there soon enough.

They cleaned off the table and gathered all their belongings. Jessica dropped her coat on the floor before Thea could stop her, thrusting her arms through the sleeves and throwing the jacket over her head just as Miss Simms had taught her. "Oh, Jess," she said, "That's not the best of ideas in a restaurant. Next time, let one of us help you."

Her daughter just stood there, one shoe lace untied, hair all over the place and said, "Why not?"

"Because the floor's not very clean, silly," Izzie said and bent down to tie her sister's shoe. Jessica didn't say anything, deciding grownups were much too confusing.

Thea gave one last look around to make sure they hadn't left anything behind, and they then all headed out into the sunshine. Once back in the car, the girls settled in for a nap and Peter checked the directions. "We're going to be on the Mass. Pike for a while, but I'll keep an eye out for the next exit."

"I'll be fine if you want to take a nap."

"No, I'm not tired," he said, and proceeded to put on his headphones and turn on his CD player. Thea sipped her coffee and kept her eyes on the road, always conscious of her precious cargo and the need to be careful. She glanced in her rearview mirror and noticed both Jess and Izzie were fast asleep. She doubted the respite would last long, but she made the most of it and enjoyed the peace and quiet. Fearful of leaving the familiar, she still had mixed emotions about the journey and what the outcome might be. If they did decide to make the break, she had no doubt the move would be hard on the kids who were even more conservative than she—they didn't like change. Jess worried her more than the other two because there was such a bond between her and Uncle Bill, although since her accident they hadn't been spending much time together. Anyway, she didn't want to create obstacles when there may be none; she would cross that bridge if and when the time came.

Peter interrupted her thoughts, "Mom, US-20, Exit 2, towards Lee/Pittsfield will be coming up shortly."

"Gotcha. Do you have the toll money?" and he opened his hand to show her the change. "Hang onto them pieces of silver until we get to the booth. I really don't want to drop them before we get there."

"Aye, aye, Captain."

After successfully negotiating the tollbooth, Peter told her she needed to keep left to take the US-20 East ramp toward Route 102, Great Barrington, and she told him his grandpa used to work at the Colonial Bank in Great Barrington, so she was now on familiar territory. They turned left on Housatonic Street, took Route 102 West and continued on that road until Peter told her to take a left onto Elm Street, which led them into Stockton, and she asked Peter to read out the directions to Ellie's house. The girls were awake by now, and Jessica was getting fidgety. Izzie had run out of ideas and Thea thought it hardly fair to expect her to entertain Jess, but she was amazed they had all done so well. "Won't be long now," she said. "Look out the window to the left and see if you can spot Aladdin's Cave. That's Ellie's store and where I used to work." She drove as slowly as she was able without holding up traffic, and Jessica, leaning as far as the constriction of her car seat would allow so she could see out of the window, suddenly shouted, "There it is, there it is." Thea decided to pull over in front of the store seeing as there were plenty of parking spaces.

"Why don't we all get out so we can at least peer in the window?" She was as excited as the children. The store seemed to be just as she'd remembered: the painted sign above the window with the Aladdin's Lamp surrounded by stars and moons and the same twinkling lights reflecting on the merchandise. The pretty notebooks, the greeting cards, the art and sewing supplies were beautifully arranged, and both Jessica and Izzie pressed their noses up to the glass wanting to see more. Peter's interest would have been spiked had the window displayed music or sporting goods, but he was bored and hung back, his hands rammed into his pockets, unable to share the girls' enthusiasm. Thea noticed her son's lack of interest, and it cast a shadow over her day; he wasn't going to be an easy sell.

Reluctantly, she dragged the girls away. She was really anxious to see Ellie, and once they were all back in the car with seat belts snugly fastened, Peter pulled the directions out of his pocket and said, "We have to find Maple Street, and according to what you wrote, it should be a left-hand turn two miles away from the store."

Thea backed up carefully, keeping an eye on the traffic, and headed out of Stockton. They missed Maple Street and had to turn back. "Where to next?" she said.

"The directions tell us to stay on Maple for three miles, and then make a right onto East Hill and Ellie's house is on the right about half way down, number 183."

Jessica sat kicking the back of Peter's seat, annoying him intensely. "Knock it off," he said. She stuck out her tongue. Thea clung to the wheel and just kept driving; it was an exceedingly long three miles. "Let's play I-Spy," she said. "Jessica, you can start."

"I spy with my little eye something that begins with B."

Peter pointed and said, "There's East Hill," and Thea turned right and told the girls to keep their eyes peeled for number 183. The numbers on the mailboxes were almost impossible to read, and they nearly drove right past, but Izzie spotted 183 and said, "Here it is."

Thea pulled into the driveway, and glanced at the clock on the dashboard; it barely registered eleven thirty. They had made good time, despite both stops, but she was still relieved to have reached her journey's end. The children were very quiet as they looked out of the car windows at Ellie's house. They took in the huge porch, noticing it was highly colorful, just like the store, with all sorts of Thanksgiving decorations and pots full of bright chrysanthemums, surrounded by pumpkins and some decidedly interesting-looking scarecrows. The house was all one level with a double garage to the right and Thea loved the soft gray siding and cream-colored trim. The bright red front door with its shiny brass knocker seemed just right, and fit Ellie to a tee. Suddenly, there she was, running to meet them, opening Thea's door and dragging her out of the car for a hug. "It's so good to see you. Why have we left it so long?"

They stood with their arms around each other and rocked back and forth, while Peter, Izzie, and Jessie looked on. Ellie eventually turned to the three of them, her arm still around Thea, and said, "I'm sorry, that was rude of me, but your mom is my best friend," and she gave them all a beaming smile and they forgot to be shy. "Come on, let's go inside, and I'll show you where you'll be sleeping. There's a play-scape out back if you want to get rid of some energy because I'm sure you're all antsy from sitting in the car. Peter, there's a soccer ball in the garage if you want to kick that around, or you can shoot some hoops."

Ellie opened the front door into a spacious hallway, and the smell of roasting turkey greeted them, and they all breathed in deeply. A bright circular rug in all colors of the rainbow covered most of the wooden floor and right in the middle of the rug sat a rather large, teddy bear of a dog. "I'd like you all to meet Honey," Ellie said, "and she will shake paws with you if you just hold out your hand. She was rather naughty when I first got her, so we went to lots of obedience classes, and now she is polite and well-behaved, aren't you, girl?" Honey's tail twitched, but she didn't move a whisker.

Ellie watched as the Chamberlin children went up to Honey one by one and shook her paw. Ellie knew, instinctively, these were good kids, and she hoped she'd be given the opportunity to get to know them. Peter, so incredibly like Michael with his shock of dark hair falling over his forehead and those intense blue eyes; Izzie, so similar to her mother with her soft reddish brown hair and her slender figure, and then there was Jessica, with her mischievous smile and mass of unruly dark curls, much stockier than the other two. Honey had broken the ice just as Ellie had planned and they all followed her out of the hallway into the rest of the house with the dog following close behind. "I'll give you the grand tour and then you'll know exactly where everything is. I have a few rules, and they're posted on the refrigerator door so you can read those when we're done. Now does anyone need a bathroom right away?" They all said they were fine, so Ellie summoned her strength and continued.

"The house is built in an ell with living space in one part of the ell and the bedrooms in the other. Mr. Blunt, the owner of Aladdin's Cave, lives with me, and he is the reason why I'm able to have such a lovely house." She turned to look at the children. "Your mom knows Mr. Blunt very well, and you will meet him later. Let's go to the bedrooms first, and you'll see I have plenty of room for you all."

Thea hadn't known what to expect when Ellie had told her about the house, but it certainly wasn't this lovely light and airy space. She glanced out of one of the bedroom windows onto a picturesque and sheltered courtyard with big pots of colorful mums and brightly painted chairs. Ellie came over to stand beside her, putting her arm around her shoulders. "It's so good to have you here," she said and Thea was touched by the affectionate gesture. Ellie seemed more brittle somehow and thinner, but Thea gave it no more than a passing thought.

Ellie had put Izzie and Jess together in one room, and they loved the bright pinks and greens. Each bed had a stuffed animal of some kind which pleased Jess no end, and Thea believed her daughter would be introducing her own bear and telling each of them they had to get along. She could tell Ellie had surprised Peter by taking them into a rather boyish room because she could only imagine how anxious he must have been after seeing so many girlie colors. The room was done out in a baseball theme, and even though she thought the decor rather young for her nearly eleven-year-old son, she could see he was intrigued by the pictures of the baseball players on the walls.

Last, but not least, came the room where Thea would sleep, and it was one of the most beautiful rooms she had ever seen. Again, there was the smooth and shiny wooden floor so unlike her old and uneven ones at home, a comfy window seat with an array of cushions in cornflower blue and a sunshiny yellow, where she envisioned herself curling up with a book. The pictures on the walls added to the color scheme with their bold flowers in vivid blues and yellows. There were no curtains at the windows, simply white fabric blinds to give privacy and keep out the sun. The room had little furniture, just an old wooden chest at the end of the bed, a dresser in soft old pine and two white bedside tables on which stood matching lamps with tall stems and stained glass lampshades in pastel hues. It was brighter and much bolder than her room at home, but she loved it. "Ellie, I don't know what to say. I always knew you had a flare for decorating, but what you have accomplished is magnificent." She went and poked her nose around the bathroom door and found the color scheme continued with bright blue and yellow towels and pretty blue and white striped wallpaper. "How do you have time to do all the decorating and run the store?"

"It's a long story, and I'll tell you all about it later when we have some time to ourselves. First, let's take the kids to see the basement, and then I've got to put on my apron and my chef's hat."

"What would you like the kids to call you?" Thea asked.

"Everyone calls me Miss Ellie."

Ellie took them on a quick tour of the finished basement and showed them the private door to Mr. Blunt's apartment. She felt sure they would be much more interested in the Ping-Pong table and TV, and gave them a list of instructions on how to work the TV and the VCR. Besides the laundry room and a storage area, there was one more bedroom with a bathroom attached and she told them her youngest brother, Robert, was living with her, too. They then went back upstairs to the brightness of the kitchen, peeking into the dining room on the way, where they were intrigued to see many place settings with lots of different names. Izzie methodically counted them, and there were nine in total.

The kids were anxious to go outside, and once they had their coats on, Ellie told them the best way to the backyard was through the kitchen and the mud room, and when they came back in they could just leave their jackets and shoes in there. Thea looked a little concerned, so she said there was nothing to worry about as the yard was totally fenced. She also said Honey would bark if there was anything wrong. So off they went with Jessica in front, Izzie in the middle followed by Peter, and then Honey bringing up the rear.

"Time to get cooking," Ellie said, opening the oven door and checking on the turkey. "We'll be eating at about three o'clock, and I have a surprise for you—I invited your parents. Robert said he would pick them up seeing as your dad's ankle is still a little sore."

"I could go get them."

"Don't you think you've had enough driving for one day? In any case, Robert is over in their direction. He's a care worker, and he pulled the short straw today, and one of his home visits is really close to where your parents live."

"It looks as though that's all settled then, so why don't you put me to work."

Ellie went to the pantry and held out a large bag of potatoes. "Here," she said. She then gave Thea a peeler and a huge pot to boil them in, and off she went to the sink to get busy. Ellie could tell she was listening for the children, and they could hear them faintly through the window. "They'll be all right out there, you know."

"I know. I'm just being silly."

"Thea, they're beautiful kids."

"Thank you. Of course, I think so, but then I'm biased, and they are good kids." Ellie watched her peel another potato and plop it into the pot. "Are we doing roast or mash?"

"Roasties," Ellie said, putting a great deal of effort into peeling a butternut squash. "And once you're done with the spuds there are some parsnips to do."

"Peter's thrilled you have a dog. He's had a dog on his wish list for the longest time, and he lives in hope because I didn't say a downright no when he asked me recently."

"Honey is a rescue dog; a year old when I got her and completely wild, but she always wanted to please. No one had ever taken the time to discipline her and, fortunately, even though the first year of her life was less than ideal, she wasn't a victim of abuse. It was just the owner's ignorance of a young dog's basic needs, so she ended up in the local shelter. As soon as I saw her, it was love at first sight for both of us, but boy was she a handful."

"Rescue dogs are always a bit of a risk, aren't they?"

"If you get them young enough I think it's okay to go that route, but you do have to be especially careful if there are going to be kids involved. That's one of the main reasons why I chose Honey. I took a couple of the kids with me who attend my after-school program and even though Honey went completely crazy, she wasn't fearful. Fear is something to look for because there are a lot of dogs that are intimidated by children, which would be a huge problem for me as my life is full of kids."

"Ellie, you made an excellent choice. I love a dog with good manners because life is so much more pleasurable for both the dog and its owners. Honey has set a very high standard, and I know Peter's going to be bugging me even more now."

There was a great deal of chattering and clattering in the mudroom. Ellie poked her nose round the door and asked Peter if he would wipe Honey's feet with the towel hanging from one of the wooden knobs. She also said if they opened the right hand lid of the built-in benches they would find lots of fuzzy socks and she promised Peter he would find some manly ones. Once they were all inside, she suggested they go off and wash their hands and then they could come back and help her put out snacks on the two tables in the living room, above Honey's nose level because, even though she was well-behaved, it wasn't fair to tempt her. She turned to Izzie and said, "If you look in the bottom of the pantry you will find a bag of dog treats and you can give her one of those."

Honey stood by the pantry door wagging her tail, and as soon as she saw the biscuit in Izzie's hand, she sat down and waited patiently. Izzie held it out, and the big golden dog took the treat gently from her fingers. She turned to Ellie and asked if she needed any help. "I sure do," she said and put them all to work. The kitchen was spacious, with plenty of room for all five of them to work together slicing cheese, washing grapes, plating crackers and getting out a crab dip which Ellie had made earlier. "This is fun," Jess said. "Thank you for 'viting us."

"You're very welcome and it's wonderful to have you all here."

They were all too busy to notice Theodore Blunt standing in the doorway. Thea saw him first and even though he had aged, he was still much as she remembered him. She went over to him and held out her hands, "Mr. Blunt, you're looking good."

"A little older and creakier but I am doing nicely thanks to Miss Ellie here, and I must say, Miss Marchant, you haven't changed a bit." Ellie looked up from where she was turning the potatoes to ensure they would brown evenly, her face flushed from the heat of the oven. "I think it's the other way around, and I agree with you, Thea hasn't changed one bit," she said.

"I think you're just being kind, but thank you."

The kids watched the interaction between the grownups and Jessica stood quietly forming her own opinion of Mr. Blunt. Always wary of men, she had to go with how he made her feel on the inside, and seeing as she didn't feel all fluttery, decided he was harmless with his tufts of spiky white hair, his round wire-framed glasses behind which twinkled a pair of pale blue eyes. He wasn't very tall, and a little bit plump, so she thought he looked ever so huggable in his soft green cardigan and slightly creased gray flannel pants. She loved his rather posh voice and hoped maybe he would tell them all stories about his life. She planned to ask him anyway.

"And, who do we have here? Won't you introduce me please," Mr. Blunt said, looking at the three children who were standing behind the table. Thea stepped forward and said, "These are my children. This is Jessica," placing her hand on her daughter's curls, "and these two are Izzie and Peter."

"I'm delighted to meet you and I understand you had quite a long drive to get here. Am I right?"

"Yes, you are," Jess said, much less shy than her brother and sister, "and we went to McDonald's, and do you know I'd never been there before?"

"Now, you've surprised me. Even I've eaten at McDonald's, but I have to confess I don't like their food very much. Why don't we take all these snacks you've prepared into the sitting room and give your mom and Miss Ellie some space?" He paused and admired the children's hard work and said, "My, you have done such a good job."

"That was highly successful," Ellie said, once they had gone. "Theodore is absolutely fabulous with kids even though as you know, he and Jenny never had any of their own. Robert should be here soon with your mom and dad. When did you last see them?"

175

"While Michael and I were still together, I'm ashamed to say. It has to be at least four years. He had to make a business trip to Boston, so he dropped me on the way and picked me up on his return the next day. I left the kids with Bill and Margaret. The visit didn't go terribly well because I was incredibly depressed and looking for sympathy, but in the end, I decided it wouldn't be fair to dump on them, so I bottled all my emotions. In any case, neither of my parents has ever been the least bit forthcoming with a shoulder to cry on."

"I'm sorry. Maybe I shouldn't have invited them without asking you," Ellie said, ceasing her stirring of the bowl of stuffing and glancing at Thea with a worried look. "I tend to jump in without thinking sometimes. I call it my 'more the merrier' complex because that's how I grew up."

"Ellie, it's all right. My father is actually a nice man, it's just such hard work to get his attention, and I have to be in the mood. I've never understood my mother, and I've always wondered whether something happened to her when she was growing up to cause her fearfulness and lack of ambition, but I don't suppose I'll ever know."

Theodore Blunt tucked himself into the comfiest armchair in his favorite room in the whole house. There was a sliding door to the ell-shaped courtyard—where he loved to sit on sunny days—and to the right of the door a huge ficus tree with variegated leaves. A deep chocolate brown sectional sofa sat in front of the large brick fireplace, and Ellie had worked her magic with all the different colored throw pillows. He watched as the children sat down side-by-side, with Honey sitting to the right of Peter with her nose on his knee and his hand on her head. He had a captive audience in the Chamberlin children, and their bright faces beguiled him as they sat waiting patiently for him to begin his story. Grateful for the distraction, he decided to forget his worries, at least for a little while.

"We'll light the fire later when it begins to get chilly," he said. "There's nothing like a real fire," and he rubbed his hands together.

"We only have gas logs at home," Peter said.

"That's nice, too, and a lot less work. I suppose you would like to know how I met your mother. I will tell you the story, but we may get interrupted, so you will have to remember where I got to because my memory isn't as good as it used to be," and he removed his spectacles, gave them a polish with a pristine white handkerchief, replaced them, and began.

"My wife Jenny and I used to run Pens & Paper—that's what the store used to be called—and we had done so for many years until, unfortunately, she became sick. I needed to find someone to manage the store because she required so much nursing, so I put an advertisement in the Stockton Gazette. Miss Ellie answered the ad, and I knew she was the one as soon as I met her, and I wasn't wrong. She was just what the store needed, and with her enthusiasm and creativity, Aladdin's Cave came into being. Initially, we managed the store together, but in the end I had to leave Ellie in charge. I then devoted most of my time to nursing Jenny because of her illness, briefly popping into the store whenever she fell asleep. Two years went by, and we both decided Miss Ellie needed to find someone to help her, so she also placed an advertisement in the Stockton Gazette—for a store assistant this time—and your mother answered the ad. She was only eighteen, but despite the age difference, she and Miss Ellie hit it off right away."

Suddenly, they heard the front door open and a male voice calling out, "Hello." Theodore heaved his way out of the chair, "Now you have to remember where I was in the story because I think we'd better go and see who's here."

Honey was sitting in her appointed greeting place in the center of the rug, and Theodore noticed she wagged her tail at Robert, but looked skeptically at the other two. The children hung back, not entirely sure what to do. Fortunately, Thea and Ellie arrived to save the day by taking coats and asking the kids whether they remembered their grandparents.

"My, how you've grown," Henry said, and Peter thought, *duh*. Thoroughly fed up, he desperately wanted to go home and he was trying to put on a brave face, but finding it difficult. He missed Ian and wanted to be with Aunt Margaret and Uncle Bill, rather than these strange people. He looked at his grandfather who was neat as a pin: his thinning hair neatly combed, his one shoe shiny as a mirror; his other foot encased in a thick and sturdy support bandage within some kind of boot with Velcro fastenings. His pants were crisply pressed, and he was wearing a shirt and a tie and a jacket! All much too formal as far as Peter was concerned, but he tried to be polite for his mother's sake, and held out his hand and said, "Hello, Grandpa." His grandmother stood self-consciously with her hands in front of her from which dangled a rather large pocketbook, and she looked as though she wished she were a million miles away. Compared to

Henry's shininess, she was drab and mousy with her plain gray pleated skirt and dull purple sweater, but Peter could relate to her awkwardness and said, "Hi, Grandma," wanting to make her feel better. She barely acknowledged him, so he gave up.

Thankfully, Ellie took over and pushed them all into the sitting room, asking Peter if he would come and help her get drinks for everyone—he nodded, welcoming the opportunity to have something to do.

"You're not having a very good time, are you," Ellie said.

He decided to be honest, "Not really."

"Tomorrow will be better, I promise. Let's just get through today, and I know you can do it," and she handed him a tray of drinks. It took all his concentration to make his way back to the sitting room without spilling a drop, and the interchange with Miss Ellie had lifted his spirits. He also decided Miss Ellie was an okay grownup, and he was pleased she had noticed he was a little down in the dumps.

All the grownups appeared to be enjoying themselves, especially once the alcohol began to take effect, with the exception of his grandma. She was sitting rather primly on the edge of the couch, clutching her purse with one hand and holding her drink in the other, and Peter went and sat down beside her. "I don't want to be here either," he whispered in her ear, and she turned and gave him a tremulous smile. He put his hand on her tiny knee and said, "It will be all right, you'll see. Miss Ellie has made lots of great food."

"I've always been shy," she said. Peter could tell he'd broken the ice, and decided to make the best out of his current situation. After all, he couldn't just get up and leave, so he might just as well try and have a good time.

"Me, too." He caught his mom's eye and she gave him a little nod and an encouraging smile, which made him feel really, really good. Izzie appeared to be talking to Robert, and he seemed like a nice guy. Jess was sitting on a footstool right by Mr. Blunt, looking up at him and chatting away. Peter could tell, even though he was across the room from him, he was one of those grownups who really listened as he appeared to be responding to Jess properly. His mom was talking to Grandpa, and they seemed to be getting along. "Grandma, why don't we go into the kitchen and see if Miss Ellie needs any help."

"What a good idea," she said, relinquishing her pocketbook, and allowing Peter to pull her to her feet. She followed him into the kitchen.

"We're here to help," he said, smiling brightly.

"I think it's time for all of us to go into the dining room and sit down. Peter, why don't you go suggest that? Oh, and bring back the rest of the crab dip and put it in the fridge for me would you, please. Enid, there's a loaf of bread which needs slicing," and Ellie proceeded to give her a cutting board and a knife. Peter noticed Ellie's hand seemed to be a little unsteady, and there appeared to be a sheen of perspiration on her face. Somehow she didn't seem quite right, but it wasn't his place to say anything, so he went back to the sitting room and told them all it was time to go eat.

Robert leaned towards Izzie and suggested the two of them go and read the nametags so each person would know where to sit. Mr. Blunt took Jess's hand; his mom walked slowly with his Grandpa as they all made their way across the hallway and into the festively decorated dining room. The room was large, unlike their cramped dining room at home, so nobody got stuck against the wall trying to get to their chairs, but Peter didn't think it was half as much fun.

Peter watched as Enid and Ellie carried in platters of turkey, a huge dish of roast potatoes and parsnips, a steaming bowl of stuffing, two casserole dishes with sweet potatoes and apples. There was gravy and cranberry sauce, delicious bread from the local bakery and real butter. Peter was in heaven. He also noticed Ellie had found a booster chair for Jess so she could sit at the same level as everyone else and his sister positively beamed from ear to ear. Seating was interesting because all the men were at the far end of the table and his sisters and the women were closest to the kitchen. He had his Grandma on his right and Mr. Blunt on his left; Robert and Grandpa were opposite. Getting food proved to be a little chaotic as plates had to be passed around and the person closest to a steaming dish would ladle out a portion and pass the plate back. Eventually, they all had food, and the time had come for them to say what they were thankful for—Peter hated this part. But when it came to his turn, he said, "I'm very grateful for the lovely meal and for Miss Ellie having us to stay," and Grandma, as if taking a cue from him, said more or less the same thing. Jessica, of course, was the most effusive of them all and nobody wanted to shut her up, although as far as he was concerned, she did go on just a little bit too long.

Peter was absolutely stuffed, having had two slices of pie for dessert, and when he glanced around the table, he could see each and every one of them looked much the same way, except for Miss Ellie. He had noticed she had eaten very little, and he wondered why. The rest of them had all eaten far too much, and if Thanksgiving here resembled anything like the ones at Aunt Margaret and Uncle Bill's, the grownups would soon be fast asleep. He pushed his chair back and started gathering plates to take them out into the kitchen. It was an automatic reaction because he was expected to clear the table at home and just walking away wasn't an option. Izzie and Jess—once her sister had helped her down from her perch—were also busy carrying the less heavy items. It was pretty chaotic, and the kitchen was a mess. Ellie's cheeks were flushed, and he watched as she tried to push some strands of blonde hair that had escaped from its neat bun away from her face. All of a sudden, his mom decided to take charge and told Ellie to go sit down and suggested to his grandma the two of them wash up. "We make a great team, don't we, Mom?"

His grandma's face lit up, and she said, "It will be just like old times," and the two of them set to work shunning any offers of assistance from anyone else. Peter initiated the help of Izzie and Jess, and between them, they cleared the table. They wrapped leftovers or put them in the plastic containers they found in one of the lower cupboards and wiped up dishes that either overflowed the drainer or wouldn't fit in the dishwasher, neatly stacking them on the table so Ellie could put them away. Peter noticed his mom and grandma didn't say anything but seemed to be comfortable enough in each other's company. Even Jess was tiring and said little. He glanced out of the kitchen window and watched the darkening sky and he felt as though the day would never end.

True to his word Mr. Blunt had lit the fire, and just as Peter had predicted, all of the grownups, with the exception of Robert, were fast asleep. He looked up when he saw Peter and closed his book and winked, "How about a game of Ping-Pong?" he asked. "Do you think your sisters would like to join us?" and Peter walked across the room, carefully avoiding his grandpa's bandaged ankle. He and Robert looked at each other and smiled. Peter thought he didn't look much like Ellie because his hair and eyes were dark, whereas she was blonde with blue eyes.

Peter put his head around the kitchen door and said he and Robert were going to have a game of Ping-Pong. "Where are the girls?" Thea asked.

"I think they went off to their room," he said.

"You go play. I'll go see what they're up to," and Peter and Robert made their escape.

Thea suddenly realized she hadn't unpacked the van so went off in search of her daughters with her mom in tow, noticing as she passed the sitting room that Ellie, Mr. Blunt and her father were fast asleep. She thought it odd Ellie was sleeping. Despite the early start and all the driving she had done, Thea wasn't tired. She had paced herself through the meal and had not overeaten, thus avoiding the post-Thanksgiving lethargy. As she had suspected, Izzie and Jess were in their room. Izzie was stretching her slender arms high above her head and then leaning forward to touch her toes, and just as they came through the door, she slid into a split. Thea, used to seeing her daughter in these uncomfortable positions, was amused by the expression of astonishment on her mother's face. "It's okay, Grandma," Izzie said, "It doesn't hurt. I have to keep stretching and stay supple because I have lots of rehearsing to do when we get back. I'm playing Clara in *The Nutcracker.*"

"I didn't know you were such a good dancer."

"It's easy to be good at something when you love it as much as I do, although I still can't believe I was chosen to play Clara, but of course I'm thrilled."

"Thea, these children of yours are full of surprises," and she turned to look at Jessica who was sitting on the bed with a picture book she had found on one of Ellie's shelves. "Do you dance, too?"

"No. I tried, but I have two left feet and I'm always tripping over things, so I'm still trying to find out what I'm good at."

"You have a really big heart, my darling, and that counts more than anything. Look how well you look after Johnny," Thea said. "Now your grandma and I are going to unload the van, so we'd be glad of some help."

Jess slid off the bed; Izzie unfolded her body from the floor, and the four of them trooped out to the hallway. "Why don't you girls stay here and then you won't have to go rummaging for your shoes and you can help us carry all the stuff once we're back inside," Thea said. They were happy to take her up on her suggestion and sat on the rug with Honey who had appeared out of nowhere and taken up her position as sentinel.

Thea helped her mom into her coat, and they stepped out onto the porch. The outside of the house was brightly lit, but once they reached the car, they found it difficult to see. She felt for the key in her pocket and unlocked the van. Once she had opened the door, the interior illumination gave them just enough light to rummage around and find what they actually needed to bring into the house. It took a couple of trips, but she and her mom soon had all their stuff, and between the four of them, they were able to make sure they left the hallway tidy. Honey, intrigued by all the Chamberlin's belongings, used her extremely efficient nose to sniff out any possibilities of food.

Eventually, Enid and Thea joined the other grownups in the sitting room; Izzie and Jess went off to the basement to find Peter and Robert, and Thea was sure they'd probably stir up trouble—at least Jess would.

"You're a lively looking bunch, I must say," Thea said, staring at the three of them lazing in front of the fire. Enid sat back down on the couch next to the pocketbook she had abandoned earlier, and relapsed into silence. Mr. Blunt rubbed his stomach and said, "Too much turkey. It makes one sleepy you know."

"I do know that," she said. "I think we all need a rousing game of cards to keep us awake." She knew the suggestion was going to go over like a lead balloon with Ellie, and sure enough she groaned.

"It's not mandatory," Thea said, pulling a face," But it might be fun. Humor me for at least one game."

Even though they were reluctant to leave the warmth of the fire, they heaved themselves out of their respective seats and traipsed off to the dining room where Ellie produced two packs of cards and a score pad. Her mom and dad were familiar with Up and Down the River, and she was happily surprised when her mom agreed to play. Ellie was rusty, and Mr. Blunt had never played the game before, but it was an easy one to learn and soon they were madly bidding on how many tricks they would make. Mr. Blunt was in his element, and Ellie, even though she pretended to be cross, wasn't really. Her mother was winning, and her father's face was a picture of contentment as he observed his wife not only joining in, but also actually enjoying herself. She noticed Robert, Peter, Izzie and Jess standing in the doorway. The card players' raucous behavior had brought them up from the basement—intrigued by the stamping feet on the wooden floor, they wondered what on earth was going on. Peter and Robert joined in, and Peter quickly explained the rules of the game. Izzie and Jess wanted no part of it, and Thea could tell Ellie wanted to make her escape, so she suggested to the girls they might like to watch a movie, and their eyes lit up. Ellie didn't come back.

Down in the basement, the girls scanned the shelves where Ellie kept all the videos, and Jessica, as usual, was having a hard time making up her mind. "Let's watch this one," Izzie said, pulling *Racing Stripes* off the shelf and reading out loud the information on the back of the cardboard sleeve. "It looks like fun, Jess. There are talking animals."

"It's a good story," Ellie said, "and if you don't like it we can always pick something else."

Izzie was relieved when Jess agreed to the suggestion as she knew how difficult her sister could be sometimes, especially when she was tired. She snuggled with Jess on the couch, and they watched Ellie as she turned on the TV and slid the cassette into the VCR. She came and sat next to them and showed Izzie how to control the volume, gave them a blanket and said she would be back in a little while to see how they were doing.

Back upstairs things were winding down. Robert said he would take Henry and Enid home and asked Peter if he would like to come along for the ride. He said he would love to and went off to retrieve his shoes from the mudroom. Robert went outside to warm up his car while Ellie helped Enid and Henry with their coats. Honey sat in the middle of the hall rug as usual, and Robert could sense she'd like to go for the ride, but it was going to be too much of a squash, so he said, "Sorry, girl, next time." He could tell by the expression on Peter's face he was disappointed. He and Honey had really formed a bond, which wasn't at all difficult as she was such a friendly dog, and unless you didn't like dogs at all, there was no way you could stop yourself from falling in love with her. Peter ruffle her ears and said, "We'll be back in a little while," to which she looked mournful and lay down with her head resting on her paws. Robert watched his sister as she stood back from the group after they had all expressed their thanks and said their goodbyes, and he sensed she was under the weather. "Hey, sis, we'll be back soon," he said, and they stepped out of the warmth of the hall into the darkness and the chill of the November evening.

Peter took his grandma's arm, and Robert helped Henry as he limped along towards the car. Their shoes made crunching noises on the gravel, and the air was cold enough for them all to be able to see their breath. They were glad to get into the warmth of the car, with Henry sitting up front because of his ankle and Peter and Enid in the back. Robert turned to look at them, handed them a blanket, and suggested they put it over their legs to keep out the chill. He heard Peter asking his grandmother whether she had enjoyed herself and she told him she had and how nice it had been to see everyone again after such a long time. Robert thought the group rather strange, but he understood why Ellie hadn't invited a couple of other people to level things out a bit—it would have been too much for her.

He drove carefully, and it wasn't long before they were pulling into the Marchant's driveway. The house was a small brick, one-story, in a row of similar houses, depressingly dreary and colorless compared with Ellie's. Robert waited while Henry fumbled for his keys. The outside light, which was on a sensor, lit up as soon as they got close to the couple of steps leading up to the faded green front door, cast in the shadow of an out-dated metal overhang. Henry unlocked the door, and once Henry and Enid were safely inside, they said their goodbyes—Peter saying they'd probably be over to visit tomorrow—and he kissed his grandma on the cheek and Robert shook Henry's hand.

Once they were back in the car, Robert sensed Peter's shyness, despite their earlier game of table tennis, and seeing as he really didn't know the boy, decided to refrain from asking any questions that might be awkward. He thought music might be a safe subject, and he was right. Peter became very animated and said three of his favorites were *Dishwalla*, *Bon Jovi* and *Metallica*. Robert responded by saying he wasn't familiar with the other two, but he did have the *Bon Jovi, Have a Nice Day* CD. He reached into the glove compartment and pulled out the disc, handing it to Peter so he could remove it from its case and insert it into the slot on the dashboard. As soon as the music began to play, Peter rested his hands on his knees and drummed with his fingers, and Robert tapped the steering wheel, both completely immersed in the energy and the raw beat of each individual song.

Honey got tired of sitting in the hallway, so decided to go off and see who she could find and happily discovered Izzie and Jess. She wasn't allowed on the couch, so she sat on the floor between the two girls with her back to them, looking at the screen and tilting her head in response to any noises that clicked with her doggy brain, occasionally giving a little whine. Izzie and Jess were thrilled to have her company, but they couldn't help being reminded of another dog—a part of their lives up until recently. "Iz, does Honey remind you of Lady?"

"Just a little bit. She's the same kind of people-caring dog just like Lady was, but she's much better behaved."

So they sat tickling her ears with their toes encased in their fuzzy socks while they watched the rest of the movie, a little puzzled because Miss Ellie hadn't returned. They also wondered where their mother was because they were thirsty and getting a little bit hungry. "Jess, I'm glad I have you with me as this day is very strange."

"It sure is," and she snuggled closer to her sister.

Thea was unpacking her toiletries, setting them out neatly in the bathroom when Ellie appeared in the doorway. "Hi," she said, "I'm not feeling so hot. I hate to be such a wet blanket, but I think I'm going to have to go to bed."

"I'm sorry you're not well. Is there anything I can get you?"

"No. I just need to go lie down. I have a rotten headache, and the best thing for me is to sleep it off. I'm sure I'll be right as rain by morning. I'm afraid I abandoned the girls; they're downstairs watching a movie. Please tell them I'll see them tomorrow. Help yourself to anything you want from the kitchen and I'm not going to hug you just in case whatever I have is catching."

"Thanks for a lovely day, and if I can be of any help, please don't hesitate to come get me. Goodnight, Ellie."

Thea went off to the basement where she found Izzie, Jess and Honey watching the tail end of the movie. She was highly amused when the dog just looked at her and then turned her gaze back to the screen. She sat down next to her daughters, and decided not to say anything until the end of the movie since she could see they were totally engrossed. She looked around her and found the decor rather dark and depressing compared with the rest of the house. She assumed Mr. Blunt had gone back to his apartment, and she thought the whole setup rather strange. The house was beautiful—there was no doubt about that—but it had no heart. Of course the newness didn't help because it took a while for a house to become a home, but there was something about the atmosphere, and unable to put her finger on it, she longed to sit down and have a long chat with Ellie. Maybe, then, she would understand why, even though the temperature of the house was warm, it gave her an underlying feeling of unease. She heard footsteps above her and assumed Robert and Peter had returned, and sure enough the two of them appeared just as the credits for the movie began to run. She turned to Robert and asked him to show her how to eject the movie and turn off the VCR since she didn't want to mess it up. He said, "Happy to be of service, ma'am," and took the remote from her hand. "You'll be pleased to know your parents were delivered home safe and sound."

"Thank you for doing that," she said. She wasn't really sure how she felt about Robert. He seemed nice enough, and he and Peter appeared to be getting along, but since her daughter's abduction she didn't trust any male she didn't know. Even though he and Peter had spent time in the car alone, Peter seemed fine, so she figured she was overreacting.

Peter, searching among all the movies stacked neatly on the shelves, found the latest *Harry Potter—The Goblet of Fire* (the fourth in the series), and even though he'd seen the movie with Uncle Bill earlier in the year, he turned to Thea and asked whether he could watch it. Thea didn't see any reason why not, and when Robert said he would keep Peter company, she could hardly say no. She asked them whether they would like anything to eat, thinking this way she could keep tabs on them, and then come back down and watch the rest of the movie with them once the girls were in bed. To add to her disquiet, Robert went off to a small refrigerator tucked under the stairs and pulled out a beer. She hadn't noticed him drinking excessively earlier in the day but who knew what his propensity to alcohol truly was. All of a sudden, she wished herself a million miles away, and wondered whether she would live to regret coming to visit.

Thea took matters into her own hands, "Robert, would you mind getting the movie set up. Peter could you come with the girls and me, and we'll put together some food for you to bring back down. How about a turkey sandwich?"

Robert settled himself onto the couch, beer in hand, and said, "I'd be happy to do that and a turkey sandwich would be great."

Once up in the kitchen, Thea talked to her children as she made the sandwiches and hunted around in Ellie's cupboards for some cereal for the girls. "I don't want you to be distrustful of all men, but I'd rather you didn't spend any time alone with Robert until I know him better. Izzie, you spent quite a lot of time talking to him. What are your thoughts?"

"He seems nice, Mom. He really listened to me, especially when I told him all about my dancing. He wanted to know all about *The Nutcracker*, and I found him easy to talk to."

"What about you, Jess?" Thea said.

"I don't know. I haven't really thought about him. I like Mr. Blunt, though. He has twinkly eyes, and he tells good stories."

"Peter, how about you?"

"He seems fine, Mom. We had a good time in the car on the way back from Grandma and Grandpa's. He had the latest *Bon Jovi* CD, and we played that—it was awesome."

She handed Peter a plate of sandwiches and a glass of milk, saying she would be down to watch the movie with him once the girls were in bed. She looked him in the eyes and said if, at any time, Robert made him uncomfortable he should just walk away and come upstairs to find her. She hoped she hadn't spoiled things for him because she understood only too well his longing for male company, and surely Ellie would have mentioned something, especially as she must have known how gun-shy they all were after what had happened to Jess. She was bolting the stable door after the horse had gone, but she was unable to stand by and just do nothing. She was overprotective for good reason—the trauma of nearly losing her youngest daughter still haunted her.

Thea cleaned up the kitchen while the girls were finishing up their cereal. Honey sat waiting patiently at the girls' feet just in case they dropped even the tiniest morsel of food, but she was out of luck. She assumed Robert was in charge of feeding and taking care of the dog in Ellie's absence, but she would check with him once she got back downstairs.

Soon her daughters were safely tucked in their beds. As always, they smelled of toothpaste and she kissed them both, telling them not to talk too much otherwise they'd have a hard time getting up in the morning. Ellie had thoughtfully supplied a nightlight, both in their room and the bathroom opposite, so they could easily find their way. Comforted by each other's company and not being enveloped in total darkness in a strange house, they let their mother go, but as soon as she'd gone, the whispering began.

"What do you think so far?" Izzie said.

"Hm, I'm not sure. I've had a nice day, but I miss home, and Miss Ellie's not as fun as I thought she'd be."

"I feel that way, too, Jess. Miss Ellie's house is beautiful, but it seems empty somehow. Do you know what I mean?"

"I do, but I can't really make the words for it. It's just how it makes me feel."

"I agree. What did you think of Grandma and Grandpa?" Izzie asked.

"They're not very friendly, are they?"

"I think they need someone to look after them. They seem kinda small, not like Aunt Margaret and Uncle Bill."

Jessica yawned. "Night, Izzie, I'm going to sleep now."

"Goodnight, Jess, and if you get lonely in the night you can always come into bed with me. Now I'm yawning, too."

"You catched it from me."

Despite Thea's misgivings, the rest of the evening passed pleasantly. She spent the time with Peter and Robert, much relieved when Robert only drank one beer. They all devoured the sandwiches she had made and enjoyed the movie. The *Harry Potter* stories were action packed, and watching any of them for the second time was certainly no chore. They had the first three at home, and she intended to buy this one for Peter's birthday to add to his collection. She couldn't believe he would be turning eleven on the third of December. Where had all the years gone?

Eventually the movie ended, and the three of them traipsed upstairs with Honey following close behind. Robert went off to feed the dog and take her outside; Peter kissed his mother and took himself to bed, and Thea made a rather half-hearted attempt at cleaning up the kitchen. She found the task unpleasant and frustrating, seeing as she didn't have a clue where anything went—but she did her best. She went into the sitting room to check on the fire, and was relieved to see the logs had pretty much burnt themselves out. She closed the glass doors to prevent the heat from the room escaping up the chimney, but she didn't linger. It felt so strange to be wandering around Ellie's house all by herself, and she felt jittery. She heard Robert return, so she forced herself to go back into the kitchen. Honey went off to her bed in the corner, and after saying goodnight to Robert, Thea thankfully took herself off to her own bed.

Tired as she was, she found it hard to fall asleep. What a strange day. She had felt an undercurrent of unease between all of them and she compared today's meal with the one she had given on Sunday. Even though MaryAnn hadn't known Jim and vice versa, and Stanley was pretty much a stranger to all of them except Nan, they had all seemed connected somehow. It wasn't something she had really thought much about, just took it for granted. Even in the midst of all the bad times, she and the children always regrouped and found solace in one another. She imagined silken threads joining them all together, and even though the kids pulled away at times, somehow she always managed to reel them back in.

She thought about Ellie and her life and wondered what the real reason was for bringing her and the children to Massachusetts. She sensed the disconnection between the two of them and she came to the conclusion she wasn't the only one to blame for the fact they hadn't kept in touch over the years. Why would Ellie ask her to come after all this time and why now? And with this thought, she drifted off to sleep...

CHAPTER EIGHTEEN

MAINE

Early Thursday afternoon MaryAnn and her boys went over to the Chamberlin's house to feed Smokey. Following the instructions Thea had given her over the phone, MaryAnn easily found the set of keys under the flowerpot. Once inside the house, they removed their shoes after carefully wiping them on the mat. Smokey, exceedingly pleased to see them, wove her way in between their legs, rubbing and purring. Johnny promptly sat down on the floor and the cat crawled all over him, kneading his legs and making him giggle. "It feels so funny, Mom," he said.

"Good thing she doesn't have any claws, otherwise you'd be like a pincushion by now, all full of holes."

When she saw how much pleasure Johnny was deriving from his interaction with Smokey, she wished her budget would run to a kitten, but it was no good longing for something they couldn't afford. Thea had left a note on the table saying they were welcome to stay and watch some of their movies—with instructions on how to operate the TV and the VCR—and had left a box of microwave popcorn to add to their watching pleasure. She had also left individual envelopes with money inside with thank you notes for the boys, saying how much she appreciated them helping her out.

MaryAnn's feelings towards Thea had taken a rather different turn after Jim had divulged his erstwhile love for her. She thought it would be awkward to strike up a real friendship with her now. She couldn't believe how quickly her rather dull and relatively uncomplicated life had suddenly come alive with all sorts of intrigue. And now she was off to a Thanksgiving with a whole host of people she didn't know. Hopefully, his brother, Ben, was as nice as Jim, in which case, they were all in for a really good time.

With Smokey all fed and watered, telling her they'd be back in the morning because MaryAnn didn't think once a day was enough, they put on their shoes and went back out into the cold. It was damp and raw, but there was still no sign of snow. Again, she had declined Jim's offer to pick them up, and she knew she was putting off the inevitable, but she didn't want him to think he had to rescue her as this wasn't what their developing relationship was all about.

MaryAnn's Thanksgiving experience was very different from Thea's. She had met Jim at his house as planned, and they had all piled into his truck. There was a space tucked behind the front seats, a little tight for Ian but just right for Johnny, and the little boy loved it. MaryAnn was a little concerned to see there weren't any seat belts, but they were so snug back there she couldn't envisage them coming to any harm. The inside of the truck was as neat and clean as Jim's house, and it was a huge relief as trucks always reminded her of her family vehicles with their messy interiors. She'd always had to shove things aside before being able to sit down and the floor was habitually littered with empty coffee cups, water bottles and candy wrappers. Besides the disgusting trash, the cab was always redolent with the lingering and nauseating odor of stale cigarette smoke and the smell clung to her clothes and her hair.

"Penny for your thoughts," Jim said.

"I was just admiring how neat and clean the inside of your truck is; a stark comparison to the ones I grew up with which were always terribly messy. It's a refreshing change," and she turned and smiled at him.

"I'm glad it makes you happy."

"It does," and she sat quietly holding the Dutch apple pie she had baked, listening to her boys chatting away behind her. It was a favorite recipe and one she hadn't made since Sam had died, but with Will's help, she was able to gather the ingredients. She certainly didn't want to go empty-handed.

"We'll soon be there," Jim said.

"What's Ben's house like?"

"It's nothing like the one I live in. Ben is quite the draftsman and much better at math than I ever was, so he decided to build a log cabin—much more practical for Maine than the drafty Victorian my grandfather built. I grew up there, the history of the house is in my bones, and I have never wanted to live anywhere else."

"I think it's a beautiful house."

"My grandfather came from England, and he had rather romantic and impractical ideas. He had no idea about the climate in Maine, but he was

191

determined to build a brick house. He certainly succeeded, but looking after it made life difficult for my grandmother and my mother. The house is a lot of work; even with the modern conveniences I have which they didn't have back in my grandmother's day. I think it fair wore my grandmother out as she was only sixty-five when she died and I never really got to know her because I was only three at the time. Ben never knew her at all. My grandfather lived to be a ripe old age, and he was a real character, but I'll have to tell you more another time as we're here."

MaryAnn, thrown slightly towards Jim as he made a sharp right-hand turn into Ben's driveway, clutched the pie tightly. He leaned sideways to steady her, and MaryAnn not sure whether the gesture was really necessary, nonetheless loved the physical contact; the brief touching of their coats caused a tingle in her arm, and her whole body seemed to glow. Jim turned his head and smiled at her, and she was sure he would have kissed her if the boys hadn't been sitting in the back. She breathed in and looked through the windshield at the house; the warmth radiating from the brightly lit windows enticed her and she couldn't wait to get out of the truck. There was a huge wraparound porch with brightly colored Adirondack chairs and a bale of straw had been placed to the right of the front door on which sat scarecrows in all different sizes: there were even fake crows perching on the railings.

"Somebody's been busy," Jim said. "Come boys, don't be shy," and he made sure they were standing in front of him when he rang the door bell, partially hidden by a huge bunch of Indian corn. Without waiting for anyone to answer, he pushed open the door, and MaryAnn looked down at two of the most beautiful little girls she had ever seen. They were identical twins and looked up at Jim with their big brown eyes peeking out from under their curly mops of bright blonde hair.

"Hello, Uncle Jim," they both said in unison. "We're wearing name tags today, so we don't get mixed up."

"Now, that's a great idea, but are you sure you got them right?"

"Course, I'm Poppy, and this is Daisy, and we're four," and she pointed to her sister.

"Well," Jim said, "I'd like you to meet Johnny and Ian, and this is Mrs. Wilkinson, their mom."

Poppy held out her hand and her tiny fingernails sparkled with bright pink polish. "Come with us," she said. Johnny was mesmerized but still managed to step forward. Ian hung back.

Ben suddenly appeared full of apologies. "Sorry, we had to baste the turkey and flip the potatoes," he said, holding out his hand. He was slightly shorter than Jim, and of a more slender build, but he had the same easy friendliness. "I'd like you to meet my wife, Jennifer," and he put his arm around her ample waist, and MaryAnn saw immediately where the twins had gotten their looks. She had the same big brown eyes, and even though her hair was a duller shade of blonde, she still had the same unruly curls.

"Welcome to our home," she said, gently pulling away from Ben. "Let me take your coats."

Johnny and the twins had disappeared, but Ian stayed with the grown-ups as they all trooped into the family room where there were more people. Jennifer said, "This is my mom, Pat, my dad, Bruce, and my sister, Elizabeth. Now what would you like to drink? There's beer, wine—red and white—and I could probably rustle up a gin and tonic, and of course there's soda."

"I'd love a glass of red wine," MaryAnn said.

"A beer for me, and what about you, Ian?" Jim said.

"I'd love some milk," he said, knowing better than to ask for soda because his mom always told him it would rot his teeth.

The family room was adjacent to the kitchen. It was a big room with a fireplace at one end, and this is where they all sat on couches and comfortable chairs, watching the logs crackle and glow. Pat, who was as bubbly and just as friendly as her daughter, immediately put them all at ease. Bruce talked casually to Ian and wanted to know whether he had ever played chess. MaryAnn's heart missed a beat because he used to play with Sam, but Ian handled his emotions perfectly and said he used to play but hadn't for a while. Bruce, oblivious to the flicker of dismay passing over Ian's face said, "Can I challenge you to a game later?"

Ian said, "I'd like that." MaryAnn knew her son was good at the game and would give Jennifer's dad a run for his money. She was also pleased he had taken an interest in her son even if it had given rise to Ian being reminded of his dad, but he had recovered quickly, so maybe the wounds were healing. Social situations were difficult and she had avoided them until recently, but they couldn't stay hidden forever. She wondered how Johnny was making out with the twins!

Ben arrived with a tray of drinks, and she decided to settle back and enjoy herself. She sat with her hand curled around the glass of red wine and sipped it slowly. Elizabeth, who appeared younger than her sister and didn't have her startling good looks, asked Ian if he would like to go play a game of Ping-Pong, to which he readily agreed.

They chatted among themselves, and MaryAnn savored the warmth from the glow of the fire and the intoxication of the wine. She could sense Jim watching her; he was certainly in his element and she could tell he was truly enjoying himself. He was nursing a beer and drinking it slowly. She didn't think he was a drinker, but it was good to be able to assess him in a social situation because if this were his tendency, she would have run a mile. The men in her family were all heavy drinkers, and having escaped once, it was something she did not want to be exposed to again. She had seen what the alcohol had done to normal, rational human beings, and she wanted no part of it.

She had managed to deflect most of Pat's questions. She had become rather masterful at turning conversations to her advantage, so people were only answering questions about themselves, and seeing as most people were more interested in their own lives, her technique worked most of the time. Disappointed to see Bruce getting a little worse for wear, she hoped the food would soak up the alcohol, so his chess game with Ian would be worthwhile.

Soon she heard the twins, with Johnny following along behind, asking their mom when dinner would be ready, and Jennifer told them it wouldn't be long. MaryAnn got up and made her way towards the kitchen, mainly to ask if she could help but also to see if Johnny needed rescuing from a world of Barbie dolls and pink nail polish. He seemed to be fine, and although Thea's daughter, Jessica, was very different from these two little princesses, she had probably initiated him into girly games. She wondered whether he was bowled over by their prettiness even at the tender age of five.

Jennifer was flushed from all her cooking and even more tendrils of her wild and unruly hair had escaped. "Would you stir the gravy? Getting all the food together, so it stays hot and is ready at the same time is the worst part of meal preparation, at least it is for me."

Picking up the wooden spoon, MaryAnn stood at the stove and stirred. "I love your house, Jennifer," she said.

"Thank you. Ben built it before I met him. I'd never thought of myself living in a log house, but when he first brought me here I so wanted the relationship to work," and she grinned at MaryAnn. "The house wasn't the only reason—I would have lived with Ben anywhere, but it was the cherry on top. Well, I think we're ready to eat. You can turn the heat off. There are two gravy boats warming in the top oven, and if you would fill them, that would be really helpful. I'll go round everyone up."

MaryAnn didn't think the dining room at all convenient to the kitchen, and it was a long walk for them to transfer all the hot dishes of food, but the room itself was a surprise—spacious and luxurious, with huge windows at the far end and along the wall overlooking the porch. Despite the log walls, the room appeared light and airy, complemented by a rather ornate and rustic chandelier hanging over the center of the huge table. A buffet ran along the wall under the windows and Jennifer placed all the dishes on warming plates so guests and family could line up and help themselves. It was so different from anything MaryAnn had ever seen, with plenty of room to move around the table. There were nametags for each person, and booster seats for the little ones. Jennifer's planning was flawless, and it seemed as though she had anticipated all her guests' needs, young and old. She was amused by the expressions on her boys' faces and their eyes almost popped out of their heads when they saw all the food, and she bent down to whisper in Johnny's ear telling him to close his mouth. He looked back at her and grinned, and she could tell he was enjoying himself. The youngest children were helped first and as soon as they were settled with their plates of food, the rest of them formed a line. MaryAnn found herself behind Ian and in front of Jim, and it took all her willpower not to lean back into him. She wondered whether he was as acutely aware of her as she was of him, and decided it was a good thing he had a plate of food in his hands.

Jennifer was a chatterer as were her daughters, followed closely by Pat, who was not to be outdone. Pat's comments were a lot more vacuous and MaryAnn noticed Elizabeth and Bruce tuning her out. As soon as everybody was sitting, they went around the table one by one and said what they were thankful for. The twins were thankful for everything, not a shy bone in either of their tiny bodies. Johnny managed to overcome his nervousness enough to say, "Thank you for 'viting us," and Ian echoed his words but added he was having a really good time. Jim was sitting opposite her, and their eyes locked at one point. She was startled by the jolt of emotion that surged through her, but it wasn't enough to make her lose her appetite, even though she was caught by surprise. Overcome with the sense of being loved, she slowly sipped her second glass of red wine and tucked into her meal. Jennifer urged them all to go for second helpings, and Ian didn't need to be asked twice. After looking at his mom for permission and getting the nod, he went back to refill his plate. Cooks always loved it when folks enjoyed their food and Jennifer looked flushed and happy, as well she should because the food was absolutely delicious.

Ian stood up to help carry plates to the kitchen, as did Elizabeth. MaryAnn was proud of her son, and she knew Johnny would have helped his brother if he could have gotten down, but he was trapped. She reassured him by saying, "It's okay, don't worry. You'll be able to help in a little while," and she saw him relax. He was such a little man and always wanted to do what Ian was doing.

Soon desserts were brought and placed on the warming plates. There was a huge bowl of whipped cream and two urns of coffee—one caffeinated and one decaf. Jennifer's earlier nervousness seemed to have disappeared, and even though she talked incessantly, she seemed much more relaxed. MaryAnn's Dutch apple pie was a huge success, and being able to give at least a little bit back for the Hudson's generous hospitality pleased her no end. Pat had thoughtfully made brownies, and the kids inhaled those, so maybe there was more than air inside her pretty faded blonde head.

As soon as the table was cleared and all perishable food put away in the refrigerator, everyone was shooed out of the kitchen so Jim and Ben could wash up. Apparently this was tradition, and there was no arguing, even though MaryAnn would have liked to help. "Absolutely not," they said, so she gave up and decided to seek out Elizabeth, thinking she might be glad of some company.

Jennifer took Poppy, Daisy and Johnny off to the den and set them up with a movie and managed to persuade the twins out of *Barbie's Summer Holiday* without too much pouting and picked *101 Dalmatians* for Johnny's sake. MaryAnn suspected they'd almost certainly fall asleep, so the movie choice probably wasn't of any great significance. Bruce snagged Ian for their game of chess and went off to the dining room to use the table. MaryAnn guessed he was escaping Pat and Jennifer who were still talking non-stop, and she just didn't know how he stood it on a daily basis. She could handle Jennifer on her own, but the two of them together was a nightmare, so she suggested a game of table tennis to Elizabeth to which the young girl readily agreed. They struck up quite a conversation, and MaryAnn discovered she was completely different from her mother and her sister, not only in looks, but also personality.

An intensely levelheaded young woman, her dark hair was pulled back from her rather ordinary but girlish face, her dark brown eyes were set rather too close together beneath heavy brows, and her nose was a little too pointy, but her friendly demeanor made up for all she lacked in physical attributes and her face lit up when she smiled, showing absolutely perfect teeth. She told MaryAnn she was a librarian, having graduated from college with a Bachelor's degree in English. "I've always loved literature so becoming a librarian was a natural progression, and I've never wanted to be anything else. Ever since I was a little girl, I've been obsessed with books, and you should see my apartment—all the walls are lined with shelves filled with every imaginable kind of book. Of course, I'm an insatiable reader which makes me rather solitary by nature, but I like nothing better than curling up with a good story on a rainy day, with soft classical music playing in the background."

"You must be older than I thought. Sorry, I didn't mean to be rude."

"It's okay. I'm twenty-eight and, yes, people always think I'm younger which is fine with me now, but it was a real pain when I was twenty and people thought I was fourteen!"

"I've never had that problem," and MaryAnn smiled at Elizabeth thinking she may have found a friend. They were poorly matched for their game of table tennis, and as she was tired of chasing balls all over the basement floor, MaryAnn said she was done if Jennifer was. "I'm sure my son gave you a much better game," she said, bending down yet again and crawling under the table to retrieve the ball.

"I am definitely done and, yes, Ian did give me a good, fast-paced game," Elizabeth said. "I'm thirsty. Would you like something?" and she headed towards a small refrigerator sitting in the corner of the rec room. MaryAnn followed close behind and said she'd love a bottle of water. They went and sat on the sofa against the wall, and MaryAnn tucked herself into the corner, and Elizabeth sat at the opposite end. "Where do you live?" the young woman asked, a question MaryAnn always dreaded.

"I live on the other side of Melford Point. How about you?"

"I live in Portland and work at the public library there. It's within walking distance from my apartment, and I love the fact I don't have to sit behind the wheel of a car for my daily commute. Don't get me started talking about my job because you will be bored to tears."

"No, I wouldn't. I'm sure there's more to being a librarian than checking books in and out and stacking shelves."

"There sure is, but let's save that for another day. I'd love you to come visit me in Portland. I could take Ian and Johnny to the library."

"They'd be thrilled," MaryAnn said. "I'm sure it's much better than the one in Melford Point. Ian is an avid reader, and Johnny is just learning, but I can tell he's following in his brother's footsteps. Being able to read opens up such a fantastic world."

"You're a woman after my own heart," and she tilted her head back and swallowed the rest of her water. "I think we'd better go be social, don't you? I'm sure the men have finished the washing up by now."

MaryAnn stood up reluctantly and followed Elizabeth back up the stairs. They peeked in on the little ones, and as MaryAnn had anticipated, *101 Dalmatians* was playing to a sleeping audience. The two girls were curled up at one end of the sofa, and Johnny the other, with blankets pulled up to their chins. She was sure her son appreciated the warmth after their cold house, and it was good to see him so comfortable with a healthy flush to his normally pale cheeks. She and Elizabeth let them be.

Bruce and Ian were still deeply engrossed in their chess game and Ian looked up at his mom and grinned, which meant he was probably winning. Bruce sat nursing another beer, and the alcohol probably wasn't helping his concentration, but her son seemed to be fine, so she and Elizabeth went off to the family room.

Jim and Ben were watching the football game and Jim glanced away from the screen when he saw MaryAnn, and smiled. She grinned back at him, but it wasn't appropriate to go and sit next to him, so she stayed where she was. Pat had produced some knitting and both she and Jennifer seemed to have finally run out of things to say. They both looked up when they saw MaryAnn and Elizabeth and asked whether they'd had a good game. "Elizabeth beat the socks off me," MaryAnn said, "But we had fun."

"Come sit with us so we can enjoy your company," and MaryAnn sat down in the vacant armchair next to the fire, suddenly realizing how tired she was. Socializing was hard work, and she was woefully out of practice.

"Thank you for inviting us. We're having a really good time, and the meal was delicious." She turned her attention to Pat. "Do you and Bruce live in the area?"

"Unfortunately, no. We moved south to Jacksonville, Florida, five years ago. The Maine winters are just too hard, but I do miss my daughter," and she dropped her knitting in her lap and reached over and took Jennifer's hand. MaryAnn thought the gesture totally lacking in tact, and a little odd, seeing as her other daughter was sitting right across from her. She didn't understand parents who played favorites. "Is your family close by?" Pat wanted to know.

"No, they're in New York State."

"How did you and Jim meet?" and MaryAnn realized, with horror, Pat was in full sail, and she was going to have to field a barrage of questions.

"We met at a mutual friend's," she said, "and how do you like Jacksonville?"

"We love it. I play tennis three or four times a week and Bruce runs on the beach most mornings. It's such a relief not to have to worry about shoveling snow any more. Bruce was let go from his corporate job, which meant he was able to retire early with a nice fat package. We also got a great price for our house here, so we're all set up," and she rattled on. MaryAnn, beginning to wish Johnny hadn't fallen asleep as he would have given her the perfect excuse to leave, was trapped.

Ian and Bruce appeared, and she could tell from Ian's face he had won the chess game, but Bruce was being a good sport about it. He put his arm around Ian's shoulders and said, "I was soundly beaten by this young man. He plays an excellent and tactical game. I'm impressed."

"Thank you, sir," Ian said. "It was a great game."

Bruce took his arm from Ian's shoulders, gave him a high five, and went and sat down with Jim and Ben to enjoy the football. Jim beckoned Ian over, and he went and sat on the floor at Jim's feet. She noticed Jim put a fatherly hand on her son's hair, and Ian didn't flinch so it must have felt good, and she was glad. She excused herself and went off to the den to check on the little kids and found them wide-awake taking in the rest of the movie. She found Johnny fidgeting because he needed to go to the bathroom, but too embarrassed to ask, so she took his hand and said, "Come with me." They ran across the hallway to the powder room opposite the dining room and he only just made it in time.

"Where were you, Mom?"

"I'm sorry, but I did come and check on you and you were fast asleep," she said, bending down and pulling out the stool Jennifer obviously had for the twins. He climbed on it and washed his hands. "Are you having a good time?"

"Yes, I am, but I like Jessica much better than Poppy and Daisy. She's not so girly."

"I know, but were they nice to you?" and she handed Johnny a fluffy pale blue towel and he methodically rubbed his hands dry.

"Yes, they were nice to me, but I got tired of playing house."

"Thank you for being such a good sport," and she bent down and looked into his face. "Can you be brave for just a bit longer as the other alternative is a boring, old football game?"

"Okay, Mom."

They went back to the den and found Jennifer sitting with the girls. "We're just going to watch the end of the movie, and then I'll get us all a snack. Is that okay with you?" and she looked at Johnny.

"Sure," he said, and sat down next to Jennifer, reluctantly letting go of MaryAnn's hand.

Jim, even though he was enjoying the feel of Ian against his legs, decided he really should get up and see how MaryAnn was doing. He leaned down and told Ian he was just going to check on his mom, suggesting he take his place on the sofa. Ian pushed himself up on his hands to get out of Jim's way and sat down in his vacant spot between Ben and Bruce. Jim couldn't stop thinking about MaryAnn and concentrating on the game was virtually impossible. He was longing to spend some time alone with her, but it was difficult. He really wanted to get to know her, but figured he was going to have to be patient. After all, he'd waited years to feel like this, and the last thing he wanted to do was scare her away.

Ben had plagued Jim with questions while they were washing up, but he had little in the way of information because he really didn't know anything about her.

"Who's the mystery woman, then?" Ben had teased, but all he could tell him was she worked in the diner on the other side of town, and they had met at Thea Chamberlin's. Ben's eyebrows shot up at the mention of Thea's name because he was well aware Jim had been in love with her for years.

"How did that come about?"

"Johnny and Ian are friendly with Thea's kids. She invited me over as a thank you for fixing her back door after Kenny tried to break in, and MaryAnn just happened to be there."

"I know, and the rest is history. They seem like nice kids."

"They really are. I like them a lot."

"And MaryAnn?" Ben turned and flipped Jim with some soapy water.

"Yeah, well, I like her a lot, too."

"Has she broken the spell?"

"I'm relieved to say she has, and you've no idea how good it feels."

"Amen to that. I never did understand your whole infatuation thing." And they said no more. They had always confided in each other, and his brother knew he would come and talk to him if he felt the need.

Jim found a very cozy group in the den, and MaryAnn's face lit up at the sight of him. Johnny looked up at him with his bright little face partially hidden by his dark hair. "Hi, Mr. Hudson," he said.

"Hi, young man." Suddenly Poppy and Daisy were all over him clinging to his legs and saying, "Uncle Jim, Uncle Jim. Where've you been?"

"Watching the football," he said, bending down and taking the two little girls in his arms, their bright curls a stark contrast to his light brown hair. He blew raspberries in their necks, and they burst into giggles, pushing him backwards, forcing him to sit on the floor. They went into attack as soon as he was down, bouncing on his legs and tickling him unmercifully, their tiny fingers finding all sorts of tender spots until Jim, overcome by fits of laughter, breathlessly begged them to stop. Eventually, Jennifer intervened and pulled the girls off. "Leave your poor uncle alone," she said.

"Aw, Mom," they said, but they did as they were told.

Jim pulled himself to his feet and sat down next to MaryAnn. "You girls have fair worn me out," he said, leaning back and putting his hands behind his head. Johnny was looking at him in amazement, and MaryAnn could feel herself falling deeply in love. Soon just the three of them remained as Jennifer had whisked the twins off to the kitchen to put some sandwiches together, and Jim moved away from MaryAnn just a little bit so he could turn sideways and face her.

"How are you two doing? Ready to call it quits, yet?"

"How long do you normally stay?" MaryAnn asked.

"Usually, long into the evening because I haven't had anything to go home to up until now," and he took her hand, "but if you need to get this young man home to bed, we can leave whenever you like."

Johnny suddenly perked up, "I don't need to go to bed. I had a nap."

"That's all settled then. If it's okay with your mom, we'll stay and have some sandwiches." He pulled MaryAnn to her feet, and if Johnny hadn't been there watching them intently he would have pulled her into his arms and kissed her. Reluctantly, he let go of her hands. "Johnny, why don't you go off and see if you can find Ian," Jim suggested, and his ploy worked—surprisingly the little boy slid off the couch and headed off towards the kitchen. Jim pulled MaryAnn into his arms and leaned down and kissed her, totally unprepared for the tears streaming down her pale cheeks. He was totally mortified and furious with himself, believing he was the cause of her unhappiness.

CHAPTER NINETEEN

BLACK FRIDAY

Thea awoke at seven thirty the morning after Thanksgiving, and when she poked her head out into the hallway, she was dismayed to see Ellie's door still shut. This didn't bode well for a fun-filled day, and she wasn't sure what she should do. There was no sign of any activity anywhere. Peter would sleep in, given half a chance, but the girls were always up, so she tiptoed off to their room.

Seeing them cuddled together in one of the single beds was no surprise, and she could tell they were relieved to see her. "I really don't know what to do," she said, sitting down heavily on the edge of the bed. "Miss Ellie's door is still closed, so I'm thinking maybe the best thing would be for us to get dressed quietly and go out to breakfast. Why don't you put on some clothes and I'll go wake up Peter."

"Is this a 'spiracy?" Jessica said, using one of her favorite words.

"Not so much a conspiracy but a plan so as not to bother Miss Ellie if she's still poorly, so we have to be quiet," and she held her finger to her lips.

Peter was dead to the world, and she hated to wake him, but she could hardly leave him behind. "Hey, Mr. Navigator, we need you."

"Why, where are we going?" and he yawned, stretched and rubbed his eyes.

"Out to breakfast as I think Miss Ellie must still be sick. There's a great place in Stockton if I remember rightly, and if not, I'm sure we'll find somewhere, so can you get dressed quickly and quietly?"

"Sure, Mom."

Thea went back to her room and threw on some clothes. The kids had gathered in the kitchen, and she told them she would go out and warm up the car while they put on their shoes and coats. Honey wasn't in her basket, and she guessed she had gone down to the basement to find Robert. She had been whining at Ellie's door earlier, and Thea was puzzled Ellie hadn't let her in. The whole situation was perplexing, and she assumed the dog was just as confused as she and the kids. She wrote a note for Ellie, telling her they were going out to breakfast to get out of her hair and were planning on stopping in at Aladdin's Cave after they had eaten. She ended the note by saying she hoped she was on the mend and left it propped against the napkin holder on the center of the kitchen table.

Tremendously relieved to be out of the house, Thea made short work of the drive into Stockton. She glanced at Aladdin's Cave as they went past, noticing the unlit window, but it was still early. She made the assumption Theodore would open the store if Ellie were still unwell. The kids were quiet; Peter still looked half asleep, and she was sure none of them had slept as soundly as they did at home. The lights of the Harvest Bakery were warmly welcoming, and she pulled off the road into the small parking lot in front of the restaurant. As she opened the door and herded the children inside, she was assailed by a million memories of the many times she and Ellie had stopped in there for breakfast. The restaurant still smelled the same—a combination of freshly baked bread, coffee, and fried bacon. There were glass cases on either side of the entranceway filled with every kind of cake and pastry imaginable, and above them were shelves with loaves of bread of different shapes and sizes. She requested a table for four and asked Jess whether she would like a booster seat—sometimes she did, and sometimes she didn't. Today was one of those days when she did! They were shown to a table in the front left-hand corner next to the window and soon they were all sitting and looking at menus. Thea relaxed; relieved to be in normal surroundings, she reveled in the aroma of the comfort foods.

She didn't recognize the waitress who came to take their orders and she was sure a great deal had changed in the way of staff since she had last had a meal there on one of the few ill-fated attempts to introduce Peter and Izzie to her parents. She looked around to see if there were any familiar faces, but didn't see any. She noticed how bedraggled her own children were because of their hurry to get out of the house: Jess's hair was a messy tangle of dark curls, and Peter definitely needed a comb run through his. Izzie was the only neat one, her long hair tied back in a sleek ponytail.

Thea took a sip of her coffee, and the kids drank their juice while they waited for their food. "What do you think's wrong with Miss Ellie?" Jessica asked.

"I don't know. It's all a bit of a mystery and rather worrying. This is not how I thought the visit would be."

"Do you think Mr. Blunt will open up the store today?" Izzie wanted to know.

"I would imagine so, as the Friday after Thanksgiving is always a busy shopping day."

"Maybe we could help," Peter said.

"What a great idea and I do plan on stopping in there after we've had breakfast. How do you feel about going and seeing Grandma and Grandpa?"

Peter said going to visit them was okay with him, but the girls were a little more reluctant. "Let's see what the day brings. And so our adventure continues, even if it isn't exactly what we thought it would be." She looked up to see the waitress balancing a big tray on which there were plates of steaming food, and she skillfully placed each of their orders in front of them one by one. Izzie and Jess had one blueberry pancake each, and she and Peter had eggs, bacon and toast. The food was delicious, and they all ate heartily, enjoying every mouthful. Thea, with the buzz of several refills of coffee, was beginning to feel she could tackle anything, although going out into the harsh reality of the world and the unknown was not a particularly pleasant prospect.

They lingered as long as possible, but there were people waiting for tables and Jessica was beginning to get fidgety, so they needed to leave. Peter took the check and the money she gave him up to the cash register, and they waited for him to come back so she could leave a tip. She just managed to stop Jess from flinging her coat on the floor and told her she would help her. "You always hold it up too high so I can't get my arms in," she said, turning with her back to Thea and wriggling madly, so helping her was virtually impossible. But Thea gladly welcomed her feistiness—she would have put up with anything from this daughter of hers—even rudeness was better than the sad and silent child she had brought home from the hospital ordeal.

Once outside, they piled into the car and drove back the way they had come. They were all pleased to see the lights were now on in Aladdin's Cave, so Thea made a left and pulled up outside the store. Fortunately, she found a space with plenty of room for her to parallel park—not one of her better skills. Peter told her she'd done a half way decent job and was only about a quarter of a mile from the curb. "Enough of your sassiness, young man," she said, turning to him and smiling.

The closed sign was still hanging on the door, so she knocked and waited to see if anyone would come. The kids huddled behind their mother in the cold, pushing against her and into each other until Peter said, "Quit it." She knocked again and saw Mr. Blunt emerge from behind a large display of greeting cards, and his face lit up when he saw the Chamberlins. Turning the lock, he opened the door and said, "Come in, come in."

Thea took a deep breath and gazed at all the merchandise within her immediate vicinity. Noticing the store was familiar and different all at the same time, she asked Theodore if he would mind if she and the children took a look around. He said, "Of course, of course," and bounced up and down on the balls of his feet as if he couldn't contain his excitement. "We don't open until ten o'clock so take your time."

Thea wanted the opportunity to talk to him, so she lingered after the children had wandered off. She could hear the girls chattering away, and she hoped Peter would find something to interest him in the book corner. "Mr. Blunt, how is Ellie this morning?" she asked, and the delight with which he had welcomed them was instantly gone, and she watched as his whole body sagged with what seemed a terrible sadness.

"Oh, Miss Thea, she's quite ill. It's not my place to tell you what's wrong, and I'm sure she'll confide in you. I do hope so," and he took his handkerchief out of his pocket and blew his nose rather loudly.

"I promise I'll try and talk to her later. In the meantime, is there anything I can do to help you here? I imagine today will be busy, seeing as it's Black Friday."

"Robert said he'd stop by if he can, but of course Ellie is his number one priority. If you could stay, at least for a little while, it would be much appreciated. It's been a long time since we've worked together, but I'm sure it will all come back to you. Not much has changed except we do have a more sophisticated cash register and billing system."

"Peter excels at anything mechanical or math related. We have friends back in Maine who own a country store, and both Peter and Izzie have been helping them out since they were little kids. It would also give him something to do, so why don't you show him how the system works?"

"What a splendid idea," he said, rubbing his hands together and smiling at her. "If the girls want to be creative, they could have a grand old time in the craft room. Here, let me show you," and he turned on his heels and shuffled his way to the back of the shop. He took out a key and unlocked the door to what used to be the storeroom, and Thea was delighted with what she saw. Ellie had transformed the dusty and box-filled space into the most beautiful and well-organized arts and craft area with a huge table in the center. There were shelves with colored bins all labeled in bold lettering, a row of pegs with brightly colored smocks hanging from each, and around the table were red, yellow and blue plastic chairs. The window, once concealed by a towering stack of boxes, was now clearly visible and beneath it rested a large white porcelain sink, snugly flanked by Formica countertops on which sat large jars full of paintbrushes. A roll of white paper for artwork was securely fastened underneath one of the countertops and two sewing machines sat on a low shelf on the wall by the stairs that led up to the apartment above. Ellie had thought of every little thing, right down to the last detail.

She turned to Mr. Blunt and said, "What Ellie has accomplished is amazing. I can't wait to show the girls. Having so much stuff at their fingertips will keep them quiet for hours. I promise you they will clean up after themselves and put all the items back where they belong," but she was talking to herself as he had disappeared, and she could hear him explaining things to Peter.

Izzie and Jess were playing 'pretend customers' and were completely immersed in their game. The pastime, a favorite activity and one the two of them had played many times before in the Country Store, involved creating imaginary people for whom they were buying gifts. Jessica had taken one of the shopping baskets from the stack by the door for their make-believe merchandise, and Thea watched her daughter struggling along with it. Although the basket wasn't heavy, it was unwieldy for someone her size, but she wasn't about to give it up. Thea went up to them and said, "When you're done with your shopping I have a surprise for you, so come find me," but they didn't even acknowledge her, they were so engrossed in their fantasy world.

The sewing section seemed to have expanded, so Thea assumed all the quilting ladies still came to Aladdin's Cave for their fabric. There were notions galore, all neatly displayed, and racks of colored threads. The most beautiful quilt, lovingly pieced together in deep purples and blues, with bright yellow stars, lay draped over a stand to the right of the cutting table. Thea thought it a shame space couldn't be found to display the quilt on the wall, but there really wasn't an inch of room. She wondered whether Ellie had finally learned how to sew, and with that thought, came the realization she had little knowledge of her friend's life and what had transpired during the intervening years. She felt sad and just a tiny bit guilty.

Peter and Mr. Blunt seemed to be getting along, which pleased her greatly. She had no doubt Peter would be able to master whatever Theodore chose to teach him, and she sensed the old man had an inordinate amount of patience. He was really sweet and she wondered what had eventually happened to Jenny, and when she had actually died, but she didn't like to ask. She wandered up to a display of what looked like items from local artisans—a completely new and smart innovation on Ellie's part. The objects were tasteful and exquisitely crafted, and she had set them out on well-lit shelves. There were a couple of lamps with pretty stained glass shades, similar to the ones in her bedroom in Ellie's house; delicate, almost translucent porcelain bowls in various shapes and sizes; wooden cutting boards, and some whimsical pottery animals. A locked glass case displayed fine jewelry, and the beautiful necklaces, bracelets and rings tastefully arranged within the brightly lit interior, sparkled their tantalizing invitation to be touched.

At ten o'clock the store sprang into life. She decided now would be the time to get the girls settled in the arts and crafts area so they wouldn't be underfoot. "Come," she said in a conspiratorial whisper. "Let me show you what I found," and they followed her without a word. She opened the door, and the expressions on their faces reflected their delight in what they saw.

"This is amazing," Izzie said.

"Let's get you started on a project and then I shall have to go help Mr. Blunt as I'm sure it's going to be a busy day. How about a collage?"

"What's that?" Jess wanted to know.

"A collage is when you take all kinds of objects and stick them onto a piece of cardboard creating a design uniquely your own. When we look at the labels on the bins we can see Miss Ellie has all sorts of stuff you girls can use," and she pulled out a bright yellow container of buttons and then one with paper shapes. "The possibilities are endless and that's the fun of making a picture with different things; it just comes to life. For example, you could draw a big tree and then just put various things on the branches. Do you get the idea?"

"I see, now," Jess said, and Thea could tell she couldn't wait to get started. They found poster board in all sorts of colors and sizes, and they each chose a piece. "Do you think the two of you could manage on your own, at least for a little while, so I can go and help Mr. Blunt and Peter?"

"Sure," Izzie said, "I can help Jess."

"Please try to put things back where you found them as best you can. We don't want to leave a big mess for Miss Ellie."

"We will," said Jess, but Thea doubted whether her younger daughter would be able to carry through with her good intentions. Hopefully, Izzie would be able to keep her sister under control. She left them busily looking in all the bins and gathering stuff as they went, including glue, scissors and felt pens. "I'll leave the door partially open, and I'll be back to check on your masterpieces soon," but immediately engrossed in their project they didn't even acknowledge her. She left with the idea they should set up such an area at home on a much smaller scale and wondered why she hadn't thought of making a craft room before. Of course, this idea was based on the assumption they would be staying in the Maine house, but she didn't really want to think about the future and the decisions she might be forced to make.

The store was busy and there were several people waiting in line to pay for their merchandise. She decided to head over to the fabric section where two or three ladies were hovering because they looked as though they might need her help. Mr. Blunt glanced over and nodded and smiled at her, and she could see he was relieved to have an extra pair of hands. One of the women turned, clutching a bolt of pretty calico in a blue and white flowered pattern. She set it down on the cutting table, asking if she could please have two yards. All of a sudden, she looked intently at Thea and said, "Oh, my goodness, Thea, is that you?"

Thea wracked her brains for the woman's name and, thankfully, she remembered, "Mrs. Johnson, isn't it?"

"Yes, my dear. What brings you here?"

"I'm visiting Ellie. She invited me and my family for Thanksgiving." She noticed the other two women were getting antsy so not wanting to hold them up, she turned her attention to the bolt of fabric. She flipped it quickly, making thudding noises on the table as she unraveled what she needed. "Two yards, you said?"

"Yes, please. Where are you living these days?"

Thea stretched the fabric along the table and measured out two yards, making sure it was straight before taking the large pair of extremely sharp shears, which cut through the material like butter. "We live in Melford Point, Maine, close to Yarmouth," she said, folding the fabric into a neat square, checking the price, writing the amount on the receipt pad, tearing off the top copy and pinning the flimsy paper to the cloth. "Here, Mrs. Johnson," she said. "Is there anything else you need?"

"That will do it for today. It was good to see you."

"You, too."

She dealt with the other two women, giving advice when asked, and helping one of them with coordinating some different colors and patterns for a quilt. She had a good eye, and the woman thanked her profusely, pleased with the choices. When both the women headed to check out, she walked to the front of the store to see how Peter was getting on. He smiled at her briefly, but she didn't interrupt as she could see he was busy ringing up items and she silently thanked Theodore for having enough confidence in her son to let him do more than put items in bags. She wasn't even going to concern herself with child labor laws!

She returned to the sewing area to tidy up, rolling the fabric back onto the bolts and placing them where they belonged on the shelves. The door-bell jangled as people came and went, and then she looked up and saw a rather nice-looking auburn-haired man—neither young nor old, neither tall nor short—just somewhere in between. He wandered over to the jewelry case, so Thea went over to see if he needed any help. He turned to look at her and he surprised her by the unusual color of his eyes—they were really green—unlike her own which were more gray than green. "Do you have the key? There's a particular piece I'd like to see," he asked.

"Of course. I'll be right back."

"It's the middle piece at the back," and he pointed to a beautifully crafted silver pendant in the shape of a tree, intricately rendered in a deli-cate filigree pattern. Thea unhooked it and carefully laid it on the black velvet pad on top of the counter so he could get a really good look at the piece. She spread out the chain with her fingers and asked whether it was the right length, telling him it could be switched if he saw another one he liked better. She didn't know whether she had the right to make such a sug-gestion, but it seemed like a good sales tactic. She noticed his hands were square and strong with a dusting of reddish blonde hair, and the nails were trimmed and clean. She was beginning to wish she'd taken more trouble with her appearance, but she needn't have worried because if she'd had the ability to read his mind, she would have known he thought she looked just fine.

"I haven't seen you in here before. Are you new?" he asked.

"I'm only here for the weekend, temporarily helping out."

"I see," he said, and a flash of disappointment crossed his freckled face. "I'll take the pendant."

"Let me go find a box," she said, not sure whether she was dismayed or relieved to find their brief conversation had petered out. She had to ask Theodore where the boxes were, and he told her they were on his side of the counter, so she had to squeeze past him and Peter. She found the boxes neatly stacked in one of the lower drawers. Now on the other side of the counter from her customer, she was pretty much face to face with him when she lifted her head, and she did like what she saw.

"Would you mind gift wrapping it for me—I'm all fingers and thumbs—while I go find a greeting card? It's for my sister's birthday. She made buying a gift easy for me because she'd already chosen what she wanted."

"Of course. Which of these papers would you like?" and she pointed to the rolls of giftwrap.

"I like the one with all the different colored cats as she's particularly fond of cats."

Thea bent happily to the task, nestling the pendant neatly within the box in a piece of soft velvet and tearing off a strip of the paper and painstakingly making sure she wrapped the gift perfectly, finishing it off with a piece of striped ribbon. She wrote up the receipt and squeezed past Peter and Theodore again so she could lock up the jewelry case. She decided to go look for the man rather than waiting for him to return because she needed to go and check on her daughters. She found him by the rack of cards, slowly turning the display as he tried to make up his mind. He had narrowed his choice to two, and when he saw Thea he asked her which one she liked best, putting her on the spot. "I don't know your sister, so it's hard for me to choose, but how about this one, seeing as she likes cats—it's whimsical and cute," she said, indicating a card with a drawing of a cat with a bird sitting on its head.

"Thank you for making my job easier," and he smiled at her, showing a row of small, evenly spaced, exceptionally white teeth.

"I've left your box on the counter with the receipt. My son will ring up your purchase for you. Thank you for coming to Aladdin's Cave today," and she walked away.

Chris stood and watched Thea walk to the back of the store. She intrigued him, and the faint scent of roses lingered in his nostrils. What just happened here? He had noticed she wasn't wearing a wedding ring, but that didn't mean anything. Somehow, he would have to find out whether she was available because, as far as he was concerned, married women were off-limits. It had been quite a while since he had felt attracted to anyone—being dumped by Meggie had taken its toll and done a real number on his self-esteem. But she was long gone and the time had come to pick up the pieces and move on, and up until now he had had little inclination, stuck as he was in his disappointment and grief. Pining for her was a complete waste of time: after all, she had a new life, was now married and even had a baby on the way, so he supposed he should be grateful at least one of them was happy. Tired of being miserable, he really wanted to get to know this young woman better. He wasn't even put off by the fact she had a son, although she certainly didn't seem old enough to be the mother of the handsome boy who had rung up his purchases. However, right now, he really had no choice but to leave the store, and he decided to mull things over, as he had no doubt if he really wanted to see her again he would find a way.

Thea pushed open the craft room door to find Izzie and Jessica still totally absorbed in their project. She was surprised Jess had survived this long as she wasn't renowned for her attention span and usually flitted from thing to thing. She went around to the other side of the table and looked at what they had done. Izzie had drawn a dancer and then used all sorts of things—yarn for hair; buttons and beads for eyes, nose and mouth; felt circles for cheeks; fabric for clothes, plus some netting she'd used for a tutu. "How clever," she said, and put her arm around her daughter's slender shoulders.

Jess had drawn a house and had used a combination of pre-cut felt and paper shapes to make a roof and a door. For the windows, she had used pale blue paper and drawn squares for panes with a blue marker. She had taken lots of different colored beads and made them look like flowers. She had even added tiny buttons in the shape of a dog, a cat and a bird in a tree. Who couldn't be creative with all these wonderful materials to hand?

"Jess, your collage is absolutely beautiful," she said. "Have you had fun?"

"Yes, but I want to eat now." The morning had completely gone and it was indeed lunchtime.

"Why don't the three of us hop down to the Harvest Bakery and pick up some sandwiches? Your pictures will have time to dry properly and we can clean up after we've eaten. How does that sound?" Thea asked.

The girls agreed. She suggested they try and wash some of the glue off their hands, so they turned to the sink under which rested a handy stool for Jessica to stand on so she could reach the faucet. Again, Ellie had left no stone unturned. They each took turns to visit the tiny bathroom under the stairs, after which they grabbed their coats and went off to ask Peter and Mr. Blunt what they would like for lunch.

Once lunch was over and done with and the craft room cleaned up, Thea asked Theodore if she could use the phone to call her parents. The girls were getting fidgety, and seeing as things had calmed down, she thought Theodore would be able to manage on his own. There was still no sign of Ellie, and even though she was extremely concerned about her friend, she needed to touch base with her mom and dad. Her dad answered the phone and she asked if it would be all right if they came for a visit, and he said, "Of course. We'd love to see you." She didn't think she and the kids would get the same enthusiastic reception from her mom, but she just couldn't worry about her reticence anymore.

Soon they were all back in the minivan and heading out of town. The road was familiar to her, and before long she was pulling into her parents' driveway. There was the big oak tree, majestic in its winter starkness, under which she had sat all those years ago, scouring the local newspaper and finding the job that led her to Ellie and Aladdin's Cave. She turned to the girls and suggested they bring stuff in with them to do, including a couple of games, so Peter grabbed *Sorry* and *Monopoly*. "The visit probably won't be too much fun, but they are my mom and dad so we have to make the best of it and I know I can depend on you."

Henry opened the door as soon as they rang the bell. His face broke into a beaming smile at the sight of them all, revealing the mostly hidden, kindly man who had surfaced briefly all those years ago when he had helped her buy her first car, and the memory tugged at Thea's heartstrings. "Come in," he said, moving back awkwardly so they could crowd into the tiny hallway, still using a cane and leaning heavily on his good leg. She looked up to see her mom standing shyly in the kitchen doorway, and she handed her the cake she had bought at the Harvest Bakery earlier.

She certainly didn't expect her mother to make them supper, but tea and cake would be nice. Peter said, "Hi, Grandma," and Thea watched her mother's face light up. She continued to be amazed at her son's ability to spark Enid's emotions, something she had failed to accomplish no matter how hard she tried, but instead of being envious, she was proud of Peter and pleased for her mother.

Her dad appeared to be in his element as he helped the girls off with their coats. Jessica chatted away as usual, and Izzie—always the sensitive one—asked him about his ankle, to which he replied, "Coming along nicely."

Enid had tentatively moved towards them, and she turned to her husband and said, "Henry, could you stay with the children just for a little while? There's something I'd like to show Thea."

"Of course," he said.

Thea's curiosity was piqued, although a little taken aback, as her mother didn't usually seek out her company. "I'll be right back," she said, "be good for your Grandpa." She followed her mother down the hallway into the room that used to be her bedroom. The room looked much the same except there were two large boxes sitting side by side on the floor. Her mother went to the first box and opened up the lid, pulling out a roll of tightly wound paper, turning and holding it out to Thea. "Here," she said, "I saved all your drawings right from when you were a little girl."

"You did?" Thea, delighted and surprised, sat down on the bed and carefully started to unroll her artwork.

Her mother came and sat down beside her and nudged one of the boxes with her foot. "I saved all your little-girl things. I never had anything when I was growing up, so I wanted it to be different for you and I thought maybe you'd like to share them with Jessica and Izzie. I should have given them to you long ago."

Thea thought if she didn't ask now the opportunity would be lost. "What happened to you?"

Enid breathed a huge sigh, crossed her hands in her lap, and looked at her daughter. "I spent my childhood in an orphanage. I was the proverbial baby in a basket left on the doorstep. I've never been able to find out who I am or where I came from and that's why it's important you have these things. There's nothing worse in the whole wide world than not having an identity. It's very difficult for me to show emotion, but I do care."

"Oh, Mom, I know you do. What you have just told me explains so much."

A brief smile crossed Enid's face, wiping away her normally sad expression. "Now, I don't want you feeling sorry for me because I consider myself blessed with good fortune, despite my humble beginnings. Meeting your father was divine providence, and gave me the nudge I needed to leave the orphanage. You see, I never managed to get away; I just stayed and helped, became a kind of poorly paid drudge. One day, I went to the bank where your father worked to deposit a check, and I tripped over the mat in the entranceway. Your father was coming in the doorway right behind me and saw me fall, so he helped me to my feet. Of course, I was terribly embarrassed, but he made light of it and asked if he could take me out to dinner. I don't know what came over me because as you know I am painfully shy, but I saw your dad as a ticket to freedom and I told him the truth right from the beginning. I wanted to be honest even though my telling him might have scared him away, but luckily it didn't. We didn't get married right away. Just took our time to get to know each other before tying the knot. He has given me a good life, and I loved you as best I knew how, but I know it wasn't enough."

"Actually, it was. I believe I'm a good mother, and I have you and Dad to thank for instilling me with good basic values. You both gave me stability, something many of my school friends didn't have. I could always rely on your being here in the house and always being consistent in the way you raised me. Also, there must be some latent artistic genes somewhere in your lineage that were passed along to me, for which I'm truly grateful. Mom, I'm so pleased you told me and thank you so much for saving all my stuff," and she reached over and took her mother's tiny hand within her own. She didn't dare hug her because she believed the dam would burst, but holding her mother's hand was almost enough.

"Your children are a credit to you. You are a good mother, and you have done a wonderful job."

"Thank you, Mom. I've made a lot of mistakes, but the kids have always come first. Shall we go see what they're up to? I'd love a piece of cake."

They found the four of them sitting around the table in the dining room playing *Sorry*. Henry had found a big fat cushion for Jess to sit on, and she was exceedingly gleeful because she was winning. Thea's heart swelled with pride at the adaptability of these children of hers. They had surpassed themselves this weekend, despite the rather strange circumstances in which they had found themselves and their adaptability had surprised her. Thea's concern over Ellie was beginning to consume her; she couldn't wait to get to the root of the problem, and planned to tackle it later. In the meantime, she decided to take pleasure in being with her parents, finally truly accepting them for the people they were, warts and all.

They all enjoyed the lemon cake and Thea could tell the kids were amazed they were being allowed to eat cake when it wasn't anyone's birthday, but she had decided being with her parents and having a good time reason enough for a celebration. Her mom even had milk for the kids, and the tea she served in the delicate china cups was hot and fragrant. How wonderful it must have been for her mother to have a place of her own after all those years in an orphanage. Now she understood the drab and dowdy furnishings and color scheme—her mother was just grateful for anything. She observed her father having a grand old time and even getting a little rowdy—most unusual for him, as by nature he was reserved and formal.

Thea didn't want to outstay their welcome, so after a couple of hours she said it was time for them to go, but they would come back tomorrow. Henry helped them put the *Sorry* game back into the box and congratulated Jessica for being the winner. She was elated by the praise and grinning from ear to ear, but Thea could tell she was tired. The last thing she needed was for her daughter to have one of her meltdowns, so she hustled them out of the house before disaster could strike. Peter, as tall as his grandma, kissed her goodbye. "Thank you for having us," he said, shaking his Grandpa's hand.

"Thanks, Mom. We'll be back for the boxes tomorrow," she said, kissing her mother on the cheek just before stepping outside. The evening sky was cloud-covered, the air brutally cold, and they huddled into the van as quickly as they could. She got the heater blasting and headed off to Ellie's, absolutely dreading what she might have to face.

CHAPTER TWENTY

JIM AND MARYANN

Jim stepped back from MaryAnn, cupping her face in his hands and wiping the tears away with the soft part of his thumbs. "I'm sorry, I shouldn't have kissed you," he said.

"Don't be," she said, giving him a watery smile.

He pulled a large, blindingly white handkerchief from the left-hand pocket of his khaki pants and gave it to her. "Do I have mascara running down my cheeks?" she asked.

"Just a little, but you look beautiful."

"I'll ruin your handkerchief."

"Do you think I care about that? Here, let me," and he softly wiped her cheeks. "Much as I would like to stay in the den with you, we really must go and find the others before they find us. Okay?"

MaryAnn parted from Jim and went to the powder room to compose herself before going back to join everyone. She remembered the feel of Jim's hands and noticed he had made a passable attempt at removing the mascara. The face reflected in the mirror seemed softer somehow, less angular, and she touched the glass with her finger just to make sure the reflection was real. MaryAnn had no illusions—she knew she wasn't beautiful—but there was no way she was going to argue with Jim if he wanted to perceive her in such a way. Jim made her feel alive, but it was her betrayal of Sam's memory that was bringing her down and causing the tears. She believed he would want her to move on, but she was finding the transition difficult. Sam had been her one and only love, and switching gears was so hard, but her love for Jim was different—raw and exciting and downright scary. Well aware this wouldn't be the last time she would cry in his arms, she hoped he was up for the emotional ride. Her lips still tingled from where Jim had kissed her, but the tingling didn't stop there and the depth of her feelings surprised her. He'd woken her up, all right! She took a deep breath, tried to wipe the silly grin off her face, left the bathroom, and closed the door gently behind her.

There was much activity in the kitchen. The football game was winding down, and there was a lot of groaning as it appeared as though their favorite team had lost. Jennifer had set out a great mound of sandwiches on the kitchen island together with the leftover pies and brownies and a huge bowl of potato chips. Jim winked at her as he held out a plate so she could gather some food, and despite all she had consumed earlier, she couldn't believe she was ready to eat again. She noticed Ben regarding her benevolently and she wondered what he was thinking. She sensed the brothers were close and believed she wouldn't be welcome if she did anything to hurt Jim. Ben eyed them both and she could tell he sensed something different between them. She wanted to tell him it was a good different, and then he surprised her by whispering in her ear, "Thank you for breaking the spell," and she knew exactly what he meant.

The boys were delighted to have more food to eat, washed down with big glasses of frothy milk. Jennifer had the three little ones sit on the tall stools along one edge of the island, a strategic move on her part to avoid spills; besides which, being so high up made them feel important, not that the twins needed any help in the self-confidence department, but it helped Johnny. After filling her plate, MaryAnn went off to find Ian who was sitting happily in front of the TV, a rare treat for him. He would have watched anything and MaryAnn chose not to play the censor monster in someone else's house. She sat down beside him and squeezed his knee. "Enjoying yourself, sport?"

"I'm having an awesome time."

"How about you?"

"Much more than I thought I would, but we're going to have to write thank you notes."

"You had to go and spoil it, didn't you? You know how I hate writing thank you notes."

"Yeah, yeah, but it's worth it, isn't it, so we get invited again."

Jim came and sat down on the other side of Ian, so her son was between them. He was playing it safe, and she was glad. She munched happily on her potato chips, a favorite food she ate rarely because they were so bad, savoring the salty crunch. What a day of forbidden pleasures and she sent up a silent prayer, "Please forgive me, Sam." She got up and went off to the kitchen for a piece of pie. Johnny was still sitting on his high stool, happily swinging his legs back and forth. His mouth was absolutely stuffed with food, and she saw his hand dart into the bowl of potato chips and grab another handful. Poppy and Daisy were beginning to get whiny and she could see how tired Jennifer was, so she sensed they would have to leave soon. Elizabeth was sitting quietly in one of the chairs by the fire reading a book, having given up totally on trying to be sociable. MaryAnn took a piece of pumpkin pie to be polite, although she would rather have had her Dutch apple, but it would have been rude to eat her own dessert, especially as there were only a couple of slices left. She went over to Elizabeth and said, "We should exchange phone numbers. I'd love to spend some time with you talking books."

Elizabeth pulled a cell phone from her bag and set up a new contact asking MaryAnn for her number. She wrote her own on a scrap of paper and handed it to MaryAnn. "Thanks, Elizabeth, we'll talk soon. Have a safe drive home."

"Oh, I'm staying over and driving back in the morning. I really enjoyed meeting you," and she went back to her book.

MaryAnn went and sat next to Pat and asked her how long they were staying. "We're flying out on Tuesday. That way, we avoid the Thanksgiving rush. Have you had a good time?"

"Yes, it was kind of Jennifer to include us. It's hard to invite strangers into your house, especially on such a family-oriented holiday as Thanksgiving."

"Hopefully, we'll see you again next year and then you won't be strangers at all," and she smiled at MaryAnn. "Don't look so surprised. I've seen the way you and Jim look at each other. Sorry, now I've embarrassed you, but please don't be shy, my dear. Jim is a wonderful man and he's been on his own for far too long, and I'll say no more because it's actually none of my business, but I'm a big romantic at heart."

"You've all been extremely generous."

"Just cherish each other and don't have expectations which can't be met. All you have to give is unconditional love—it's as simple as that."

Suddenly MaryAnn wasn't hungry anymore and she glanced down at the pie on her plate with distaste.

"There's been a lot of sadness in your life hasn't there, but it's going to be all right now, you'll see," and Pat reached over and touched her hand. "It's okay, you don't have to say anything. Just stop trying to go it alone."

For all Pat's airy chatter earlier in the day, MaryAnn recognized one astute woman.

"Thank you. I really appreciate your taking an interest. I'm so pleased we came today, but now I must go rally the troops," and she leaned over and kissed the older woman on the cheek, not only surprising Pat but also herself.

Poppy and Daisy were close to meltdown, and Ben was attempting to calm them down by promising piggyback rides and their favorite bedtime stories. Somewhat mollified they quieted down and Jennifer stayed with Daisy while her dad played giddy-up, cantering down the hallway with her sister. Once he came back to retrieve Daisy, she went off to the girls' room to get them ready for bed.

MaryAnn told the kids it was time to go home. Elizabeth had dragged herself away from her book and she and Pat were cleaning up the kitchen. Jim went off to find coats and shoes and soon they were all dressed to leave with MaryAnn clutching her empty, but now clean, pie plate. Jennifer came back to say goodbye, and MaryAnn gave her a hug and told her how much they had enjoyed themselves. The boys said thank you and Jim leaned over and kissed his sister-in-law on the cheek, said goodbye to the rest of the family, and then the four of them were out in the dark and the cold.

MaryAnn sat deep in her own thoughts. It was hard to leave the warmth of the log house behind when the only thing greeting her and the boys was her dark, cold and dreary rental. Convinced the boys were experiencing the same reluctance to go home, her bubble of happiness rapidly deflated.

Jim looked at her with a worried expression on his face, wondering what had happened. It seemed as if they had all left their lightheartedness behind in Jennifer's kitchen, but he wasn't going to give up. When they arrived at his house, he parked the truck beside MaryAnn's car. Turning to the boys, he asked them to stay there just for a second because he wanted to ask their mom a question. He left the engine running so they wouldn't get cold and went around to the passenger side and opened her door. She swung her slender legs out and stood up.

"MaryAnn, I can't let you go home tonight. Would you and the boys please stay? I won't pressure you into anything, I promise. I just want to talk. I want to get to know you."

She was so tempted, and she suddenly thought, why not?

"I have spare toothbrushes if you're worried about not being able to clean your teeth," he said in the hope she would say yes.

"If the boys agree, we'll stay."

"Thank you. Will you ask them or shall I?"

"Let me," she said, opening the passenger door and sticking her head inside. "Mr. Hudson has asked us to stay the night. What do you think?"

There was absolutely no hesitation on their part and Johnny was bouncing up and down on the seat going, "Yes, please, but I don't have my PJs."

Jim had opened his door by this time and said, "I'm already ahead of the game because I was hoping you might sleep over, so I have everything you need. Let's get you in out of the cold and I know Carrie is going to be really pleased to see us all." He leaned the seat forward and reached in to take hold of Johnny who put his arms around Jim's neck and allowed himself to be carried into the house, and MaryAnn relinquished whatever doubts she had about her decision.

She and Ian followed Jim around to the left-hand side of the house. Johnny looked back at them over Jim's shoulder, grinning madly, and MaryAnn thought this has to be the right thing to do if staying over made her younger son so happy. Jim set Johnny down gently and reached into his pocket for his keys. The outside of the house was brightly lit, so he didn't have any problem finding the lock. Carrie had heard them and was making soft whining noises on the other side of the door. The warmth of the kitchen hit them as soon as Jim opened the door and they all hurried inside out of the bitter cold. Jim flipped a switch, and the illuminated room was just as she had remembered when they had stayed for supper earlier in the week—clean and neat and shiny with nothing out of place. Carrie was excited to see the boys and the three of them were all over each other. She even tolerated Johnny putting his arms around her and giving her a gentle hug.

"Let's go see where you're going to sleep," Jim said, and they all went out into the hallway. He took each of their coats and hung them in the closet, and MaryAnn was relieved to see the contents of the closet in a bit of a jumble. They had already taken off their shoes and placed them on the rubber boot mat by the kitchen door, and she had a moment of panic, hoping the boys' socks matched and were without holes, but she needn't have worried—Jim wouldn't have cared anyway.

They padded up the stairs behind Jim, and Carrie waited patiently at the bottom step emitting little whines of protest. "She's not allowed up the stairs because I'm afraid she'll slip and hurt herself, so I trained her to stay down there. She doesn't like being by herself, but she wouldn't like a broken leg either, so it's best she stay where she is."

Ian said, "I think that's a really smart idea."

They reached the landing, walking past the picture MaryAnn had so admired, and up the second set of stairs bringing them into a long wood-paneled hallway with several doors on either side. Again, there was an oriental rug, and this one stretched the full length of the passageway. There were old-fashioned sconces on the walls giving off a soft peach colored light. The boys were in awe and looked around them. There were pictures all along the walls and she couldn't wait to get a better look at them in the daylight. The long window at the far end had a built-in window seat and she could just imagine herself sitting there all curled up with a good book. Jim kept walking until they came to the last bedroom on the left. "This is your room, and I put you both in here as I thought you'd like to be together. If not, there's plenty of space if you'd like to each have a room." Both the boys glanced around in wonder, taking in their surroundings, and Ian turned to Johnny and said, "We'd like to be together, wouldn't we?" and his brother nodded, reaching over and rubbing his hand over the bright red fuzzy blanket draped over the bed he was standing next to. "This is so soft," he said. The room was plainly decorated in pale blues, navy and red and on each twin bed there were books and Ian's face lit up when he saw one of them was *Harry Potter and the Half-Blood Prince*. "Mr. Hudson, how did you know? I've had my name on the waiting list at the library for the longest time."

"Lucky guess, and I'd like to read the book when you're done. I'm a fan!"

"Have you seen all the movies?"

"Sure have. I'm a bit of an Anglophile, as you will soon find out, which means I like anything to do with England," he added by way of explanation when he saw Ian's puzzled expression.

Ian picked up the book and started thumbing the pages, pulling out the bookmark Jim had thoughtfully included. "I'll take good care of it, I promise."

There were two books on the bed where Johnny would sleep, and Jim had placed a bookmark in one of those too. He sat down on top of the fuzzy blanket and picked up one of them. "This was my book when I was a little boy. Enid Blyton, the lady who wrote the book, is from England and so was my grandfather, and he loved her stories so much he made sure we had copies of all her books when we were growing up. She was born a long time ago and she died in 1968, but the really great thing about writing stories is no one ever forgets you, especially when the stories are really good. There's a library here in the house and I'll show it to you tomorrow. In the meantime, I chose *The Magic Faraway Tree,* and I'm sure Ian would be happy to help you with the words. The other one is another favorite of mine, but it's yours to keep, and he handed Johnny *The Enormous Crocodile* by Roald Dahl.

Johnny, although almost speechless, did manage to say, "Thank you, Mr. Hudson." MaryAnn just stood and watched, pinching herself every now and again to make sure she wasn't in the midst of some incredible fantasy.

"You are very welcome. Let me show you where the bathroom is and then I'll leave you with your mom to get settled. She'll be in the room right next to you and the lights will be on in the hallway so you'll be able to find your way around."

The bathroom was huge and very white. MaryAnn expected the decorations to be manly, but they weren't—the room was a complete surprise and, again, spotlessly clean. There was a huge claw-foot tub, a pedestal sink with a medicine cabinet above, and a toilet in the corner by the window over which hung a soft pleated shade. There were three huge plants absolutely thriving and those, together with the warmth of the old wooden floor, created an atmosphere of total luxury. Jim broke into her thoughts, "Welcome to the guest bathroom," he said. "A few years ago, I added a bathroom off the bedroom I use, and there's a shower in there if anyone doesn't like baths. Jennifer worked her magic, and there's the whole kit and caboodle in here, and he grasped the glass knobs and pulled open the two doors of the floor to ceiling closet to the right of the tub revealing every toiletry imaginable. He reached in and extracted three toothbrushes and a tube of toothpaste, pajamas for the boys, and much to her embarrassment, a nightgown for MaryAnn. "It used to be my mother's," he said, "And somehow, I didn't think you'd mind."

MaryAnn held the garment to her nose and breathed in the faint scent of lavender. "It's so soft," she said. "I'd be honored to wear it." He looked at her and smiled and she believed she had made him happy with her genuine and enthusiastic response. They were both feeling their way, testing the waters, and so far she was willing to keep her toes in, but only on the edge.

"Okay. I'm going to leave you to it. Goodnight boys. I'll see you in the morning."

"Goodnight, Mr. Hudson, and thank you."

MaryAnn looked at her boys and said, "Can you believe all this? I feel as though I'm in a wonderful dream. Just the heat from this radiator would be enough to satisfy me," and she leaned back against it to feel the warmth through her clothes. Reluctantly, she pulled herself away and said, "Let's clean our teeth."

Johnny had wanted the red toothbrush; Ian took the blue, and MaryAnn the yellow. She would come back later and gaze at the treasures in the closet. She had noticed a whole shelf of lotions and cosmetics and she couldn't wait to explore, but for now, she wanted to see the boys tucked snuggly in their beds. The pajamas were a perfect fit and almost as soft as her nightgown and she wondered if they, too, were old, but she didn't think so. Jim must have washed them to get the stiffening out.

She stood at the end of their beds and told the boys they could read for a while. They each had a lamp within reach, and with ample light from the hallway they wouldn't have any trouble finding their way to the bathroom, but she doubted either of them would get up. "I'll be right next door if you need me. I expect Mr. Hudson and I will sit and talk for a while, but when I come to bed I'll be close by, and if you want me for anything before I come back upstairs, please don't hesitate to come and find me. Okay?" They nodded absent-mindedly and were immediately engrossed in their books—they didn't even notice her leave.

Still holding the nightgown, she wandered into the bedroom where she was to sleep. She turned on the light to see the room better and again, there were two single beds. Noticing the tasteful decorations in various shades of lavender with deep cream accents, she wondered whether Jennifer had also had a hand in this. If so, the woman had exquisite taste as the room was pretty and elegant without being fussy. She gently laid the nightgown on the bed nearest the door and made her way down the hallway and back downstairs.

Jim heard her coming and walked across the hallway to meet her just as she reached the bottom of the stairs, Carrie trailing at his heels. "I guess we have a chaperone," he said, and MaryAnn laughed. "Would you like anything to drink?"

"I'd love a long tall glass of water. After the wine and too many potato chips, I'm really thirsty."

He opened one of the cupboards in the kitchen and pulled out two tall shiny glasses and proceeded to fill them with tap water. "Would you like ice?"

"No thank you," and she took the proffered glass from his hand and drank deeply.

"Come, we'll go sit somewhere more cozy so we can talk," and MaryAnn's heart sank as she suspected she was going to be coaxed into revealing even more of herself.

Jim opened one of the doors off the hallway and MaryAnn found herself standing in the doorway looking into a small room with a TV in one corner. A plaid sofa ran along the back wall, mostly in blue with a deep red and gold stripe running through the fabric; a burgundy chair in the corner sat diagonally from the TV, and a chunky coffee table in honey-colored pine resided on a dark red braided rug. Again, another of those big fat, deliciously warm radiators sat under the window. Jim crossed the room and pulled the drapes across. They were plain blue and matched the sofa perfectly. He lit the lamps on either side of the couch and said, "Please don't be shy. Come and sit down." He made no attempt to touch her for which she was grateful. Now they were truly alone, physical contact would be dangerous, and she didn't want to reignite the fire, especially with the boys upstairs. This wasn't why she had agreed to stay. She wholeheartedly believed if the relationship was to move forward she had to be honest with Jim, but it was going to be difficult and she was apprehensive.

She sat on the edge of the couch and placed her glass of water on one of the coasters on the side table to the left of her. She felt awkward and nervous and suddenly aware of how little she knew Jim. After all, she had only met him less than a week ago and she hoped her intuition had been right to trust him. MaryAnn watched Jim sit down in the chair and lean back, and she wondered how to break the ice. She looked sideways at him through the fronds of her hair, and he said, "Can you tell me why you were crying earlier? I didn't mean to make you sad."

"You didn't," she said. "It's complicated."

"Do you trust me? I know we're just getting to know each other, but you have nothing to fear from me."

"I know. And, yes, I do trust you. I wouldn't be here now if I didn't. I don't really know where to start, but you deserve to know the truth. As you can probably guess, the boys and I have fallen on hard times. I'm struggling to make ends meet, and I live in a dump I can't afford to heat properly. I can't invite you over because I'm afraid you'll want to rescue us and that would start our relationship off on the wrong footing. You have so much in the way of material comforts and the boys and I have so little, but we manage. Not well at times, but we get by."

"Can I ask what happened to the boys' dad?"

"Sam died of cancer three years ago, and when he died something in me died, too. I've just been going through the motions, carving out an existence for us, but that's all it is. Even without the shadow of my grief, constantly living from hand to mouth wears you down. Social situations are especially hard because I don't want to reveal my circumstances. I'm afraid I've been hiding, but it's no longer fair to isolate the boys just because it's easier for me. This is the reason why I accepted Thea's invitation to have dinner last Sunday and your invitation to spend Thanksgiving with your family, but the only problem is it makes going home so much harder. When you kissed me, I felt so disloyal to Sam even though I know he would want me to move on. You've stirred up all these deeply buried emotions, and I don't know what to do with them. I don't want people thinking you've taken on the boys and me as some kind of charity project. What you gave my boys today was..." and choked up, she just couldn't go on.

Jim pushed himself out of his chair and came over to kneel in front of her, tipping up her face with his fingers, and reaching into his pocket for his handkerchief. "I guess you need this again," and she took it gratefully, wiping her cheeks and blowing her nose.

He sat down beside her and took her hand. "Let's get things straight right from the start. You and the boys are not a charity project. I am spend-ing time with you because I want to be with you. You have awakened something in me, too, and of course I want to make things better for you, but it has to be on your own terms. I won't do anything you don't want me to, but for the sake of the boys, please let me help you."

"I'm so afraid of this deep attraction I have to you. Sam and I built our relationship over time. We met at college; we were both the same age, and it all seemed so simple compared with this. He was the only man I had ever been with, and we waited until we got married before we made love. We were both really career-minded, and I had to keep my grades up because of my scholarship, so we buried the passion we had for each other at the beginning. He was my best friend, and by the time we consummated our love, our coming together was comforting and good, but I can't say there were any fireworks. But we were so happy, and our marriage was rock solid. We ran a successful photography business out of our home, looked after our boys, and I never wanted for anything. Then Sam got sick, and we lost everything. I had to sell the house, the goodwill for the business and all the equipment to pay for the medical bills. We were left with nothing except our clothing, a few pieces of furniture, and the boys' books and toys, and I wasn't going to let anyone take those."

"What about Sam's parents?"

"Initially, they were really helpful. At least George, Sam's dad, was. They came to stay during the last few weeks of Sam's illness and he helped me with making sure I got a good price for the business, but Sandy, Sam's mother, couldn't bear to be around Ian. He is the spitting image of Sam and it was all too much for her—she couldn't stand the constant reminder. I was so sad for Ian: not only had he lost his dad, but he also lost his grandparents. We never see them. They send birthday and Christmas cards and some money, which helps, believe you me, but I don't spend all of it. I put what's left into a savings account for the boys. To tell the truth, it's really our emergency fund, something to fall back on should, heaven forbid, any of us get really sick."

"What about your family?"

"They live in New York State and I did think about going and staying with them, but it wouldn't be practical. I'm the oldest of seven and the house is already bursting at the seams. My mother would have taken us in out of the goodness of her heart, but my parents don't have any money either and my father drinks rather too much, as do a lot of my uncles. It's not the best of environments and I left because I was determined to better myself, so thrusting Ian and Johnny into a less than ideal situation would have been worse than us attempting to make it on our own."

"You've got a lot of spunk, MaryAnn Wilkinson, and I admire you for it. Thank you for being so honest. Do you have any questions for me?"

"Please tell me about Thea. I bared my soul, so now it's your turn."

"There's not much to tell. I met her when she first moved here after her marriage to Michael Chamberlin. I was instantly attracted to her, but she was married, and unreachable. I would never go after another man's wife. I only ever saw her when she came into the store, which was hardly ever, once she became pregnant with Peter. Eventually, the marriage collapsed; she and Michael divorced and she took up with one of my employees—Kenny Evinson. The relationship was a total disaster, but there was nothing I could do about the hole she was about to dig, and it was really none of my business. Our paths crossed after she asked Kenny to leave. He showed up in the Country Store that same day and frightened both

Jessica and Thea badly, and I accompanied the two of them home and stayed with her and the kids while the locks were being changed. Then, I tried to help out at the time of Jessica's abduction, and just recently after Kenny tried to break in during one of his drunken rampages. I returned to her house the next day and replaced her back door which had been damaged during the fight, and as a thank you, she invited me over for dinner last Sunday, and that's when I met you."

"Thank you for telling me. I feel so much better now things are out in the open. Are you sure the boys and I aren't a poor substitute?"

"MaryAnn, what do I have to do to make you believe me?" She felt Jim put his arm around her, and he leaned back into the sofa pulling her gently with him until she was lying against him with her head on his shoulder. "You can't tell me our being together like this isn't right and you don't have to worry about Thea. I thought the life I had envisioned with her was real, and yes in my mind it was, but it was just a fantasy I created for myself, and I never held her in my arms, never kissed her. You can't make someone love you, and our feelings for each other would have been lopsided so it would never have worked. As I said before, you broke the spell and the relationship we are creating together is factual and not some figment of my imagination," he said, squeezing her tight. "Anyway, you smell different," and he buried his nose in her hair, "of shampoo and toothpaste and a little bit like turkey and gravy."

She bent forward and pulled away from him so she could look into his face. "Well, that's nice. I'm never going to stir gravy ever again," she said, appreciating his humor. "I think you and I are going to have a lot of fun together. Just remember I grew up in a big family and I can throw a punch with the best of them, but not tonight. I really need to go to bed. I'm sorry, but I'm absolutely exhausted and I have to go to work tomorrow. Will's been very good to me and I can't let him down."

Reluctant to move away from the warmth of Jim's body, but knowing out of self-respect she had no choice, she leaned forward and pushed herself up from the couch. He got to his feet and said, "Can I kiss you?"

She was so tired she was almost swaying on her feet, but she rested against him as he put his hands on either side of her neck, moving his fingers gently up into her hair and tilting her face to meet his. The kiss was slow and lingering and aroused so much passion. Jim's kisses were nothing like the ones she had shared with Sam—for one thing Jim was clean shaven, although a little prickly this late in the day—and Sam had had a beard. MaryAnn unwillingly pulled herself out of his embrace, placing her hands on his chest and pushing him firmly away. "Being so close to you is dangerous, Jim. I would never be able to forgive myself if things got out of hand. I have my sons to think about."

"I know. You go on to bed. What time do you need to be woken up, and I'll set my alarm?"

"Really early I'm afraid. Let's say six thirty?"

"Why don't you let the boys stay with me tomorrow."

"Don't you have to work? Remember, it's Black Friday, and having two kids underfoot might not be such a good idea."

"You're right, but I don't have to be there all the time. There are advantages to being the boss man."

In reality, MaryAnn didn't want to leave Jim and go off to her lonely room, but she knew it was the right decision. She reached up and lovingly touched his cheek, gave him a soft kiss, and said, "Thank you for everything. You are a thoughtful and kindhearted man."

"And you are a lovely woman," and she could sense him watching her as she climbed the stairs, so she turned and blew him a kiss when she reached the landing. She was weary, but it was a good kind of tired. Instead of being drained and hopeless, she was filled with warmth. This inner glow was a tangible thing, and she smiled. When she turned off the light she'd probably glow in the dark, just like the fluorescent stars on Ian's ceiling in the house where she had lived with Sam. Even thinking about Sam did nothing to quench her newfound hope because she had to believe he would approve.

Jim, finding it difficult to fall asleep, lay on his back with his hands under his head and stared at the ceiling. He couldn't believe how much his life had changed in less than a week. He loved MaryAnn—there were no two ways about it—he admired her courage, her moral principles, and the way she was bringing up her boys. Knowing she was just down the hallway was exquisite torture, but there was no way he would go to her. He respected her for her strength of character, and she was right, the boys did come first. To send them mixed signals would be completely unfair and he suspected it would take Ian a long time to accept him as a father figure, so he wasn't going to push his luck. Johnny was a different story. He was so little when Sam died and Jim sensed he had already won his heart. The little boy trusted him completely so he certainly wasn't going to betray his trust by making moves on his mother before she was ready and before both Johnny and Ian understood completely what their plans for the future were. Eventually, he rolled over, pulled the covers up around his neck, and fell into a deep and dreamless sleep.

The alarm startled him awake at six thirty. He unhooked his robe from the back of his bedroom door, shrugged into the soft fleece, and then padded quietly down the hallway to MaryAnn's room. Instead of one blonde head on the pillow, there was a small dark one as well. Johnny had found his way into MaryAnn's bed; he was snuggled up against her, and they were both fast asleep. She looked so peaceful, and he hated to wake her. He walked around the other side of the bed and leaned over and kissed her on the cheek, whispering in her ear, "MaryAnn, it's time to wake up."

She groaned, "Okay. I won't go back to sleep, I promise, and by the way you're very stubbly," and she grinned. "You need to leave now so a lady can have her privacy."

"Yes, ma'am." He wanted to tell her he loved her, but he didn't dare.

CHAPTER TWENTY-ONE

THEA AND ELLIE

It was almost dark by the time Thea and the kids got back to Ellie's. The house appeared to be all lit up and she felt a little spark of hope—she so wanted Ellie to be better. She and the children huddled together on the porch, the cold of the evening seeping into their clothes. Thea reached up to ring the doorbell, but Robert must have heard them coming because just as she was about to push the bell, the door opened. Robert stood there looking tired and drawn, with Honey at his heels, and Thea sensed the reason for his downtrodden appearance was not a good one. "Please come in," he said. They trooped in one by one—decidedly glad to be in the warmth of the hallway. Even Honey seemed subdued, and not really wanting to know what the answer would be, Thea asked Robert how Ellie was.

"She's still not very well, but I know she wants to talk to you."

Thea nodded. The situation was exceedingly awkward, and she would soon have three children to feed because a slice of cake wasn't going to last them until morning. She tried, but failed, to break through Robert's hopelessness and he seemed overwhelmed by the sight of these virtual strangers standing in his sister's hallway.

"Have you had any supper?" she asked.

"*Non*," he said, reverting to his native language.

"Would you mind if I fixed us all something to eat?"

The children were standing huddled together completely at a loss. Even Jessica stood quietly, although she was getting very hot and would have liked to take her coat off, but she didn't dare move.

Robert looked at them and Thea wondered whether he had even heard her question. She turned to the children and said, "Why don't you take off your coats?" Jessica didn't need to be told twice and unzipped her jacket, unwinding her scarf at the same time and getting in a terrible mess. Peter stepped in to help her and she didn't make any of her usual comments about being able to do it herself. Izzie methodically hung up the coats as they were handed to her and Thea suggested the children go off and find something to do for about half an hour. She noticed Robert had wandered away, leaving a little pool of sadness in the hallway and his despondency was bringing them all down. "I'm sorry about this," she said. "I've no idea what's going on, but I'll go find something for us all to eat and then I'll come and get you, unless you want to sit in the kitchen with me. It's up to you."

"It's okay, Mom. We'll be all right," Peter said and he reached out and grasped his sisters' hands, gently pulling them in the direction of the bedrooms.

"See you in a little while," she said, and went off to the kitchen where she found Robert sitting on one of the stools at the breakfast bar with his head in his hands. Honey lay glumly at his feet.

"Is Mr. Blunt here?" she asked.

"I would imagine so," Robert said.

"Does he normally eat supper with you and Ellie?" She was concerned about him and wondered how he had made out at the store after she and the children had left.

"Sometimes."

She walked across to the refrigerator and opened the door. The contents seemed pretty much as she had left them yesterday. "I'm just going to heat up some of these leftovers," she said, bending over and retrieving the platter of turkey. "Would you like me to put a plate together for you?"

"I don't feel much like eating."

Thea folded her arms across her chest and vented her frustration. "Neither do I, but I do have to feed my kids."

Robert slid off the stool and started to walk away. "I'm sorry, Thea. I just can't talk to you right now."

Thea was suddenly overcome by a sense of total desperation. The situation was just so horrible and she had absolutely no one to turn to, but she had to pull herself together and put on a brave face for the children's sake. She was actually relieved to see Robert walk away as his melancholia triggered her own despair—she had no desire to travel down his dark road. She busied herself getting plates out of the cupboard and portioning out the food onto each one, heating them in the microwave and then putting them in the oven to keep warm. Once all the plates were done, she put the remaining food back in the fridge and went off to get the kids.

She sat them around the kitchen table, finding a pillow for Jess to boost her up and they all ate silently. She could tell the kids were tired, hardly surprising considering the day they'd had, and even Peter made no attempt to stifle his yawns. They cleared the table mechanically and put their plates in the dishwasher. "Baths and bed," she said. She ran a bath for the girls in the bathroom off her own bedroom, and Peter went to take a shower in the bathroom across the hall. They were all terribly subdued, no one made a fuss, and the girls were super-quiet without having to be told. They could all sense things weren't right and they didn't want to make the situation any worse by being noisy and misbehaving in someone else's house.

Soon they were all snug in their respective beds and even Peter didn't make any objections to an early night. She said she would find out what was wrong, get to the bottom of it, and tell them all about it in the morning. "Thank you for being so good," she said to the girls. She went off to Peter's room and sat on the edge of the bed and commended him for all the help he had given Mr. Blunt. He gave her the slightest hint of a smile and said, "I loved it, Mom. He's a really nice man."

"He is, isn't he? I always enjoyed working with him."

"I loved Aladdin's Cave. It's a really neat store, and I had fun using the cash register."

"I'm pleased you had a good day, and you know you've stolen Grandma's heart, don't you? She seems to come alive when she sees you."

"I really like her and Grandpa," and he leaned back against the pillows and put his hands behind his head and looked at his mom. "Despite things not being quite right, I'm glad we came."

"I was, too, up to this point, but now I'm not so sure."

"I'm so pleased I'm not a grown up."

"I hope you remember that the next time you ask for something you can't have or want to do something I can't allow!"

"Aw, Mom."

She leaned over and kissed his cheek, and for once he didn't object. "Goodnight, champ. I'd better go get this over with and see if I can find out what's wrong with everybody. If you wake up and need me, you know where I am."

CHAPTER TWENTY-TWO

JIM AND MARYANN

MaryAnn decided it was too much of a temptation not to take advantage of the lavishness of Jim's bathroom. She managed to slide out of bed without waking Johnny, and after grabbing her clothes, tiptoed across the hallway in her bare feet. How heavenly to just be able to walk about and not be freezing to death. She closed and locked the door, inserted the plug in the tub and turned on the faucet, allowing the water to run over her fingertips in order to get the temperature just right. She would have to kneel up to wash her hair, but that would be a novelty in itself. She tipped in a little of the bubble bath and breathed in the fresh and alluring scent of lavender. She found shampoo and conditioner and two really fluffy towels. She spread the bath mat, sinking her toes into the silky softness. Oh, she could get used to this.

The bath was exquisite—there was no other word to describe the luxury—and she lay back in the warm softly scented water, allowing herself to daydream just for a little while. Appreciating such a simple pleasure of a bath when the treat had been denied to her for so long threatened to undo her resolve to remain independent. She and the boys only took showers at the rental house because the thought of sitting in the pitted and iron-stained bathtub gave her the shivers. Reluctantly, she stood up and let out the water, reaching for the towels, pleased she had maintained her slender figure even after giving birth to two strapping infants. She wrapped one towel around her head and one around her body and decided to go check on Johnny before turning on the hair dryer as she wouldn't be able to hear him if he called out for her. She didn't want him to be scared if he didn't know where she was. She opened the bathroom door and stepped out into the hallway, surprised to see Jim walking towards her. He stopped before he got too close, and looked at her with intense concentration. "You're taking my breath away, woman," he said.

She felt languid and sultry, and grateful her sons weren't too far away, otherwise who knows what would have happened. She grinned and said, "I had to wash away the smell of gravy!"

"You certainly succeeded," he said. "Even from here, I can tell you smell absolutely wonderful and seeing you wrapped in nothing but a towel is driving me crazy."

"I'm sorry, it wasn't my intention. I just wanted to make sure Johnny was all right before I turned on the hair dryer."

"I just checked on him and he's still asleep. I'll stay within earshot until you've dried your hair."

"Thank you for solving my dilemma, kind sir," and she started to inch her way backwards as he moved a little closer. "Don't you dare," she said, quickly stepping into the bathroom and closing and locking the door.

"No fair," he said, walking into the room where Johnny lay sleeping. He looked down at the little boy in wonder, and he just couldn't believe his good fortune. Not only had he found a woman to love—a beautiful, but spunky, capable woman for whom he had great respect—but also two fatherless boys. He hoped, in time, he would be able to fill the void in their hearts as they were certainly filling his own. He sat down in the chair by the window. The room was illuminated by the waning reflection of the moon as the sky began to lighten, and Jim, always sensitive to his surroundings, was pleased with what Jennifer had accomplished with the decor she had chosen. The bright and pretty colors were much too feminine for his liking, but they brought the room alive and made it absolutely perfect for guests. The fact he'd had Thea in mind when he'd asked Jennifer to help him redecorate the house seemed ridiculous now, but the long overdue facelift had given him something to do. Now he was pleased he'd made the effort and also extremely grateful Thea had never actually come to the house. Everything would have been tainted somehow, overshadowed by her lingering perfume, and he leaned back in the chair and closed his eyes, reveling in the knowledge he could now identify his obsession as a thing of the past and tuck it firmly away.

Jim heard the bathroom door open and watched as MaryAnn walked quietly into the room. She had tied her silvery blonde hair up in a high ponytail and her bangs fell gently on a level with her eyebrows. Even in the moonlight, he could see the desire on her face and as she backed into the hallway, he tiptoed out to follow her. Even in just the dim glow of the wall sconces, Jim noticed she was still flushed from her bath and he pulled her to him, and she offered absolutely no resistance. They fit perfectly together. A head and neck taller than she, he was able to bury his nose in her hair. "You smell absolutely delicious!" he said.

She made no reply but lifted her face to be kissed. She just couldn't resist him any longer, and even though he wasn't Sam, it was okay, and she didn't feel like crying any more. She just responded to the warmth of him and her arousal matched his own—the physical contact exquisite torture as they pressed as closely together as they could—and she whispered, "Oh, Mr. Hudson, what are you doing to me?" But the spell was broken by a little voice calling out for his mom and she said, "I'm right here." She reached up and touched Jim on the cheek, "You're a dangerous man," she said, reluctantly pulling out of his embrace.

"Me, dangerous! You're a temptress and I don't even think a cold shower would help. I'll go make us some breakfast," he said. "All this exercise has given me an appetite."

MaryAnn glowed from head to toe, and she felt like a giddy schoolgirl. Her attraction to Jim was incredible and she had a hunch they would be insatiable, but now she needed to turn her attention to her son who was sitting up in bed looking somewhat bewildered. "I thought I was in a room with Ian," he said.

"You were, but somehow you found your way into my bed in the middle of the night. It's a good thing Mr. Hudson left lots of lights on," and she leaned over and kissed him. "Guess what? The whole house is warm, so if you need to go to the bathroom you won't have to make a mad dash."

"That's good," he said, grinning from ear to ear. "You smell nice, Mommy."

"I took a bubble bath and washed my hair with the fancy shampoo I found. The towels are really fluffy, too. Are you hungry, because Mr. Hudson is downstairs making breakfast? Why don't you go to the bathroom and I'll go check on Ian. Okay?"

"Yes, Mommy."

Ian, her mini version of Sam, was still fast asleep, his curly head pressed deeply into the pillow. He looked so warm and comfortable, and knowing he was mature enough to find his way downstairs, she let him be.

MaryAnn and Johnny went down the stairs hand in hand and were greeted by Carrie sitting by the bottom step. She stood up and waved her plumed tail in an enthusiastic greeting and MaryAnn watched her son's face as he tenderly stroked the dog's soft fur between her ears. She pushed her long nose under his arm making him giggle, and they could hear her padding along softly behind them as they made their way into the kitchen.

Jim turned to greet them, spatula poised in mid-air as pools of batter sizzled on the griddle. "Good morning, young man," he said.

"Hello, Mr. Hudson. Those pancakes smell yummy."

"Sit yourself down and they'll be ready in two shakes of a lamb's tail. MaryAnn, please help yourself to coffee and Johnny would you like orange juice or milk?"

"Two shakes of a lamb's tail!" she said.

"It's one my grandfather's English sayings and there are plenty more!" Jim was in his element and it made MaryAnn feel so good to realize she was the cause of his lightheartedness.

Johnny, perched high on his cushion, sat quietly eating his pancakes, enjoying every mouthful. He looked back and forth between the two grownups and knew something was different, but it was a good different. He was only five after all, and as long as all his needs were being met he was exceedingly contented. Both his mother and Mr. Hudson seemed to be very happy and he thought this was great, so he gave up trying to figure it out.

Carrie, still missing one member from her newfound family, went back to her vigil at the bottom of the stairs. She didn't have to wait long, and she looked up and gave a little whine as Ian stumbled sleepily towards her. "Hello, girl," he said, and sat down and fondled her ears. Reveling in the warmth of the house, he couldn't quite believe he wasn't dreaming, and the tantalizing smell of pancakes lured him to the kitchen. He and Carrie walked across the hallway and Ian pushed open the door. Three smiling faces greeted him and he noticed his brother's was covered with syrup and butter, but nobody seemed to care. He still felt as though he was in a dream, but not one he wanted to wake up from. His mother looked wonderful. It seemed as though all the sadness she had carried around for the past three years had magically melted away, and if this was how Mr. Hudson made her feel, he was all for it. Mr. Hudson seemed to have a permanent smile on his face, so he guessed he and his mom liked each other a lot. He looked at them all, with Carrie standing at his side, and said, "Hi."

Mr. Hudson stood up and said, "Come and sit down. Would you like some pancakes? I know, what a stupid question."

"I'd love some," and Ian went and sat down next to his mom. He noticed the maple syrup and the butter was the real stuff, so much better than the fake syrup and the tubs of margarine they had at home because it was all they could afford. He didn't say anything since he didn't want to hurt his mother's feelings, just complemented Mr. Hudson on the pancakes by saying they were absolutely delicious, and they were. "These are so good, not like regular pancakes, which are usually so stodgy. How do you make them?" he asked.

"Ah, it's a family secret. It's all in the beating of the eggs. You beat the whites separately until they are really stiff and then add them to the batter. You should try it next time you make pancakes."

"I will. It makes a huge difference."

MaryAnn was warm and comfortable and the last thing she wanted to do was to upset the apple cart by saying she had to get to work, so with little enthusiasm, she said, "I'm sorry to be a wet blanket, boys, but you need to get dressed because I have to work today."

They both looked at her, and even though they were too polite to say anything, their body language spoke volumes. Ian stood up, pushed back his chair and started to clear the table. Johnny slid off his cushion with a great deal of wriggling and went to help his brother. Jim got up and went over to MaryAnn and whispered in her ear. "Can I have a word with you in private?" he said, walking out of the kitchen with her following close behind. She knew what he was going to ask, and she could feel her resolve crumbling.

"Why don't you leave the boys with me today. I'd love to have their company and get to know them a little better."

MaryAnn chewed on her lower lip. Jim put his fingers under her chin and forced her to look him in the eye. "I won't eat them, you know."

"I know, but they're my children and my responsibility."

"What are you afraid of?" Jim said, standing back from her and pushing his hands in his pockets. "What can I do to make you trust me?"

"This is all happening too fast. I'm so confused," and to MaryAnn's dismay, she started to cry. "I want to trust you, but don't you see, I don't really know you. I'm sorry if it's hurtful, but I'm not sure I can leave the boys with you all day. They're always with me, you see, except when they're at school."

"I guess you need my handkerchief again," he said, pulling it out of his pocket and holding it out to her. "Can I make a suggestion?"

"Sure," she said, wiping her eyes.

"Why don't we ask Ian and Johnny what they would like to do?"

"That's not fair," she said, giving him the first glimmer of a smile. "You know exactly what they're going to say."

"I only know what I hope they're going to say. If they don't want to stay with me, then we have a problem. I'll wait here while you go and talk to them."

MaryAnn balled up Jim's handkerchief and went back into the kitchen. The boys were sitting on the floor by Carrie's basket and the dog looked up and twitched her tail when she saw MaryAnn. She decided to sit down on the floor with them. "I have a question to ask you," she said. "Would you like to stay with Mr. Hudson while I'm at work today?"

Ian said, "That would rock if it's okay with Johnny."

"How about you Johnny? Would you like to stay?"

"Won't Will miss us?" he asked, always the sensitive one.

"I think he would understand, especially when I tell him who you're with. He and Mr. Hudson are friends."

"Then, I'd like to stay."

"What about the Chamberlin's cat? We were supposed to go to their house and spend time with her," Ian said.

"I hadn't forgotten and I will feed her on my way to the diner. Maybe Mr. Hudson would bring you there after I get out of work, and we could all stay with Smokey for a little while just in case she's lonely. Is the problem solved?"

"I think so," Johnny said, sliding across the floor and snuggling up against his mom.

"Now, are you both sure about this? I only want you to say yes if that's what you really want to do. If you need to talk to me, you can call the diner at any time. Okay?"

"Yes, Mom. We're okay, right Johnny," Ian said to his brother and Johnny nodded enthusiastically in return. Even Carrie seemed to have perked up, sensing she wasn't going to lose her newfound companions.

"Let's go give Mr. Hudson the good news and then I really do have to get a move on."

Jim was sitting at the bottom of the stairs, and MaryAnn thought he looked like a man waiting for a jail sentence. She handed him back his handkerchief and said, "A white flag of truce, and the boys would love to stay with you." He exhaled in quiet relief and stood up. "I'm so pleased," he said, looking at the three of them with a twinkle in his eye.

"I've told the boys they can call me any time at the diner if they feel the need, but judging by the look on all your faces, I don't think it's going to be necessary, and now I really have to scramble. I'll see you all later at the Chamberlin's at about three thirty."

Jim turned to MaryAnn and said, "Off you go." He took Johnny's hand and said, "Why don't we go back into the kitchen and see what kind of job you did cleaning up!"

"Uh-oh," Ian said, and MaryAnn suddenly felt superfluous. She had only ever left the children with Sam and, of course, she had never given it a second thought. The current situation was entirely different and would take some getting used to, but she had no doubt in her mind Ian and Johnny were in good hands.

CHAPTER TWENTY-THREE

THEA AND ELLIE

Thea left Peter's room, and with her heart full of trepidation, walked down the hallway and stood outside Ellie's door, holding her breath. She could feel the tension in her neck where she'd raised her shoulders—a bad habit of hers—and she forced herself to relax. She was so afraid of what she would find, and mustering all her courage, she raised her hand and knocked gently. She thought she heard her say, "Come in," but the softness of Ellie's voice was barely audible. She slowly turned the doorknob, pushing the door open inch by inch. Ellie was sitting up in bed, and she looked ghastly. Her eyes were closed and her face was creased with pain. Robert was sitting on a chair to the right of the bed with his head in his hands. The room smelled of sickness and Thea couldn't help noticing the large enamel bowl, and she didn't need to be told what the bowl was for. What on earth was going on?

Robert looked up at Thea and shook his head. Now, what was this gesture supposed to mean? Should she just leave without making an attempt to talk to her friend? She was standing there awkwardly when Ellie suddenly opened her eyes. "Hi, Thea," she said, her voice barely a whisper. "Robert, why don't you leave us just for a little while. I'll be all right."

He stood up and leaned over and gave Ellie a kiss on the forehead. "If you're sure," he said, and she nodded. Thea watched him shuffle out of the room like an old man, and he closed the door quietly behind him.

"Come sit close so you'll be able to hear what I have to say and I'll try not to throw up while you're here, but there's no guarantee. I'm sorry I can't make what I am going to tell you any easier, but I don't have the energy to spin a sugar coated story about what's happened to me. The truth is I have an inoperable brain tumor."

Thea gasped and took Ellie's hand. "But you seemed fine on Thursday," she said.

"Steroids. I don't know if you've ever taken them, but they give you superhuman strength. I've been doing good, and I would never have asked you to come had I known I was going to go downhill so fast. I'm so sorry." She took a deep breath and leaned back against the pillows closing her eyes. "The morphine is going to kick in soon and then I won't make any sense, but I'll keep talking while I can."

"What can I do?"

"There's nothing anyone can do and that's why Robert's here. Unfortunately, he's taking my illness badly, so I'm trying to be the strong one, and poor Theodore, we had such plans." Her face contorted in pain and the tears rolled down her cheeks. Thea took a tissue from the box on the bedside table and gently wiped Ellie's face.

Thea had so many questions, but she didn't want to tax Ellie's waning strength, so she sat quietly waiting for her friend to tell her what was on her mind. Once Ellie had fallen asleep, she would tackle Robert and make him talk to her.

Ellie seemed to gather her strength again and she said, "I've always loved you. I could never find anyone to replace you after you left for your life with Michael. I've never had much interest in finding a man and having a family after seeing what child bearing did to my mother." Her lip trembled and her eyes filled with tears, and Thea really had to lean in close to hear what she was saying. "I just wanted a life with you and Theodore and Aladdin's Cave, but you went away."

Thea felt terrible, but affronted at the same time. Why on earth was Ellie laying all this on her now? Had her anger at Thea festered all through the years and did she now want to tell the truth before time ran out? Was it the influence of the morphine?

"Thea, I'll soon be asleep, but I just wanted to let you know I've written you a letter which will explain everything. Robert will give it to you when the time is right. I'm so terribly sorry things have turned out so horribly and I'm..." Her final words were slurred and Thea had a hard time understanding what she was saying. She noticed Ellie had fallen asleep, so she leaned over and kissed her and quietly left the room.

Robert was sitting on the floor outside the door looking just as miserable. "Is she asleep?" he asked.

"Yes. Robert, talk to me. I know it's difficult for you, but I have to tell you I'm pretty mad right now and totally confused."

"Come sit down beside me and I'll tell you what happened."

Thea slid down the wall and sat, bending her legs and folding her arms around her knees, and Robert continued. "Ellie called me about a year ago to ask my advice. She said she kept getting these headaches and they weren't responding to the usual headache remedies. She assumed they were migraines, but I urged her to go and see a doctor, especially as she also told me she sometimes experienced tingling in her arms. She chose to ignore me. Theodore was frantic because, as you know, Aladdin's Cave doesn't run itself and he's not getting any younger. He noticed mood changes in Ellie, compounded by the fact she didn't seem to be able to concentrate on a given task for any length of time. He called me and said I'd have to try harder to get Ellie to go see a doctor, and believe me I tried, but it was all to no avail until she had a seizure and ended up in the emergency room. Fortunately for Ellie, Theodore was with her and it happened here in the kitchen, but she still had some nasty bruises as she fell against the counter as she went down. Theodore called 911 right away but he was truly shaken up as you can well imagine. I immediately understood something was seriously wrong, so I started putting the wheels in motion to transfer my job with the Visiting Nurse Association in my hometown in Maine to one in Massachusetts. I also had vacation time owing, so I packed up my belongings, stowed them in my car, and drove here as quickly as I could."

Thea sat quietly and listened, even though she found sitting on the floor extremely uncomfortable, but she didn't want to interrupt Robert's train of thought.

"Ellie underwent all sorts of tests. She was given a CT scan of the brain—the scan is like an X-ray but shows more detail in three dimensions. A harmless dye was injected into her bloodstream to highlight any abnormalities on the scan and our worst fears were realized as the scan indicated the presence of a brain tumor, something I'd suspected all along. At this point, Ellie was given a prescription for Dilantin, an anti-seizure medication, and sent home with the name of a neurologist with whom she was urged to make an appointment, which she did the next day. To cut to the chase, she was given an MRI and diagnosed with a Glioma type tumor—an Astrocytoma, grade two. We were devastated, but somewhat heartened as it is considered very slow growing, but because of the location and type, not a good candidate for surgery. We were thankful the tumor wasn't on the left side of her brain because, had this been the case, it would have affected her speech, and we were pathetically grateful for any small glimmer of hope. Her initial treatment was six weeks of daily radiation and she did well, and a subsequent MRI showed the tumor had shrunk a little. She was back at the store and giving it as much energy as she could. Fortunately, Theodore was practical and told Ellie she needed a backup for the days when she wasn't strong enough to work, to which she agreed. She told me many times, Thea, she wished you were closer, but wishing wasn't going to solve anything. She had become well acquainted with an older woman, Dorothy, and she hired her to help with the after-school programs. She's away this weekend visiting family otherwise you would have met her. She's widowed and she and Ellie have become firm friends, and I don't know what we would have done without her. Finding her was a stroke of luck. She's absolutely marvelous with the kids, but she's useless when it comes to running the store, and I'm not telling tales out of school, she would freely admit it herself. This is where you come into the story."

"But how can I? I have three children to consider. I already told Ellie when she offered me the partnership, even if I agreed, I wouldn't be able to come until the end of the school year, which wouldn't be until June."

"I know, but she didn't expect to go downhill so fast. She thought she'd be able to hang on until you could got here."

"I can't just drop everything. The kids have commitments. My older daughter is playing Clara in *The Nutcracker* and she would be heartbroken if I pulled her out. There are a million other things besides. If I didn't have the children to consider, I wouldn't hesitate, but don't you see, it's just not possible. My kids have suffered a hell of a lot already through no fault of their own and to thrust them into a situation such as this would be totally unfair. I'm sorry if I sound uncaring because I'm not, but my family has to come first," and she reached over and gave Robert's hand a quick squeeze. "I can only imagine how terrible life must be for you and Ellie. Your grief is seeping into my bones and dragging me down. I'm familiar with that sinking sensation of wallowing in a bottomless pit of despair, and it's a terrible place to be."

Robert turned to look at Thea and said, "I know. I'm just grasping at straws, looking for lifelines anyway I can. Ellie's undergone so much, and after fighting so hard, I can't believe the tumor has finally gotten the better of us. We both believed she was going to get better and the periodic MRIs did show the tumor was shrinking, but the prognosis was never good. She may rally again, but I doubt it, and sometimes it doesn't help being in the medical field because I just know too much."

"I just can't believe the difference between yesterday and today. She cooked a whole Thanksgiving meal, for goodness sake. How on earth did she do it? I thought she seemed a little off; not her usual bubbly self, but I didn't really pay much attention. Then when she said she was going to bed early with a headache, I thought she was just a little under the weather, but when she didn't appear this morning I was truly concerned."

"She made every effort to appear as normal as possible for you, and to be truthful, we did much of the cooking on Wednesday night in order to conserve her energy. She so badly wanted to give you a nice Thanksgiving, but even with all the prep work we did beforehand, obviously she over-did it. Sometimes, even when our body is tired and sick, we are able to put mind over matter and achieve superhuman things, and I'm sure that's exactly what happened with Ellie yesterday. Of course, the steroids gave her a boost, at least for a little while."

"What can I do to help?" Thea asked. "At least let me get you something to eat. It won't do Ellie any good if you don't keep up your strength."

Robert let out a huge sigh and said, "You're right."

Thea pushed herself to her feet and it was a relief to stand up. Her rear end was numb from sitting on the hardwood floor and she rubbed it vigorously. Robert grasped her hands when she held them out to him and she leaned back and pulled him to his feet. He was about a head and neck taller than her, and even though the hallway was dimly lit, she could see how tired he was. His skin above his neatly trimmed beard was almost gray with fatigue, and his soft brown eyes were terribly blood-shot. She let go of his hands and said, "You look pretty terrible, you know. When did you last get any decent sleep? At least let me look after you while I'm here."

"Oh, *merde*," he said, running his hands through his neat dark hair. "I really don't know."

"Why don't you take a peek at Ellie and then come into the kitchen and I'll heat up some leftovers for you and make us some tea. A hot drink will do us both good. I can then sit with Ellie while you get some rest. Does that sound like a plan?"

Robert looked down at Thea, and she was pleased to see a glimmer of a smile. "It's a good thing I have a beard, huh? Otherwise, I would look even more unkempt than I already do."

"You look fine to me. I'll see you in a few minutes," and Robert watched her retreating figure as she walked off towards the kitchen. Left with Thea's lingering scent of roses, he tried to take the fragrance with him when he returned to Ellie's bedside. What just happened here? He had enjoyed his conversation with Thea and he was saddened by the realization she wouldn't be able to stay. Relieved to find Ellie sleeping peacefully, he made sure her cell phone was right by her hand, so she could call him the moment she awoke. His was snug in the pocket of his jeans and fully charged. The communication system worked well for both of them, and although it gave him peace of mind, it gave him little opportunity to rest. He knew he would have to ask for extra help and being an employee of the VNA worked to his advantage—there were always people who could pick up the slack. Up until now, he had managed on his own and Ellie hadn't wanted anyone else, but the situation would have to change if she didn't get any better.

Robert arrived in the kitchen just as Thea was pouring boiling water on the tea bags in the two mugs she had set side by side on the countertop. She was concentrating on her task but heard him coming, so she looked over her shoulder and said, "Hi." She removed the plate of food she had fixed for him from the microwave, her tiny hands encased in Ellie's huge oven mitts. "Why don't you sit here," she said, indicating one of the bar stools with an inclination of her head. He opened his mouth to say something, but she jumped in saying, "No arguing. Please let me wait on you."

"Okay, I give up," he said, slumping wearily onto one of the stools, picking up the knife and fork she had already set there and starting to eat, realizing as he chewed the first mouthful he hadn't had anything since breakfast.

"How do you take your tea?"

"Normally plain, but I think milk and sugar are what I need right now."

She set the steaming mugs next to Robert and sat on one of the stools, and again he was aware of her subtle perfume. Steeped in his own misery, he had failed to truly look at her up until now, and he suddenly noticed how incredibly attractive she was. "Where's Theodore?" she asked.

"He must be in his apartment. He keeps very much to himself these days."

"Isn't he terribly lonely?"

"I'm sure he is. Nothing turned out as Ellie had hoped. She was the one who was supposed to be looking after him, not that he currently needs care, but they were both planning for the future when they designed the house together." Robert stopped eating and picked up the mug of tea: it was hot, sweet and comforting. "Thank you for being here. It's helpful, even if you can only stay for a little while."

He set his mug down and she reached over and touched his hand. "I'll do what I can. The children will understand. They're good kids."

"Yes, they are. I enjoyed my time with Peter yesterday. Did he tell you we share similar interests in music?"

"He did. He was very impressed you had the latest *Bon Jovi* CD. You definitely won brownie points there! Look, even though I'd love to sit and talk to you, you need to get some rest. You look as though you're about to fall off the stool."

"I know. Could I ask you a favor?"

"Sure."

"Could I leave my cell phone with you? If the dang thing is anywhere close to me, I won't get a wink of sleep, but please promise me you'll come and get me if it rings."

"I promise. Just show me how to use the offending object. I'm ashamed to say I have yet to get myself a mobile phone, but it's the first thing I'm going to do when I get home."

"It's easy. Just flip it open if it rings, and that's all there is to it. Okay?"

"Gotcha. Now off with you," and she took him by the shoulders and pushed him gently out of the kitchen. Thea's kindness was almost Robert's undoing, but he managed to keep his composure. He was dizzy with fatigue and as soon as he reached his room in the basement, he fell onto his bed and was instantly asleep.

Thea glanced at the kitchen clock and saw to her surprise it was almost nine o'clock. The cell phone sat on the counter. She thought it was scary-looking and she told herself she would have to get over her irrational fear if she was going to have one of her own. She cleaned up the kitchen and decided to go seek out Theodore. She felt bad for the old man and thought he must be pretty lonely. She gingerly picked up the phone and carried it off with her as she made her way through the hallway and down the basement stairs. As she passed Robert's room she could hear him snoring gently, and this made her smile. Hopefully, he was sleeping deeply and she was glad she had at least been able to give him a brief respite. She walked to the far end of the basement, knocked gently on Mr. Blunt's door and stood back and waited. She heard his shuffling footsteps, and he said, "Who is it?"

"Mr. Blunt, it's Thea. I know it's a little late, but I just wondered whether you would like some company."

The door opened slowly and there he was dressed in his robe and slippers, grinning at her and saying, "Come in, come in," as he always did.

She wasn't sure what to expect as she stepped into the small entryway in which stood a large and old-fashioned piece of furniture with a mirror in the center and hooks on either side. At the base of this, sat a small built-in wooden box with a lid—a great storage place for scarves and gloves. Still clutching the phone in her hand, she followed the old man into his sitting room.

"Please come and sit down. Just let me turn off the TV. I was trying to distract myself, but except for PBS, the programs are all useless drivel and I have no tolerance for the ads."

Thea sat down on the edge of a rather ornate sofa with a carved back and Queen Anne legs. Upholstered in a pretty pale blue, it was exceedingly feminine, and in stark contrast to the rather ordinary dull brown recliner in which Theodore sat. "The fancy furniture belonged to Jenny and I just couldn't bring myself to get rid of it, so the room is a bit of a hodgepodge, but it suits me down to the ground."

Thea looked around her and noticed some fine paintings on the walls, a beautiful oriental rug beneath her feet, and various small tables and lamps. Tucked into a corner was a gleaming, deep mahogany, upright piano on which stood a couple of silver-framed black and white wedding photographs of Theodore and Jenny. She wondered whether Jenny had been musical.

"You've found yourself in a bit of a pickle, haven't you?" he said, looking at her intently with his faded blue eyes.

Constantly amused by his Dickensian turn of phrase, she never quite knew what he was going come up with next, but she always understood perfectly what he meant. "Her illness has certainly taken me by surprise, and I'm shocked and sad. I also feel rather useless, as I can't stay. I'll do what I can while I'm here, but as I explained to Robert; my children have to come first. I will talk to them in the morning and explain how sick Miss Ellie truly is. I know they will want to help, but I honestly think they will be in the way, so we should probably just head home. How are you holding up?"

"I put on a brave face and be as cheerful as I can, but it's hard to be optimistic any more. She's put up such a good fight, but now her good days are outweighed by the bad. We had such plans, and we had so much fun designing what we called 'our home.' At one time, the house was always full of children, the less fortunate ones, and they looked to Ellie as their mentor and friend. Having all this space meant a lot to her. She created somewhere safe where the children could come after school rather than going home to empty houses. She'd also applied to be a foster parent, but that's all gone up in a puff of smoke now. Ellie's the daughter I never had and I've grown to love her very much over the years. I keep praying for a miracle, but I'm afraid we're all out of miracles now." He pulled his handkerchief out of his pocket and blew his nose loudly, a gesture with which Thea was familiar.

"I don't know what to say. I hate to think of you being all by yourself."

"I manage to amuse myself and I'm quite tired after a day in the store, so I usually sleep pretty well, although lately I find myself waking up in the middle of the night unable to get back to sleep. The mind plays horrible tricks in the dark, so I find it's better to get up and make myself a hot drink. Sometimes I read for a bit, and more often than not, I fall asleep in my chair."

"Now, if you're sure you're all right, I think I should take myself off to bed. I have Robert's cell phone and if Ellie calls, I'll be right across the hallway from her. I'll see you in the morning." She could see he was about to get out of his chair, so she said, "Please don't get up. I can see myself out," and she leaned over and gave him a soft kiss and his cheek was wet with tears.

"Goodnight, Thea, and thank you for coming to visit me."

"Goodnight, Mr. Blunt." She walked away, and as soon as she closed the door quietly behind her, the phone buzzed inside her hand like an angry insect. She flipped it open as Robert had instructed and said, "Hello."

"Thea?"

"Yes, Ellie, I'll be right there." She hurried through the basement and up the stairs, moving quickly until she reached Ellie's room. She opened the door warily. "Is it okay if I come in?" and Ellie beckoned to her.

Thea noticed she looked more relaxed and the grimace of pain she had worn earlier seemed to have gone. "How are you feeling?" she asked.

"A little better."

"Tell me what you need," Thea said, standing awkwardly at the end of the bed.

"If you could help me to the bathroom, that would be good for starters," Ellie said, giving Thea a brief smile.

She went around to the side of the bed and waited while Ellie pushed back the covers, turned little by little and painstakingly lowered her legs until her feet touched the floor. "I have to stand up slowly because I get so dizzy."

"Take your time," and Thea bent over and gently pulled Ellie's nightgown down around her legs.

Eventually, Ellie was able to stand and Thea stood right next to her so Ellie could put her arm around her shoulders. Thea tried not to recoil from the smell of sickness and it was if Ellie had read her mind because she said, "I've lost my sense of smell, which in my current situation is a blessed relief, but I'm sorry if all this is offensive for you. Are you still wearing the same scent I always remembered?"

"It's only rosewater, but yes I still wear it. I never changed it."

They inched their way slowly across the floor and into the bathroom, and Thea made sure Ellie was sitting securely on the toilet before giving her privacy. "Call out when you're ready. I'm not going to close the door all the way."

"Okay."

Thea leaned against the wall and waited. She suddenly longed for the familiarity of home, but compared with Ellie's situation, hers was a heavenly existence and she was suddenly grateful for all she had, especially her health. She would be able to walk away from all the sickness—not so her friend, and this made her feel terrible.

"I'm ready," came Ellie's soft voice and Thea went back into the bathroom. Ellie was standing with one hand on the sink and she said, "I'd like to clean my teeth. My mouth is like the bottom of a bird cage."

"I think you've been with Mr. Blunt too long; his funny way of speaking has rubbed off on you. Here, let me help you." It was pathetic to see the one lonely toothbrush as it seemed to be so symbolic of the narrow life in which Ellie was forced to live. Putting those morbid thoughts aside, Thea picked it up and squeezed on a healthy dollop of toothpaste. "Here," she said, holding it out to Ellie.

Ellie took the toothbrush and stood looking at herself in the mirror, steadying herself on the sink with her other hand. "I look terrible, don't

I?" she asked. "It's okay, you don't have to say anything. I can answer my own question."

Thea looked at their two faces side by side, the contrast between her reflection and Ellie's like night and day. Her eyes were clear and shining, and even though her complexion was naturally pale, she still had a healthy glow, whereas Ellie's pretty blue eyes were dull and lifeless and her skin had a slightly grayish tinge. Her friend lifted the toothbrush carefully to her mouth and brushed slowly. To Thea, it seemed as if even this simple task took a superhuman effort. "Would you like me to do that for you?" she asked.

"No thanks, but I would like a glass of water."

Thea picked up the tumbler on the counter, bent over the sink, turned on the faucet and handed the full glass to Ellie in exchange for the toothbrush. Ellie first rinsed her mouth and then drank thirstily. "Could you help me back to bed?" They shuffled their way across the floor with Ellie leaning heavily on Thea just as she had done before. Ellie seemed frail as Thea put her arm around her waist to give her extra support and she still couldn't believe she hadn't noticed anything yesterday, but then again she had no reason to believe anything was wrong. On reflection, she had thought her friend looked a little tired and a little thinner, but that was all.

Once safely back in bed, Ellie lay back against the pillows and closed her eyes. "Is there anything else I can get you?" Thea asked.

"Just a glass of water and do you think you could stay with me for a little while?"

"Sure," and she went off to the bathroom to refill the glass Ellie had just used, placing it carefully on the bedside table.

"Is Robert sleeping? I assumed he was because you have his phone. Poor man, he gets no relief and I know this can't go on."

"Yes, he's sleeping. I went to see Theodore, although I still call him *Mr. Blunt*. I just can't bring myself to call him by his first name."

"Why is he here? Why isn't he at the store?" A puzzled expression came over Ellie's face and Thea's heart sank when she perceived just how sick her friend really was. She played along with it and said, "Because the store is closed for the day."

"I get so confused," she said, wringing her hands together until Thea couldn't stand it any longer, so she reached over and gently put her own hand over Ellie's to still them. Thea was finding it almost unbearable to see her friend so distressed and her heart was racing. All of a sudden, she heard little snuffling noises at the bottom of the door and a tiny whine. Ellie heard it, too, and she smiled. "That must be Honey," she said. "Please let her in."

Thea had never been so relieved in all her life to have a distraction. She had completely forgotten about the dog and now here she was in all her golden glory, making a beeline for Ellie's bedside and resting her lovely head on the quilt. "Hello, girl," Ellie said, and leaned over to rest her hand on Honey's silky fur. "Thea, you can leave me now. Honey will come and find you if there's anything wrong. Just leave the door open a little bit."

Thea remembered to pick up Robert's phone from where she'd left it on the dresser, made sure Ellie's was within reach and quietly crossed the room. Ellie was coaxing Honey onto the bed and the big dog did a running leap, landing carefully away from Ellie's legs. And this was the way in which Thea left them—Ellie resting easily with Honey snuggled up against her.

Thea went off to check on Robert and found he was still sleeping peacefully. She had a sudden urge to snuggle up with him, which caught her off-guard. He must have become aware of her presence because he opened one eye and said, "Hey, you," as if it was the most natural thing in the world. "Come and sit down. I won't bite! I feel like a new man after all that sleep."

"All that sleep. At the most, it was an hour and a half, maybe two. Robert, it's not enough, and you know that."

"At least it's a start," and he pushed himself up, pulling the pillow up behind him until he was in a sitting position. "What have you been doing? Did Ellie call?"

"So many questions. Are you always this demanding?"

She was still standing and he repeated his request, asking her to sit down, so she sat at the end of the bed as far away from him as possible. It was late, she was tired and vulnerable and horrified to find she was really attracted to him. She took a deep breath, turned sideways a little so she could look at him, and said, "I went to see Mr. Blunt as I felt the least I could do was to pay him a visit, but we didn't talk for long. Just as I was leaving, your beastly phone did its buzzing thing. It was Ellie and I went to her."

"Is she all right?"

"I helped her to the bathroom, then back to bed after she had cleaned her teeth and consumed a large glass of water. She asked me to stay with her. She's terribly confused, isn't she? She couldn't understand why Mr.

Blunt wasn't at the store, but seemed happy when I said the store was closed for the day."

"Unfortunately, her confusion is all part of the way the tumor presses on her brain. It's gotten a lot worse. Go on."

"She seemed really agitated until we heard Honey whining at the door. She asked me to let the dog in and Ellie's face lit up as soon as she saw her. I left the two of them snuggled up together and I guess the "no furniture" rule doesn't matter any more."

"Do you know how good it is for me to have a normal conversation? I've had no one to share this with except my family, but they are too far away. Will you stay in touch with me when you get back to Maine?"

Thea sensed the intimacy between them brought on by the burden Robert carried and the incredible sadness she felt for her sick friend. She was overtired and looked at him with tears gently rolling down her cheeks. "Of course I will," she said.

"There's something going on between us, isn't there? You feel it too, don't you?"

"Yes, I do, but now isn't the right time."

"I agree, but knowing you care gives me hope," and he climbed off the bed and came and sat beside her. She leaned into him and he put his arm around her shoulders and rested his head against hers; they sat in silent companionship and it was enough...

CHAPTER TWENTY-FOUR

JIM AND MARYANN

Jim went out to warm up MaryAnn's car for her. The sky was overcast, the cold damp and penetrating—the sort of weather that usually preceded a snowstorm. He hoped not. He shivered and wished he'd put his jacket on. He turned the key in the ignition and the car purred into life. The vehicle seemed sturdy enough, but it was old. He turned on the heater full blast, but MaryAnn could have told him the exercise was futile, it had long given up working at full capacity. He worried about the car breaking down, but his intuition told him to back off. It would be inappropriate to offer a solution this early in their relationship; he didn't want to damage her pride. He'd just have to keep his fingers crossed the poor old banger kept on going. MaryAnn was putting on her coat when he got back into the house and the garment didn't look substantial enough for a Maine winter, but he wisely kept his thoughts to himself. "Where are the boys?" she asked.

"In the kitchen brushing Carrie and she is loving the attention. Come here," and he held out his arms, and she walked into his embrace. "It feels so good to hold you," he said as he kissed her softly, being careful not to mess up her hair. "But you're wearing too many clothes."

"What am I going to do with you? You're nothing but trouble," and she put her gloved hands on his chest and pushed herself away. "Now, I really do have to leave and I won't be able to concentrate on my driving if you get me all hot and bothered."

"Okay, I give up," and he held his hands in the air in mock surrender. "Away with you."

MaryAnn put her head around the kitchen door and said goodbye to her sons. They were completely engrossed in their task and seemed perfectly content, so she left the house with a happy heart. She waved at Jim as he stood in the doorway and she watched him in her rearview mirror as she drove away.

There was little traffic and she made good time to the Chamberlin's. Smokey was prowling around the kitchen looking a little lost, pleased to see MaryAnn. As she did with anyone who came close, she attempted to weave her way through their legs and MaryAnn was no exception. She bent down to stroke the cat and was rewarded with the little head pushing firmly against her palm. She put out fresh food and water, took a quick glance around Thea's bright kitchen with all her children's colorful artwork, and felt a little odd being there because of her burgeoning relationship with Jim. She wondered how Thea would feel now Jim was lost to her. How could anyone not love Jim? She crouched down and stroked Smokey and told her she would be back later and then she'd have lots of company. The cat looked as though she understood because she seemed to be totally content and ate heartily in the finicky way cats always seemed to have. MaryAnn firmly locked the door and slid the keys back under the flowerpot just in case she was delayed. Ian and Johnny were aware of the hiding place.

Even in just those few moments the car was cold again, but fortunately, started right up. She wound her scarf more tightly around her neck in an attempt to stay warm, but her feet were freezing by the time she reached the diner and its welcoming lights. She pulled past the building and parked out back. She was half an hour late. Matt, the high school kid who bused for Will, was standing on the steps by the back entrance smoking a cigarette, and he said, "Hi," as she approached him.

"Did you wonder where I was?" she asked.

"Will's been slapping stuff around on the grill even more than usual, and the slapping got even worse when he couldn't get any reply from your house."

"Thanks, Matt. It's nice to know Will was worried about me, but I should have called."

"Uh-huh," he said, breathing out a cloud of smoke and leering at her evilly.

"Smoking will stunt your growth," she said, but she was wasting her breath. The acrid smell of nicotine stayed in her nostrils as she brushed past Matt, heaved the door open, and went into the building. She never had understood why people smoked.

The odor of cooking smells overwhelmed her as she hung up her coat and thrust her arms into her work uniform, buttoning up the front. The coverall did little to protect her from smelling just like a diner at the end of the day and she could just imagine Jim teasing her about that, too. She smiled, and her heart did a little flip-flop of happiness. She walked down the dark hallway, past the storage room and the bathrooms and out into the brightness of the restaurant. Matt was right. Will was definitely in a snit, but she knew his bad mood wouldn't last long. "Hi," she said. "I'm sorry I'm late."

Will turned and glared at her. "I've been worried sick. You're always on time, and I was about to send Matt to go looking for you. Don't ever be late again without calling me," and he turned back to the grill and continued to murder some very innocent looking sausage patties. He filled a couple of plates with the breakfast special and turned and said, "Order up," and Evelyn, the other waitress, hurried over. "MaryAnn, where have you been?" she hissed under her breath. "I'm run off my feet."

"Sorry. Who are these orders for?"

"Table ten, and don't expect to get their tips."

MaryAnn didn't care everyone was so grumpy. She blithely went about her work, smiling at all the customers and refusing to rise to either Evelyn's or Will's angst. Yes, she was sorry she had gotten in late, but there was nothing she could do about her tardiness now except work extra hard. Evelyn, grim at the best of times, had altercations with all the staff. She complained constantly her feet hurt, her back hurt, and life had just dealt her a rotten deck of cards. She was slow but she was a fixture, part of the diner's furniture, and the place wouldn't be the same without her. It was a standing joke and the regulars would have wagers as to who could make old Evelyn smile first, but her face was set, her lips in a permanent pout with wrinkles running up to her nose. No one had seen her break a smile, yet.

MaryAnn waited until there was a lull after the breakfast crowd and went to talk to Will. He seemed to have calmed down somewhat, as he wasn't buttering toast quite so ferociously and he wasn't scowling. "I truly am sorry," she said.

"Where were you?"

"Can I ask you a question?"

"You have to answer my question first."

She ignored him. "How well do you know Jim Hudson?"

"Ah," he said. "That's how the land lies," and he raised his eyebrows and looked her straight in the eye. She didn't waiver, giving as good as she got, staring straight back at him into his small dark brown eyes, like a couple of boot buttons. Everything about Will was small. He was compact, slender and boyish, with skin that seemed permanently tanned. He rubbed his fine-boned hands down his grease-spattered apron and asked MaryAnn to come sit in a booth with him. She followed meekly behind, and once they were sitting opposite each other, he said, "Now, what do you want to know? Are the boys here?"

"No. That's why I wanted to ask you about Jim. I guess I'm looking for a character reference. It's kind of important as I left Ian and Johnny with him today."

"Okay. I will put you out of your misery. Jim Hudson is a fine man. Of good solid Maine stock and I've never heard anyone ever speak an ill word. Has he captured your heart?"

She nodded. "You are one lucky woman, and judging by the smile on your face, he is one lucky man."

"It took us both by surprise. Can I ask you about Thea Chamberlin?"

"Now she's a whole other kettle o' fish. Jim's carried a torch for her for years, but it was never any good."

"It frightens me. I'm worried I may be a poor substitute."

"MaryAnn, now you're just being plain dumb. You put her in the shade, believe me. Look how you've cared for your boys since Sam's death..."

"In the dreadful rental with no heat. That's looking after my kids? I don't think so."

"Come on. Now I'm losing patience with you. I've always admired your spunk. Those kids love and respect you, and a little hardship hasn't done them any harm. Yeah, yeah, I know, before you say anything about Johnny's weak chest, but I don't honestly think your living conditions have anything to do with it. It was grief that did that, losing his daddy, and Sam's death wasn't your fault. So buck up and just be thankful you have a second chance. They don't come any better than Jim Hudson, mark my words."

"I'm just scared. It just seems too good to be true."

"Fairy tales with happy endings do happen, you know. Somebody has to fit the glass slipper."

"Thanks, Will, for listening to me and for all you've done for me and the boys."

Now it was Will's turn to look embarrassed, but he still looked MaryAnn in the eye and said, "You and the boys are worth it and don't let anyone ever tell you different. It's time you got a break. Anyway, I hope you can rest easy now because we need to get back to work or Evelyn is going to deck one of us with whatever weapon she can lay her hands on!"

"You're too darn right."

The rest of the day went by quickly. The diner, busy with folks coming in for a quick bite to eat between their Black Friday shopping trips, was a popular hangout for the locals because they could always rely on Will to give them a reasonably priced and hearty meal. He always made time to welcome all his patrons, and like the Country Store, Will's Diner was part of the charm of Melford Point, even though it was further out of town. MaryAnn's shift was over at three, and she said goodbye to Will. He said, "Be good, now," and gave her a wink. Evelyn had long since gone, taking her sour expression and general miserable outlook on life with her. Miranda, a cheerful high schooler, replaced MaryAnn, and she certainly lifted the spirits of the place. She and Matt, the busboy, were friends, so Will was probably in for some trouble-making, but he liked having young people around and only kept Evelyn on out of the kindness of his heart.

MaryAnn hung up her uniform and shrugged into her shabby coat: it wasn't even fit for good will—the navy faded, the lining torn, and the ends of the sleeves worn. She wrapped her scarf around her neck and pulled on her gloves, bending to pick up her pocketbook just as Miranda came through the door. "Perfect timing," she said. "We're like ships passing in the night."

"Brrrrr, it's cold out there. How are you, MaryAnn?"

"I'm fine. Yourself?"

"I'm good. Where are the boys?"

"They're with a friend today. Makes a change from them being stuck in the back room. Anyway, I must dash."

MaryAnn opened the door and stepped outside into the parking lot. Miranda was right, it was cold, absolutely freezing in fact, and she was surprised it hadn't snowed, despite Jim's earlier prediction. The sky was leaden with low hanging clouds, and it was beginning to get dark. She hurried towards her car, looking down at her grease spattered sneakers and wishing she had boots: long luxurious boots, lined with soft lamb's wool, reaching all the way to her knees. She wriggled her toes in anticipation of the pretended warmth. She was so tired of being poor.

Fortunately, it didn't take long to drive to the Chamberlin's house—easier for her to think of it as that, rather than Thea's house—but she was still pretty darn cold. She reached the house before Jim and the boys, so she parked well over to the left of the driveway to make room for his truck. She didn't bother to lock the car, hurried around to the side of the house and retrieved the keys. Smokey greeted her as soon as she stepped through the door and MaryAnn reached down to fondle the cat, and said, "I told you I'd be back."

The house felt deliciously warm even though the thermostat only said sixty-five degrees and she reveled in the treat of being able to walk about in a constant temperature. MaryAnn unwound her scarf and took off her coat, laying it over one of the kitchen chairs. "I'd better go check your litter tray," she said to the cat, amused to find Smokey following her. She was surprised to see part of the basement was finished with an area for dancing. A huge floor to ceiling mirror flanked one wall, along which ran a long wooden barre specifically designed for ballerinas. MaryAnn loved to dance and standing there looking at her reflection, her hands resting lightly on the barre, she was immediately transported back to her childhood and how much she had longed to be a ballerina, but she had never had the opportunity. She glanced down at her feet in their grubby sneakers and had she had more time, she would have been unable to resist the temptation to remove them and dance in her socks to the imaginary rhythm in her head. She wondered whether Jim liked to dance—Sam had been hopeless. The highly polished hardwood floor was a little worn from what she assumed would be hours of practicing. MaryAnn was intrigued. Who was the dancer, she wondered? A stereo system had been placed on a shelf to the right of the mirror, well within a child's reach, so she thought the dancer was probably Izzie. MaryAnn reluctantly pulled herself away.

To the left of the dance area was a space filled with exercise equipment and beyond that a laundry room, where she found Smokey's litter tray. MaryAnn hummed happily as she went about her task, quickly scooping up the clumps of soiled cat litter and dumping them into the trash can. Smokey sat in silent vigil on top of the dryer watching her the whole time with her bright yellow eyes. "There, all done," she said, scratching the cat beneath the chin. She returned the bag of litter to its allotted space, went over to the sink to wash her hands, and rubbed in some of the lotion Thea had thoughtfully provided.

MaryAnn went back upstairs with Smokey close behind. She would have liked a cup of tea but decided against it, afraid something might break. She remembered a holiday cottage she and Sam had rented one summer. They had only had Ian then. She had not only managed to break the glass carafe to the coffee maker, but also the toaster. Ian had collected shells from the beach in which he had quickly lost interest so, without thinking, she had thrown them in the outside trash barrel. As the week wore on and the weather got hotter, the smell from the trash barrel became so bad they could hardly bear to lift the lid! Even paper towels soaked in a hastily purchased bottle of *Febreeze* did little to dispel the nauseating odor. Other than these events, the three of them had a fabulous week, and she had replaced the carafe with a whole new coffee maker, offered to buy a new toaster, and apologized for the smelly garbage, but despite all MaryAnn's worries, the owner, completely unfazed, happily refunded their rather hefty security deposit. She thought about Sam and how Johnny had been conceived during the holiday, surprised to find the memories less painful. Was this just the passing of time or the distraction of her newfound love for Jim? She wasn't sure.

Where were Jim and the boys? Now she was getting worried, and even though it was only just three thirty, she thought they'd be here by now. She stood in front of the sink looking out of the window willing them to appear, and her whole body sagged with relief as she saw his truck turning into the driveway. Forgetting her coat, she went out to greet them. Jim was pulling his seat forward so the boys could scramble out from their cozy space in the back of the cab, and his face lit up when he saw her, but scowled when he noticed she wasn't wearing a coat. "You'll catch your death, woman," he said.

Ian reached the ground first and Jim carefully lifted Johnny and placed him next to MaryAnn. The little boy threw his arms around his mother's legs and said, "Mommy, Mommy, we've had such a 'citing day."

"Come on, let's go inside as my teeth are beginning to chatter and you can tell me all about what you've been up to. How about you Ian? How was your day?"

Using one of his favorite expressions, and being a boy of few words at the best of times, he just said, "It rocked."

Jim walked along behind the three of them and he loved to watch the interaction between MaryAnn and her sons. She had done an incredible job of raising them, and even if they had been his own he couldn't have done any better. She had instilled them with good values, and he believed they would grow up to be fine young men. He prayed silently MaryAnn would allow him to be part of their life, but he understood he would have to be patient and only time would tell what the future held…

CHAPTER TWENTY-FIVE

Margaret

On Saturday evening, Margaret was sitting by herself in the living room and mulling over the last few days. Surprisingly, she and Bill had enjoyed their rather quiet Thanksgiving with just Nan and Stanley and she had quickly gotten over the disappointment of not having the usual crowd. In a way, she was relieved MaryAnn had refused her invitation because, had she accepted, she would have been obliged to ask Jim. She wasn't sure how Nan would have coped with this, seeing as she had once been in love with him. Margaret remembered those awkward times when Jim would come into the store making a pretense he was there to see Nan, when all he really wanted was to find out how Thea was doing after her stay in the hospital. He took Nan to dinner a couple of times, but his heart wasn't in it, and Nan would come home looking sad and disheartened. Not anymore, though, now Stanley was part of their lives, and it warmed Margaret's heart to see her daughter so contented and settled with a man both she and Bill liked. Margaret was still highly amused Nan rhymed with Stan and Stan rhymed with Nan. Stan, himself, hadn't failed to see the funny side of this, too. In fact, he always saw the funny side of life and after all the drama they had endured with Thea, Stanley was a breath of fresh air. Margaret was of the opinion he had his head screwed on right, and his love for Nan was healthy, not obsessive. She had watched the interaction between Stanley and her daughter and realized with great relief Nan had finally found her man.

Thursday turned out to be a truly relaxing day. They all pitched in with the meal preparations, and even though there was too much food, it was so much easier to cook for just the four of them. It was a blessed relief not to be on her feet all day, and she took full advantage of Nan and Stanley's offer to wash up. They had pushed her and Bill gently into the living room where they promptly fell asleep. The four of them had played Rummy in the evening, and even though Stanley was familiar with the card game, he lost miserably, but he didn't seem to care—another good sign as far as Margaret was concerned.

She leaned back into the corner of the couch and wished Lady was still with them. She missed the big black Lab, but not nearly as much as Bill did—he still grieved for her. The sight of her empty basket in the corner of their bedroom was a constant reminder until, finally, she couldn't stand it anymore, and she quietly took it away. Bill had never mentioned the basket since, but she thought he was secretly pleased she had made the decision for him. She wondered whether they would ever have another dog, but she doubted it. Of course, Margaret would always be eternally grateful Lady had saved Thea's life, but even taking into account Lady's heroism, the loss was still hard to bear. There was something exceptionally reassuring in the loyal companionship of a dog and she missed her dreadfully.

She was overcome with sadness, which was unlike her, but the apartment felt empty without Nan and Stanley and she had been sorry to see them leave. Bill had gone to bed to read, and she suspected he was probably asleep by now, so she was left alone to ponder. She was looking forward to seeing Thea and the children when they got back from Massachusetts. She wondered how they were getting on and whether Thea had come to a decision about Ellie's offered partnership. The Wilkinsons also came to mind with the surprising news MaryAnn and her boys had received an invitation to spend Thanksgiving with the Hudsons. There seemed to be so much happening all at once and her mind was buzzing. Her thoughts turned to Nan and Stanley—when would they get married, and what kind of wedding would they choose? There was her own life to consider, and she was fully aware she and Bill needed to put their heads together and make future plans for the store. He had so wanted an heir, and they had certainly planned to have more than one child, but it wasn't meant to be. It certainly wasn't for lack of trying, and she smiled to herself. The stars had most definitely been in alignment on that fateful day when she had walked into the Country Store as a visitor to the area and locked eyes with Bill. She was always amazed at how things happened and how people's paths crossed, all with perfect timing so it seemed. She hoped in her heart of hearts the Chamberlins would choose to stay because she and Bill loved them all, but the decision was in the lap of the gods and all her praying in the world wouldn't make it so. Eventually, she took herself off to bed, counting her blessings and thanking God for the richness and the fullness of her life, but she couldn't help wondering as she walked towards her bedroom, just what was in store for all of them. She hated change, but she knew it was inevitable...

AUTHOR'S NOTE

I have included these recipes just for fun and also the rules for Up and Down the River, simply because you might want to give the game a try. I hope you enjoy making the recipes and playing the game as much as I enjoyed writing this book.

Jim's Pancakes

Ingredients for one small serving:
1/2 cup milk
1/4 cup wholewheat flour (or an equal mix of wholewheat and white flour to make a lighter pancake)
1/2 cup powdered milk
1 egg yolk
1 egg white
Method:
1. Combine milk and yolk of egg
2. Stir in flour and milk powder
3. Beat gently until mixed
4. Fold in stiffly-beaten egg white
5. Cook on moderately hot griddle pan, using a drizzle of oil. Use two tablespoons of batter for each pancake. This makes four small ones.

Serve with fresh fruit and a dab of butter and honey or maple syrup.

Thea's Pavlova

Ingredients:
3 egg whites
1 level teaspoon of cornstarch
1 teaspoon of white vinegar

1 teaspoon of vanilla extract

Slightly less than 1 cup of white sugar (7 oz.)

Method:

1. Prepare a cool oven (300 deg. F).
2. Cover a cookie sheet with parchment paper.
3. Whisk egg whites until stiff but not dry.
4. Mix cornstarch, vinegar and vanilla together in a small bowl and whisk into egg whites with sugar until well blended. The mixture will be heavy and smooth.
5. Spread mixture on cookie sheet to an even circle about 1" thick, leaving a hole in the middle.
6. Place in the oven and immediately turn heat down to 275 degrees. Cook for one hour, after which pavlova should be crisp on the outside and marshmallow-like on the inside.
7. Turn oven off and leave to cool in the oven without opening the door!
8. Serve with whipped cream and fresh fruit. Raspberries work well as the tartness of the fruit complements the sweetness of the meringue.

MaryAnn's Dutch Apple Pie

Ingredients:

9 inch unbaked pie shell (prepare and refrigerate until ready to use.)

Note: *Jiffy Pie Crust Mix* works really well.

Topping:

2/3 cup sifted all-purpose flour

1/3 cup butter or margarine

1/3 cup light brown sugar, firmly packed

Method:

Combine flour and sugar and cut butter into mixture until consistency of coarse meal; refrigerate until ready to use.

Filling:

2 lb. cooking apples (MaryAnn used Macintosh)

1 tablespoon lemon juice

2 tablespoons flour

3/4 cup sugar or honey (MaryAnn used sugar)

Dash salt

1 teaspoon cinnamon

Core and pare apples. Slice thinly into large bowl and sprinkle with lemon juice. Combine flour, sugar or honey, salt and cinnamon, mixing well. Toss lightly with apples.

Turn filling into unbaked pie shell, spreading evenly. Cover with topping.

Preheat oven to 400 deg. F and bake for 40-45 minutes or until apples are tender.

Rules to Card Game — Up and Down the River

1. Create a score sheet by numbering the amount of rounds you and your opponents will play. Four players will play a total of 22 hands, five players will play a total of 20 hands, six players will play a total of 16 hands and seven players will play a total of 14 hands. In the case of four players, you should mark a column along the left side of the paper from 1 to 11 and then 11 to 1.

2. Determine the player who will begin as the first dealer by dealing out cards. The first person to be dealt a Jack will start off.

3. After shuffling the deck, deal out the cards according to the round you are currently on. When in the first round, you deal each player a single card. In the second round each player will get two cards and so on. The number of cards for each round will continue to increase until you are all the way up the river. Once up, the number of cards for each round will decrease until you are all the way down the river.

4. After cards for that particular round have been dealt, the dealer will set the remaining cards to the side and then flip over the top card to indicate trump for the round. You can make one of the rounds a 'no trump' round just to make it more fun.

5. Once trump has been decided, take a look at your hand and bet the number of tricks you think you can take during the round. In order to score, you must take exactly the number of tricks you bet, not over or under.

6. As players bet the number of tricks they will take in any given round, the scorekeeper will note this on the score sheet under the name of each individual player.

7. The player to the left of the dealer starts. It is up to him, and his bet of tricks, how he'd like to lead. No one may lead a trump in any round until it is broken and those are the only cards remaining in his or her hand. Also, you must follow suit. If a diamond is led, you must play a

diamond from your hand. If you do not have one, you can either lay trump or discard.

8. After everyone has laid a card, the player with the highest card or highest trump card takes the trick and places it in front of him. Laying the tricks in front of you is a good way to track the number of tricks you've taken for the hand.

9. After all the cards have been played for the round, each player will indicate if they've either gotten their tricks or busted. For those who made the tricks they bet, the scoring is as follows: 0=10 points, 1=11 points, 2=12 points and so on. If a player were unable to take the proper number of tricks, they would receive zero points for the round.

10. Play continues around the table, either dealing more or less cards, depending on where you are in the game, in a clockwise direction following the same rules as previously described as you go up and down the river. The winner is the one with the most points.

A Scary Kind of Honesty

A Novel

Pamela Frances Basch

A SCARY KIND OF HONESTY © 2014 Pamela Frances Basch
All rights reserved.
ISBN: 1495439216
ISBN 13: 9781495439216
Library of Congress Control Number: 2014902709
CreateSpace Independent Publishing Platform
North Charleston, South Carolina

About the Author

I grew up in England and immigrated to Canada by ship in 1970. It took six days and we arrived in Montreal on a foggy, September morning after a rough trans-Atlantic crossing. After the birth of my second daughter, my then husband was offered a job in the United States and we moved to Connecticut where I have lived ever since.

A long time ago when I was between jobs, I started to write a novel. The years went by and the novel lay idle—my characters stuck in time—until September 2012 when I finally found time to finish EACH TIME WE SAY GOODBYE.

I love to write and find the whole process absolutely fascinating. I have no plot line and the story just develops as I sit at my laptop and find myself laughing and crying along with my characters. I never know until I start to write exactly what my characters are going to be doing next. How their lives evolve never fails to amaze me. I try and write every day for at least a couple of hours.

I have been retired since 2009 and writing has become my obsession. I do believe stories connect humanity and this inspires me to create my novels, together with all the support and encouragement I receive from friends and family. All the hours I spend are made worthwhile every time I hear—"I thoroughly enjoyed EACH TIME WE SAY GOODBYE and can't wait for the next one."

A SCARY KIND OF HONESTY is the second in the trilogy and continues the saga of the Chamberlin family. Now I just have to knuckle down and finish the third book because I can't wait to see what happens!

If you enjoyed this book, please recommend it to a friend and post a review on Amazon. Please feel free to contact me at StoriesConnectHumanity@comcast.net.

Made in the USA
Lexington, KY
30 March 2014